THE TINSMITH'S APPRENTICE SERIES

BOOK ONE

A

PARTIAL

SUN

A Novel

LAWRENCE REID BECHTEL

BQB

Virginia

A Partial Sun (Book 1 in The Tinsmith's Apprentice series)
©2019 Lawrence Reid Bechtel

While this book is based on true events and real people, the story itself is a work of fiction.

Published in the United States by BQB Publishing
(an imprint of Boutique of Quality Books Publishing Company)
www.bqbpublishing.com

Printed in the United States of America

978-1-945448-39-3 (p)
978-1-945448-40-9 (e)

Library of Congress Control Number: 2019940384

Book design by Robin Krauss, www.bookformatters.com
Cover design by Rebecca Lown, www.rebeccalowndesign.com

First editor: Caleb Guard
Second editor: Michelle Booth

PRASIE FOR
LAWRENCE REID BECHTEL AND
A PARTIAL SUN

"Isaac's adventures and misadventures highlight the complexities and nuances of slavery, even in the North. Bechtel's deep research brings gravity and authenticity to that twisted American social culture. Isaac's harrowing adventures on his trip to Philadelphia are worth the price of the book. I was truly sorry to find myself at the end of Isaac's journey, and I welcome the author's promise of a sequel."

- Rod Barfield, author
America's Forgotten Caste
Thomas Day, Free Black Cabinetmaker

"[The author does] a wonderful job shaping Isaac's character and sculpturing a plot that's thoroughly engaging. [His] characters, good and bad, are all convincing, and the atmosphere and setting feels vivid and realistic."

- Ed Falco, Professor
English Department
MFA Creative Writing Program
Virginia Tech

This book is fondly dedicated to the memory of
Nannie B. Hairston (1921-2017)
"Praise the Lord!"

ACKNOWLEDGEMENTS

Many persons have been instrumental in the writing of this book, which originated with a sculpture project of mine in 2008; namely, portrait busts of Thomas Jefferson and one of his slaves, Isaac Granger Jefferson. In 2017, Terri Leidich, of BQB Publishers, lifted me from my largely solitary labor of writing the manuscript into the dynamic process of getting it into print and marketed. My developmental editor, Caleb Guard, helped me immeasurably in transforming the narrative's structural form, and copy editor Michelle Boothe significantly assisted in improving the prose. My brother, the freelance nonfiction writer Stefan Bechtel, shared the lessons of his experience with publishers, listened attentively to my reading of Part I, and offered valuable suggestions on titles. The Pennsylvania Historical Society, in Philadelphia, provided key pieces of information, and access to editions of the *Philadelphia Gazette* from the eighteenth century. Dr. Edward Falco, head of the Creative Writing Program at Virginia Tech and his colleague Dr. Virginia Fowler, my graduate professor for Victorian Literature, offered comments and encouragement of early draft segments. Becky Cox, who had typed out my first novel, *The Favorite*, which I wrote while teaching at Virginia Tech, came to my aid once again in preparing, organizing, and proofreading the first complete digital version of this book. Dr. Rodney Barfield, author of *America's Forgotten Caste*, film maker James Crawford of *Swinging Gate Productions*, and Thomas Orman Knight, a longtime friend and book lover, read and perceptively commented on versions of the full manuscript. Dr. Wornie Reed, Director of the Race and Social Policy Center at Virginia Tech, and Bennett Johnson, President of PATH Press Inc., provided invaluable advice and counsel regarding use of the word "nigger."

I love reading aloud to audiences and there is no better method for gauging whether a story "works," and two audiences have favored me with their warm attention and valuable comment: a reunion of Wheaton College friends in Blacksburg, in the summer of 2015, and the "noble band" of Etaturk XLVIII, at the Wytheville House in Virginia.

Of the many books which informed and enhanced my writing of *A Partial Sun*, three deserve particular mention: *Jefferson at Monticello: Recollections of a Monticello Slave and of a Monticello Overseer*, edited by James A. Bear, which contains Isaac Granger Jefferson's recollections of his time in Philadelphia; *Forging Freedom: The Formation of Philadelphia's Black Community 1720-1840*, by Gary B. Nash, which provided indispensable details for some of the episodes I enlarge upon; and Lucia Stanton's, *"Those Who Labor for My Happiness": Slavery at Thomas Jefferson's Monticello*. Ms. Stanton's rich, nuanced understanding of Jefferson and slavery, gained from a lifetime of scholarship, was vital to me.

I cannot close these acknowledgements without expressing my gratitude to the late Carmen Gaudio, of Chicago, under whose rare tutelage and protection, in the mid-to late '70's, I was able to work and live in an African American neighborhood on the Near West Side, where I drew inspiration for two characters fundamental to the development of my protagonist.

At my side and having my back through everything has been my spouse and closest friend, Ann Morris Shawhan. Without her sustaining encouragement, extraordinary patience, thoughtful commentary, and general management of our affairs, I could never have written this book.

Finally, I thank you, my Dear Readers. May the sun in your firmament prove not to be partial but full of light!

NOTICE TO THE READER*

Isaac Granger, Thomas Jefferson, James Hemings, Mr. Bringhouse (or "Bringhurst," as he is listed in Philadelphia records), Billey Gardner, the Reverend Richard Allen, Reverend Charles Campbell, and certain other characters which appear in this novel were real people, and certain historical events which inspired the plot really happened, but the book itself is a work of fiction. References to real people, events, or locales are intended only to provide a sense of authenticity, and are used fictitiously; all other characters, incidents, and dialogue are drawn from the author's imagination and are not to be construed as real, or to be read as history. The language used in the book includes crude idioms and epithets that reflect what the author believes would have been authentic to the period and characters. The author intends no offense, disparagement, or hurt.

*I am indebted to Ross Howell, Jr., author of *Forsaken,* for the substance of this Notice.

* "We know that as early as the 17th century, 'negro' evolved to 'nigger' as intentionally derogatory . . ." (quoted from Arizona State University Dr. Neal A. Lester, who twice taught courses on the n-word; Teaching Tolerance, (Teaching Tolerance is italicized) Issue 40, Fall 2011, tolerance.org)

* ". . . W.E.B. Dubois announced to the world in 1898, 'I believe that eight million Americans are entitled to a capital letter.' Dubois was not the first to raise the point that the spelling of Negro with a small 'n' was a gratuitous insult, but it was a long time before white publishers and editors abandoned the practice." (from a preview of journal article, "Some Notes on the Capital 'N'," by Donald L. Grant and Mildred Bricker Grant, published in Phylon, (italicized) Vol. 36, No. 4; previewed in JSTOR, jstor.org)

INTRODUCTION

by Reverend Charles Campbell

In the year 1847, to distract my grief from events which even now cause me to shudder, I cast about for a fresh historical subject upon which to concentrate my attention, one that would be of interest to the reading public and offer the chance of an income, of which I was desperately in need. Providentially, I chanced to hear of an old Negro, one Isaac Granger Jefferson by name, working as a blacksmith in Petersburg, Virginia, who had for most of his life been bound a slave to the late Thomas Jefferson. It was said that this fellow could ruminate at length upon his experiences at Monticello, sprinkling his reminiscences with rare glimpses of the great man.

So excited I became at the prospect of speaking with this venerable gentleman, and gleaning from him more of these rare glimpses, and assembling this material in a book, that I packed my portmanteau and notebooks that very day and set off by coach for Petersburg. I shall not trouble you, dear Reader, with details of my journey, which included a broken axle, violent thunderstorm, and attempted robbery, but will instead present myself as having arrived, weary but unharmed, at my destination, a city which sits astride the Appomattox River, about twenty-four miles south of Richmond. I found it bustling with activity, and peopled with a remarkable number of Negroes, many living as Free Blacks, and engaging in all manner of trades. After numerous inquiries, and vain searches, I located Isaac Granger's workshop on Plum Street, one block back from the railroad line. It was a modest structure between a cobbler's stand and a cooper's stall. The door was open, and Isaac, his back to me, was working at his forge. I entered and stood quietly to one side and watched. He was at that time about seventy-one years of age, and though somewhat stooped, still remarkably robust, with large shoulders and muscular forearms, and, I noticed, the end of one finger missing on his left hand. At last, he put down his hammer and tongs, turned to me, and in a deep and resonant voice inquired what business had brought me to his door. His face, black as coal, creased with lines, and glistening with sweat, wore an expression deeply somber, as though it registered all the sufferings of his race. I expressed to him my fervent hope that he would share with me his memories of Thomas Jefferson, and Monticello, that I might publish these for the edification of the citizenry. Having completed my entreaty, I stood uncomfortably waiting for his response, as he watched me with his deep-set eyes. Finally, he said that "Old Master" had been dead twenty years or more, and that he, Isaac, had already spoken of him and life at his plantation to white men on several occasions, and saw no reason to bring up the business yet again. Then he spread open his arm to show a cluttered work bench, and said he was "full up with work," as I could plainly see.

Fearful that he would turn me away, and that my hopes would come to naught, I begged him to forgive my intrusion upon his business, and said that I expected my anticipated book of his recollections would turn a tidy profit, and that I would dispense to him a percentage, if he would only be so good as to humor my questions and allow me to take down his answers. His grave expression visibly softened at this, and we managed to come to terms. There in his rude shop we made ourselves comfortable on two stools, and he began to talk, and I to write in my notebook—a difficult enterprise, I found. Having warmed to his subject, he was animated and voluble, and I was obliged to my pencil fairly flying along the page to keep up. I returned a second day to complete the transcript of his reminiscences, and we then parted amiably, with a firm handshake and my promise to notify him when the book was in print.

Alas, I could find no willing publisher. I was told the material was curious, but antique; that the modern reader was no longer interested in pedestrian details about the Patriarchs of the Republic; that books of practical advice were wanted, commentary on topics of the day, and for ladies, novels—always novels, full of romance and intrigue, sufficiently weighted with instruction on probity and good manners. I despaired, and the manuscript languished in my cupboard desk for nearly five years, until early in 1852. By then, abolition was the hue and cry, and southern states were marshaling arguments in defense of their "peculiar institution." A lively market for slave narratives emerged. In these narratives, the protagonist typically detailed his many excruciating ordeals and grisly injustices under a cruel slave master, before escaping at last to the bounties of liberty. While browsing one of these, I suddenly recalled, from Isaac's recitation to me, his brief account of having been taken by Thomas Jefferson to Philadelphia, where he had been apprenticed to a tinsmith, "one Bringhouse by name." Though I had passed over this scanty account with little thought while writing it down,

because it had little to do with Mr. Jefferson, it now awoke
an idea in me: might it be enlarged, and made into a kind of
slave narrative? For Isaac had been verily transported from
one world to another and altogether different one. From the
proscribed world of a Virginia plantation, where he could have
expected to live and die as a slave, to the busy, prosperous
world of a northern city—and not just any city, but the
capital of the country at that time, extolled as the "Athens of
America," seat of a thriving and dynamic Negro community
of some two thousand souls; a city, and a state, founded upon
Quaker ideals which included an aversion to slavery. It was
to such a world that Isaac had been suddenly admitted, at
the impressionable age of fifteen, and where he remained
for nearly four years, growing into his manhood, with all its
attendant desires: philosophical, moral, and sensual.

What, pray tell, had he seen, and heard, and felt, in
such a world, and at such a time of life? Philadelphia was a
well-known destination for escaped slaves. Had he met one
of these? Conceived his own ideas of escape? The tinsmith,
James Bringhouse, was likely Quaker, and if so, had Isaac
ever attended a Friends Meeting? Pennsylvania had passed
a law providing for the gradual abolition of slavery—the
first such law in all the nation. Had Isaac learned of this
law, somehow? The city housed the first African Methodist
Episcopal church in the country. Had Isaac ever attended this
church? Surely, I thought, the sum total of these and other
circumstances, and the novel experiences which arose from
them, must have had a profound effect on Isaac as a young
enslaved man. Yet in the end he had returned south, whether
by force or personal volition. Returned to Thomas Jefferson's

plantation, returned to the proscribed life of a lifelong slave, having left behind all the opportunities which must have beckoned him in Philadelphia. How had he faced this? Did he ever have regrets? Had he struck some kind of bargain with Mr. Jefferson?

Oh, how I wished to know the answers to these questions! I believed that a healthy number of sensitive readers would also wish to know. Though not perhaps distinguished by beatings and torture, followed by a wild escape, the story I foresaw would be uncommonly interesting, intimate and full of particulars, featuring a young Negro of conscience and sensitivity, who would stir in the attentive reader the deepest concern. However, to bring such a story to the publisher, one which was credible and attractive, I knew that I would need to visit again with Isaac and get from him the full story of his time in Philadelphia. Yet when I arrived at his door once again, with deep apologies for my long absence and failure thus far, but with enthusiasm for this new enterprise, I found him deeply reticent. Therefore, I took lodgings in the city, and visited with him nearly every day for three weeks, imploring him to cooperate, until at last he relented, not, I think, on account of my importuning, but from the simple fact that he was now clearly ailing, and no longer the vigorous man I remembered from my first visit. He knew his days were numbered.

"My story won't do me no harm nor good when I am laid in my grave," he said. "Might as well get it off my chest." He expressed a wish that his percentage of any monies gained from the book go to his "poor Mrs.," who suffered from gout. This I ardently promised to do, and with that assurance—

he in a ladder-back chair, and I, with my notebook open and seated at a plain deal table—Isaac told me his story. He sometimes cried, and often laughed, or shook his head, as it all came back to him, as vividly as life itself, though it were so many years gone by. In this way, meeting as his work would allow, over a period of three months, he completed his recitation, and I my notes-taking. On one point only, Isaac and I vigorously disagreed; namely, in regards to his inclusion of the word 'nigger' when quoting the speech of the despicable Daniel Shady. "The word is coarse," I objected, "an emblem of bigotry, and will offend the gentle ears of my readers!" He only laughed at my objection. "Let it offend!" he retorted. "If I have been required to bear the sting of that word upon my ears time and again all these years, then your readers must learn to bear it too, in all its savagery! Besides, I have been considerate of your readers more than you know, for if I were to include every instance of its use, why this proposed book of yours would require *fumigation* upon every readin'!" He watched for my reaction and then smiled. "So sweeten your pages for me, will you? Put a capital letter at the front of the word, *Negro*." It was a request I heartily agreed to. Over the following two years, as ominous clouds of impending conflict began to darken our nation's skies, I labored to assemble those notes into a passable narrative and submit them for the publication of the book which you now hold in your hands.

With these remarks, I shall conclude this introduction, begging you, kind Reader, to forgive any errors or inaccuracies as being solely mine. It is my fervent wish that this narrative will preserve some moving semblance of Isaac Granger Jefferson's life and experience. A thousand, thousand enslaved persons have lived and died, with no record kept of their time on earth. May it please God that I have given this good man his due opportunity to speak and be heard.

Composed on this fifth day of June 1855.
—*Reverend Charles Campbell*

PART I

ONE

How it all begun

"Now then, Reverend Campbell!" Isaac began, leaning back in his chair, the cane bottom creaking under his weight, "so you have come to hear about my adventures in the great city of Philadelphia, have you?"

"Yes, and record them for posterity," I added, lifting my pen over the notebook which lay open before me.

"Well," he said with a slow smile, "I can remember as if it were yesterday, though in truth it was now more than sixty years ago, when I set off down Master Jefferson's mountain on old Beulah, my travel satchel tied on behind, one fine September month in the year of seventeen and ninety."

I bent over my notebook, taking down every word, excited to begin recording the narrative I had so long anticipated, and knew would be historic.

"But this is too hasty a beginnin'!" he said.

I looked up at him, baffled, and for a moment my spirit wilted within me, fearing that he had for some reason changed his mind, and would after all not share with me his recollections. Then he turned in his chair, pulled open a small drawer under his workbench, and took out an oiled paper. This he unfolded and lifted up in his thick fingers something which looked like a piece of old leather, dark with age, crinkled, and roughly eight inches square. "Break you off a piece," he said. "Go ahead!"

I put down my pen, reached out, and somewhat tentatively did as he commanded.

At once, my nostrils were filled with the strong, intoxicating, and unmistakable odor of tobacco.

Isaac then broke off a corner, too, and held it up. "This," he said, "is tobacco leaf grown on Master Jefferson's main plantation, under the watchful eye of my own father, who managed the crop that year from planting to harvest. He was the only black man ever to be appointed overseer by Master Jefferson."

"What an honor that must have been for him," I said.

"Oh, it was a hellish honor, Reverend Campbell, hellish! Pinched as he was by the demands of Mr. Jefferson, and the hatred of the field hands, who could not abide the rule of a black man like themselves."

I looked again at the piece of tobacco in my hand, as if its veined surface were somehow inscribed with that anguish.

"Now crumble it up," Isaac said, "and put it on your tongue."

I watched him crumble up his piece, open his lips—noticing as he did so that he was only missing but one tooth—and lay it on his pink tongue. Then he closed his lips and massaged the tobacco around in his mouth. "Come on, now," he said.

But I was loath to, for I was opposed to the use of intoxicants of any kind. Yet I had come a long way to record Isaac's recollections. This small transgression against my principles was a small price to pay, I told myself, and so I crumbled up the piece, seeing as I did so that it stained my fingertips with a color dark as umber. Then, begging God's forgiveness, I opened my lips and dropped those crumbles upon my tongue. Instantly, my whole mouth burned with the taste. It stung, it bit, it seized the very seat of my perceptions with a terrible intensity. Only by sheer force of will was I able to keep my mouth closed and look at Isaac a moment and prove to him irrevocably by my cooperation that I was committed to our enterprise.

"In this pungent plant," he said, looking at me calmly, "is contained much travail of the slave."

Momentarily, I was overwhelmed with a feeling of revulsion for that unfathomable travail, and then I broke from my chair, pushed open the door, and retched in the gutter. I thought my guts would come up. I spat repeatedly and rinsed my mouth with water from the well pump before I at last felt reasonably restored to myself, returned to my seat, and took up my pen. Isaac watched this whole miserable experience I had endured without a word, then calmly spat his wad of tobacco in a small tin and neatly wiped his lips with one finger.

"Now my father," he said, taking a deep breath, "was George Granger. Great George, he was called. Sometimes King George. Not only because he was great of stature, but because he was great in his capacities and responsibilities. He rose from leadman to foreman and then to overseer—the only Negro ever to attain that station under Master Jefferson, as I have said, with the duty to supervise half of all his farms and hands, the raising of crops, especially tobacco, the money crop, from planting to harvesting to shipping in their hogsheads to market. My father's tobacco brought top dollar, for it was clean, fully dried, and of a good color. He was loyal to Master Jefferson, my father was, and worried himself sick to please him. Certain hands hated him, whether he was light with the lash or heavy, for they expected he should go easy on them, even if it meant leaving good leaf to rot in the field. It was on account of him that I did not toil in the tobacco fields, worked to death, dawn to dark, under the active lash of an overseer like Mr. Paige, neither me nor my brothers.

"My mother was Ursula, known as Queen, for her grandmother had been a true queen back in the mother country, and the title of royalty naturally passed down, and she was spoken to as such by the field hands, for it was understood she had powers, both to heal and to harm. She was so beloved of Master Jefferson's wife, Martha, that she had him fetch her back from a man in Goochland County, who'd bought her when Ms. Jefferson's first husband, Batter Skelton, died from an accident. My father was also bought special by Master Jefferson, and brought back to Monticello, for he was married to my mother, but bound slave to a different master than she was. My mother was in charge of the pastry kitchen, a vital position, believe you me, for Master Jefferson he did love his pastries! She had responsibility for the laundry, too, and preservation of the meat, and she was the only person Master Jefferson would trust with the making and bottling of cider. She was wet nurse to Master Jefferson's eldest daughter, Patsy, at the same time she suckled me."

"Excuse me, Isaac," I interjected, "but I am skeptical that your mother suckled both you and Patsy Jefferson. You claimed this likewise in your first narrative, and I calculated out the dates, which simply do not bear the correspondence, as she was born in 1772 and you in 1775."

"Young man," he said, taking from his bench a small-headed hammer, each head rounded, like a half-ball, "were you there, or was I?"

Stung by his rebuke, mild though it was, I apologized for my intrusive question, yet making clear that I considered factual accuracy as vital, and a duty to readers and to myself as historian.

In response to my remarks, he briefly smiled. "This here," he said, "is a hollowing hammer." Then he held his hand out flat. "It works like so." He pounded lightly on his hand with the hammer, gradually curling up his fingers into a cup as he did so. "You got to be careful so as not to thin the tin sheet unevenly and weaken it."

I supposed his action with the hammer held some message for me, but what it was I could not ascertain. So I merely nodded, dipped my quill pen, and waited. He put the hammer down, settled more comfortably in his chair, smiled for a moment all to himself, and then continued with his narrative, lapsing into the amiable and unlettered speech of his youth as he did so.

CHAPTER TWO

*This man, he goin' to Philadelphia—
on Beulah, for goodness' sake*

Oh, I was all on fire that mornin' I set off on old Beulah
for the great city of Philadelphia to become a tinsmith. I could
hardly wait to get there and begin work! I knew I could make
Old Master Jefferson proud. Had to. For I was a Granger, and
that meant somethin', and I aimed to prove it.

But I was not a Hemings, who of all the bound families
was closest to Master Jefferson, Sally most of all, as you may
have heard. So I knew full well, as I walked up through the
quarter that mornin', with a cloth satchel packed by Mama's
own hands slung over my shoulder, that I would be up against
it with James Hemings. For he was manservant to Mr.
Jefferson at that time and would for that reason also be going
to Philadelphia. I hated that I should have to travel with him
all that way. Even Mama's warm, buttered corn cakes wrapped
in oil paper tucked in my satchel didn't help my mood much.
And sure enough, when I came up to the grand east door of
the Big House, there sat James high and mighty up on the
coachman's seat, the team all harnessed up and ready to go,
with Master Jefferson's riding horse, Odin, tied on behind.
He was eatin' a jam muffin and sippin' coffee from a mug. He
was a handsome man and knew it. "About time you got here,
Granger," he said. "We near ready to ride off."

James was just being irksome, as usual, for I saw no sign

of Mr. Jefferson, who was likely havin' his regular morning foot bath just then, and after that a proper breakfast, which he lingered over. He was a man of order and habit.

James bobbed his head toward an old cart horse, tied to a post and switchin' her tail. "Take your mount," he said. "You're not riding in the Master's coach, that's sure."

"Beulah?" I said, in consternation. Why, she was the boniest old thing you ever seen, sunken where she ought to be thick, bumpy where she ought to be trim. "Did Master Jefferson assign me to ride that animal?" I needn't have asked, of course.

James inspected his fingers. "She's saddled, ain't she?"

"You sure this animal can make it all the way up to Philadelphia?"

"I would say you had better make damn sure she does, because if she don't, you walk."

"I don't like this arrangement," I said.

James shrugged. "Can't be helped."

For a moment, I thought to bolt back down to our cabin and bring Mama back with me. Now, she would give James what for, be he a Hemings or not. But then the thought of her carryin' on in my defense, and apt to draw the whole breakfast party, napkins still tucked under their chins, out onto the porch, Master Jefferson included, to see what the devil was going on, was altogether too embarrassin' to contemplate. So I said nothin', lest I should give James one more chance to rib, and simply walked on over to old Beulah just as indifferent as could be. I tied on my satchel, took her loose from the post, led her out onto the gravel drive, and climbed on. She went about five paces, then put her head down and kicked up her hind legs. Right off I went, bangin' my left knee, and got up hobblin'. Still to this day that knee bothers me on a cold mornin'.

James poured the dregs of his coffee into the grass. "You're a fine horseman," he said. "Fine."

"I'm glad you enjoyed the show," I said, and got back up on Beulah. Or tried. Got one foot in the stirrup and went to pull myself up, but she did a two-step away, and I had to hop after, on the one foot that was still aground, and so went hopping about and couldn't get that one foot out, nor swing the other up. Worst of all was James up on his high seat, laughin' like a lunatic. I am no horseman.

Finally, he called out: "Click of the tongue, boy, click of the tongue! I have had all the fun I can stand for one morning."

I hated that he called me "boy," but click I did, and sure enough if Beulah didn't stop. I got on. She stood still. Well, that was progress. But she did not move. I snapped the reins. She paid no attention.

"Dig in your heels," said James. "Make it hurt. *Persuade* that animal that the pain of your heel is worse than the pain of going forward."

I didn't want to hurt poor old Beulah, but I didn't want to look the fool, either, so I done as James said. Beulah began to move, and I hung on tight lest she buck.

"Don't stop now," said James, waving his hand, "keep a-going. We shall be along shortly, after Mr. Jefferson finishes his breakfast."

"Which way?"

"Down. Down the mountain, what other way is there? Then toward town."

I was only too happy to get away from James, so down the mountain we went, me and Beulah.

"If you see Mr. Rattiff, tell him we on our way."

Beulah was as rough and awkward a ride as a man could well endure, besides stoppin' every so often to stamp her foot and shake her head until I got her nudged into action again. Yet when we had wound far enough down the road that I could turn around and not see Old Master's house, and the road ahead was empty and all my own, with the sun beginnin' to light the world and the trees in color, my spirits began to rise. I was well and truly pleased to be travellin' away to a far country and the big city.

Then all at once Beulah came to a dead stop, and no heel nor click of the tongue could make her go. She did not share my cheerfulness about a long journey. But this would not do! For wouldn't I look the fool, when James showed up, high on his coachman's seat, driving the matched pair, with Mr. Jefferson looking out to see what had brought their progress to a stop. So I climbed down off Beulah and considered this animal which was to carry me, and now had decided not to. She turned her head and looked at me with her big watery eyes. I reached out my hand to rub along her neck, but she nipped at me.

"Beulah," I said. "You and me got to come to an understandin'. We got a long road ahead, and you got to carry me the whole way, like it or not. Now, I'd rather not ride. I'm better on my feet, yes ma'am, I am, and would stay on 'em and off your back, except that is not how it's supposed to be. If we stay stuck here long, why, Old Master will come along and bump up against us and we *both* be in trouble. So the sooner you get me to Philadelphia, the sooner I can get off your back, you hear?"

Beulah she switched her tail and shifted her ears and

bobbed her head. I reached out a hand again, and this time was able to stroke down along her neck all the way, and she did not try to nip. I kept my hand goin' to her scratched and bony rump, where the hair was all worn off from the traces, and then as my hand moved down over her thin belly, I began to feel the burden of her animal life, which she had borne soundless, until all the spirit was beat out of her, nearly. I supposed she wanted no more than to be put to pasture, where she could lay down in the long grasses and warm sun, and there bob her head a time or two and breathe her last. Instead of that, here she was a-carryin' me, how far she got no idea, only every step of it pain.

I took her whiskered ear in both hands. "Beulah," I whispered. "You old beast. You pitiful, you know that? Pitiful!"

I got out from my sack one of Mama's buttered corn cakes, broke loose a fair portion, laid it in my open hand, and let Beulah gobble it up, to the last crumb, in her slobberin' way. I broke loose another bite, and she gobbled that, too. "Now," I said, "let's you and me get on down the road."

Then I hoisted myself into the saddle and onto her back once again, and but lifted the reins. With no heel nudge at all, forward she went at a decent pace. "Hallelujah," I shouted out. "Oh, halle*lu*jah!"

CHAPTER  THREE

Here come Mr. Ratliff, and I got no pass so must wait, then commence to dream

Beulah and me went on together happy from there, all the way to the bottom of Master Jefferson's Little Mountain, and so I decided to keep right on into town and wait there. Wouldn't James be surprised, I thought with satisfaction. But we no sooner hit the public road, when here came a white man, in a long travellin' coat, atop a big bay gelding, with a box tied on behind his saddle.

"Hold there, nigger," he said.

Oh, I held, believe me, as the man rode his horse up close. Beulah, though a good two hands shorter, was not spooked, and showed her teeth, and the man's horse backed up a step.

"You got your pass this morning, nigger?" said the man.

I dropped my eyes. "Sorry, Marse. I got no pass, this mornin'. Forgot it, silly me."

"Forgot it? Don't you know it's a crime not to have your pass, nigger? Why, I could have you arrested. Who do you belong to?"

"Mr. Thomas Jefferson, he my Master. He sent me to scout the road ahead," I said, which wasn't bendin' the truth too awful much. I gave him a foolish grin. "We on our way to Philadelphia."

"Oh!" he said, pushin' his hat back. "Why didn't you say so, nigger? Save me all this bother arguing with you. I shall be traveling with Mr. Jefferson and his party. Goin' up the mountain just now to meet him for breakfast. Now I'm late, thanks to you."

"Sorry, Marse."

"Address me as Mr. Rattiff."

"Yes, Marse."

"Did you not hear? Address me as Mr. Rattiff."

"Mr. Rattiff."

"Rat*tiff*. Mr. Rat*tiff*, in the French manner."

"Mr. Rat*tiff* in the French manner," I said, all in one go. That got his goat, as intended.

"No, no, goddamn it. *Just* Mr. Rat*tiff*."

"Mr. Rat*tiff*."

"Finally!" he said, slapping his pant leg. "God, I hate to deal with dumb niggers. Breakfast is probably cold by now, with all this frittering around." He broke his horse into a trot and turned up the mountain road. "Don't you be going on farther without your pass," he called back. "You ought to know that much at *least*."

Just as the man got out of sight, Beulah lifted up her bushy tail and peed. Then shat.

"Thank you," I said, pattin' her neck. "My sentiments exactly."

But it was true what he said about havin' no pass, so I got down off Beulah, tied the reins to a branch, and set myself on a tree log close beside. I would just have to wait 'till Mr. Jefferson showed. He and James and Mr. Rat*tiff*. Beulah pushed her nose around in the leaves to forage.

I watched her. "*You* may be happy to just stand around

and eat," I said, "but it galls me to set here idle. For I am full of adventure for the road!"

Beulah lifted her head, and took a good look at me, but kept her big teeth grindin' away, grass stems hangin' from her lips. When she had done, she dropped her head and pushed around in the leaves with her nose for more.

"Any chance you get, you eat," I said, disgusted. "You know that?"

But watchin' her made me hungry, so I got from my sack another of Mama's corn cakes, and nibbled away at it, little by little, so it would last. The cake was still just a tad warm and smelled of her hearth, which sent a pang of homesickness through me. And here I was barely started. So I began to consider the long road ahead in a more resolute manner. Except tiredness crept over me, for I had lain awake a long while the night before, thinking of this very morning. Now that I was in it, I could hardly keep my eyes open. Figurin' that Mr. Jefferson would not be along for some time, I pulled my coat around me, slid back off the tree log and lay in the deep leaves, lookin' up through the tree branches and red leaves to the blue sky where slow clouds drifted peaceably by.

So on that deep bed of leaves, in the quiet morning, I fell asleep. Shouldn't have, but I did. Slept deep and dreamed. Dreamed myself right back to where this expedition had all begun, one sunny afternoon three months before. I was pumpin' the bellows in my brother's smithy. Little George— my brother—he was at the forge fire, hammer in hand. We was forgin' chain. Then all of a sudden in walked Master Jefferson. Walked in and came over right close to me, saying not a word, only watchin' just exactly how I pumped the bellows, what color flame I kept, how much charcoal was left. Every little detail counted with him, and I was terribly afraid there must be some detail I had wrong, only I didn't know which. Then he went over and watched my brother real close up, same as he done me, and got out his stick rule and measured to the inch how much iron rod we had used, to figure wastage, and wrote in his vest pocket notebook with a stub pencil. I could see the sweat on Little George's brow, for Master Jefferson he did not like wastage.

Then he said, in a perfectly usual voice and lookin' straight at my brother, "Send Isaac up to the house."

I nearly fell against the bellows. What had I done so very wrong that I must go up to the Big House?

Little George he put his hammer right down. "Yes, suh. Now?"

"When you come to a break point," said Master Jefferson. He stood a moment longer, inspectin' us both, then turned out the door, blockin' the sun as he done so, and was gone.

I looked at my big brother. "I pumped the bellows even as could be, two counts on the downstroke, two counts on the up."

Little George held open his hand to show a length of iron rod no longer than two thumbs end to end. "This is my only wastage and was going to use it as a door bolt."

I flung up my arms. "So why does he want me up at the Big House?"

"You tell me. I hope to God you ain't got us both in trouble. Did you get the wood split?"

"Split and stacked."

"Carry up the water?"

"Twenty buckets."

Little George chewed his lip. "You didn't get into Mr. Jefferson's ice cream again, did you?"

"No."

"You ain't lying to me, is you?"

"I only took a finger swipe."

"How many times I got to tell you, Isaac," exclaimed my brother, pushin' at his sleeves and tuggin' at his apron as he would do when upset, "stay out of Mama's pastry kitchen. You know Mr. Jefferson don't want no black finger in his ice cream. It's bad luck."

"Don't you think I know that by now?" I said, agitated by his tone. "I'm fifteen, or near. Besides, how's he to know?"

Little George shook his head. "You know as well as I do Old Master seems to know about everything that goes on anywhere on this big ol' plantation of his."

I couldn't argue that.

"Now, pick up your tongs and get a bite on that link."

So I done, and Little George he forged the link. "Go on then," he said and waved a hand. "Go on to Old Master, but don't dawdle."

I run all the way, hoppin' over the big rock and swingin' 'round the sassafras tree just where the path bent, and only when I came to the trim-cut lawn did I slow to a walk and catch my breath. There I stopped a moment to settle my jitters, then stepped around the corner of the Big House. At the east front, under the tall columns, stood Master Jefferson all by himself.

He was still plain dressed in scuffed boots, worn trousers, and open shirt, not yet suited up for dinner. Even so, he had a bearing about him, whatever clothes he wore. I badly wanted to turn right around and run back to the smithy, but said to myself, "stand firm now and take your medicine." I drew a deep breath and walked slow across the raked drive and right up under the columns and stood quiet to one side, at a respectful distance. He was hummin', which eased my mind a good deal, and though he saw me come up, kept on hummin' a while yet.

Then he folded his long arms across his chest and looked over at me. "Isaac," he said, "I have been studying you."

"Yes, sir," I said, nervous as could be. "I hope what you have been studyin' of me pleased you."

"It has, Isaac. It has. Among all my young servants, you stand out as the one most diligent and capable."

I was afraid then he was going to hire me out.

Instead, he asked me a most unlikely question. "How would you like to learn a trade?"

I was caught off guard. "Little George he already teachin' me to blacksmith."

"I mean in a formal sense. As an apprentice, under a Master Craftsman. Would you like that?"

I fairly leaped in the air. "Oh, yes sir," I said, "I would, I truly would!" Then felt how foolish I must appear to him, standin' there so tall and grave, and settled myself. "If it please you, Master." For suddenly I wondered what trade it would be, if not blacksmithin', and just who the Master Craftsman was to be.

"It does please me," he said, watching me close. "So I have considered what trade. Tinsmithing will do for you, I think."

"Tinsmithin'?" I asked in surprise. "Anybody 'round here do that?"

He rubbed his hands together. "No, Isaac. Nobody."

"Who would teach me then?"

Old Master smiled and laid his long-fingered hand on my shoulder. "Isaac Granger, son of Great George and Queen Ursula, faithful servants to me, lo these many years, I have arranged for you to be taught by none other than Mr. James Bringhouse."

I felt the weight of Old Master's hand on me. "Never heard of that man."

"That's because he lives in Philadelphia."

"Philadelphia!" I said, plain shocked. "But that's nearly another country, ain't it?"

"Some would say so," he said, "with its Quakerism and mercantile obsessions. But I wish you to learn from the best, and James Bringhouse is the best tinsmith in the whole of eastern Pennsylvania."

That sounded to me like a mighty big territory. "He a pretty important man, then," I said, hardly able to believe that Old Master would choose out such a man, from such a distance, to teach me in particular his solemn trade.

"An important man, for an important future," said Master Jefferson, puttin' out his hands as if to take hold of that future. "Tin ware, my boy, is no longer just for the military. The country is growing, and the demand for tin with it. There's money to be made in tin and I want you in it. I *need* you in it."

"Yes, Master," I said. "When this Mr. Bringhouse show at your door, I shall be ready to learn."

Master Jefferson looked at me and smiled. "Oh, he's too busy to come all the way down here just now, Isaac. I mean for you to work under him at *his* place of business."

I am sure my mouth must have dropped open. "You don't mean up there in Philadelphia," I stuttered out, "do you?"

"I do," he said, his face almost radiant with that smile of his.

The prospect scared me. "I could get lost goin' up there, Master," I said. "Or nabbed. It's such a long ways. I never been any such distance all by myself."

"Oh, I wouldn't send you out on the road alone, you should know that," he said reassuringly, as if it was no trouble at all, me leavin' hearth and family and friends and my set ways. "No, you shall go with me, for I must go to Philadelphia, too. Though in truth I should rather not. The dam needs repair. Our farming methods must reform. And I have designs for my house."

Mr. Jefferson he was never done with his house. Always buildin' it up and tearin' it down. Why, Polly, his youngest, she fell through a door one time. Didn't know the steps was gone.

Old Master he sighed. "It shall be no pleasure, being Secretary of State. But such is duty, Isaac. Duty."

The word fell heavily upon me. "Yes sir, duty," I said. "The very word."

"So, it shall give me pleasure," he said, "while I dutifully grind away at the business of government in the State House, to think of you some blocks away profitably at work learning the useful trade of tinsmithing from Mr. Bringhouse. You shall find no rascals in his domicile. He is Quaker through and through: sober, devout, and keeps his shop as clean as a church pew."

I knew nothin' about Quakers at that time except two things: they were said to quake and shiver in church, and they was all against slavery. Old Master would send me up there to work with such a man? Now, that was a mystery.

"We shall leave for Philadelphia the first week of September," he said, looking into the distance. I looked out upon that distance, too, green first, then blue beyond. When the leaves turned, I would be headin' off into that beautiful distance. Suddenly I had a hankerin' to go. To leave all behind and strike out new.

"Now you best return to the smithy," said Master Jefferson. "Lest your brother get behind on the chain work."

"Yes, Master. I is off to it, right now." Then I took off running.

"Isaac Granger, Tinsmith!" called out Old Master after me.

But soon as I got 'round back of the Big House and on the footpath through the woods, I slowed. Questions sprung up in me. Philadelphia, way up north, with me in it, at a trade I knew nothin' of, under this Mr. Bringhouse? What if I did poorly? What if he was ornery and took a dislike to me? Would there be others learnin' the trade in his shop, or just me alone? Would there be any other Negroes around, and if so what did they do? There would be no Papa to speak on my behalf, no Mama to settle things with a hot pastry. I stopped at the sassafras tree and hung on the limb. I didn't want to go, no I didn't. I had it good right where I was and didn't want no change. I was a Granger, after all. Not a Hemings, but still. I would beg Mr. Jefferson to send somebody else, I thought. Maybe Aaron. He would go. But namin' that boy changed my mind, right off. He would leap at the chance, he would, and leave me to feel left behind. That was no good. So my thinkin' on the matter shifted. I was up to it, sure I was. I was tired of this old mountain, seven miles from anywhere. Let me try my hand at the tinsmithin' trade up there in Philadelphia.

I let go the sassafras tree, hopped the big rock, and ran, full of myself, then slowed once again. Where would I stay all that time up there, I wondered. With Mr. Bringhouse and his family, I guessed. That's what 'prentices did. But they was white people, had to be. Now how could I live in the same house with white people?

So my thoughts went, 'till I came to the back of Little George's shop, with old barrel staves propped against the chimney.

Little George was waiting for me when I got inside. "Didn't I tell you not to dawdle?"

"I didn't dawdle," I said. "Old Master had a lot on his mind."

"I'll bet he did. Was it about the ice cream? Or something worse? Probably something worse."

"No," I said, going to the bellows, "nothing of the kind."

"Well, what was it?"

"Big brother," I said, and began to pump air into the forge, "I am goin' to Philadelphia, to be a proper tinsmith up there."

"I told you, don't lie to me."

"I ain't lyin'."

"Does Papa know?"

His question fell on me like a weight. "I don't know. I didn't think to ask."

"So, he is going to have to suffer the indignity of learning this from you—or somebody else."

I shrugged. "I can't help that."

"He's not going to be happy, you know. Not happy at all."

"I know."

Then Little George got downright mad. "Damn it," he said,

"quit pumpin' that bellows. Fire's hot enough. Get yourself around here and pick up them tongs."

His tone made *me* mad. I set my fists against my hips and stuck out my elbows. "I don't want to pick up no tongs," I shouted out. "This man, I say *this* man, he goin' to Philadelphia!"

Suddenly, I was most rudely awoken from my dream by James Hemings, who stood over me pokin' at my chest with the butt end of his horsewhip. "Asleep already are we, Granger?" he said, and poked.

I jumped to my feet, or tried to, but slipped on the dry leaves and fell down.

James looked back to the coach and matched pair standing impatient in the road. "No, Master," he called out, "the Granger boy is not hurt. Just asleep, if you can believe that."

I got to my feet this time and brushed the leaves off. Both Mr. Jefferson and Mr. Rattiff were turned in their seats, watchin' out the window.

James dropped the horsewhip and got me by the collars with both hands. "You're an embarrassment to our race, you know that? Now get your poor black ass back in the saddle. And don't you lag, for God's sake. Mr. Jefferson keeps a brisk pace."

"I got no pass," I said.

"You don't need no pass. Keep up."

"But if I should need one."

"I said, keep up. We going the Fredericksburg Road, and shall put up tonight at Old Nat Gordon's place. Simple as that."

"Yes, but suppose I do get behind. You think Mr. Jefferson

would like it if paddyrollers nabbed me as a runaway, because you set me on a nag that couldn't keep up?"

James gave me a hateful look. "Damn you," he said. He let go my collars, got his horsewhip in hand again, stomped back to the coach, and stood there talkin' to Old Master. Some moments later he came back and slapped a paper in my hand. "You owe me," he said, then stomped back to the coach again. He took his seat, snapped the whip, and away the whole party went at a good trot, with much creaking of the axletree and pounding of hooves.

I have that paper still. It was torn from the little book Mr. Jefferson always kept in a pocket and written out on it were these words in pencil: *This man Isaac Granger is the property of Thomas Jefferson, who hereby gives permission that said Negro should travel the Fredericksburg Road without hamperment*, and signed by him. But I wasn't no man then, oh no I wasn't.

CHAPTER FOUR

The road to Ol Nat Gordon's Place, with recollections how I almost came to blows with Papa

Beulah and me done our best to keep Odin's rump in view, but James drove the coach hard. Every time the road dipped, it disappeared, then showed again at the rise, only smaller. I felt for Mr. Jefferson's pass in my pocket, for fear we should be stopped, but there was little traffic those long miles. Fall time was land clearin' time, for the best tobacco only grew in fresh ground, so all the brush was burnt on either side of the road, trees girdled and dead. Gray ash and red ground, and the smell of smoke. Then storm, and a hard rain. Beulah would rather wait it out, rump to the wind, so I had to sweet talk her to keep movin'. We waded a branch which ran muddy and crossed a rough bridge over a larger, just as muddy. Sun beamed out through the clouds, enough to dry me mostly, and we came to a spring trough, well-built. Beulah drank, while I walked about to stretch my legs and nibble on one more of Mama's corn cakes.

Then on down the road again we went, me and Beulah, mile after mile. I thought back to those three months right after I'd stuck out my elbows like a young fool in my brother's smithy and said, "This man, he goin' to Philadelphia." For afterwards I had soon wished I'd said no such thing, nor been picked by Mr. Jefferson to go, because word of it got all through the Quarter, and along the Row, and even out among the field hands on the quarter farms. I guessed James Hemings was responsible, but I had a part in it, too. I told Aaron, who cut wood for the charcoal kilns, and Kip, who worked for the cooper. Well, more than just told—boasted, I guess.

By nightfall that very day, Papa gave me a tongue-lashing, soon as he came in the house. "Cannot you keep your damn mouth shut?" he demanded to know.

I said I was sorry in every way I could think of.

"Sorry don't help," he said back. "Cat is out of the bag now, and *I* got to deal with the consequences."

Mama stuck right up for me, as she always did. "He only proud. What other boy did Master pick to be a tinsmith? None, George. You ought to be proud, too."

"Proud?" He waved his arms about. "Why, Queen, I don't need that kind of proud. *That* proud only bring me trouble with Saul. You know he'd just as soon see me dead as look at me. *His* son only shovels out the barns. And I got to rule that Saul."

He complained again the next night. "Don't you know I got to get the tobacco baled and shipped? Mr. Jefferson is anxious *every* damn day, lest the prices fall still further. I got a hogshead or more of leaf still in the fields, yet can I get my hands to hurry and get it cut and hung up in the smokehouses? No. Not unless I stand over 'em with the lash. And not just threaten, but use it till the blood run. God, I hate that."

As if I was responsible for the fallin' price of tobacco, or his troubles with that Saul. Why did he not blame Little George? Or Bagwell? But it was never them, it was always me he laid into. *I* was the one he would blame for his troubles. No matter what I said or did to try to please him.

Add to that was the teasin' and guff I had to put up with most anywhere else. Like for instance when I went up to the icehouse. There would be Sam, shovelin' in more sawdust to keep the ice blocks from meltin'. "I wouldn't go up North," he said, puttin' his shovel down and wipin' his brow with the back of a hand. "Them people not like us. They crazy up there." He screwed up his face at me. "You ain't crazy, is you?" Then he poked at me with his pipe stem, as if he could tell by this. I would've liked to tell him *he* was crazy, the way he put teeter bugs in his biscuit dough, to ward off the ague he said.

Or when I took a cartload of staves down to Hickman, the cooper. He waited till I had piled 'em up where he told me, and then he said, "You ain't going to get fancy on us, is you? You hung a yellow scrap out your back pocket, once. That's fancy."

"Well, then, maybe I will come back dressed *all* in yellow. Would that be fancy enough for you?"

Then there was old Jerry, too lame to work, except to set on the big maple stump and braid rope. I went by him with a cartload of firewood one day and he said, "Keep your eyes on the street up there."

I set the cart down. "Why should I do that?"

"Because there's money to be found, that's why. White people got so much money up there it just fall out their pockets and they don't even bother to pick it up."

I tried to picture that. A whole street littered with dropped coins, and white people walking back and forth over 'em, hands in their pockets.

"I'll be learning the tinsmith trade," I said proudly, "not walkin' around lookin' for dropped money."

"Aw, Isaac, don't be so high and mighty. Send a coin home to old Jerry. Just one of all your hundreds. Is that too much to ask?"

If I went up to the Big House, Doll with her sharp eye always had a word for me. One time, she was out back, sweeping. James Hemings was there, too, and his sister, handsome Sally. Dolly stopped her sweeping. "Isaac, he going to work in the government," she announced. "Going to live in a palace. Have a golden chamberpot."

Sally clapped and laughed. "Don't you go getting yourself in trouble, now," she said.

As if that was my natural bent, to get in trouble. But I smiled anyway, for she was so handsome, with long straight hair down her back, she could say anything to me and draw my smile.

"He won't," said James. "I shall be there, too, don't forget, and keep an eye on the boy, as Mr. Jefferson require."

I had to remind him yet again that I was not a boy.

He spat tobacco into the flower bed, then pushed dirt over the spot with the toe of his shoe. "Then how come you don't have more to show for yourself?"

James meant to provoke me, but I was not about to let him and just walked off. Yet I could picture myself, experienced from my years in a great city, with new shoes on, and a hat, as I had seen a drover wear once, set a tilt, with a tassel off the back brim, yes, and a silk kerchief tied 'round his neck.

But the worst of it was at the supper table my last night before leavin'. Mama had made a rabbit stew, with root vegetables from out her garden, and herbs only she knew, crumbled up from bunches hung off a rafter. We set down to the table at dark, not one candle stub lit but two, waiting on Papa. When at last he pushed the door open and stooped under the lintel with his big shoulders, he stumbled on the step and had to catch himself with both hands, droppin' his lash. He tossed his hat at the wall peg, but missed, and it fell on the floor, where he left it. Then he settled down heavily on his seat. I was sure he'd got into the liquor, with some of the hands, which a foreman must never do, as he told us, but still he would from time to time.

We all sat quiet. Mama filled his bowl and set it in front of him, but he pushed it to one side and looked across the table at me. He smelled of the liquor and tobacco leaf. "Now why in the hell didn't you say *somethin'* to Mr. Jefferson," he said, putting his fists together under his chin, "before you agreed to go on up there to Philadelphia with him?"

It was a foolish question, and he was just bein' objectionable to ask it. "What could I say?" I replied. "Old Master he had the business all settled up in his mind."

But he paid no attention to what I said. He laid his hands flat on the table and leaned over at me. "You *could* have said, 'let me go ask my father. Let me go see what he says.' *Something*."

"Like I said, Papa, he had the business all settled up. You know how he is. There was not a thing I could say, except, 'Yes, sir.'"

He got to his feet, holding onto the table with both hands. "My own son. And wouldn't put in a *single* word for me." He raised a finger in the air. "Not *one* word."

Everybody at the table had bowed their heads, so they would not see him in this condition. Everybody but me.

"My God," he said, strikin' his chest. "I would never have *dreamed* of treatin' *my* father this a way."

I shook my head. I shrugged. I turned up my hands. "He's Master Jefferson."

He struck the table. "Don't you think I know that?"

I thought he would strike me.

"Not one goddamn word."

Mama got to her feet. "George, George," she said, takin' his hand. "Sit down, now. Have supper."

So he sat down again, and we all waited for him to lift his bowl, and only then would we lift ours, for that was the rule. Which he did lift, but then set back down. And so we did the same. We all sat there in silence awhile. "Isaac," he said at last, as if there was nobody else at the table but me, "it's a big city."

"I know."

"No, you don't. You know *nothin'* about that city."

I looked down at my soup bowl. I wondered how *he* could know.

"All kinds of people there," he said. "Some good. Some not so good. Some *bad*."

"Like those Irish masons, always drunk?"

He laughed a little, which was good. Maybe he was sobering up some.

"No, not the same. I mean bad *Negroes*. *Free* Negroes."

I pictured that drover again, with the tassel hat. Rode his own horse and whistled as he went. He was bad. Maybe free, too. And fine. "You mean like that yaller man that comes in to slaughter hogs? He's free, ain't he?"

But Papa had not heard me or didn't care to answer. He

struck the table with his fist, and all the bowls shook. "I don't *trust* 'em. Once they get free, they act all high and mighty."

"But they earned their freedom, George," said Mama. "Or bought it. What's wrong with that?"

Papa turned his bowl. "Man's got a right to better himself, I know that as well as anybody. It's what I done. Gone from field hand to leadman to foreman and hope to rise to overseer."

"Well, there you are," said Mama, with a big smile.

Papa slapped his chest. "But I *understand* my position. That I am *beholden* to Mr. Jefferson. And must *do* as he *say*. *That* is how a man rise in this world. But those *free* Negroes make it *hard* on everybody."

"Stew is going cold," said Bagwell.

Now Papa looked at Bagwell. "Well, take up your bowl then, son," he said. "You too, Little George."

I lifted my bowl as my brothers had, but Papa pushed down my bowl with his big hand. "I ain't done with you."

I drew back my hands, and watched my brothers suck in their stew and then grin at me.

"There's a whole *nest* of Free Blacks in Philadelphia," said Papa, his voice risin'. "'Black Town' they call it. Cobblers in there. Tailors, butchers, bankers. *Lawyers*, even."

"Could be they need a tinsmith in there, too," I said, to rankle. "I might ought to check, once I'm up there."

He pointed his big finger at me like a gun. "Don't you dare."

"Oh, well, then," I said, "I shall keep to my bench and not raise my eyes for seven years, till I come out a tinner, then trot right back home here, and say no more about it." Then out of spite, I lifted my bowl.

Papa struck it from my hands. Soup went everywhere, splashing my brothers, which took their grin off.

"Oh, George," said Mama, mopping the wet table with her apron, "why'd you do that?"

"I *told* him not to mock."

What could he expect? Why, I hadn't taken even one step off the plantation, and here Papa talked like I would bring down ruination and judgment upon the whole family the minute I did.

He shoved his bowl away and stood up, then strode to the hearth, turned, and spread his arms. "Look at this here snug cabin we are in. Got a real door on swing hinges and table bowls sent down by Mr. Jefferson's own daughter."

Chipped and cracked bowls, I wanted to say. Everything she sent down from the big house was broke or tattered, and we yet must be forever grateful. Which I was, I was, and very few other families got anything at all sent down, I knew. But it irked me that Papa should make such a point of it now.

"And you," said Papa, pointin' at each one of us, "you sons of mine. Every one of you has been known to Old Master from the time you was born. Ain't a one of you sweated in the fields, as I have done. Ain't a one of you worked under the lash. Ain't a one been sold off." Then he came back to the table, lookin' at me the whole time. "And now you, Isaac," he said, grippin' the table edge with both hands, "my youngest, who's had it better from day one than even your brothers here. Plucked from my house to learn a trade by Mr. Jefferson himself, and bound in the morning for a far city, to live without no supervision of any kind. So, I mean to *impress* upon your forgetful mind not to take up *notions*."

"Notions," I said, being both exasperated and hungry by then. "What notions?"

"Ain't you been listenin', boy? Notions that once you leave this house you can run around all cocksure and troublesome, and just do what you *please*. My God, if *I'd* a talked to Mr. Jefferson, I'd a told him to keep you home. For you are nothin' but *young* and *ignorant*."

That done it. I jumped to my feet. "Well then, you're old and set in your ways. All *you* care about is what Mr. Jefferson think!"

Oh, that did rile up Papa. He got me by the shirt front and shoved me against the wall. "Don't you *ever* talk to me that way again. *I'm* the boss in this house."

Then I got riled, too. I broke his grip, which surprised him. I could see it in his eyes, this son of his that was no more a boy. My shirt tore, but I slid away. He got me again, but I pushed him off. I could smell the liquor on his breath, and that made me madder yet. I got a hand loose, made a fist, and would have struck him straight in the mouth, but Mama pushed her whole self between us. "Now stop!" she screamed, pushing us away from each other. "I'll have no fighting under my roof. Peace, for God's sake, peace between you two."

Papa threw open the door and pitched himself out into the night. Mama didn't even call after him, but pulled the door shut and hid her face. Little George shook his head. "That was pleasant," he said. Then he went off to our pallet bed, Bagwell after him.

Mama looked up from her hands. I could see the tears. "Why must you be so cruel?"

"*He*'s the cruel one," I said, pointing to the door.

She went to the hearth stone and sat, then patted the place beside her. "Come set."

I didn't want to. For I knew how she would love me up, and turn my heart from hard to soft, and I didn't want that. But she patted again and waited, and so at last I set.

"It's true what your father says, that some hands hate him."

"I know that."

"They say he's no more than a white man's nigger."

Though I had nearly struck him but moments before, now I felt such anger over such an accusation against my Papa, I hit a fist into my palm. "That ain't so."

"No, but that is what your father must live with. Every minute of every day in the fields he must watch his back."

"Why take it out on me?"

"Because he favors you."

I looked at Mama. "Favors me? He sure has a strange way of showin' it."

Mama pulled me close, and got her arm around my middle, which tickled. I pulled away, but she only laughed, and so I gave in and let her squeeze on me as she would. "He's always known," she whispered, "that of you three boys, you'd be the one that might prosper."

I looked at her. "You mean that?"

"I do. He has talked to Mr. Jefferson many a time about it. And here you are going to be a tinsmith, in *Philadelphia*."

"Apprentice tinsmith, you mean."

"Apprentice tinsmith, then," she said. "Main thing is, your father believes in you, but fears for you, too. Fears for himself, for all of us, if you do badly, or act foolish."

"I shall do no such thing."

She looked at me a long moment, gauging, I knew, just whether or not I would do such a thing. Then she brightened. "Look how my boy has grown," she said, and squeezed again. "Come back, he will be tall and strong and good-lookin'. A man your father be proud to call his own." Mama leaned into me then. "When you in Philadelphia, walk about for me, will you?"

"Sure, Mama," I said, suddenly full of myself. "I'll walk about for you. I'll walk all over that city. I will learn the ins and out of it, as if I was born there."

She laughed a little, then grew quiet. "Carry no troubles with you up there, my son. Just *live*. And if that be a notion, why then Isaac, *take* it."

She got to rockin' then, and got me to rockin' with her, till finally I got restless and stood up.

"Look at your torn shirt. And your pants, with the knee ripped. Oh, I got to fix those. Got to make some corn cakes, too, and pack your travel sack."

So I took off both shirt and pants, and went to the pallet bed, and squirmed in beside Bagwell and Little George. I lay there in the warm darkness, and heard an ember pop in the hearth, Mama singin' low as she stitched, a fox bark in the distance. Little George pulled at his edge of the quilt, and I pulled back on my edge, the old habit between us. In the mornin', I would be gone from all this, I thought, my place in the bed an' at table empty of me. Maybe for good, who could say? Tears came to my eyes. I wanted so badly then to just stay in that place, my home, for good or ill, until I was laid in the grave. But then I felt again how Papa had pushed me up against the wall, and wanted more than anything to get away, and prove myself. Tomorrow, I had said to myself, tomorrow it would be me and none other, Isaac Granger Jefferson, youngest son of Great George and Queen Ursula, proudly gone away to that far city with never a look back.

And so there I was, in the actual fact of it, on that journey, but hungry and tired by then, it bein' late in the day, an' Beulah cranky, too, when finally, we came to ol' Nat Gordon's place, and glad of it. Nat Gordon is long gone, but in them days his tavern was well known. It set at a crossroads, with a town built up around it, even a post office and dry goods store and tolerable stable, but mostly taverns. A long slope ran down to a pond, with campsites, some neat, some not, staked out around it. By a patch of woods was a stretch of level ground, and horse races, with bettin'.

On the road just in front of Nat's tavern was a dance of sorts goin' on. Rough and bearded white men, tall or broad, mugs in hand, hopped about to the squeak of fiddles and stomp of feet on porch boards. A few women even joined in and got twirled about. But what mostly caught my eye was a thin girl, black as me, not much more than a child, in poor rags, standin' off to one side. I caught her eye, too, and held it, and she began to move sideways toward me.

Then a hand squeezed my elbow. "What do you think you're doin', fool?" It was James. "That whore will take every penny in your pocket."

"Don't have a penny in my pocket, James," I said.

"That don't matter. What *do* matter is Mr. Jefferson's reputation. You are his property, remember? Wherever you go and whatever you do, his reputation goes with you. Now get that nag of yours stabled."

I had forgotten about Beulah. With all the commotion and goings-on, I'd got down from her and dropped the reins. I

looked around, but she was nowhere about. I took off runnin'
in search, and about wore myself out, frantic with lookin', but
come upon her at last, at the far edge of the pond, head down
in tall grass.

"Beulah!" I shouted.

She raised up her head, a whole clump of long grass dang-
ling from her lips.

"Get yourself over here, where you belong." I pointed to
the ground at my feet. "Now!"

Beulah kneaded the grass in through her teeth until it was
all gone, and then put her head down to tug at more.

I tromped over the soggy ground and got her by the halter.
"You don't listen very well, you know that?"

She just snorted, and back up the hill we went to the
stable, which was mostly full. Horses, two mules, a team of
oxen, even. Odin stood tall in his stable and had a cover over
his back. I found a back corner, got good hay for it, and tied up
Beulah there. Took off the saddle and blanket and rubbed her
down. "You already ate," I told her, "but I ain't, so I'm going
to find some supper. Behave yourself."

She just looked at me and stamped her foot, then swished
her tail.

From the kitchen boy at the back door I got watery stew
in a cup, and a hard crust. Nothin' like Mama's supper! The
porch was full of Negroes passing the whiskey jug, and some
smoking clay pipes. One man bragged how he made off with
his Master's horse. "It was a fine horse, too," he said, "sixteen
hands, and *speckled*."

Finally I walked back up to the stable, lay down in the
hay near Beulah, and was almost asleep when I heard a voice,
hardly more than a whisper—"Here, horse, here!" I turned to

look, ever so careful, and there in the moonlight that shone
through roof cracks was that poor thin raggedy girl. She had
climbed up on the stall boards and reached her hand out
toward Beulah.

I sat up and she pulled back her hand. "I like your horse,"
she said.

"She's a trial. But we get on." I could see sores on her arm,
and a scratch across her neck. "Ain't you got no home?"

She shook her head. "*You* can be my home."

I looked at her bosom, which was barely hid.

"I can make you happy."

"I'm happy as is."

"I mean *happy*."

She had the saddest face I ever saw, in one so young. I
shook my head.

"Can you borrow me some money?"

"I have no money."

"Something I can pawn?"

I looked at her small hand held out to me. "All I got is this
travel sack, and ain't nothin' in it, hardly."

"You must have *something*," she said as she wiggled her
fingers.

"All I got is this hammer," I said, and drew it out. "It come
from my own hand, forged in my brother's smithy."

"Can I hold it?"

I ran my finger along the smooth handle. "Only for a
minute."

She reached out and took hold of the one end, and pulled
it slow from my hand, then lifted it to her mouth and touched
her tongue to the hammer head. "Iron?"

"No," I said, "it made from steel."

She licked around her lips with her pointed tongue. "Can I have it?"

"No, you cannot have it."

"What's your horse's name?"

"Beulah," I said, patting her at the shoulder. "Means 'Promised Land.'"

The girl pointed at Beulah. "She lookin' at you."

I looked, and she was, and that's all it took, for the girl jumped down off the stall boards and ran off into the night. I got to my feet and went after her and crashed around in the thick briars where I had seen her go, but it was no use. I came out at last all cut and scratched and went back into the stable. "Aw, Beulah," I said, "that girl stole my hammer!"

But Beulah only shook her head and pawed at the hay.

CHAPTER FIVE

I break Mr. Rattiff's eyeglasses, and nearly get struck with a spit wad of tobacco

I was bothered in my sleep by a naggin' dream of that girl with her bosom scarcely hid, with one hand on my pants and the other in my travellin' sack. So I woke tired, as well as hungry and cold, and was only too happy to saddle up Beulah and get on up to the inn. But no sooner was I settled on her back than she wheezed out a long fart and bolted clean past the inn. It was all I could do to get her turned around and brought back to the front steps.

"Lord!" I said, "what's got into you?"

But she trembled so that I slid off her back and rubbed down along her front legs.

That's when James came out the front door onto the porch. "Quit messin' with that nag," he said. "Get in here and help with the baggage."

So I done, but Mr. Jefferson was still not ready, for no doubt he was takin' weather measurements and markin' these in a book, which gave me time to run around to the back door of the kitchen and bargain for a pair of ash cakes from the slop boy there, and a strip of hog bacon.

When I got back, James sat up in his coachman's seat. Mr. Rattiff, still in his night dress, came out the front door. "One of you boys go fetch my eyeglasses," he said. "They're in Mr. Hollingsworth's high spring phaeton, the one with red cushions."

Of course, James would not fetch 'em. He ordered me to. So I went, though resentful, and sure enough found 'em, stuck in the crease of the red cushion seat. Sat on, it looked like, which had bent the frames. I took 'em in hand and rode back up to the inn.

"Where's our friend Mr. Rattiff?" I asked.

"He went back inside to get dressed," James said.

I handed the eyeglasses to him.

"They're bent."

"Bend 'em back."

James handed the eyeglasses back to me. "I give that honor to you."

I took 'em in hand and looked 'em over. Mr. Ra*ttiff*. Then right quick, before my better judgment could take hold, I gave the eyeglasses a sharp twist. One glass fell to the ground and broke. "That should do."

"Have you lost your mind?" James hissed at me. "Now we *both* in trouble!"

I shrugged. "Can't help it. Like my Papa said, I'm young and ignorant."

James grabbed back the glasses and threw 'em way out in the yard. "They're lost, hear? You looked, but they were not to be found."

Mr. Rattiff fumed and fussed when he was told. "I'm an educated man," he said. "No educated man can be without his eyeglasses." He demanded we look again, and this time we both went, and sat a spell under a corkscrew willow that hung out over the lake, and had no ill words for each other, for a change.

At last we walked back up to the inn again, sad-faced. "No luck, Marse," said James. "Though we nearly took apart Mr. Hollingsworth's red cushion phaeton for lookin', no luck at all." Finally, Old Master loaned Mr. Rattiff a pair, and he was satisfied enough that we could go on.

The road to Fredericksburg was long, with some miles good, some not. Where good, I mean level and smooth, for the most part. Where bad, rough, rutted, and muddy in the bottoms. Beulah and me had a time keepin' up. In the late afternoon, we came to a stoned road, which took us into town, and lodgings on Charles Street. A stable boy climbed up in the coach to drive it around back, but insisted James give him a coin first.

"I will give you no coin," James said. "Don't you know this coach belongs to Mr. Thomas Jefferson? Just drivin' it to the stable should be payment enough for a ragged boy like you." Still, the boy would not go until he was paid. I walked Beulah by the bridle behind the coach, for she'd had enough of me in the saddle for that day.

The stable master showed me where to bed Beulah, and where the feed was, and so I got her settled good. Then I took the saddle blanket and my travel sack, went up to the inn, and laid out my bed just outside Mr. Jefferson's door, in case he should need an errand run, or his slop pot emptied.

Then this bent old woman came up the stairs, with a branch broom in hand. "What you doin', nigger boy?" she said.

"I mean to sleep here." I laid my hand on the door. "This is my Master's room."

"You cain't sleep there, naw you cain't. I don't sweep around no nigger."

The woman was poor white, but so dirty you might think she was mixed blood. I was tired and not about to take commands from such as her. "Don't you tell me what to do."

"I will. You in my hall, and this be my floor to broom."

"Do you run this inn?" I asked.

"I run the broomin'," she said back, then reached into her apron pocket and pulled out a twist of dark tobacco. With what teeth she had, she bit off a length and began to chew.

I pointed to the door. "You got any idea who my Master is?"

She stopped chewin'. "Who?"

"Mr. Thomas Jefferson, that's who."

Raising up both elbows, she spat out a wad of tobacco and a stream of juice so close I had to jump aside. "Don't know the man," she said, wipin' her chin. She raised the broom back over her shoulder. "Now git from this hall, nigger, or I shall strike."

Then Mr. Jefferson's door opened a crack and James showed his face. "What's all the noise out here?" He looked at me, then the woman. "Are you the trouble?"

She brought the broom down and shook her head. "Oh, no," She pointed at me. "It's him. He the cause."

James closed the door a moment, then opened it again. He had a chamber pot in hand, which he held out to the woman. "Dump this."

"I don't dump no pots. I only do broom work. And dustin'."

I heard Mr. Jefferson from inside the room. "Any trouble out there, James?"

James turned his head back into the room. "No, Mr. Jefferson, everything's in order out here, just as you like it." He looked at the chamber pot, and then at the woman. "Now, you want your job here, or don't you?"

The woman's mouth dropped open and tobacco juice ran down her bony chin. "Oh, yessir, I want my job here. I sure do." Then she began to cry and sniffle, most pitifully. "My husband is halt and mute. One child daft. I gots to have this job."

"Then dump this pot. Bring it back clean as a dinner plate."

The old woman dropped her broom, snatched it from his hands, and rushed down the steps.

"As for you, Granger," he said, glarin' at me, "who said we need you here? Now take up your bed and walk yourself back to the barn and sleep with that nag, where you belong." He pointed to the stairs. "Now."

Someday, I said to myself, someday I will get even with you, James Hemings. But now was not the time, not with Mr. Jefferson in that room blocked to view by James' own self, with his hand held tight to the doorknob.

"Beulah," I said, when I came back to her stall, "I don't mean this unkindly, but I hate that I am made to sleep by you in the barn, for a second night."

She pawed the hay toward her, and I grabbed some back, to make my bed. "And another thing. *Try* not to pass gas for a few hours, will you, please?"

What did she do? Stretch out her neck, lay over her tail, and do just *exactly* what I had politely asked her not to.

"You ornery beast," I said. "That does it for this night." So up I got, took my sack, and went all the way to the other end of the stable, and there made up my bed yet again, this time right under Mr. Jefferson's coach. Slept good, too.

CHAPTER  SIX

*Beulah gets a loose shoe, and
I meet "Hot Stuff"*

I woke to a voice. "Well, now, what have we here?"

The words froze me, and I kept my eyes tight shut, and tried almost to stop breathing, as if this would hide me. Was it the stable master that had found me? A constable?

"Is it a gypsy I see under there?" came the voice again. "A soldier? A man about town?"

"Uncle Bob!" I blurted out, as I opened my eyes. I was happy to see him, only I wished he wouldn't tease me that way. But it had been so long since he'd seen me, he thought I was still a boy, I guessed. I hiked up on my elbow, or tried to, and banged my head on the front axle, then crawled out between the wheels and stood up. I rubbed my head with one hand and picked the hay stems from my trousers with the other.

Uncle Bob stood there with hands on hips, beaming a smile. "Your pants are unbuttoned," he said.

I looked. So they were. I buttoned up and tucked in my shirt.

Now, Bob, he was not really my uncle, but of the Hemings brothers he was the one kindly to me, and so from the time I was a boy, I called him uncle. He always dressed lively and today more than usual, with a broad hat on, puffed shirt and close vest, trim-cut trousers, and of course, good shoes. "If you want to separate the wheat from the chaff," he would say, "look at a man's shoes."

"What you doin' here?" I asked.

He smiled broad. "Oh, I heard from Mr. Jefferson in a roundabout sort of way. He said my brother could maybe use some help navigatin' this party."

"Where did you come from?"

"Not far." He never would say for sure just where he went, nor how long he would be gone. Master Jefferson himself generally didn't seem to know. How he managed that, I had no idea, but because of it held him in a sort of awe, as a man who could somehow keep his distance from Old Master, but not annoy him so much as to get himself sold off.

"Do you mean to go all the way to Philadelphia with us?" I said. "I wish you would."

Uncle Bob shook his head. "Not that far. Got business elsewhere." He always did seem to have business elsewhere. "Now get yourself ready. We have the Rappahannock to cross this morning and then Georgetown to go through. Be good if we could get across the Potomac, too. So go on and get your horse saddled."

I found Beulah standin' with her right foreleg raised up, the toe of her hoof barely touchin' the ground. "What'd you do, dance all night?" I asked her and got down close to see what was wrong. At first, she shied away, but then she let me take hold of the hoof, and I found her shoe loose, and two tacks dropped down into the hay. She could not get me to Georgetown, or even as far as the Rappahannock on a loose shoe, that was sure. I patted her shoulder. "We're gonna take care of that shoe," I said. "You wait." Then I ran back to tell

Bob. He and the stable boy had the breast collars on both coach horses and were just then backing the one horse into its place and buckling the harness to the pole shaft.

"Uncle!" I said, "my horse has a loose shoe." I held up the tacks. "She can't walk. What do I do?"

He looked at the tacks. "You in luck, young man," he said. "There's a good farrier about four blocks from here, on Hanover Street. He's an old friend of mine, goes by the name of Raymond." He pointed how to get to Hanover Street. "Tell him I sent you." Then he took a roll of paper money from his pocket, stripped off one bill and gave it to me. "Bring back the change," he said.

He had enough of that, too, as always, his own money, mind you. How he made it, nobody really knew, and he wouldn't say. He gave me one bill, which I rolled up tight in my hand.

Four blocks may not sound like much, but coaxin' a horse that distance, especially Beulah, with a loose shoe, was a slow business, I mean to tell you. I fretted that James and Master Jefferson would leave without me. So I tugged and prodded and begged her to come on, but it was only when I got out the last of Mama's corn cakes that I was able to bribe her forward, by holding out a crumb until she hobbled up to get it with her big, wet lips, then backing up and holding out another.

I heard the hammer against the iron as we got onto Hanover Street, and smelt the forge when we came to the shop with the double doors thrown open, and saw the fire when I peeked in. A big-shouldered man in a good leather apron was heating a rod, the tip red.

"Excuse me, sir," I said, holding Beulah by her bridle, "I have a horse here with a loose shoe. Can you fix it?"

He did not answer, but poked the rod farther into the coals, and pumped the bellows a couple of times.

"The horse belongs to Mr. Thomas Jefferson," I said, "He's my Master."

This made no impression on him. "Come back at noon," he said, without turning.

"But noon will be too late!"

He said that couldn't be helped, in a matter-of-fact tone of voice, and I thought to raise my voice and object that he must attend to Beulah's shoe, and right that minute. But then I thought a minute. "Bob Hemings sent me," I said.

At once, the man Raymond let go that rod and turned right around. "Bob Hemings, you say? From Virginia?"

"Yes, sir, the very one."

Raymond smiled then and shook his head. "Bob Hemings is the most travelled man I know who is still in servitude. Why is that?"

"I don't know. He stays mum about his business. Will you please fix my horse's shoe?"

But he ignored my request and asked another question instead. "Can't he buy his freedom? I did. Took me ten years to get up the money, but I did."

I thought of myself working for ten years and then buyin' my freedom from Master Jefferson. Seemed an awful long time, though. I'd be somewhere around twenty-five.

"Well," said Raymond, and waved his hand. "I owe ol' Bob a favor. Bring that horse of yours over here and let me take a look."

Beulah would not take another step, but stood where she was, foreleg bent. So Raymond walked over to her and got his big arm over her neck and rubbed down along her cheek. "I'll bet there was a time," he said to her, "when you had every stud in the barn after you. Ain't that right?" She nuzzled Raymond's hand, and that made me mad. For here I had spent these last days with Beulah, and I thought she was as good as my horse, and now this man did a little sweet-talkin' to her, and not a single corn cake as bribe, and she acted like she had plain forgot all about me.

Raymond let go and looked at me. "Get hold of her bridle again. Hold her steady." And I did, and scratched behind her ear, which she liked better than a rubbin' down her cheek, I knew.

He ran his hand down along her foreleg, bent it at the hock, and inspected both hoof and shoe. Then he set down that foreleg, and lifted the other, and inspected that hoof and shoe, too. Then her hindlegs, first the right one, then the left. After he set the left hindleg back down, Raymond stood up straight again and looked at me. "How far do you mean to go on this horse?"

"Philadelphia," I said, and puffed my chest a little. "Yes, sir, the great city of Philadelphia."

Raymond raised an eyebrow. "Not on this horse you ain't, not with those shoes. Every one is thin and wore, and got tacks missin'. Hooves need to be trimmed, too."

"But I don't have time for all that," I burst out.

"Better that than get twenty miles down the road somewhere and find yourself on a lame horse." He eyed me. "You still in a slave state, you understand."

"I got a pass."

He laughed.

"Well, then," I said, growing impatient, "how long is it going to take to fix her shoes?"

"About an hour, maybe more, bad as she is."

"I could get left way behind in that hour," I objected.

"Look, son, it's got to be done."

I wondered just how long it would be before people quit calling me "son." But he was right. "Go ahead then," I said.

He asked if I had money, and I said yes, Uncle Bob's money, and plenty of it. Then I stuck out the bill.

Raymond took the bill and laughed again. "You go back and tell that Bob Hemings he shorted me by half! Go on, now. By the time you get back, I should have one hoof and shoe about finished."

So I dashed out of his shop, down Hanover Street, and then to the barn. But the coach was gone. Had Mr. Jefferson and his party left town already? I flat out ran up to the inn, and found the coach parked out front, thank goodness, Uncle Bob loading luggage. He put down a snap bag and smiled. I tried not to show how scared I had been that he and everybody might have been gone. He asked where my horse was, and I said with Raymond, who said she needed all four shoes fixed, not just one, and hooves trimmed, too.

"Oh," he said, and set up the snap bag on the box trunk. "When will he be done?"

I told him an hour. "Also, he said—well he said you shorted him by half."

Bob cursed under his breath, took out his roll of money again and then laughed. "You tell that Raymond I shall take it out of his hide, next time," he said, and stripped off another bill.

I grabbed the bill and turned to run, but Uncle Bob caught me by the arm. "Listen to me, Isaac. We can't wait for you as Mr. Jefferson is eager to push on. And we will with luck be across the Rappahannock by the time Raymond is done with your horse."

I didn't like the sound of that at all. "You sure you can't wait for me?" I said. "It's only an hour."

He shook his head. "If it was up to me, we'd wait. But it's not. You must catch the ferry yourself. Go straight down Commerce Street here, right to the river. Ferry dock is on the left. I shall pay your fare ahead. Tell the ferryman you are with Mr. Jefferson's party." He took me by the shoulders. "You got that?"

"Yes, Uncle, I got that. But I still don't see why you can't wait."

"Now, Isaac, go on. The sooner you get back there and get your horse, the sooner you can come on."

Raymond was hard at work, I was happy to see. He had the one forehoof well trimmed and was just then pulling from the red coals with tongs the new shoe. This he fitted to the hoof just so, pounding it in place. Then he dipped it into a bucket of water, where it hissed and steamed, until he drew it out, set it to the hoof again, and tacked it in place, neat and tight. He set Beulah's foot down.

"I got Bob's money," I said, and held out the second bill. "He said he's going to take it out of your hide, next time."

Raymond took the bill and put it in his pocket. "Just let 'im try."

I couldn't tell whether he was jokin' or not.

Then he went back to work. But I was too restless to just stand and wait, so I went outside and stood where I could see the river and looked for the ferry. I couldn't see it, though.

Good, I thought, maybe I can catch it before they go. I went back inside, and watched Raymond at the other foreleg, then the right hind leg. I could barely stand still and went out to look for the ferry again. But there was still no sign of it on the river, thank God. I rushed back into Raymond's shop and fidgeted until he had the last shoe done. He stood up and stretched his back. "Now," he said, "you and that horse can get to Philadelphia."

"Yes, sir!" I said, "and thank you!" I took Beulah by the bridle.

"You could do me a favor," he said, "when you get up there."

I wanted desperately to tell him that I had no time to talk about favors, for I had to get down to the ferry, but he had gotten serious all of a sudden. "What favor?" I said.

"Look up a woman for me."

The way he said it, I didn't know if he meant a wife kind of woman, or some other kind.

"A woman called Marge," he said. "Though mostly she is known as *The Boss*."

"I never heard a woman called the boss, Raymond. I probably won't be able to find her."

"Oh, you'll know her when you find her, believe me," he said. "Because, little brother, when she get aholt of a man, you *know*, she *The Boss*." Then he just burst into a big laugh.

I imagined this big-bosomed woman catching me in a corner somewhere, squeezin' me so tight I like to die, and then doing some other things with me. "Look, Raymond," I said, "Philadelphia is an awful big city, you know."

"Oh, little brother, she be easy to find, don't worry. Just ask for the Dempsey place. It's a huge ol' house up on a high hill. She's the *main* house servant there. Marge, she run the place. Them white folks, they pure helpless without her. She add up the money, hire the help, run the kitchen. Like I say, she The Boss." Then he caught hold of my hand. "You will look her up for me, won't you? Promise me that much."

All I could think was, *I got to get down to the ferry*. But I couldn't, not until Raymond let go, and so I promised.

He gripped my hand and looked at me almost fierce. "Tell her, *Hot Stuff* sent you." Then he laid back his head and just hooted.

CHAPTER SEVEN

*We cross the Rappahannock—and
the sore trouble we encounter*

I fairly jumped onto Beulah's back and lo and behold, happy in her new shoes, she broke into an honest trot. Maybe I could yet make that ferry boat, I thought. But soon as I turned down Commerce Street, and the river lay in full view at the bottom, I saw the white top of Master Jefferson's coach, bright in the sun, just toppin' the first rise on the other side of the river, with Old Master himself out front, riding handsome on Odin. My heart sank. If James drove as hard as he had so far, how many miles would the coach be out front of us when finally we did get across?

I slowed Beulah to a walk, for I would rather that, than speed down to the river bank and just have to stand waiting. I watched the ferryman workin' his winch, as the ferryboat cut across the river current toward us at an angle along its iron cable. At last, with painfully slow exactness, the ferryman nosed his flat boat to the near shore, threw a cable over a post on either side, opened the wide gate at the shore end of the boat, latched it in place, and dropped the ramp. By this time, Beulah and me had come right up to the dock nearly, and stopped. The ferryman leaned against one cable post, took a short knife from his pocket, unfolded the blade, and began to clean his nails, which were dirty. He paid no mind to me at all.

I waited as long as I could stand. He was white, after

all. "Mr. Ferryman, Marse," I said, "can I board, now? Bob Hemings he paid my fare ahead. He's with his brother James, the coachman, and my Master, Mr. Thomas Jefferson. That you just took across." I pointed to the far bank.

The ferryman folded up his knife, put it back in his pocket, spat tobacco in the river, and squinted up at me. He had so much beard I could hardly see his face. "If'n you want to talk to me," he said, "you git down off thet horse. I don't talk to no nigger thet sets up on a horse."

I got so mad, so quick, I could have clubbed him with a post if I'd had one. But I settled myself, got down off Beulah, and looked straight at the man. He had on a broad hat and showed red in his eye whites. "I am with the Thomas Jefferson party, that you ferried across the river just now. The coachman, Mr. Bob Hemings, paid you my fare. So I request passage on your ferryboat."

"Oh," said the man, spitting into the river again, "you mean the white nigger. He lied. He didn't pay me nothin'."

"That's not so!" I burst out. "Mr. Bob Hemings told me he would pay, and he's a truthful man!"

The ferryman scratched at his crotch. "I say he lied. All niggers lie."

I could hardly hold back my anger. "My Master, Mr. Jefferson, is a powerful man. He will not like it when I tell him you delayed my passage."

The man tugged at his beard and pulled at the brim of his dirty hat. "I don't give a good god damn who your master is. I'm the master here. Now pay your fare, or I shall fetch the constable on you."

"Mr. Bob Hemings paid my fare, I told you that."

The ferryman shook his head. "And I told you he lied. You

got to pay, same as every man. Jes' cause you a nigger don't mean you is special and don't have to."

Oh, I hated that ferryman. His dirty shirt, his body smell, his fat hands, his small, red eyes, the tobacco spittle in his beard. I could have killed him, killed him! "How am I supposed to get across the river if you won't take me?" I said at last, musterin' all my self control.

He loaded his lip with another wad of tobacco. "Well," he said, "you kin ford your horse, *if* you got the gumption. Most niggers don't." He opened his mouth in a sort of grin, and black teeth showed.

"Gumption?" I said. "You lookin' at gumption, mister."

"All right then," he said, and spat. He pointed to a path just along the shoreline. "You see this towpath here? Foller it all the way to that riffle up there, see it?"

"I see it."

"Walk your horse 'cross that riffle, jes at the island head. Other side of that island is a narra channel to the fur bank. Stiff current run through there."

"So?"

"So that's where the gumption come in."

I got back on Beulah. "That's it? A channel? That ain't nothin'." I sat as tall in the saddle as I could and walked her on up the towpath. The ferryman shouted after me, but I ignored his insults and watched the river ahead, the way it divided around the island head. When we got up that far, I turned Beulah to face our crossing. The water looked shallow, and very passable.

"C'mon, girl," I said to her, "let's show that bastard."

Beulah stepped right down into the water, got her feet solid, and went ahead, step by step. I could see the bottom was stony, and feel it was slippery. "Easy," I said, "easy now." I was glad she had on new shoes. We worked around a pair of big rocks, and then Beulah splashed out of the water onto the island, which was also stony, and white as bone in the sun. I let her stand quiet for a moment. "There now," I said, scratchin' along her mane, "we doin' it."

Then I walked her to the far side of the island, where the channel ran. The current was stiff, sure enough, and hard to tell how deep. The far bank was cut sheer. Where could we cross? Upstream, the channel was slower, but broader, too, and the bank as steep. No good. But downstream, just t'other side of a big rock, the bank did not look to be cut. I walked Beulah down that far, to get a look. A game trail came right down by the rock. Good. Though the current was strong, the channel from where we stood to that game trail, I judged to be no more than twenty-five feet across.

I leaned forward and rubbed behind Beulah's ears. "All right then," I said, "let's show some gumption."

And then with no more urging from me than a click of the tongue, Beulah stepped forward to the very edge of the water, bobbed her head, snorted, and stepped in. But there was no bottom, and though she pushed off strong with her hindquarters, her front half was turned downstream at once, and her head went under. I nearly pitched out of the saddle, but hung on, and drug back on the reins to get her head up, she meanwhile strugglin' with all her might to get turned toward the far bank. But we were carried downstream anyhow, and came around a sharp bend, where a tree had fallen across, no more than a foot above water. Beulah's head crashed straight into that tree trunk, blood burst from her nostrils and I felt her whole body go limp, and then slide under the tree. I would have struck, too, but let go the reins and grabbed hold of that trunk with both arms. My left foot had got so stuck in the stirrup I thought it would be wrung off, but I got it free somehow, as Beulah washed on down the river, leavin' me to work my way along the tree trunk arm over arm to the far bank. There I let go and crawled on all fours up the muddy game trail and lay down at the top, heavin' for air, and feelin' like my hip bone was about pulled from the socket. When at last I got my breath back, I burst into tears for poor old Beulah. Just that mornin', she had new shoes put on, and trotted almost like a show horse. Then I worried over myself, for here I had lost one of Mr. Jefferson's own horses, even if she was old and sometimes cantankerous. What would I say to him of the loss? If I caught up to him, that is. But with no horse, how could I?

Oh, I felt the fix I was in. But I got to my feet, as a man must do, and limped down along the river some ways, shivering in my wet clothes as I went, but saw no sign of Beulah's body. Then sat down, in another burst of tears, and tended to my achin' foot. There was no break, thank goodness, but some skin peeled back at the ankle bone, and the whole business, foot and ankle, red and swollen. From high water debris nearby, I pulled loose a sturdy stick to use for a cane, and then, utterin' up one more prayer for Beulah and her sorry end, I hobbled out from among the trees. Some way off there stood a shabby cabin, smoke risin' from a clay chimney, and so I struck out for it, hopin' I could find a decent welcome there, and get warm at the fire.

CHAPTER EIGHT

Me, Sam the Runaway, and on the road in a coffin box

It was a long cold hobble to that cabin, my foot tender with every step. Then my stick broke and I had to crawl the last yards through a field of corn stubble. Dragged myself to the door front and knocked with the heel of my hand. I knocked again, harder. Door but cracked open, and a mulatto woman looked out at me.

She frowned. "Sam?"

"I'm froze," I said

She shut the door.

I knocked again and kept knockin' until she opened, and when she did she asked once more if I was Sam, Sam the Runaway, and though it was a lie I was too cold to argue the point, and agreed heartily through chatterin' teeth that I was the very same and could she please let me in to get warm.

She hesitated, then swung the door wide. "Josh!" she called out. "Help me here." A strong boy with drool at his lips grabbed hold my arm, jerked me in, and dragged me over to the fire, where he and the woman stripped off my clothes and wrapped me in a blanket. They made me drink hot tea, but I retched it up. Thought I would shiver to pieces till Josh lay out close beside me and put his head upon my chest. My shiverin' began to ease then. Warmth crept back into me at last and I fell off to sleep and knew no more till the woman shook me by the shoulders. "Sam. Sam! It's mornin'. You must rouse up now. A man comin' soon with a wagon. He going to take you."

I sat up then. "Take me? Take me where?"

She frowned at me again, as she had at the front door. "Gracious, son. Did the chill drive it out of your head? Freedom Land, that's where. North ten days to Chillicothe. Cross the Ohio River and you in Freedom Land."

Freedom Land? Freedom land! All at once I could see myself in that land, with my own piece of it. Bottom land, with a clear water river through it. Good timber right up to the ridge top. And a view west to lands some said went on forever.

The woman shook me again. "Get up."

The one foot was tender when I stood, and that brung it all back, how Beulah cracked against the tree and then went under, my shoe stuck in the stirrup. I began to cry, I did.

"What's wrong, son?"

"Just a near escape."

"Don't use up your tears yet," she advised. "You got more near escapes ahead."

She held out my clothes, dry and clean, even drawers. Josh stood close by and watched me pull on my shirt. He touched my sleeve.

"What shall I do for shoes?" I asked, lookin' at her. "Wear but the one and hope to find another? Go barefoot?"

"Take these," said the woman, and held out a pair of shoes with thick soles and good heels. "They're fitted, right foot and left. Hardly wore. Made for my husband, but he shall git no use from 'em where he gone. Nor from these socks."

I never had had socks. Not like the ones she held out, made of wool.

"Don't just look, put 'em on."

So I did, and the shoes after, then stood and walked about, testin' the foot. There came a knock on the door just then, a rap of three.

"Out to the wagon you go," she said and handed me a paper, wrapped. "Bread and bacon."

Josh swung open the door and I saw outside a stout wagon, with a team of big horses. The driver, a white man, stepped over the seat and stood in the wagon bed. He lifted a box lid. "Climb in, and I shall pull the canvas over top."

I looked at the woman, anxious.

She nodded. "You can trust 'im."

I looked at the driver. "Must I travel in a coffin box?" For I didn't much like the prospect, with a canvas over top, in a wagon drove by a white man to parts unknown.

"If you will travel in my wagon, you must," he said. "Get comfortable in it, for it's thirty miles till I pass you off to the next man. You travel in a whiskey barrel then." He laughed and slapped his knee. "You shall wish you were back in my coffin."

I was not comforted by his laughter, and hesitated to climb into his wagon, and just peered over into that coffin box. There was a blanket laid on the bottom, and a view hole cut in the front end.

"See that latch there?" he said, pointing. "When it comes time, I shall rap three times on the wagon seat. Throw back that latch and the bottom shall swing open. Just drop on through to the ground, you hear?"

I nodded.

"Don't go to sleep on me. When I rap, drop through at once."

"Are you goin' north on the Georgetown Road?"

"Some miles, and then I turn west and head for the Gap."

I didn't know what the Gap was, but knew I didn't want to go through it, nor turn west, but hold tight to the Georgetown Road. "Will you rap just as you make the turn?"

He got a puzzled look on his face. "Why?"

"'Cause it mark a turn in my life, that turn in the road."

The driver shrugged. "I guess. Three raps, a skip, and rap twice again. That shall be the signal." He leaned over and rapped on the seat just so.

I turned and looked to the woman, who stood half out the door, with Josh, mouth open, close beside. "I have somethin' I must tell you."

She waved at me. "Shush you. I know."

So I had not fooled her at all, I thought. Yet she had taken me in. "Thank you for your kindness," I said. "You and Josh both."

"Then do a kindness for some other, when the chance come around."

"I will," I said, and lay down cautious in the coffin box. The driver set the top in place above me. I heard the canvas pulled over it, and then the noise of harness chains and axle tree, and the wagon got underway.

CHAPTER   NINE

*I travel in my coffin box, then
limp along on my own feet again*

O h, then I wanted to burst from that dark coffin box,
rattlin' down this road to God knows where. For how did I
know this white man was not takin' me straight to the auction
block? Get the nigger in a box and go sell 'im, that was his
plan. Sure, it was. That old woman and her Josh were in on it
all, and would take their cut, too. What a fool I had been. I got
hold of the wood handle beside me and made ready to pull it
back. Let me drop down out of this wagon right now! But wait
there, Isaac, I told myself. Suppose farmers were right then
balin' hay and should see me high tail it across their fields. Or
suppose we was just then comin' to a crossroads, and a patrol
of horsemen was gathered there. They would like nothin'
better than to catch me. Chase me first, make sport of it, then
run me to ground. I hated to think what would happen to me
then. Or suppose we were just then comin' to a town, and a
merchant's wife and children stood on the porch of their dry
goods store. "Look, Mama, what's that nigger runnin' for?"

So I talked myself down, and only pushed the coffin lid
up a mite. Enough for a little air, a little light, which made
me feel some better. Until I thought, "You are the one that
got yourself into this mess." Why had I not said, right off,
"No, I am not Sam the Runaway"? But I hadn't, and so here I

was. I badly wanted to be astride old Beulah once again, ridin'
happy down the road, having crossed that channel after all. I
cried in the darkness for that old horse, and for myself, too.

Just then the wagon slowed and came to a stop. What was
going on? One of the horses stamped. A harness shook.

"What's your load here, Mister?" came a rough voice. It
was the ferryman. But of course! This wagon had to get across
the Rappahannock, too.

"Coffins, brother," said my driver. "We shall all end up in
such a box, when our time comes."

"Where you bound to?"

"Wherever death rules."

Laughter.

"Now level with me, where to?"

"Lewisburg."

"That's a fur piece."

"Yes, it is, but they like fancy coffins there."

Fancy coffin, I said to myself. It's a hard-on-the-bones
coffin, is what it is.

"Not carryin' any niggers in 'em, are you?"

"Oh, hell no. I got an honest business to run."

"Mind if I look?"

"I'd rather you didn't. I got a funeral to make. Town
mayor, no less."

"I got a business to run, too, you know. And don't want
no trouble with the law, for lettin' niggers sneak across my
river."

There was silence a moment. Then I heard the canvas bein'
laid back, and the rap of knuckles on my coffin lid. I clutched
the latch handle. Let him not catch me trapped in here!

"It's fair work," said the ferryman, so close I could hear

him spit. Spit on my coffin box, he did. Oh, that made me so mad I wanted to burst from the box and give him such a fright as would kill him. I heard him lay the canvas back over. "Guess you got no niggers in here, then. If you had, I'd have smelt 'em. I can smell a nigger."

Silence again.

"Your horses shy of water?" asked the ferryman.

"No."

"Then come aboard, but easy."

There passed some fussin' and bother as the wagon was rigged for passage, and I heard the wheel chocks go into place. Then at last I heard the squeak and groan of the cable winch and felt the ferry boat, with the heavy wagon aboard, press forward across the current. And so I crossed the river Rappahannock after all, under the very nose of that dirty, filthy, hell-bound, tobacco-spittin' ferryman. Oh, I could have fairly sung out when I felt his boat nose the far shore, and heard the gate open, and the ramp drop down.

"Good day to you, sir."

"Good day, coffin man."

As the wagon, creakin' and groanin', got underway again and I bounced along over a rough road, I thanked my wagon driver from top to bottom. He was a good man after all, even if he was white. He had lied to protect me and put himself in danger at it. He was well and truly bound for the Freedom Land, just as he had said. Then I smiled to myself, travelling in my own coffin box. Yes, I decided, I liked adventure. Was made for it. And there was some reason for pride in myself, yes there was. Enough pride that I began to wonder what if I was to just go on to Freedom Land after all. How would that be? I pictured myself in store-bought clothes, standin' on the porch of a brick house—well, maybe not brick, but clapboard at least—lookin' out over a prosperous farm all my own, with a river full of fish. Then in my picture, I went back inside, to my library, with books to the ceiling, where I dictated a letter:

"Mama, Papa, this is Isaac. Many are the adventures I been through, but in the end I have done very well for myself here in Ohio. So I say, come out to Freedom Land, you and Little George, and Bagwell, for I have room enough for all. And could use the help, as my holdings are large and business strong." I imagined Master Jefferson reading over my letter, James Hemings at his shoulder, both of 'em in shock. What a pretty picture that was to me.

Then the front wagon wheel on my side must have dropped into a hole, for there was a terrible bang, and I thought for a moment the whole load of coffins above me would shift and slide out, but what happened was I banged my head good, and felt of a sudden rather poorly about my future in Ohio. I would have no big farm there. It would be field work for me, that's all. Grub roots. Hack weeds. Shovel barns. Work to the bone, but rags on my back, dirt for a bed. Lose a good Master—a fine Master—to get stuck with a whip-happy field boss. No, no, that would not do. I must get on my way to Philadelphia, as planned, and learn the tinsmithin' trade. That was the only way to come into Freedom Land, with a *trade* in hand, for goodness' sake. I got myself so worked up, I put my hand on the latch handle again. Let me drop through and get on my way. This ol' wagon was *too* slow. I could hardly bear to lie in that box one minute more, I would run the distance to Philadelphia. Run! But sense came to me. "Come now, Isaac," I said aloud to myself. "Run to that city? And just how far do you think that might be?" No, no, no. Let this wagon carry me as far down the Georgetown Road as it would. No use goin' them miles on foot, for I shall get all the walkin' I want after that. And anyway, was I for sure my swelled foot was up to walkin' just yet?

So I lay quiet instead, eager to hear the raps that would mark the wagon's turnin' off the Georgetown Road. *Then* let me drop through. And only then. But the road had gotten fairly good, no drops or bumps, and I only rocked back and forth, as if I lay in a baby cradle. "Don't sleep," I told myself. "Don't you sleep." But I did. For try as I might, I just could not stay awake.

A jolt woke me. But for a moment, I did not know where I was. I had been dreamin' of back home, and tryin' to get out of our cabin door, which wouldn't open whether I shoved or tugged. Then another jolt came, and I knew *exactly* where I was. No cabin, but this wretched coffin box. Had we passed the Georgetown Road? I was sure we had, or was I? If so, how far back? Might be I had only been asleep a minute. But how could I know? I was just all confused and thought I must ask the driver. But show myself? Goodness, no.

Then, oh then, I heard it: three sharp raps, a skip, and then two raps more. This was it, the turn off from the Georgetown Road. I had to get out. So I got hold of the latch handle and pulled—and pulled and jerked and then pushed on that handle for all I was worth but could get no good purchase on the thing and it would not budge. The wagon slowed, the shaft creaked in the hub, and the driver called out to his wheel horse. Still jerking at the handle, I felt the wagon straighten, and the horses pull forward together. Trapped, I was. Tricked! And soon shackled up and carted south, I was sure. So I twisted around as best as I could and slung both hands in a double fist against that handle, and just like that a trap door bottom popped open and I fell out. Fell through and hit the hard ground with my full weight, and only barely ducked my head before the rear axle passed over me, and I was left groanin' on the stones. I looked up to see that wagon load of coffin boxes turn a bend, then ran, or rather limped, with my still-swollen foot and now banged shoulder and hip, fast as I could get out of sight into the roadside brush and brambles. Then pushed through that tangle, and stood a little while under a bunch of sumac, their berries all furry red. I wasn't no fugitive, but I sure felt like one just then. I stretched, and rubbed, and felt of my ankle, then came back careful through the tangle, checked to see there was no traffic either way, foot or wagon, and stepped boldly out into the road. Glad I was to be on my own feet again!

CHAPTER TEN

*I meet the Quack, am healed, then
rescued by Uncle Bob*

I walked back to where the wagon had turned off, where stood a tall post with a signboard, and leaning against it a Negro man, with a tattered coat on and a fiddle and bow in hand. He looked up the road and then down, as if he was waitin' for somebody.

I came up to him and said, "Is this the Georgetown Road?"

The man looked at me. He had a double scar on his forehead. He said, "Why yes, it is." He pointed his finger up at the signboard. "Can't you read?"

My ears got red. "I mean to, in time."

"Well, young man, there's no time like the present. Let me teach you." So he turned around, and holding both fiddle and bow in one hand, reached up with his other and traced out the letters, one by one, saying each one as he went. Then he had me repeat after him, and trace the letters as he had done, and imitate the dignified way he spoke the words, which now seemed to me glorified: *Georgetown Road.*

He was all for going on with the lessons, too, as for example readin' the worn label on the inside pocket of his coat, but I was anxious to know how far ahead Master Jefferson was. "Have you seen a white-topped coach go by here," I asked, "pulled by a matched pair?"

The man tugged at his chin whiskers. "Well, I have seen an

ox cart, the right-hand ox with a horn broke off," he began. "I have seen a gentleman's carriage, with family crest embossed in gold on the door. I have seen a wagon with but three wheels and a peg with a skid to drag the ground where the fourth wheel ought to have been. I have seen families with no cart or wagon at all, dressed in black from head to toe but for the women's bonnets, and I have seen two boys pushin' hoops, and an Indian in buckskin and feathers, and a Scot in his colors and kilt, and a woman with a wooden leg, and a dog with but one ear, and two hogs loose, and a man with a wicker box on his back bigger than himself, full of quacking ducks."

I thought he was done with his recital of travelers. But he drew a deep breath, and in a deeper tone he said, "And I have by God seen a coffle of four slaves, shackled together at the neck and short-shackled at the ankles, half-running in step, and with the man over 'em on horseback." He shook his head. "But no, I have seen no white-topped phaeton."

His mention of the coffle made me shudder, and I checked in my pants pocket for Master Jefferson's pass. It was there, thank goodness, though wrinkled from the river soaking and the ink bled out in places.

The man then put his fiddle under his chin, took up his bow, and commenced to play the mournfulest tune I ever heard, and so with his music in my ear I joined the traffic going north on the Georgetown Road, favoring my foot as I went, almost in time to that man's tune. I began to think that if he had seen no white-topped coach but had been there long enough to see such a deal of traffic, that Mr. Jefferson might be a day or more ahead of me, and that I might just have to walk all the way to Philadelphia on my own. But how far was that, exactly? I thought I'd better know, so I watched for a Negro to come my way that I could ask but saw none. Then a white man came up beside me, pushin' a barrow with an old woman in it, her shawl pulled down over her bonnet so close that only her eyes showed, and the tobacco pipe in her mouth.

"'Scuse me, kind sir," I said, "but can you tell me how far to Philadelphia?"

The man set down his barrow and looked at me. "You don't mean to walk it, do you?"

"I may have to."

He turned to the old woman in the barrow. "Mother, lend me your pipe."

She scowled at him. "What fur?" she said, without takin' the pipe from between her clenched teeth.

"I got some thinkin' to do for this unfortunate darkie here."

She grumbled, but then handed the pipe to him. "Don't smoke it all up, son."

The man took the pipe from her hand, clenched the stem in his teeth, and packed the tobacco in the bowl with a nail head he drew from his pocket. Then he stood smokin' for several minutes. He looked so satisfied, puffin' out smoke rings slow and easy that I wondered if he would ever speak again.

At last he took the pipe from his mouth. "To Philadelphia from here I judge to be about two hundred miles," he said. "Now, if you average three to four miles per hour, and keep right at it, you can make twenty to thirty miles a day."

"Give the pipe back, Henry," said the woman, holding out a bony hand.

"Which means," he said, takin' one more draw before

handin' it back, "you got six to ten days walking ahead of you. That don't account for terrain, of course. Or calamity of some sort."

I didn't know what *calamity* meant but didn't like the sound of it.

"Are we going," groused the old woman, through a puff of smoke, "or do you mean for me to die here?"

"Yes, Mother, we're going," said the man, who picked up the barrow handles and went on his way.

I felt lonely all at once, and sorry for myself, to see that pair go. Add to that, I felt dog-tired, to think of all the distance I had yet to go. Six to ten days. My foot was not up to such a journey. I would have to rest now and then, which would only put me farther behind. And how was I to eat, through all them days on the lonely road? For I had no money. I pictured myself days or maybe weeks from now, pulling into Philadelphia little better than skin and bones and dressed in rags. Mr. Jefferson would probably turn me around and send me back home. But I dared not face Papa, if that was to be. What then? Wander the earth and play a mournful fiddle like the signpost man?

I got so down-hearted that I just set down right there on a big rock, as if I was never going to take another step until finally I said to myself, "Isaac, this will get you nowhere. You *must* get up and on your way. Somethin' good shall happen along." So I pulled myself to my feet and went limpin' onward. Just a little farther on around a bend, I saw a big coach, painted all red with yellow letters on the side, parked at the roadside. Standin' on the rooftop was a white man, in a red coat to match the coach, with a tall hat on. A crowd had gathered, lookin' up at that man, who strode from side to side and pointed here and there.

"Do you suffer from gout?" he cried out. "Catarrh, boils, weeping sores?"

The crowd kept gettin' bigger, to see the way he flung out his arms as he talked and shook his hat in the air. "I say friends, are you afflicted with rheumy eyes, constriction of the bowel, inflammation of the joints, pressure on the brain pan?" He raised his long arm into the air, shakin' his finger at the sky. "Then *Science* is your answer!" Reaching inside his coat, he took out a little blue bottle, and held it up for all to see. "*This*, friends, is my patented *liquid science*. Product of my *years* in the laboratory. Got my *very* last bottles for sale *today*, at a *steep* discount."

"Patent my arse!" shouted out a short man nearby.

The woman beside him spat. "The man's a quack."

They both turned and walked off. And since they seemed so sure, I turned back to the road, too, but had not gone three steps before the man up on the coach box called out, "You there, Blackie! You with the limp!"

I turned around.

"Dear God, help me citizens! Fetch that poor black boy up here."

I was at once grabbed up by many white hands, lifted clean off my feet and carried bodily to the coach. I feared to struggle, lest I be taken for a runaway, and so let myself be passed right to the top, where the quack got me by the hand and pulled me to my feet. He laid his arm along my shoulder. "Dear friends," he said, in a voice that sounded as though he was mournin' a loved one, "just look at this poor child of God, black though he be." He knelt down and pressed his thumbs hard upon my foot.

I cried out and jerked my foot away.

He shook his head. "A terrible case!" he called out. Then
to me he whispered, "Nepholis. Pretend you got *Nepholis of
the foot bone*. Sing it out when I pinch your ear, and you shall
get a penny."

A penny. That might get me a meal.

The quack stood straight again and looked out over the
crowd. "Oh, the boy is frightfully bad. *Mortal* bad. I never
seen *worse*. He has *Nepholis,* curse of the ages. Nepholis of
the foot bone." The quack pinched my ear. "Is that so, poor
boy?"

"Gad, yes, it's so," I said and pulled away from him. And
then I don't know what got into me, maybe it was the sight
of all those white people gawkin' up at me, but I went on in a
wavery sort of voice. "Nepholis of the foot bone, sure enough!
Since *birth*. And seepin' into my leg bone, too."

The doctor looked at me in surprise. "Two pennies," he
whispered. Then he held up the blue bottle for all to see. "Let
Science banish this awful disease!" He pulled out the stopper
with his teeth, which he spat away in a long arc, and made me
take the bottle. "Drink up, and you got a third penny."

I stood with that bottle in hand and looked out over the
sundry crowd all gathered up in silent waiting to see what
I would do. I smelled from the bottle, and wondered if three
pennies, or any number of pennies, was payment enough.

"Go on now, Blackie," said the quack, pressing my elbow.
"Don't you be shy, drink up your medicine."

So I drank, and wished to heaven I hadn't, for the bitter
taste of it on my tongue, and the sharp fumes in my nose,
and the feel of it burnin' its way down inside me. I looked at
the quack, with his long, bent nose and tall hat with a yellow
band. Then I turned again and looked out over the crowd,

which it seemed to me stretched out in every direction and all the faces looking up at me as if I was about to become a miracle, a poor Negro soon to sprout angel wings. I saw the roadway with its traffic goin' north and south, windin' its way far, far off into the awful distance. So many people, and each one bound to his own fate. I saw the hills out beyond, and the mountains in color beyond them, and the sky above, with clouds booming up, and a golden sun breakin' through. It was all a wonder, it was. The whole of life a *wonder!* And then I saw, comin' down the road at a full gallop, a fancy horse, head held high, mane flung out behind. People rushed to get out of the way, for that horse and rider were flat flyin'. Somehow, I *knew* this horse. Why, it was *Odin*. Mr. Jefferson's own riding horse, and on his back Bob Hemings, yes, Uncle Bob Hemings in his felt hat with the rolled brim.

I leaped into the air at the sight of 'em, both man and horse. "Healed!" I shouted out. "Healed!" Then I scrambled down off the coach and jumped to the ground, foot not hurtin' atall, and ran through the crowd, still shouting as I went. "Healed! I'm healed!"

Bob saw the ruckus by then and brought great Odin to a mighty stop, snortin' and backin' on his haunches. "I have looked everywhere for you, Isaac Granger," he said.

I looked up at him, and felt a mighty big smile come into my face. My whole body felt like it was smiling. "Uncle, you just weren't lookin' in the right place," I said. "For I have always been where I am, and where I am is always good, can't you tell?"

Bob got a puzzled look on his face.

Just then the quack rushed up, out of breath. "Let me buy this boy."

"No, sir," said Uncle Bob. "He's coming with me."

"But he's a born showman . . . I need him."

"Sorry, I need him more."

"But he's just a nigger boy. And I pay in cash."

Bob reached a hand down to me. "Grab hold."

I did, and he gave a great heave, and I scrabbled up onto Odin's rump.

"I shall give you double his worth," said the quack, holding out paper money.

Bob did not answer, but spun Odin right 'round, pretty as can be, and off we went at a fine rate. "Science!" I shouted out, and pointed my finger at the sky, "Science!"

CHAPTER ELEVEN

The love of Mr. Jefferson, and thoughts of slavery, comparative and absolute

"Hang on back there, Science," Uncle Bob shouted over his shoulder. "Hang on with both hands."

But there wasn't much to hang onto, so I locked my hands around his middle, and we galloped on down the road for a mile or more, until the quack and his wagon were far behind us. He brought Odin down to a trot, then a walk, and finally stopped the big horse to water at a creek. My hands were so clenched together Bob had to pry 'em apart, and when I slid off Odin's rump, I was so sore in my own hindquarters I could hardly walk. I tottered around in a circle like an old man. Bob watched me while Odin, his forefeet in the creek and head down, sucked up water.

"I was told you were travellin' by horse," said Bob.

"I was," I said, ashamed to say more.

"Well, what happened to it?"

I stopped walkin', shook my head, and then told him the whole miserable story of Beulah, and came near tears, all over again.

"One day," said Bob, in a perfectly calm voice, "that ferry-man is going to end up face down in the Rappahannock."

I got a picture of that in my mind of a sudden, the man's arms and legs spread wide and his hat gone, rockin' in the ripples at the river edge, and nibbled at by fishes. I had never thought of Uncle Bob as dangerous, but now knew different, and because of me, too. I didn't know what to think of that.

"What shall I tell Mr. Jefferson?" I said.

"You best let me handle that. The horse was old to begin with and not fit for the journey."

I was not entirely comfortable with his answer. "What if Old Master gets mad at me, even after your explanation?"

"Oh, well, now, Isaac," he said. "Mr. Jefferson has an interest in seeing you get to Philadelphia, don't forget, and learning the tinsmith trade."

"And I mean to prove his confidence in me, uncle, I truly do."

Bob nodded. "Of course you do," he said. "It's what he expects."

I was disgruntled by his easy tone and dismissive wave of the hand.

Uncle must have seen that in my face, for then he said, "Mr. Jefferson, you see, he wants his people to *love* him. At least certain of his people, and you are one. And so am I. All of us Hemings are. And you Grangers. Burwell. Some others. He will go a long distance in forgiving us some wrong or other and grant us unexpected favors. All so we will love him back."

I went over and stood by Bob, without looking at him, and scratched Odin's hide, just along the edge of his saddle blanket. "What's so wrong about that?" I asked.

Bob drew a long breath, as he ran his fingers through the reddish hairs of Odin's mane. "You just got to understand there is good and bad in his love, all tangled up together. It's the *worst* kind of bondage, I can tell you."

"The worst kind of bondage," I repeated, hardly able to believe my ears. For Bob, it had always seemed to me and most others, lived as if he were nearly free of Old Master, the way he travelled about the country. What would he know of bondage?

"And the best, too," he added, "if bondage can be said to have gradations."

This confused me even more, and I said so.

"I mean," said Bob, "that it's the best a slave could ever hope for from a Master, to be loved. Never any whippings, no bein' hired out, or driven to the worst chores, or shorted on rations, or any such thing. Just the opposite. You wear good clothes, eat better food, don't have hard work to do."

I thought of Papa standin' at the fire, countin' out for Little George, Bagwell, and me, how good we had it—the fine cabin with a swing door, the plates and bowls Ms. Martha had sent down from the Big House, how we had never worked in the fields, and so on.

"But it's the worse of bondage, too," Bob went on, letting go of Odin's mane, and rolling his hat brim. "Because Mr. Jefferson *makes* you want to love him back. And a *part* of you wants to. You *know* he's a good Master. You *know* you got advantages." Bob let go of his hat brim. "But you just don't *want* to give in." He slapped his trouser leg. "You just don't want to hand over to him every last part of yourself." He slapped his trouser leg again. "*Definitely* not hand over love. That is *mine* to give, not *his* to take." Uncle shook his head. "So I resist. Politely as I can, damn me."

I stood there in the hot sun, staring at Bob with his rolled brim hat, big Odin at his side slick with sweat, and thought that now I maybe understood why it was he never seemed to be around Mr. Jefferson's plantation much, but was frequently out on "business," or away on "errands."

"Well," he said, drawing in a big breath, and slowly letting it out again, "we are a day at least behind Mr. Jefferson, and must stop jawing here, and cover some miles."

So on we rode, in the late afternoon crossing the Potomac into Georgetown, with big brick houses side by side and only stopping when we got to Herring Hill, where the Negroes lived in their shanties, some worse than the Quarter cabins at home. There we stayed with Mama Smith, close by Rock Creek, and fed on her hot herring pie. It was only because I was hungry that I could stand to eat all them tiny fishes between crusts, but Uncle Bob tucked right into it, talking with Mama Smith half the night, and other friends of his that came by.

Then in the morning it was on to Baltimore, where we stayed at Fells Point, for Bob had business there, meetin' a man aboard an old boat at the end of a long dock, while I held Odin on the street. Bob came back smiling. "I love a port town," he said. "Let's go celebrate." So we went into a grog shop around the corner, where Bob knew the keeper. The man set us out a great bowl of what looked like rocks, which Bob called *mussels*, and then showed me how to pry 'em open and scoop out the slimy stuff inside and wash it all down with ale. I needed more ale than was good for me on that business, and Bob had to help me upstairs to the bed, singin' as he did.

We got a late start in the mornin', but made up for it, going hardly without a stop till we came to what I thought was a river, much bigger than the Potomac.

"This is no river," said Bob, "this is the mighty Chesapeake Bay, which empties into the ocean itself. And see over there? That's Havre de Grace, just at the mouth of the Susquehanna."

I had never seen so much water.

We had to go upstream a ways to cross the Susquehanna at what Bob called the Lower Ferry. Once over, we walked Odin up the hill to Rodgers Tavern for a room. A white man with but one hand stood on the porch. He was as friendly almost as a brother, until Bob said I would be boardin' the night, too.

"You know I can't do that," said the man. He pointed his stump at me. "He's too dark."

Bob shook his head. "Too dark for what? To sleep? To eat? To travel?"

"Ah, Bob, it's about the rules. I don't make 'em, but I can't break 'em. You can pass for white, but not him." He pointed at me again. "Now, I could let him stay in the barn. That I could do."

But Bob got mad and raised his voice. "Me in the tavern, and Isaac here in the barn? No sir, that would never do."

The man shrugged and held up both his good hand and the stump. "Look, Bob, I got a business to run."

Bob would not listen though, and mounted Odin without a word, pulled me up, and on we went, Bob still grumblin'. "Damn it," he said. "Man thinks that just because General Washington stayed in his tavern, his bed and board is too good for the Black Man."

"It's all right, Uncle," I said, and thought he was mainly embarrassed to be treated so in front of me.

Down the road a half mile or so was another inn, set off in

the woods, and not much to look at. But there was a big fire
in the hearth, the smell of meat, and a table where men were
seated all around playin' cards.

"Ho there, Bob Hemings," called out a big man with an
apron on. "Set in here and play my hand. I must stir the
chicken pot."

"And lose my money to your poor hand?" Bob answered
back. "Not likely." All the men laughed at this, but Bob sat in
anyway, and took up the cards. I stood by to watch.

"Any word?" said one man, slapping down a card, face up.

"No," said another, slappin' down his own card, which
matched the first.

"Sheila got through," said a third man. He drew a card
from the spread in his hand, then put it back and drew another. "But not Sam."

I stiffened up.

The big man in the apron came back to the table. "Somebody told. Must have. Slave catchers were waitin', I'll bet.
Poor Sam."

"Where was this?" Bob asked.

"Just outside Fredericksburg."

I watched the card play for a long minute and wondered
whether I should speak up. But I thought of Poor Sam,
whoever he was, and decided that at least on his account, I
ought to. "I know of this Sam," I said.

All the men looked at me.

"I was mistaken for him and traveled in a wagon bound
for Ohio."

Bob looked at me in surprise. "You did what?"

I smiled at his surprise. "I think the woman that took me
in knew I was not Sam."

"Whoa, there," said the big man, and put up his big hands, palms toward me. "Start from the beginning."

So I did, and told it out, and how I was put in a coffin box to travel.

"How'd you shit?" one man asked.

That got a big laugh.

"Now that you mention it, Mister," I said, warming to my situation, "I was pretty much like a big turd myself, when I dropped out the bottom of that wagon box."

That got an even bigger laugh. The card game stopped, and bowls were brought to the table, and the chicken with fixins' ladled into 'em, and all at once I felt very comfortable among these men and liked that feelin'. I had shared an adventure and become in their eyes no longer but a youngster, untraveled and untried.

In the morning, Bob and I got off at daylight and rode long.

"We gettin' anywhere near Philadelphia?" I said at last, hoping Uncle Bob would bring Odin to a stop, and let me get down off his rump for a while.

"This day we make Wilmington," he called out, "and tomorrow we are there."

"Tell me about Wilmington," I said, to pass the time.

Bob slowed Odin down to a walk, which I could better tolerate. "Oh, Wilmington's a pretty town," he said. "It's where the Christina River joins with the Brandywine and they flow together into the Delaware."

"A port town again."

"That's right. A port town."

"No doubt you have business there."

"I do. Must see a Swede, and collect my money, as agreed."

We rode on, still at a walk, along an empty stretch of road, with the brush cut back on both sides. "Oh, I see now," I said at last.

"See what?"

"See why you have no need of Freedom Papers."

Bob reined Odin to a stop, and I took that chance to slide off, and rub my rump, and then my thighs.

"Why do you say that?" he asked, lookin' down at me.

"'Cause you're free already, or nearly so. You go where you please, and stay where you will, and carry on business all your own. You don't need no Freedom Papers."

Bob dismounted, and walked over to me, Odin tailing after him by the reins. "Listen, Isaac," he said. "It's like this. When it comes to Freedom, there's the *comparative*, and the *absolute*."

I was proud of myself, just then, for having prodded him to talk, finally, and explain the principles upon which he operated. "So what's the *comparative*?" I asked.

"The comparative is, that compared to the field hand, I am free, or nearly so. Or so it appears to that field hand, who is always under the eye of an overseer, dawn to dusk, and fears the lash and whipping post, and is liable to be sold off at any time, for all his labor and suffering. Yes, as to the comparative, I'm free and he's not."

"Then what of the absolute?" I asked, stretching up first one arm and then the other.

Bob dropped the reins and held out both hands. "The *absolute* is simple. You either free or you ain't. It's one, or the other. *Absolute*. So now by *that* measure the field hand and I are just the same, though he dress in rags, and I wear suits. We are both properties. We both owned. We both shackled."

"I don't see no shackles on you."

"Of course, you don't. My shackle is as fine as a spider's thread, and it will stretch as far as I can go, and still not break. But when Old Master tug, I feel the pull, no matter how far I have pulled that thread. He just *reel* me in, no matter how I squirm to get loose—and worse of all, I *let* him." Then all of a sudden, he stepped up into the stirrup and sat himself in the saddle. "Let's go," he said, "I have done all the talkin' I mean to."

But instead of reaching down a hand to hoist me up, he took a short ridin' whip from its holster just at his right knee. "*God*damn it," he said and struck Odin a stingin' blow with that ridin' whip, just at the shoulder. And what did Odin do? He didn't buck, nor rear, nor back away, but only stood where he was, and trembled all over.

"You cut 'im!" I said, shocked that he would do such a thing. "That's Mr. Jefferson's favorite riding horse."

A welt raised up where he had struck, with a trickle of blood.

"I know, I know," said Bob, pulling a kerchief from his pocket and daubin' at the wound.

INTERLUDE

by Reverend Charles Campbell

At this juncture, dear Reader, I felt compelled to interrupt Isaac's narrative with a question. "Did you also feel," I asked, "as your traveling companion did, that Mr. Jefferson's love, or desire for it, was entrapment?"

Isaac hesitated, then took from his workbench the tinsmith's hammer again, and rolled the handle through his fingers for a minute or two, looking at the motion as he did so. Then he looked at me, with those dark, penetrating eyes of his. "I have meditated upon that subject all my life," he said.

I nodded, waiting for him to continue.

He laid the hammer in the lap of his apron, and massaged for a moment the finger without its last digit. "Let me tell you a story," he said, drawing a deep breath. "Mr. Jefferson, when he went to France as ambassador, stayed away so long from the plantation that rumors sprang up among us. Some said he had grown to like France so much he contemplated staying there for good. Others said that he had discovered his accounts were in arrears and that when he did return, he would be obliged to sell off some of us, to square up his books. Still others said he would soon become president and move to the capital, leaving the affairs of his plantation in the hands of his daughter Martha, who was more strict than he was, or worse, to an overseer like Mr. Lilly, who was all meanness and cruelty. You can hardly imagine how fearful we all were! So when there came word that he had after all chosen to return home and then had arrived at the bottom of his little mountain, why, we all rushed down to greet him. Or all of us that could get away. Such was the rush of bondspeople that the carriage could not proceed. When tall Mr. Jefferson bent himself over to get out the door, he was taken hold of by many of us, I among them, and carried bodily up to the house. Others unharnessed the horses, and themselves got into the traces and pulled that carriage, loaded with all his trunks and baggage, on up to the Big House."

"Did he object to any of this?" I asked.

"Oh, no! He did not. I fancy he liked it, the being buoyed up on all of our black hands as we sang our way uphill, right on into the house and set him down on his favorite sofa. Someone even fetched his violin and put it into his hands."

"Astonishing," I said. "Was he loved so well as that, by you and so many others, who were indeed enslaved to him?"

"It was the fear of losing his love, Mr. Campbell, which impelled us," he said. "We were all of us desperate to demonstrate to Old Master that our love for him knew no bounds, so that should there come a time when he chose to sell off property that it would not be one of us, but another."

I sat quietly, contemplating the scene which Isaac had described for me. It had appeared to me at first almost bucolic—the great man and his adoring subjects—but now struck me as quite awful.

"Mr. Jefferson was the sun, you see," said Isaac, "and we his bondsmen circled around him like planets. We remained in our orbits by the force of his place and his power. If unable to get free, we had at least the comfort of order and safety. If Mr. Jefferson our sun were ever to withdraw his power, exit his place, or even expire, as he did on July 4 in the year of Our Lord eighteen and twenty-six, what would become of us, his planets, do you think?"

His metaphor was striking—and surprising—as I had never supposed he would know anything of the planets or astronomy, and remarked on this. He took offense and reminded me that he had often been around Mr. Jefferson, who was conversant in many subjects. I hastily apologized, and returned to the contemplation of his question. "Disharmony among you would be the result, I suppose," I said.

Isaac picked up the hammer from his lap, and twirled it in his hands again. "Much weeping and gnashing of teeth is what happened," he said. "Nearly everybody had to go up on the auction block."

"You, as well?" I asked.

Isaac set the hammer down in his lap once more and shook his head. "I was one of the lucky ones. I, my wife Iris, and children, Squire and Joyce, had become the property of Mr. Thomas Mann Randolph, Master Jefferson's son-in-law, well before that calamity."

"What of the magnificent house?"

"Everything inside was sold at auction, and it fell into ruin."

"Well," I said, and heaved a sigh. "You have given me an awful lot to think about."

We were both silent for a time.

"Shall I go on with my story?" he said at last. "My younger self is about to arrive in Philadelphia, you know."

"Yes," I said, taking up my quill pen again, "please, continue."

PART II

CHAPTER TWELVE

I enter the great city at last on Master Jefferson's riding horse

By the time we got to Wilmington, which was only one day's long ride from Philadelphia, I was all for pressin' on, but not Bob. "I can feel Old Master already," he said. So we took a room for the night above a grog shop on the waterfront. After we had stabled Odin, he wanted to tour me around the city, but I was hungry, so he took me to a Swedish place he especially liked. The menu was pea soup, mashed carrots, and fishballs, which I only picked at.

"You need to expand your palate, young man," he said, with some heat. But we got up and left anyway, and he took me to a little place hardly more than a shed roof and wattle chimney, with food I could recognize—smoked hog. Uncle insisted on loin, which we pulled ourselves, dipped in a mustard sauce, and ate with cornbread. We hardly spoke, and I didn't consider myself finished until I had licked my fingers. It all had the taste of home, and we reminisced about the annual Christmas hog, fed on apples all fall, and roasted on a spit for three days. From Christmas to New Year's, there was not a lick of work done on the plantation, or no more than was necessary. I got to feelin' how far away from home I was, and how very long it would be before I would get back and grew mournful over this.

Bob ordered whiskey. He went on about his brother James, sayin' he could be prickly, all because he'd never gotten over the disappointment of having to come home from France with Master Jefferson. "He was free by the law there," Bob said, turning the tumbler in his fingers. "So just remember that. He *can* be helpful, if he's a mind to."

I was up and packed in the morning at daybreak, but Bob dawdled over breakfast, which I could barely tolerate, and then said he had to go see a Swede on business. "He built a flour mill, and I invested." He sent me to groom Odin until he got back. "Be good to polish his hooves, too," he said, before going out the door. "And salve that welt."

Odin was a tall horse, and apt to be skittish, especially under strange hands. So I sang to him, and he settled enough that I could get the curry brush on his hide after all, though he still swung his head around twice and tried to bite me. But when I salved that welt he stood as quiet as an old mare, and so at last I could communicate with him, and whisper in his ear, and tug gentle on his mane. I was even able to polish his hooves.

That's when Uncle Bob finally showed back up. "Brush out his forelock again, if you don't mind," he said, "Mr. Jefferson is particular about that."

I did, and Bob watched. "Would you like to handle the reins today?"

"Me?" I asked, putting up the curry brush. "The reins for Odin?"

"You're not going to drown the animal, are you?"

"*Drown* him!" I said in surprise. "Oh, no, Uncle. I would drown myself first."

"Little chance of that. There are no rivers to speak of

between here and Philadelphia. Saddle up, and I shall settle with the tavern keeper."

"Now, Odin," I said, after Bob had left, "what I just sung, about no more saddle upon your back? That's for a future time, you understand. In this here time, I got to put the saddle on you, and you got to mind, hear?" He wasn't so sure about that at first, but I got him to concede by scratchin' behind his ears, and when I had got his gear on properly, I led him out into the stable yard and prepared to mount.

But Bob came through the yard gate just then and made me hand the reins over to him. So he mounted into the saddle, and I took the miserable rump seat once again. Even so, I was mighty glad to be on our way. We crossed the Market Street bridge, passed the flour mill, and trotted on out of town. The road by now widened out to a good thirty feet and sloped to either side for water to run off, with the brush cut well back on either side and cabins along the way, with animal pens and outbuildings here and there, taverns wherever there was a crossroads and water.

At last, Bob slowed Odin to a walk. "Now then," he said, "lean over my shoulder and watch." Then he showed how to hold the reins, just so, and how to control the horse with 'em. "Odin is a light touch. You lay the reins over so they just touch his neck, and he turns." He did this a couple of times, and Odin turned, neat as could be, right and then left. "If you need to stop, give the reins an even tug, just with the wrist, like so. To change gaits, give the reins just a little flip, and tap his belly with your heels. But only a tap. One to trot, two to canter, three to gallop." He counted one and we trotted, two and cantered. But traffic there was too heavy for three taps and a gallop.

We went on some miles yet, and I wondered if I would ever get a chance to climb into the saddle and take the reins. Maybe Uncle had second thoughts about himself ridin' the rump, with me in charge. Finally, Bob brought Odin to a stop and dismounted. "Well," he said, "come down off that rump and take these reins." He held them out.

I slid off and took the reins.

"Pull yourself up smooth," he said.

So I did. But the stirrups were short, so Bob spent some minutes adjusting them while I got the reins in my hands just as he had showed. When he had done, he stepped back, looked up at me thoughtfully for a moment, and then pointed down the road. "Keep right on a-going and you shall come to Philadelphia."

I looked down at him, and I'm sure I must have had a look of astonishment on my face. "You don't mean for me to go on alone, do you?"

"I do."

"But this is Odin I'm ridin'."

"You look just fine in the saddle. Ride that way, and you will be all right."

I asked what in the world I was supposed to say when I showed up at Mr. Jefferson's door on his prize riding horse with me in the saddle, and no Uncle Bob with me.

"Just tell our Old Master I am detained on business," he said.

I could feel Odin restless beneath me. "But how shall I ever find him," I objected, "in this great huge city up ahead I have never been to in my whole entire life?"

"Ride straight to his address, is all. Every house has an address. His address is 274 Market Street."

"Two Seven Four Market Street," I said. "Is that all you have for me to go on?"

Bob raised a finger to quiet me. "Now, Isaac," he said. "Settle down. I wouldn't have let you get up in that saddle if I didn't think you could find your way. So listen."

I nodded, determined now to prove myself, and listened. He told me to follow that very road until it jogged left. That was where the road got its own name, *Passyunk,* he said, and I was to follow that right on into the city proper, where I should turn left on Fifth, then count off nine cross streets, and then turn left again onto Ninth, or Market as it was mostly called, and look for Mr. Jefferson's address. I got a little uneasy, then, and said so, but he assured me that while Philadelphia was the biggest city in the country, it was an easy city to know because it was laid out in a grid. Half the streets, he said, mostly named for trees, ran east and west—east being straight to the wharves along the Delaware River—with the other half of the streets being numbered, and running crosswise, north and south. That didn't sound too complicated, and I felt better.

"Of course," he added, "what would be First Street is called Front Street, because it fronts the Delaware River."

"I thought Market Street must be the exception," I said, "if it runs east to the river, but is not named for a tree."

"All right, two exceptions," he said, with a wave of the hand. "Well, also Broad Street. Three exceptions."

"Any *more* exceptions I should know about, Uncle, before you send me alone into the biggest city in the whole country?"

"Oh, Isaac, don't be so. You got a good head. Just count off nine blocks like I say, to Market. You will know you're at Market because if you go right some ways, you shall come to the Wharf Market for which the street is named. There is a water pool there, with the statue of a woman holding a goose in it. That's *if* you go right. But *don't* go right, go left. Then go down as far as Eighth Street. Mr. Jefferson's house will be on the left there."

"You give me any more directions," I said, "I shall get lost for certain. You *sure* you can't come with me?"

"No, no," said Uncle. "I got business, like I said, and I'm just not ready to face Mr. Jefferson. Now repeat back my instructions."

I did, word for word, for all my complaints.

"Then go on," he said, waving. "Go on to Philadelphia."

And so, turning my head to the road, I gave Odin's reins a little flip, tapped his belly once with my feet, and he promptly set to walking.

"Oh, now, Isaac," called out Uncle Bob, "you go at that speed, it shall be Christmas before you arrive."

That irked me, as it was meant to, so I tapped again, and Odin began to trot. Shortly, I tapped again, and he changed gait to a canter so smoothly I could barely feel it. But when we got to a rise, and I could see the road was clear ahead for a long stretch, I bent to Odin's ear. "Come on, Champ," I said, "give me some speed." Then I worked my feet tight into the stirrups, settled myself firmly in the saddle, and tapped again. Odin he flat took off. I loosened the reins and gave him his head, and we just flew. And I howled! Me. Isaac Granger, born of Queen Ursula and Great George, headed now at last and on my own to the great city of Philadelphia after so many days and much adventure.

What I saw first way out ahead of me was smoke. Not the wisp of smoke here and there from a cabin chimney, but many wisps, some from very tall brick chimneys, all risin' up to make one huge, broad cloud. There was nothin' but tree stumps on both sides of the road, mile after mile, with here and there log piles and dray horses hooked to heavy wagons, loading those logs. What a city Philadelphia must be, I thought, to demand such a quantity of fuel. For I had been to Williamsburg, and to Richmond, but they were nothin' compared to this.

Odin was winded, so we slowed to a walk, and I stopped at a muddy stream for him to water. I could see that we would not make it into the city before dark, due to our late start that mornin', from all Bob's dawdlin' and business, and so just about dark I found a small barn, well off the road, and we passed the night in there. I woke to the sound of bells, and went outside in the dim light, hands to my ears, and listened. Church bells they were, but other bells, too. A confusion of bells, large and small, the sound of a city wakin' to the workday. Odin, I found, had broken into a feed sack, and I let him continue until he was satisfied, then saddled him, led him to water at a creek, and on we went.

By the time the road jogged left, as Bob said, and became Passyunk, the land all about was more settled, with the farms smaller, the houses and outbuildings closer together, and in places actual streets laid out, but not cobbled or even gravelled. Then I began just barely to smell the waterfront—fish and tar, mostly—and saw white birds with narrow wings circling in the sky. I had made it, I thought, feelin' proud, made it to Philadelphia!

CHAPTER THIRTEEN

A jumpin' boy guides me, and I encounter Mr. Peipur

My feelin' proud shortly collapsed when I discovered a problem with Bob's directions—Passyunk Road ended in a long, crowded marketplace, and I could count out five side streets comin' into it up along the left side. Five! Just exactly which was the one I was supposed to bear left on? Not to mention the four side streets comin' in from the right side. I sat still on Odin and wondered what I was to do and watched the scene. Hawkers stood on every corner, cryin' out their wares. Loaded carts pushed this way and that through the crowds of people gathered around sellers' stalls. Most everybody was white, and here I was, settin' up tall on this fine horse, me a dark Negro, lost. It was an awkward situation, if not dangerous. Suppose some of these white people dragged me down out of the saddle, and stole Odin away? Even if I walked my way through these people, pullin' Odin behind, I might look suspicious, especially if I was to ask too many questions, or maybe any question at all. I dearly wished Uncle Bob was with me and then got peeved at him that he wasn't.

All at once here came a boy, a thin white boy with blond hair and a curry brush in hand. "Groom your horse for a penny, Mister," he said, jumpin' up and down, his hair floppin' as he jumped. "Groom your horse for a penny!"

I showed the flats of my hands. "I don't have no pennies."

The boy stopped jumpin'. He was awful thin, and ragged, too.

"Anyway, I don't need my horse brushed," I said. "But I do need to know what that first street there to the left is called." I pointed.

"German Street," said the boy and started jumpin' again.

"German Street," I said. "Well now. That's good enough for a ride on this tall horse. Would you like a ride?"

The boy's eyes got wide. Then he started jumpin' all over again.

"Jump on over here," I said, "and let me catch you up."

So he jumped on over, sure enough, and I reached down and got him under the arms, and lifted him off his feet, and set him right down in front of me. He was no more than a twig, except for his floppy hair.

"Set still, now," I said, "Odin don't like no wigglin'."

I felt a lot more comfortable with this white boy in front of me. People looked up, saw him, and made way, and so I was able to walk Odin slowly past the street called German, and on to the next one, where I asked again. "What street is this one?"

"Plum," shouted out the boy, bouncin' up and down.

"Easy now," I said. "You remember what I told you about this horse."

I walked Odin on to the next street. "This one?"

"Shippin."

So far, not a single street named for a tree, or a number. Just how many exceptions had Uncle Bob failed to tell me about, anyway?

A cart and horse blocked our way ahead. Two women, both

stout, unloaded winter squash from the cart box, one by one, and walked 'em to a stall.

"This a tall horse," said the boy, lookin' down over both sides. "How tall?"

"A good sixteen hands," I said.

"I seen a taller."

"Oh? How tall?"

"Tall as a house."

"That is tall," I said. "What do you feed a horse that tall?"

"Trees. He gulps down a whole tree in one bite." The boy twisted in his saddle and looked up at me, to see what I thought of that.

"That's some horse."

The women had finished unloading their squash and got the horse and cart out of the way. I walked Odin on to the next street. "Now, what's this street?"

"Cedar. My friend he lives on Cedar Street."

"Finally," I said, "a street named for a tree. Oh, it's good to have a friend on Cedar Street, I'd say. Now what about this street up ahead here? What's that one called?

"Fifth."

"Oh, now," I said, "I *love* a street named Fifth."

"Any more streets you need to know, Mister?"

"Not today. This is the very one I was looking for, boy."

He twisted in his place and looked up at me with his big eyes again. "You sure? I know all the streets. Every one."

"Tell you what. If I do come back this way—and have a horse under me—we will take a ride again and you can show me some more streets. How would that be?"

I supposed the boy would be most thankful, but just then another boy dashed across the street, with a dog after him.

"Rafe!" called out the boy. "Rafe!" He squirmed one leg from over Odin's neck and slid down to the ground. "Bye," he said, looking up at me one more time, before dashin' and dodgin' after that boy down an alley. I had been such a boy, once, I thought, though never in such a city as this one, nor so able to be on my own, as he appeared to be.

Cheerful, I bore left on Odin up Fifth Street, counted off the nine blocks, just as Bob said, and came to what I hoped was Market Street. It was a broad street, and when I looked to the right I could see, down a ways, wagons parked along each side of the street, and people bunched around these wagons. If that was the Wharf Market, then the water pool, and that statue of a woman holdin' a goose with water streamin' from its beak, must be there somewhere, too, and I was sorely tempted to go down there and look. But I thought better of it, being anxious now to arrive at Mr. Jefferson's house, and so turned left, growing more uneasy with every clip clop of Odin's hooves on the hard cobbles. Would Old Master be standin' on the porch, and would he go flush in the cheeks when he caught sight of me? For not only had I lost Beulah, but here I was astride his own ridin' horse. I should get down, I told myself, and walk, but didn't know how far I had to go yet, so stayed in the saddle and watched for the address numbers on each house. Numbers I had no trouble with, as Little George had taught me the one to ten, for the cutting to length of iron rod. And these numbers were painted in black, above each front door. Only they didn't go in much of an order, house to house, that I could see, so I had to look close at each one.

When I did get to the house with number 274, I thought at first I had made a mistake, and maybe numbers were somehow different here in Philadelphia. For the front door was propped open with a chunk of plaster debris, and two men were just then carryin' into the house a stack of boards. A white man in a good coat stood on the front porch, swatting a rolled paper against his hand.

Uneasy, I climbed down slow off Odin, looped the reins over a post, and went in the gate and up to the porch, where this man was now pacing back and forth, still swatting the paper. I waited for him to turn and come back my way. I had to speak up, for there was much noise from inside the house. "Excuse me, sir," I said. "Excuse me. I am here to report to my Master, Mr. Thomas Jefferson. Is he anywhere about?"

The man squared around to me. He had bushy eyebrows and long creases in his cheeks, and glasses set on the very end of his nose. He frowned down at me. "Of course not. Can't you see?" He half turned and opened his arm toward the door. I tried to look past the man, enough to see one workman hammerin' on a wall, and another bent over a buck, sawin'.

"It was a perfectly good house," said the man, not waiting for me to answer and raisin' his voice. "One of my best properties. But was it good enough for your *esteemed* Mr. Thomas Jefferson? Oh, no. He must have a Book Room built out. Pantry by the kitchen. Dining room enlarged. Antechamber added. Do you have *any* idea of the trouble this has put me through?"

I could have added that Old Master would probably want yet more changes, then probably yet more after that, and most likely changes until the very day he quit livin' in this house. "No, sir," I said, "I don't have any idea of the trouble you been through. Awful, I'm sure."

The man pushed his glasses back up his nose and looked hard at me. "Who did you say you are?"

"I didn't, sir. But since you kindly asked, I am Isaac. Isaac Granger Jefferson. Mr. Jefferson he is my Master, and I am to report to him here."

"You're awfully shabby, to be bearing such a distinguished name."

"I been on the road, sir. Brung Mr. Jefferson's ridin' horse." I pointed to Odin. "His *favorite* ridin' horse."

That was the wrong thing to say, for it set the man off again. "And that's another thing," he said, raisin' up his hand with the rolled paper in it. "Your *Master* requires a stable for *three* horses, *and* a carriage house. Where exactly am I supposed to put those on a city lot?"

I shook my head, "I wouldn't know, sir. But you ask a good question. *Very* good."

"Then for goodness' sake, convey to him my earnest desire that he present himself to talk with me in person. I don't need one more letter from him with diagrams, thank you." He shook the rolled paper at me.

"Yes, sir, I shall most certainly pass the message," I said, though of course I would never dare to pass any such message on to him. "That is, if I know where to find him."

"Mulberry Street. Your Mr. Jefferson has taken temporary lodgings on Mulberry Street."

"And where do I find that street?"

He threw up his hands. "Must I draw you a *map*? Go back one block to Eighth, then turn left and go one block, and there you are—Mulberry. Simple."

"Yes, sir, simple. Except maybe for some poor Negro that never been in this city before and must follow directions that turn out not to be so simple after all. But I will find it even so, I'm sure, sir. And who may I say wishes to convey this message?"

The man stood as tall as he was able, which was not as tall as Mr. Jefferson, not by a head. "Leipur," he said. "Mr. Thomas Leipur, real estate agent—and, regrettably in this instance, *contractor*."

I bowed, and turned to go, but Mr. Leipur reached over the porch railing and caught me by the shoulder. "*Also* mention his proposed Garden House," he said. "Where he expects to 'retire in the evenings with his books, unseen and undisturbed, even by his servants.'" He slapped my head with the rolled paper. "If he wanted a Garden House, for God's sake, he should have taken a country estate." He hit me again with the paper, then let me go.

I backed up and turned around. "Yes, sir," I said. "You are mightily displeased, I can see that, and don't blame you *one* bit, and will let Mr. Jefferson know, in such terms as he will *never* forget."

"Good God, don't you dare!"

A big-nosed man came out the door just then. He had a mallet in one hand, and chisel in t'other. "That plan you showed me?" he said, standin' square to Mr. Leipur, "for the funny bed?"

"Not *funny* bed. Alcove bed. *Alcove* bed. How many times must I tell you?"

"Funny bed no good. Not work. I show you." The man got hold of Mr. Leipur's arm with a big hand and fairly dragged him into the house.

I walked down the steps and back out to Odin. "Well," I said, unlooping the reins, "that was interesting." I swung up into the saddle. "No telling what we shall find on Mulberry Street."

CHAPTER FOURTEEN

Master Jefferson's crates of books, a heated James Hemings, and "I-O-P"

I was only too happy to get away from Mr. Leipur and his troubles, so I trotted Odin the block back to Eighth, then turned left, and settled him into a quiet walk while I tried to prepare myself for Mr. Jefferson again. What should I say to him? How about, "I have made it." No. That would show too much pride in myself. Then maybe, "Guess you thought you'd never see me again." But no, he wasn't much for humor, at least from his Negroes. Well, then, how about, "Master, please forgive me, it has been trial and tribulation on the road. But I am here at last, and most grateful to lay my eyes on you once again."

I thought this might do, though wordy and heavy on the sweetness, when I came to the street which had to be Mulberry, if Mr. Leipur had told me right. I turned Odin left, and we walked on about three blocks, and though the street was well paved that whole distance, the houses on either side petered out, with the blocks ahead being only weedy fields and but a tree or two here and there. But where for goodness' sake was Old Master's house? Was this to be my fate, having so proudly arrived in this great city, to just wander about, looking for it?

I turned Odin around and went back the way I had come, and as I came past Eighth, I saw ahead of me, about two blocks down, a man in the street with his coat off and shirt sleeves rolled up, wavin' his arms all about. Somethin' about the man reminded me of James Hemings, maybe the way he stamped his foot. But he was far enough ahead that I thought he could have been a white man. Yet when me and Odin got closer, there was no doubt it *was* James Hemings, and he was shoutin' at some other men who stood by a wagon, with the tailgate off, parked at the curb. Up in the wagon was a big wooden crate, and on the ground was another.

Odin snorted just then, and James turned, saw me, and at once stopped shoutin' and wavin' and rushed down the street at me. When he got up close, he set his hands on his hips and opened his mouth, but no words came out.

"Good afternoon there, Mr. Hemings," I said with a smile.

James sputtered and spat. "Don't you *dare* 'Mr. Hemings' me. What—what the *devil* are you doing riding Odin?"

"Oh, your Uncle Bob told me to ride him on in to Philadelphia. Odin is a light touch, James. And gallop? Why, he was made for it." I leaned forward and rubbed along Odin's neck. "Yes, he's a fine mount."

James stamped, and flung up his arms. "Get—get your sorry black ass down off that horse," he said. "Now!"

I got down, but slow, and then reached up to scratch behind Odin's ear. He turned and bowed his head, so I could scratch behind the other.

"Granger, don't you mock me, now."

I dropped my hand down and looked at James, all red in the face, just like a white man.

"He likes a good scratch," I said. "He's come to expect that from me."

James ignored my comments. "Now," he said. "You walk Odin up to the corner. You take him around back to the stable.

You give the reins over to the man there. Then you walk back." He pointed to the ground. "To *here.*"

So I led Odin by the reins back to the stable—he would have followed without me leadin' him that way, I knew, but I didn't want to aggravate old James any more than I already had. The stableman was an old Negro with white hair, and half bent over. I didn't see how there was any way he could get Odin's saddle off, so I done it, and the blanket, and took off his bridle, too, and hung it up, for which the man was grateful.

Then I went to fill Odin's feed bucket, but the old man caught the scoop from my hand. "Don't think me invalid, young man," he said. "In my day, I was a jockey."

So while he filled the bucket, and then brought a pail of fresh water for the water trough, I stroked down Odin's neck one last time. "To think," I said, untanglin' some of his mane hairs, "that I should have begun my journey on old Beulah and ended it on a race horse like you."

Then I turned from the stable and went back to the street, where James was at it again with the two men and their crates, one of which was now up on the house porch, right at the front door. A heavy man in a dirty stockin' cap stood on one side of it, James on the other. "Did you *roll* this crate from Virginia?" said James.

"Nope," said the man, reaching behind his ears where his black hair was pulled together, and hung long down his back.

"But it lays on its side, for God's sake."

The man shrugged.

"Can't you see?" said James rapping the side of the crate with his knuckles. "*This* is the top. It says so, right here." He read out the word, letter by letter, pointing with his finger. "T-O-P. TOP. Can't you read?"

"Nope," said the man. "Nor them." He nodded at the other three men, standin' in a bunch by the wagon. They all looked dangerous to me. One had a big knife at his belt.

James slapped the crate. "Precious books are in here," he said. "Mr. Thomas Jefferson's precious books."

"You not like," said the man with the stocking cap and long hair down his back, "we take back."

"By God, you shall not. Mr. Jefferson *must* have his books."

I decided it was time to make myself useful, and to practice the letters James had so kindly pointed out. Two of 'em, "T" and "O," I knew from the Georgetown Road sign which the Negro in the tattered coat and with a fiddle had taught me. So I walked to one side of the wagon, and then around to the other side. "You might have the same problem with this one, James," I said. "I see no T-O-P." I jumped up in the wagon and looked at the top, then on the side that faced the wagon seat. There was no T-O-P on any side, or the top. I turned back to James with the unhappy news. "This box is upside down."

James was fairly beside himself. "I packed the books in these crates myself. Exactly in order as Mr. Jefferson instructed. From anthropology on down to zoology. And now look what these numbskulls have done. Got my packing *all* messed up."

"Well, James," I said, "we just got to get these crates right side up, then, and get 'em through the door."

"They don't fit through the door."

"Then they must be opened on the porch. And the books taken inside by stacks."

James glared at me, then turned to the heavy man in the stocking cap. "You heard him," he said.

The man in the stocking cap did not move. "Nope."

"What?"

He pointed. "Bring to house only. No take inside."

I thought James would tear his shirt off he was so mad. "'*No take inside*,'" he said. "What did my Master pay you for, then? To stand around and watch *me* break my back carryin' 'em in?"

I saw that the three men in the street had begun to murmur among themselves. They were all big men, especially the one with the knife.

"James," I said, "I think we ought to just let these men go on about their business. My back can help out."

"Oh, well," said James, with a toss of the hand, "that's the *easy* part. The *hard* part is sorting them back onto the shelves, in proper order. You ain't up to that."

I wondered for a moment why I had not just continued on down the road with Odin, for all the bother and adventure I'd had to get here, only to be bossed around by James Hemings, same as back home. But I kept still, and we got that second crate up on the porch, and both of 'em turned right side up, and the tops pried off.

That done, the man in the stocking cap and his helpers went off in their wagon, all of them crowded together on the seat. Such slow horses they drove, even when whipped.

"Damn savages," said James.

CHAPTER FIFTEEN

I put up with James' instructions, and Master Jefferson surprises me in his library

Now I had been in Master Jefferson's library back home many a time, though only when he was present, of course. Once, I found him down on all fours, books laid out all around him, readin' from first this one and then that, excited as a child. Never did I myself put a hand on his books, for that was not allowed, not even to his domestics, which made me all the more long to handle one, as if it were a medicine plant which simply in the touching of it would prove beneficial.

Yet here before me was a whole crateful of Master Jefferson's books, two, in fact, which James himself had responsibility for, and to get them into the library had even ordered the gloomy movin' men to do it, except they had refused. James he must be desperate to get the task completed, I thought, and so reached right into the first crate to get my arms under a whole stack of Old Master's books, almost as if they belonged to me. But James he didn't like that, and slapped my arm, and reprimanded me, then had me put on gloves while he explained in his high-handed way that he had a whole system of arrangement for packin' those books, which must therefore be unpacked letter by letter accordin' to his system. Then he proceeded to show me how a piece of paper lay on each stack, with a letter on it, and that all the books under each paper must be kept to just that order, letter to letter. But he would not tell me what the letter was, written on each paper, only that I must tote in the books with the greatest care or answer to his switch, which he shook at me, and then made clear that he—and only he—would put them up on the shelves. His whole manner aggravated me, but I held my feelings in check, for the chance even to hold Mr. Jefferson's books, even just to carry them, and explained the advantage of teachin' me each letter as I came to it, so's I, too could put the books in order up on the shelf, and save him the labor and backache of doin' it all himself.

"I know what you're doing," he said, eyeing me suspiciously. "You're trying to get me to teach you to read. Well, I won't do it. Mr. Jefferson would be highly upset with me, if I was to do that."

I objected that I already knew "T," "O," and "P," and some others, and that hadn't constituted any threat to him, had it? I added that surely there couldn't be that many more letters.

That was just the prod he needed. "Oh, there are many more," he said, and laughed.

"Hundreds?"

"No, not *hundreds*."

"More?"

"Good gracious, no."

"Then just one hundred?"

James folded his arms. "I ain't saying."

It was like pullin' hen's teeth with him. "More than a hundred," I asked, "or less?"

James tapped his foot. "Fewer than one hundred. *Fewer*, not *less*."

I got exasperated, then. "James," I said. "Here I have offered you my help getting all of Old Master's precious books out of the crates here, and into his library, I would guess before he comes here and finds the job unfinished. The *least* you can do is just tell me how many letters there are. If you do, that still don't mean I can read. Even if you teach me the letters one by one, Mr. Jefferson need never know."

James swatted his hand at the air. "Never mind about that," he said. "All you need to know right now is this one letter, 'A.' The first letter. 'A' for *anthropology*. Now, take up the first stack of books beginning in the corner up here, until you have brought in all the stacks, down to the next paper. Then I shall teach you the next letter."

I toted books for the next two hours or better, James teaching me, though begrudgingly, each letter as I came to its paper, and where to put the books up on which shelf, while he stood by to oversee, which of course guaranteed he would criticize nearly my every move. I never thought I would get to the end of "H": history-ancient, history-modern, history-British, history-American.

I got as far as bringing in the last stack of the "P" books, when James told me to go out on the front porch and wait there until he came back from the Necessary, as he didn't want me "meddling unattended" in Mr. Jefferson's library, and then lectured me once again how there was nothing Old Master treasured more in all the world than his books. "He ain't a churchman," he said, "but if he were, his library would be his church."

So I went out on the porch as instructed to enjoy some fresh air and time to myself. But the way he had steadily talked down to me so rankled that after a minute I went back inside, just to be contrary. But hardly could I stop there, and so tiptoed down the hall and into Mr. Jefferson's library. It did feel like a holy place, a place no Negro was allowed in, especially all alone and without permission. Oh, I longed just then to read from books as I had seen Mr. Jefferson do! And so, gathering courage, I stepped forward, looked over the many books on their shelves, and then with tremblin' fingers took down a small one, with a dark blue cover and gold letters on the spine. This one in particular James had plucked up himself from the crate and carried in. It was so small that I thought, in some crazy way, that Mr. Jefferson would not be disturbed in his mind if I looked in it for just a minute. The cover was smooth, and soft, the pages inside barely rough to the touch, and ragged along the edge. Every page, front and back, had a block of tiny letters all tight together, with a blank border around the edges. I could make out no words—not "TOP" or "Georgetown Road," or anything—but felt as if I soon would, if I searched and stared long enough. I imagined, as I turned the pages slow, what it would be like to be behind the eye and inside the mind of Master Jefferson, and take in these lines of words, page after page. To understand their meaning and connect their meaning to the meanings of the pages of words in other books, and be able to quote from those pages while in conversation with other men so able to read, as Old Master could do. In the middle of a left-hand page, I found three blue ink lines, drawn straight across, as with a rule, one line under one row of words, another under the next row of words below, and the next below that. Old Master's ink lines. I felt like I had fallen upon a secret of his.

Just then, from behind my right shoulder, I heard his

voice, very soft, hardly more than a whisper: "Well, Isaac, are you now to be my new librarian?"

I snapped the book shut, and he came up beside me.

"Oh, no, Master," I said, ashamed, "not me."

He smiled, ever so slightly, and held out his hand for the book, which I gave over to him at once. He took it carefully in his long, clean fingers, as if it were a small and fragile bird, then riffled through the pages as easily as if they were a deck of cards. I was afraid he might be searchin' for the pages I had touched and hoped my fingers had not damaged them somehow.

"*Stanley's Lives of the Philosophers*," he said. "How fitting. Do you know what a philosopher is, Isaac?"

I shook my head.

"A philosopher is a *lover of wisdom*. Are you a lover of wisdom, my boy?"

I tried to think what the right answer might be. "I hope so," I said. "I try to be. Might not be old enough, though. Might be too foolish still. Foolish enough to look into one of your books, Master Jefferson, which I oughtn't to of, I know, but forgot myself. It shan't happen again, no it won't, not ever." At last I got my mouth to stop talking, and just stood there, looking at Mr. Jefferson, with his long nose and hair not tied up but loose behind the ears.

"We learn by mistakes," he said, "what is our place in the world. Such as my place in this library, and your place at the tinsmith's bench."

For once I was happy to hear James angry at me. "Granger!" he said, from behind me. "what the devil are you doing in here?"

But Mr. Jefferson raised a hand. "Now James," he said, "Let me ask Isaac a question." Then Old Master turned full to me. "Where is Bob? I sent him to find you, which he evidently did, but he has not presented himself to me."

I looked at the toe of my shoe for a moment. "He told me to tell you that he was—*detained on business*."

Mr. Jefferson looked at James, who shrugged, then at me. "What business?"

"He did not say," I answered. "But it would be business you approve of, I would think."

"Now, Granger!" burst in James, as he got hold of me by the sleeve. "Get out to the porch like I told you." Then he drug me down the hall. So it was true, I thought, as he opened the door and pushed me out, what Bob had said about James: he *could* be a help, if he had a mind to.

CHAPTER SIXTEEN

I am brought to Mr. Bringhouse's place by Mr. Jefferson at last, and become a surprise

I was three days in that house, totin' books, movin' furniture—you never saw so much furniture, I lost count of the crate loads—and sundry other novelties including four stone heads and six skins of animals. I about concluded all this was Mr. Jefferson's punishment for me putting my black hands on his *Stanley's Lives of the Philosophers*, or reporting that Bob was detained on business, and began to fear that Old Master might just have decided against my bein' a tinsmith apprentice at all and would soon send me home, though only after all the unpackin' and so forth was done, of course.

But then, on the fourth morning, just as I set about carefully unwrappin' a framed picture of Mr. Jefferson's poor deceased wife, Martha, James told me to collect my things and go stand out at the curb, for I was going to the tinsmith man, he said.

"You for sure about that?" I asked, skeptical.

James stamped his foot. "Don't you argue with me. Mr. Jefferson is taking you and he don't like to wait."

So, wishing again for my travel satchel lost in the Rappahannock, I rolled up what I had—one pair of underdrawers and a shoelace—in my coat, and went out the front door.

"I got no idea why Mr. Jefferson himself should bother to take you," said James, standin' on the porch. "That should be *my* job."

I looked at him. "Pretend you're the man of the house, why don't you."

He swatted at me as I went by.

I ducked. "Enjoy the moment, for a change." Then I stepped out to the curb, happy. Behind me I heard the door slam shut, but didn't look around, for I just knew James would go to the window and watch.

I stood there, lookin' up and down the street at the buggies going by, the two women arm in arm, the Negro boy with a broom over his shoulder and wooden bucket in hand, the several hogs driven by a small boy with a hazel switch. So I would get to be a tinsmith, after all, and this was the day for me to begin. I fancied myself already well-accomplished and respected, with fine tools and my own shop, good as any white man's, and dwelt on this picture as I stood there in the warm sun. Then here came a high-spring phaeton, pulled by a spotted mare with a long mane, swinging around the corner and straight down the street toward me—driven sure enough by Master Jefferson himself. He brought his buggy to a neat stop, just where I stood, looked at me, and said, "Isaac, my boy, climb up."

Understand that I had not seen Old Master since that day in his library, when he took the book from my hand and spoke to me of wisdom and knowing my place in the world. Yet here he was, patting the seat beside him, and saying, "Don't be bashful now."

I still hesitated, for it just didn't seem right. "Oh, Master, I couldn't," I said. "Let me run behind. I'll keep up, you know I will."

He smiled. "No, no. I mean for you to ride beside me." He patted the seat again. "Come now, we must go. I am due at the State House before long."

So I gripped the brass hand hold, stepped onto the fancy footrest, and pulled myself up into Mr. Jefferson's phaeton with extravagant caution, lest I tarnish or scratch anything, and then set myself down ever so slowly on the leather cushion seat, feelin' the springs give with my weight, and holdin' my things, what there was of them, wrapped in my coat and close to my chest. That seat was so comfortable it almost made me uncomfortable.

Mr. Jefferson snapped his ridin' whip and off we went at a brisk pace, so brisk I thought he would hit that poor Negro boy with broom and bucket.

"A rare opportunity awaits you, Isaac," he said, holding the reins high, and turning toward me.

"Oh, yes, sir," I answered back with enthusiasm, though wishin' he would keep his eyes on the traffic in the street.

"Indeed, among all those persons who have labored for my happiness," he said, swerving left around a slow ox cart, "in my fields and gardens and workshops, and even in my home," he went on, swerving right around two children jumping rope, "there is only a handful to whom I have seen fit to offer such an opportunity as the one I am offering you."

He had told me this before, and him remarking on it again made me anxious for what he would expect of me. Still, I was happy for the chance, though I clung to the arm rest, as he dodged left past a honey wagon pulled by a sway-backed mare.

"You can best express your gratitude," he said, slipping the phaeton, still at a trot, between a horse cart and a vendor's stall, with hardly a handbreadth to spare on either side, "by diligently applying yourself."

"Oh, yes, sir," I said, as a little dog chasing after a tall goat dashed out in front of us, "I intend to."

A work wagon blocked the street ahead, and a gang of men were pulling up cobbles. "I might be able to get around," said Master Jefferson, but I guess he thought better of it, for he slowed his horse to a stop, thank goodness. "Now what is going on here?"

Water welled up from the ground where the cobbles were taken away.

"A main break, it looks like," said Mr. Jefferson. "Old lines, no doubt." He shook his head, then got down out of the phaeton to go inspect. I sat watching, feelin' foolish on my leather cushion, as he talked with the men pulling up cobbles.

"*If* we are to have cities," he said, climbing back up into his seat and takin' the reins, "which I suppose we must, we ought to design our utility lines so they are *accessible*." We waited our turn to get by, and were made to turn on Fifth Street, which I recognized from my ride in on Odin. "Too bad we must detour," he said. "I had thought we might go by the Goose Fountain. It is a small marvel of engineering."

The Goose Fountain again, I thought, and decided I must see this thing which was so talked about.

"No, I am not fond of cities," said Mr. Jefferson, going along at a more moderate pace, for there was more traffic here, "for they promote unhealthy habits of mind. And distractions, especially for the young." He nodded over toward a corner, where two women, one dark and one pale, stood with headcloths of bright colors, and dresses hitched up. "So watch yourself, Isaac."

"Oh, yes, sir," I said and looked back over my shoulder toward the women. One lifted her leg and shook it.

We turned east again, and now I could smell the salt air of the river and hear the squawk of birds overhead. "Yet withal," said Mr. Jefferson with a sigh, "I do cherish my memory of Philadelphia in the '70s. Those were memorable times." A block on, Mr. Jefferson slowed the phaeton, to get by people crowded around a vegetable truck.

Then we came in sight of the river, and Mr. Jefferson drew the phaeton to a stop. "The Delaware," he said. "Rising in the Catskills, to empty into Delaware Bay, and thence into the Atlantic, and so join the other oceans, which encircle every continent on earth."

He said all this with such enthusiasm that I thought for a moment he would leap from the phaeton and rush straight into the water. He was that way, sometimes, when not borne down by work, ready in a sudden moment to take pleasure in the world, even if it was only one springtime flower just poking up at the door of Little George's shop.

Many docks were built out into the river, with boats tied up everywhere, large and small, and wagons pulled up as close to the water as they could, to load and unload, with shouts and commotion.

"This street along here," said Mr. Jefferson, "is Front Street."

Which ought to have been called First Street, I almost said, then thought I better not.

About four blocks down, after we had gone by two sail-making shops and one for making and repairing rope and nets, then a boat yard, saw mill, and printing shop—all of which I could tell from the picture boards hung out over the street—Mr. Jefferson brought the phaeton to a stop at a corner house, two stories tall, with a steep-pitched roof. "Here we are," he said, pointing to yet another picture board hung out. On it was shown a cup with two crossed hammers and behind them a sun, with words over top and underneath, which Mr. Jefferson read aloud for me: *"Master Tinsmith James Bringhouse Quality Work. Best Prices."*

Most of the big letters I could make out, though not so the words.

No sooner had Mr. Jefferson set the brake and wrapped the reins, than a plump woman with big forearms opened the door and came down the steps at a half run, holdin' up her gray skirts so they wouldn't drag. She wore a sparklin' white apron, and white bonnet tied under her chin. "Thou must be Mr. Jefferson," she said, bending to him twice. "I am James Bringhouse's wife. He's not here, but he said to expect thee."

I got out of the phaeton, and stood to one side, head bowed, both hands holdin' my rolled-up coat, as Old Master stepped down onto the walk. He bowed his tall self to her short self in return, then stood straight again.

"Shall we see our new apprentice soon?" she asked, tilting her head a little.

Master Jefferson put his hand on my shoulder. "This is he."

Mrs. Bringhouse looked at me in surprise.

Master Jefferson took his hand away. "I thought I had mentioned his color in my letter to Mr. Bringhouse."

"I suppose thou did," she said. "But I am not privy to my husband's correspondence."

"I am sorry for the misunderstanding, Mrs. Bringhouse,"

said Old Master, bowing his head a moment. "He has promise, believe me, more than you might suppose."

"But he is *so* black," she said.

"Madam," said Mr. Jefferson, reaching out and patting her hand, "please don't let his color discourage you. You will grow accustomed to it. Consider rather his character. He is obedient, and not inclined to laziness. Nor dishonest. Nor troublesome. Unblemished by the usual peculiarities of his race. And his mental faculties are perfectly adequate for the tinsmith work which, I trust, your husband will set out for him."

I felt so very alone just then, though I had looked forward to this day for many months and taken considerable trouble on the road to arrive here, too, when I could have run off. But now that I was in truth at the very door of the house where I was to live, and learn a trade, I was more aware of my color than I had ever been on Old Master's plantation, and felt I had no proper business here, and wished I could roll myself up in my coat and disappear.

"Oh, Mr. Jefferson," said Mrs. Bringhouse. "Thou need not enumerate these characteristics for me. I am aware of how the Negro is viewed. But I am Quaker, you understand, and believe that every human soul bears the light of God within."

I looked at her in surprise, for never had I heard anyone say such a thing. It sounded so outlandish at first, that every human soul bore the light of God within. I could think of more than a few souls, like dry old Mr. Cary who found sport in whippin' me, that could hardly have much light of God in 'em, in any at all. Yet this Mrs. Bringhouse had spoken very frankly, and in my hearing, too. Oh, I liked her very much for that.

Mr. Jefferson bent his head. "Pardon me, Mrs. Bringhouse. I intended no disrespect."

She nodded and looked me over. "Is this young man pure African?"

Old Master laid his hand on my shoulder again. "His forebears were, naturally. But he was born on my plantation, as were his brothers. His parents have been with me for years. Bringing the boy here, to live in your household, and learn from your husband, is my way of favoring them, for their good service to me."

"Then he speaks English?"

Master Jefferson patted my shoulder and took his hand away. "Why, of course he does." He turned to me. "Demonstrate, will you? Speak to the good Mrs. Bringhouse."

I rummaged in my mind as to what to say, whether I should speak in what Master Jefferson called "the Negro dialect," and by that indicate a simple and untutored mind, or whether I ought to express more complicated sentiments and thereby indicate how my association with Old Master had generally refined my character. I chose instead to speak plainly. "Mrs. Bringhouse," I said, and bowed, "I am most happy to be here, and grateful to my Master that he should allow it. I mean to do well at the tinsmith trade and promise to do my chores."

"My," said Mrs. Bringhouse, "thou art a serious young man." Then she folded her hands together, just where her apron tied around her middle, and bent toward me. "What is thy name?"

It was such a simple question, but asked so earnestly, that I was silent for a moment.

She looked at Master Jefferson. "Has he a name?"

Master Jefferson nodded to me. "Go ahead, Isaac, tell Mrs. Bringhouse your name."

I looked at Mrs. Bringhouse. "My name is Isaac."

"Your whole name," said Mr. Jefferson.

"Isaac Jefferson," I said. "Isaac Granger Jefferson."

Mr. Jefferson looked at Mrs. Bringhouse, and she looked at me. "Good, good," she said, clapping her hands lightly together. "Isaac Granger Jefferson. That is quite a name."

"Yes, ma'am."

She bent toward me again. "Hast thou manners?"

I looked at Old Master again, for I wasn't sure if I did or not. Not his manners, I knew, nor hers, I supposed. Mama taught us her own way how to act. Did that count?

Master Jefferson smiled at her. "I had hoped, Mrs. Bringhouse, that you might instruct him in the niceties of the table. You will find him docile and teachable. If not, please ask Mr. Bringhouse to communicate with me by post."

Then he turned to me and laid his hand upon my shoulder. "Now then, Isaac," he said, "son of Great George and Queen Ursula, do as this good lady and Mr. Bringhouse require. *Apply* yourself, *gain* knowledge, *prove* my confidence in you. And every Sunday morning, report to me at my lodging."

"Nay, Mr. Jefferson," said Mrs. Bringhouse. "On First Day our family goes to the Friends meeting, and our apprentices with us."

Mr. Jefferson nodded. "Would there be time in the afternoon, then?"

"I will ask Mr. Bringhouse, but I think yes."

"Well, then, that is settled. Now, I must go."

"Oh, Mr. Jefferson," said Mrs. Bringhouse, touchin' his

sleeve with her two hands, "so soon? Can thou not stay for tea at least?"

Old Master climbed back into the phaeton and took up the reins. "Sadly, no," he said. "President Washington expects me." He looked at me. "Remember, Isaac, *to whom much is given, much shall be required.*"

Then he lifted the reins, snapped his whip, and set off away from me at a trot. I watched his straight back lightly bobbin' above the high spring box, saw him turn the corner, and the horse, head high, disappear behind a building, and soon Mr. Jefferson after him on his cushion seat. I felt both free and lost.

CHAPTER SEVENTEEN

Mrs. Bringhouse welcomes me into her house, and I put on new clothes

"We are simple here," said Mrs. Bringhouse, as she let me in the front door—the *front* door, mind you—and closed it behind her. "It is the Quaker way to be simple."

I nodded and looked around. It was a tidy room, nearly as big as our whole cabin in the Quarter, with a woven rug on the floor, padded chairs in three corners, a tall bookshelf, and brick fireplace in the fourth corner.

"This is the sitting room," she said, "for guests and reading." Then she frowned and pointed at my rolled-up coat. "Is that all thy luggage?"

"Yes, ma'am," I said. "Coat and drawers and a spare shoelace."

Her eyebrows rose. "Mr. Jefferson provided thee with no more than these paltry things?"

"Oh, no," I said, anxious lest she rebuke my Master in person, "he is not to blame. I started with more. Mama packed me a full travel satchel, socks and patched trousers included."

"Well," she said, putting a finger to her cheek, "that's something, I suppose. But where is it?"

"Lost, ma'am," I said, and avoided her eyes. "Lost in an accident on the way."

She put her hands together at the breast. "Oh, I'm so sorry. What sort of accident?"

I didn't want to say, but felt I must give some explanation, at least. "My horse drowned," I said. "Well, she wasn't my horse, but she felt like mine. We got on good together, once I scratched her bony hide, and gave her bites of Mama's corncakes. Beulah was her name. She was old, yes, but sturdy for her years. I am sorry she is gone. Very sorry." I bent my head, for I felt the tears come into my eyes. As usual, I had said more than I intended.

"Oh, I am so very sorry, too!" she said, in a voice that sounded like she meant it. "But I shouldn't think that means thee must go about in a single suit of shabby clothes for the rest of thy life!"

I hadn't supposed my single suit was shabby, and had expected that more or less I would be wearing the same clothes most of my days. But here she had put me in a different frame of mind about that.

"Thou must have some proper clothes, Isaac Granger Jefferson!" she said. 'Well-clad is well-seen.'"

Then she rushed out of the room, through a door in the far wall, and I looked down at myself, wondering if I had scared her out. Then looking up, I knew myself to be standing entirely alone, here in the quiet sitting room of this white man's house. Now *that* would put a fright in a body, and I nearly bolted out the front door! But I got hold of myself, and turned slowly about, examining every crack and crevice in that room. The walls, though brick, were smoothly plastered, and plaster between the ceiling beams, too. All of it painted a dove gray. The floorboards were polished, and so tight you couldn't have slid a knife between any of 'em. The padded chair set in the corner to my right, and the one to match it in the corner to my left, had matched, stitched designs in the seats. The rug was woven in broad bands of color, the outer bands dark, the inner bright, or at least some brighter. The bookshelf had glass doors, and across from it, by the opposite wall, was a small writing desk, proper chairs with backs on either side. A paper of some kind, framed like a picture, hung on the wall above the desk. The small brick hearth in the far corner was connected, I guessed, to the main hearth. This was no Big House, like Mr. Jefferson had built, but it was snug and comfortable and well-furnished. I felt how poor our cabin was, with its dirt floor and clay chimney, that forever needed patchin'.

A quick knock startled me from these thoughts, and in through the same door Mrs. Bringhouse had gone out of came a short, neat-built man, with leather apron on and sleeves rolled back. He came straight to me and held out his hand. "Thou must be Mr. Jefferson's boy," he said.

I wasn't for sure he didn't take me for a servant boy, as his wife had done, but took his hand, which was strong.

"Good to have thee here, Isaac," he said. "I am James Bringhouse, Master of this house and a Tinsmith by trade. Thou shalt make a fine apprentice, I have no doubt."

I was glad to hear him say so, not sure if I should smile or not. "I hope to."

Then he caught hold of me with his second hand, too, and looked up at me most earnestly. He had an honest face, and eyebrows that curled up. "Slavery is an abomination before God," he said. He dropped my hand, strode off a few steps and then turned back to me. "Just know that we Quakers, from the time of William Penn, have fought against that evil institution."

I had known that Quakers were opposed to servitude, it

was generally known to be so among us, but never had I heard the actual words spoken to my face, meant for me to hear and understand, and I was shocked. They were dangerous words and dangerous for me to hear. Did Mr. Jefferson have any idea that the Tinsmith he had sent me to held these ideas so strongly? I had not come here to make trouble, or be invited to be part of trouble, only to learn the trade of tinsmithin' from this man, and feared that even as Papa warned, I might be takin' *Notions* just bein' here, which Old Master would learn of, sooner or later.

But I could bother myself no further with these thoughts for in through the door came Mrs. Bringhouse, with folded clothes on her arm. "Mr. Bringhouse," she scolded, "art thou preaching already at the poor boy? He isn't even properly dressed yet."

Mr. Bringhouse turned to her. "I wanted him to know he is welcome here, that anybody is, who lives decently and works hard."

"Isaac," said Mrs. Bringhouse, holding the clothes out to me, "take these up to thy quarters and change."

I took the clothes from her and felt how clean and pressed and soft they were. Then I asked where my quarters were.

"Hasn't my husband told thee?"

I was embarrassed that she should ask, and knew not what to say, even more so when he rebuked her, if politely. "All in good order, wife, all in good order," he said, pulling a watch from the high pocket of his apron. Then he turned to me. "Your quarters are in the attic."

I supposed that by "attic" he meant "loft," and my quarters were in a barn. Where else would they be?

"Goodness, James," said Mrs. Bringhouse, "he needs more instruction that! Isaac, follow me, please."

"Don't let him dally," said Mr. Bringhouse. "Isaac, come straight out to the shop when thou art done."

"Yes, sir," I said, turning back from following his wife.

"We have no 'sirs' in this house, young man. A decent, 'Mr.' will do."

"Yes, Mr. Bringhouse."

He turned on his heel, and went out the door, and a moment later I followed Mrs. Bringhouse out that same door into her big kitchen, past the stout hearth where a stew pot hung simmerin'. Bread dough lay restin' on a pantry table, and herbs hung from the rafters, just like what Mama would do. Mrs. Bringhouse pointed to steep steps built against the far wall and told me to go up three flights to just under the roof, pass through a narrow door, and look for my bed at the far end, with fresh sheets and a blanket. "Our other apprentices quarter there, too," she said.

I thought to ask her did she really mean for me, *me*, to quarter in her own house and under the same roof. Maybe, I thought, the other apprentices were Negro, too, strange as that did seem. But she had been so surprised by my color when first I came to the door with Master Jefferson that I then thought, no, they must be white. Quarter with white boys? That didn't seem even allowable!

"Hurry now," she said, then added that she and Mr. Bringhouse had their bedroom off the first landing, and that their daughter, Rachel, was minding children in the other bedroom off the landing, so I should be quiet going by. So I started up the stairs, she telling me as I went that a wash basin and towels were on the bureau. "Bring down thy dirties," she said.

When I got to the first landing, sure enough I heard children through the left side door, which was open a crack. "She's bothering me!" "He started it!" "No, she did!"

Then another voice interrupted, the voice not of a matron, like Mrs. Bringhouse, but a girl's voice, not a child's, though. "Jacob, Lydia," said the voice. "Guess what I have in my hand." The argument over who started what stopped, and I tiptoed by the door and rushed up the narrow steps two at a time to the attic quarters, only to find the narrow door stuck. But by liftin' the latch, I could keep the bottom edge from draggin', and in I went.

These quarters were just under the roof, which came down steep on both sides, so that I could only stand up straight underneath the ridge beam. Halfway back, the stout brick chimney came up out of the floor and rose through the roof. This great chimney divided the attic into halves, with two dormers, a sash window in each, on the one side, and two dormers with sash windows on the other, with under each window a frame bed. Belongings of all sorts were lined up or scattered around each bed, except the one in the far-left corner. That one, I supposed, had to be meant for me, so I stooped around the chimney and went over to it. It was a real frame bed, apparently to be all my own. The pressed sheets and blanket were neatly tucked all along the side, and a second blanket was folded up at the foot end. And there was a pillow. I put the clothes down and picked up this wondrous thing and saw a small feather jutting from a seam. A *down* pillow. I thought for a minute that I must have stopped at the wrong bed, and looked again at all the other beds, which were occupied, sure enough. I had made no mistake, then. This frame bed with a down pillow was mine. I stood there in simple amazement for some minutes.

Then I remembered that I was up here to change clothes, not to dally, so I knelt down to untie my shoes—I just couldn't bring myself yet to sit on this frame bed of mine—and saw, underneath, a pot. It was an actual *chamber pot*, ceramic, and painted, with a lid, and also apparently for me, alone. I was amazed all over again until I heard a knock on the door.

"Isaac?" said Mrs. Bringhouse, "Is anything the matter?"

I stood up. "No, ma'am," I said, "I be right down. I almost finished in here."

In a hurry I stripped off my old clothes and dressed up in the new and looked down at myself. The shirt was some long in the sleeves, and broad in the shoulder, but I had no doubt I would fill it out in time. And the breeches, why, they had suspenders, of leather, and two front pockets, and one back. Nearby, against the end wall, was the sideboard, with two washbasins, and on the wall above each basin a mirror, and not a broke off piece as at home, but a full square mirror, in a painted frame. I stood and looked at myself, but it wasn't me anymore that stared back. Or anyway not the me that first climbed on Beulah in front of Master Jefferson's pillared Big House way back in Virginia. I looked to myself bigger and more serious, with eyes deep in their sockets that saw more than they let on, and strong lips that didn't say much yet, but could.

I replaced the oldest shoelace with the new one, balled up my dirty drawers and old coat and went quick down the steep stairs.

At the second landing I heard the older girl's voice again,

through the door still ajar— "Now, do we remember our lesson from yesterday?" A sweet voice it was.

I tiptoed by, and went down to the kitchen. Mrs. Bringhouse was just then using a long board to slide a bread loaf into a small opening in the brick hearth built for the purpose, to the side of the main hearth fire. I waited until she finished. When she stood up, set the board aside, and looked me over, she to my surprise began to cry.

"Don't mind me," she said, drawing up her apron and dabbing her eyes with it. She drew a heavy sigh, and dropped her apron, then pressed it down along her skirts. "There are some things too hard to bear. Losing a child is one." She sighed again. "Oh, my dear Joshua." Then she straightened. "It's good to see his clothes put to use, at least."

I trembled all over at what she said, and looked down at myself, dressed in her dead son's clothes. I felt sorry for Mrs. Bringhouse, but uncomfortable to be entangled in her sorrow, because of the clothes she had given me to wear. My own, though dirty, were suitable, and I would rather have changed back into them just then, but there was no doin' that now.

Mrs. Bringhouse pointed to the kitchen door. "Get thyself out to the shop, Isaac. Mr. Bringhouse doesn't like to be kept waiting." Then she went to stirring the stew pot with a long-handled spoon.

I rushed out the kitchen door, but stopped just beside the well pump, for there was a lot to take in. This was no plantation, with thousands of acres to work, only a fenced city lot, no more than a half acre, if that, yet packed full. There was a wood shed, chicken coop and run, hog pen, tool keep, a Necessary in the back corner with a rooster perched on the roof. Along the right-side fence was a line of covered stalls for animals, a wagon with high sideboards, and two stalls for tack and gear such as harnesses, wheel spokes, and barrels. But the biggest building by far extended from the end of the animal stalls, all the way to the back corner of the property.

There could be no doubt this was Mr. Bringhouse's tin shop, that I had come so far to enter, and so I made at once for the end door, took a deep breath, slid the bolt, and stepped inside.

CHAPTER EIGHTEEN

*I survey Mr. Bringhouse's tin shop,
and am rudely greeted by Daniel Shady*

My first thought was, wouldn't Little George love to see this shop! But my second thought was, no he wouldn't, for if he did, he'd never be satisfied workin' in his own rude shanty ever again. For this was a shop with a plank floor and snug walls. Not a hole nor gap in the chinkin' anywhere. No bird nests in the rafters, no roof leaks. This shop had windows— yes, *glass windows*—that let in good light and would keep out the cold. A sturdy work bench, a good two-foot-wide and waist high, ran all along the right wall. Oh, yes, Little George would have been mighty envious. What he wouldn't have liked, and what I would have to learn to deal with, were the other apprentices, three of 'em, about my age I guessed, and every one white, workin' at their separate stations at that long bench. I felt again how very out of place I was. Then I saw that there was one open station, and supposed that would be mine, and wanted desperately to be set to work there at once, never to raise up my head but only stick to the business and be no bother to anybody.

I was shortly a bother to everybody though, for Mr. Bringhouse, at the far end of the shop, turned, saw me at the door, and sharply clapped his hands. "Now, then, fellows!" he called out, "turn about, if you please." He clapped his hands again.

Two of the apprentices, one very fair-skinned with sun-shine hair, and the other sunburnt, tall and strong and wearing a headband, put down their tools, turned around as told and looked at Mr. Bringhouse. The third, the darkest of the three, stocky and with bushy hair, did not obey, so Mr. Bringhouse had to call him out by name, not once, but twice: "Daniel! Daniel Shady, turn thee around, please." This Daniel Shady finally did. But he did not look at Mr. Bringhouse, he looked at me. His eyes *fixed* on me. I knew the look, knew it well. It was not condescension. No, nor hatred, exactly. It was distaste. Distaste and contempt. My presence in that shop—nothing more—was distasteful to him, so unbearably distasteful that there was nothing, no particle of air, even, between those four walls nor under that roof that was not tainted by my simply being there. He had a small hammer in hand, and tapped the head into his open palm, and would as easily have struck and killed me with that hammer as you or I would bat at a fly.

Mr. Bringhouse walked over to where I stood at the door, took me by the elbow, and drew me to the center of the shop. Then he stepped aside and held out his hand as if putting me on exhibit. "I should like to introduce our new apprentice, Isaac Granger Jefferson," he said, "here by permission of the distinguished Mr. Thomas Jefferson."

Shady quit tappin' his hammer into his hand. "Say that again?"

So Mr. Bringhouse repeated himself, adding that he expected each of them to treat me with the decency and respect, which he, Mr. Bringhouse, treated each of them.

"That's not going to be possible," said Shady promptly.

Mr. Bringhouse, surprised, turned to him and asked why not.

Shady shook his head, as if the question was so elementary, he need hardly answer. Then he pointed his hammer at me. "Because he's a nigger," he said.

"Yes, he is a *Negro*," said Mr. Bringhouse, "but that makes no difference to God, nor to me, and should make no difference to thee. Now, the decision has been made that he shall be an apprentice in my shop, and I expect thee to abide by it. We shall learn, day by day, to work alongside each other as equals."

Shady struck his hammer against the bench top. "I will do no such thing."

I was shocked how he spoke back to Mr. Bringhouse, and expected Mr. Bringhouse would deliver a sharp rebuke, if not a whippin'. Disobedience was the one cardinal sin on Master Jefferson's plantation, or any other, that I knew of. Now a rebuke of some kind was sorely needed, for otherwise how was I to work in this shop alongside this man? But Mr. Bringhouse did not rebuke, nor even reprimand. Instead, he only counseled. "Now, now, Daniel," he said. "The light of God is in him just as surely as it is in thee."

This just set off Shady again. "Whose god, I should like to know? Not ours, who elevates the civilized white man and subjugates the barbarous black. Read your Bible, Bringhouse!" He pointed at me with his hammer again. "Just look at him," he said, nodding at the other two apprentices to also look, "with his swollen lips and beetle brow. Look!" He bared his teeth, fairly foaming at the mouth, looking the savage himself, then flung down his hammer and rushed from the shop, slammin' the door behind him.

I hung my head, not wanting my face to be seen, and shrunk into myself. Never had I been singled out like this for such hatred! On Mr. Jefferson's plantation, the black man and the white, howsoever deeply divided, had some common cause to see the crops harvested, the animals foaled, the hogs butchered, the tobacco baled for shipment, and much else accomplished, lest all go hungry, the place fall into ruin, and much worse circumstances result. But here! Here in this Quaker city I had heard so much about, and now, in the presence of the very man who not an hour before that announced to me what an abomination slavery was, I had been most poisonously reviled. And there was no escape for me! I would have to stand where I was, and act as if Shady's words were no more bothersome than chimney soot.

"Well," said Mr. Bringhouse, looking at the slammed door, "we must believe that Daniel, too, is a child of God, even if wayward." Then without a pause he introduced the two other apprentices to me. I struggled to listen, and just hoped these two did not share Shady's feelings against me. The sunshine-haired apprentice was named Charles Shippen, from Delaware, I was told, and the tall, strong one with the headband was William Wharton, of Lancastershire, across the Schuylkill. Most often, said Mr. Bringhouse with a smile, he was called, "Little Will." I tried to smile, too, but could not.

This Little Will then said that Shady, for all his turbulence and accusations did have a point, which was that should I learn the trade of tinsmithin', I would take decent jobs away from good men at lesser wages.

Mr. Bringhouse responded that he, Little Will, needn't worry about that, saying that I would be returning to Virginia when I had completed my time in the shop, rather than seeking employment in Philadelphia, or anywhere in the state. This seemed to satisfy Little Will, but it made me most uncomfortable, as though my time there, and even my very self, could be easily endured because I was only temporary, a passing inconvenience, and that afterwards I would be returned to bondage, and all would be as before. Maybe to you, Reverend Campbell, it seems that I have made too much of this small occasion, but to me it was deeply hurtful, and for the first time I felt within myself that I was not so ready to accept my fate as a slave and no more than a slave. I did not want to be simply temporary, and I did not want to return to Old Master's plantation in Virginia, even if I did have advantages as a Granger. Never before had such ideas come so clearly into my mind. Up until that moment, I judged my condition by the "comparative" of Uncle Bob, and mainly thought of myself as fairly well off, compared to most of the bondspeople on Master Jefferson's plantation. Now, I felt more akin to the "absolute" of slavery. All of this led me to resolve that no white man, however hateful, and no shop owner, however lukewarm in my defense, must prevent me from learning the tinsmith trade. To excel at the tinsmith trade, rather. So I said to Mr. Bringhouse, "Show me my bench and tools, will you?"

Mr. Bringhouse looked at me, surprised. Though he was mostly bald, gray hairs curled up around both ears, in a comical kind of way. "Gladly," he said, then added, "Daniel will settle, if treated kindly."

That, I knew, would never happen. "Is this my bench here?" I asked, going to the open station between Shady's and Charles'.

Mr. Bringhouse slapped his hand down on it. "It is, indeed! And these are thy tools. Here I shall teach thee, and here thou shalt learn to be a proper tinsmith, if thou have the patience and the gift for it."

Oh, I had the first in abundance, and would prove I possessed the second. "What is this here?" I asked, pointing to a little box, about the size of a lantern, with a glass door on the front, and a pipe out the top that went up through the roof.

"This is thy soldering stove," said Mr. Bringhouse, opening the little door. Gray ashes lay inside. "And this," he said, holding up a long metal rod with a wood handle at one end, "is your soldering iron." He handed this to me, then cast his hand over the bench, scattered with tools and bits of tin. "First rule," he said, picking up a hammer that lay by the window, "keep your tools in good order, and ready to hand." This hammer he laid down close to another smaller hammer, then took up yet another even smaller hammer just by Shady's station, and put it with the other two, so arranging the three in a neat row. Then he showed me what he called a *stake*, which was a small, shoe-sole-shaped anvil fixed to the top of an elbow-high steel pole. "In smithy work," he said, "the iron is shaped hot upon the anvil, but tin is shaped cold." Then he took up a strip of tin and demonstrated, neatly bending the strip with quick, light hammer strokes as he pulled the tin down along the edge of the stake. The work looked easy in his hands, but was devilish-hard to learn well, I found out.

Then the shop door opened and in came Shady, smokin' a short clay pipe.

"Daniel," said Mr. Bringhouse, putting the tin strip and hammer back on the bench, "you know the rule. No smoking in here."

I expected another outburst, but instead, Shady opened the door, knocked out the bowl, ground the ash underfoot, put the pipe in his shirt pocket, all without a word of complaint, and came directly over to where we stood. He put his elbow on the stake and turned his back on me as if I weren't even there.

"You have your principles," he said to Mr. Bringhouse, "and I have mine. You have your obligations, and I, being the eldest son of a prosperous mercantile family, have mine. So I am prepared to give ground."

As he spoke, I watched a small spider crawl along the edge of his shirt collar, just at the back of his neck. He must have felt the creature on his skin, for he suddenly brought up his hand, and sqashed it with a finger tip.

I was sorry for that spider.

"If," he said, raising a finger, "you were to employ the *Negro* in sweeping the floor, or emptying ashes from the solder stoves, or even, on occasion, sorting tin from the scrap box, why then, I suppose I could make allowances for his limitations and tolerate his presence. To keep the peace, you understand, despite my *profound* reservations. It's a generous offer, wouldn't you agree?

Mr. Bringhouse waited a long time before he answered. He pulled at the lobe of his ear, stroked his chin, ran his fingers through his thinning hair. I was really afraid he would accept Shady's offer, and prepared myself to protest, though I had no idea what I would say, nor if it would matter.

Finally he drew a long breath. "I appreciate thy willingness to compromise, Daniel," he said. "It speaks well of thee, yes it does." He drew another long breath and blew it out. "But no, no I don't think I can do that. I promised Mr. Jefferson that I would teach his—servant—tinsmithing. I musn't go back on my promise. Mr. Jefferson is Secretary of State under President Washington, as you may know. He is a man of power and prestige, and it is a privilege to perform this favor for him. Business can flow from my cooperation. Business is good for all of us, you included."

Shady got more and more fidgety as this explanation went on, until at the end, he suddenly spun around and faced me. I would be a poor judge of the matter, but I think he may have been handsome, at least by the standard of white people, if his features were not so twisted by anger. "If you so much as touch any one of my tools," he said, pointing at my eyes, "I shall by God find a way to *kill* you."

He struck fear into me he did, for he had a killer's eyes.

"I think that is manageable, keeping the tools separated," said Mr. Bringhouse, as Shady let go the stake and moved to his station. "Dost thou not think so, too, Isaac?"

It was a wretched and unfair question, and I did not want to answer, but I did not have to, for Mr. Bringhouse began moving tools from off the one open station over onto Shady's station. The tools he moved had red marks on the handles, I saw, and the ones left behind, blue marks.

Shady stood with his hands in his pockets and watched. "My father will hear about this," he said, "how you have sided with the Negro against me. You can see I am crowded."

Crowded with work half done, I said to myself, crowded with tin scrap and torn paper and a broken pencil, and a hammer head without a handle.

Mr. Bringhouse asked if I wouldn't mind Daniel Shady leaving a few of his tools on my bench, at least for a little while, until he got his station organized. I said I guessed not, except what if by accident I picked up that hammer there, or those shears. Why then the metal would be contaminated, and likely to spread disease if another apprentice chanced to use the tool after me.

Shady eyed me suspiciously, and I was sure he knew I was mockin' him with such talk, but his contempt—and fear—of me was so deep it amounted to superstition, I could tell, and he didn't dare take a chance. "Hellfire," he said, grabbing away both hammer and shears. Mutterin' and cursin', he pulled the rest of his things off my bench, too.

"Shut," said Charles, from the other side of me. "Shut your mouth, Shady, and go to work."

"So now you are takin' up for the damn Negro, too?"

"He's done nothing to you."

I looked more closely at this Charles, who had come to my defense. He had a thin nose and a scrawny neck, which made his Adam's apple look like the biggest on the tree. His hair was cropped close around his head, except at his forehead, where it hung over nearly to his eyebrows.

Mr. Bringhouse motioned to me to follow him out of the shop, which I did, fearful that I was about to get a private scolding. On my first day! Once the door had shut behind us, Mr. Bringhouse touched his forehead, rubbed his hands together as though washing, took out his timepiece, and put it back. "Daniel is—difficult, at times," he said, looking at me and then looking away. "And it appears that your presence makes him more so. Now, I am happy to take thee on, as Mr. Jefferson requested. Indeed, I see it as my obligation, as a Quaker." Here he hesitated. "But your being here is, I fear, going to be rather more burdensome than I had expected."

He looked at me again, hoping for signs of sympathy.

Nodding was the best I could do, though I felt more miserable and unwanted with every word of his speech.

"Perhaps if thou were to remain out of the shop for a while longer," he said, "I can more effectively address Daniel's apprehensions. It is too late in the day, after all, to begin thy training." To my surprise, he recommended I walk five blocks up to the Wharf Market and see one of the "city sights," which was the Goose Fountain, only warning me to return by dusk. Then he pointed the way, went back inside the shop, and pulled the door shut behind him, as if he would rather I never came back.

Almost in a daze, I walked out to Front Street. A wagon went by, then a carriage, then two white men arguing, then a boy with a stick and hoop. I was afraid at first to walk all alone up the street and checked for Master Jefferson's safe pass in my pocket—and realized I'd left it in my old pants' pocket. Dare I go on up the street without it? But I remembered how I'd promised Mama that I'd walk all about this city for her and was ashamed of myself. Had I not come through many adventures to be here? And would I now, after all of that, quail on the curb? Let that hateful Shady stew at his bench! Leave Mr. Bringhouse to tremble over my presence.

So then I stepped boldly out into the street, turned north, and joined the traffic going toward the Wharf Market, eager to see this Goose Fountain.

CHAPTER NINETEEN

The Goose Fountain, spilled apples, and I meet Miss Rachel Bringhouse

All thought of either fears or boldness shortly disappeared in the simple business of tryin' to keep from gettin' maimed or killed on Front Street. What with the heavy wagons and big horses, the gentlemen in their fast coaches, the shoutin' workmen with their overloaded carts, the old people with their sticks and canes, the women in bunches with baskets on their arms, the ragpickers with their pointed pokers, and the beggars pullin' on sleeves, it was all I could do to make forward progress and not get run over. Added to that was the noise of river business—the ships and boats with their bells and horns, the noisy seamen, the shoutin' fishmongers, the squawkin' gull birds overhead circlin' and divin'.

There was a freedom in all of it, too. For with all the clamor and traffic, and people of every race and color eager to do their business, I felt almost invisible. Nobody seemed to care or even notice who I was or where I came from, or what color I was, which was an altogether new experience to me, and so I jostled my happy way up the crowded street. I began to think I could *love* this city of Philadelphia in which I found myself. "Mama," I said aloud, "look at me now!"

Then a mulatto man with a wrinkled face and broken straw hat and teeth missin' from his smile caught hold of my sleeve and slapped a log laid out on sawbucks. "Go ahead, young man," he said. "Cut off a block and you got yourself a penny." He twanged a long saw with his knuckles. "A penny a block, many as you can cut." He held up the saw. "Like to try?"

I told him no but he wouldn't accept my refusal. "A young buck like you I could keep in work cuttin' wood until spring."

I said again no, saying I already had work as apprentice to a tinsmith, which impressed him some, but still he badgered, pointing out that chances were I would get no money for my labors, but that he would pay me in coin then and there. He twanged the saw blade again, but I pushed off into the crowd, hoping he would not come after me.

Two blocks on, tents and stalls and wagons were set up here and there, narrowin' the way for traffic. By the fifth block, when I turned left onto Market Street, they were on both sides, from the waterfront on back, and sellers in aprons were shouting their wares—potatoes, apples, cabbages, all sorts of nuts, butters, cheeses, flayed fish, leather britches, beaver top hats, tin whistles, lace-up shoes and boots, pistols, knives, and under one tent, some dozen of those little blue bottles of *Science*. I was tempted to drink, except the price was fifty cents. Three Negroes, with string gourds and drums, played on one corner, a banjo man on another.

There was so much to see that I hardly paid attention to where I was goin', and so found myself at last in a more or less open space—with right in the middle a round pond, walled up about knee high, and in the middle of that pond, the *Goose Fountain*. This fountain was a statue of a woman, taller than any woman in life, and with hardly a stitch of clothing on. Under her arm she had hold of a fat goose, with a great long neck stretched out, and beak wide open. And from that bird's beak streamed out water, going a foot or more forward, before falling all noisy into that pond, which was a good twenty feet across. I came right up to the pond wall, half expectin' that woman to move, she was made to look so real, and walked in a full circle around the pond, to see this wonder from every angle.

Where the water came from, that spilled from the bird's beak with such force, I could not figure. No creek fed into the pond, and there was no water wheel nor mill race anywhere about. Just as puzzlin' was how that pond did not overflow its wall; if water came in, it had to be goin' out, but where from, and where to? I walked all around the pond a second time, lookin' for some pipe or drain, and got so caught up in my search that I backed up and bent down all heedless of the people goin' this way and that. Suddenly, apples tumbled all about me, a girl cried out, and I fell down upon skirts.

"Shameful!" said somebody.

"You two should be a travellin' act," said another somebody.

I scrambled to my feet, tearin' the knee of my new britches on a sharp cobble and faced about—and saw that I had knocked down a *white* girl! I thought I ought to hold out my hand to help her up, that would have been the respectable thing. But oh, I could not do that, not with so many people around to see. Her bonnet had got crooked, and stray hairs showed from under it, just at the temple. For a moment I couldn't do anymore than look at her in surprise, and she at me with just as much surprise. Then I knew better and looked away and went about stoopin' to pick up her scattered apples, but not before a heavy-shoed dray horse crushed one under foot, and a stray dog with but one ear ran off with another. I picked up a good dozen in my arms, and turned back to see her, basket in hand, gettin' up the rest.

"I's sorry, Miss," I said, "didn't mean to. Wasn't payin' no attention, and should have been, and will next time, which there won't be no next time, but if there was—"

She held out her basket and I funneled in my apples, under the handle held in her small white hand. It scared me, that hand of hers, so close to mine.

"*Gently*," she said, "lest they bruise."

Never was a man so gentle with apples goin' into a basket as I was then.

"Thou art bleeding," she said, and pointed to my knee.

I saw my pant leg was torn, and skin peeled back. Blood welled up from the scrape.

The girl pulled from her apron pocket a kerchief, but I would not take it, and pulled up my trouser leg so the cut would not show. She folded the kerchief, though, and herself pressed it to my knee, and the pressure of the cloth felt good. But I could not have her tend me like that in public, so I pressed the kerchief with my own fingers, careful not to touch hers, and she let go. Then she instructed me to wash it well and often, and daub it with aloe, and I told her I would, oh, I would.

"Keep the kerchief," she said, "in case it bleeds again."

But I did not want this white girl's kerchief in my pocket! For that was bound to be trouble, some way or other. But then it had my blood on it. So I wouldn't want her to have it in *her* pocket, either. I lifted the kerchief off the wound, and found the bleedin' had stopped, thank goodness. So I folded it neat and pressed it deep into my pocket.

"Look!" she cried out, "one more apple."

I looked where she pointed, and sure enough, there in that little pond, stuck in place by the water streamin' from out the goose's beak, was one more apple, rollin' around and around.

"Let me fetch it, Miss," I said.

She said that wasn't necessary, that she had apples enough, and lifted her basket to show me. But that apple would bother my mind, and who knew what she might tell her friends or parents of what this thoughtless Negro had done, so I at once took off my shoes and socks, rolled up my pant legs to the knee, even with her present, and stepped out over the wall into the little pond. The water was cold, deeper than I expected, and the bottom slick, so I slid my way out careful to that rollin' apple. I got just close enough to reach out my long arm, and get my fingers on it, when my feet went out from under me. I didn't want to strike my hurt knee again, nor go completely under, and so managed to just catch the goose's beak with my other hand and hold myself up. Still, the most of me was wet.

"Hey!" said a man from the other side of the pool, "get outta there, black boy. Don't you know this here is city water? You're going to poison us all."

I splashed back to the wall and climbed out. "Here's your apple," I said, holding it out all shiny with water.

The girl smiled, and may even have laughed a little, and held out her basket, and I nested that wet apple in with the others. Then she asked if I had dry clothes. Well of course I had none, but said she needn't worry, and so she nodded, looking at me as I stood drippin' wet on the cobblestones.

"God bless thee," she said, and passed away into the crowd.

CHAPTER  TWENTY

Dinner disrupted, Mr. Bringhouse delighted, and Mrs. Bringhouse suspects

It was almost dusk by then, and I was both cold and wet, and sure didn't want to present myself at Mrs. Bringhouse's supper table in such condition, not to mention in her dead son's pants torn at the knee. So I ducked up an alley and in the narrow space between two buildings took off my clothes, a piece at a time, wrung 'em out, and got back into 'em. Then I ran, in part to keep warm, only slowin' when I came on a respectable lookin' white man in a tall hat and long coat, and slowed down goin' by, with head bowed, then ran again. But my speed got me in trouble, for Front Street did not look the same goin' back as it had comin', especially not in darkness, and I went three blocks too far and nearly fell over a dead horse and had to double back. Got to Bringhouse's place at last—I knew by the big signboard, dim in the moon just risin'—and went in the front door quiet as could be, then through the front room and into the kitchen, following the scent of good soup 'round the chimney and through an open door into another room, where all were seated at table. On my side, backs to me, sat the three apprentices on a bench, the damnable Shady in the middle, with Mr. and Mrs. Bringhouse in chairs at the table ends.

On the far side, between two small children, her face aglow in the candlelight, sat the very girl I had bumped into at the

Goose Fountain, and whose kerchief spotted with my blood was folded into my right-side front pocket. I knew at once that she could be none other than the daughter, Rachel, who I had heard the night before, with the children, behind the left-hand door. What had she told about me to Mr. and Mrs. Bringhouse? Was I now that clumsy Negro who had knocked her down and spilled the apples? I wanted to run from that house just then.

But there was to be no runnin', for the children had spied me. The little boy pointed and said, "Who's he?" And the little girl said, "He's black."

Everyone then turned to look. Mr. Bringhouse got up from his chair. The girl bowed her head.

"I told thee to be home at dusk," said Mr. Bringhouse. "Could thou not obey even so simple an instruction as that?"

"Simpleton," said Shady, who swung around on the bench, pushing Charles aside as he did so, and faced me squarely, with arms folded across his chest. "Or criminal. Too bad he didn't run off!"

I almost did, I wanted to say, the more so seein' you.

Right quick, that girl jumped to her feet and slapped the table with the flat of her hand. "Daniel," she said, with such anger he turned around. "How dare thee insult him so!"

Her rebuke warmed my heart but frightened me, too, lest her defense of me appear altogether too personal and raise suspicions.

Mrs. Bringhouse got to her feet and came over to me. "Dear boy," she said, "what hast thou done to the fresh breeches I gave thee just today?"

"I fell," I said, which caused Shady to burst out laughin',

the girl to slap the table again, and Mrs. Bringhouse to wring her hands.

"Your humor bothers my digestion," said Charles, glaring at Shady, before getting up from his place.

Mr. Bringhouse told Shady to please leave the table, which caused him to jump to his feet and demand to know why, then seize his bowl of soup and the bread loaf and stomp from the room, shoutin' that he would *never* eat at table with a nigger.

"Pass the soup please," said Little Will, as if nothin' at all had gone on.

The girl pulled both children to their feet and went a different way out of the room.

Mr. Bringhouse put his head in his hands. "For pity's sake."

But Mrs. Bringhouse took me by the arm and brought me to the table, and invited me to sit down. Then she ladled up some stew for me, with pork meat in it, which was nearly as good as Mama's.

Charles took his bowl and spoon, rinsed them in the sink, and left the room, Little Will after him. Mrs. Bringhouse went to a cabinet and got out another loaf and cut me a slice, and slathered it with butter.

"How did you fall?" she asked, handin' me the slice and sittin' down.

"I fell from figurin'."

"Figuring?" said Mr. Bringhouse, raisin' his head.

"Figurin' how the Goose Fountain worked. Or trying to. I could not see where the water came from, nor why the pond did not fill up and spill over. I just forgot myself, with all that figurin', and fell."

A smile came to his face. He pushed his chair back and stretched his legs.

"I expect Mr. Jefferson would have done the same," I said, "figurin', that is, not fallin'."

Mr. Bringhouse laughed then, really laughed.

Mr. Jefferson," I said, relishin' both stew and bread, "is surely a man who loves to figure. Keeps a pocket notebook and pencil handy, just for the purpose."

"Well," said Mr. Bringhouse, puttin' his thumbs in his two vest pockets, "I was involved in that project. It was quite a task to figure how to circulate the water for that fountain, I assure thee. We finally settled on a double action pump." He began to elaborate.

"Oh, James," said Mrs. Bringhouse. "Must thou begin on this subject? Isaac needs to get into bed. And I need to mend his breeches."

Mr. Bringhouse paid her no mind, for he was warming to his subject. "The principal problems we faced," he said, sittin' up straight in his chair, "were two: the distance the water was required to travel from the waterworks' trunk line; and the height to which the pump was required to lift the water, with *sufficient* force to produce the stream of water from the goose's mouth which so *mystified* thee, and, I suspect, caused thy fall." He patted his belly contentedly with both hands and smiled at me.

"So *that's* how you done it," I said, pleased—surprised to have hit on a subject by accident which interested us both. "Oh, I will tell Mr. Jefferson all about that pump of yours, I surely will," I said, smoothing butter onto my last piece of bread. "He will be *most* impressed with your genius, I'm sure, and may just want you to draw it out."

He patted his belly again. "Be happy to," he said. Then he leaned over the arm of his chair toward me. "As for where the pond drain is located," he said, almost in a whisper, "it's just under the raised heel of her left foot." He winked.

"Oh, that is clever, Mr. Bringhouse."

"I thought so," he said, getting to his feet and stretching his arms. "Well, wife," he said, "I'm up to bed. Good night, Isaac."

So saying, he left the room, and I soon heard the stair treads squeak. I sat and finished my bowl of stew, and that last piece of bread. Mrs. Bringhouse sat and watched me, but I did not feel uncomfortable.

When I had done, she took up my bowl and spoon, and Mr. Bringhouse's, and those of the girl and two children. "After a meal," she said, "take thy dishware and silver, and rinse them in the sink. Then set them in the drainer here." This she did, and then picked out Charles' and Little Will's bowls from the sink and set them in the drainer, too. She opened the ice box and took out an apple, cut it into wedges, and brought these on a dish back to the table. Then she sat down. "Go ahead," she said, "take a wedge."

I did and held it a moment between thumb and forefinger. I could see a dark skin bruise.

"Rachel bought these apples at market just this evening."

"Rachel?" I said, pretending ignorance.

"Our daughter. Who had the Dempsey children at her side this evening at table."

I looked at her, pretending my interest was only from politeness, and took an apple wedge. "Daughter, you say."

"Yes, our dear daughter. Who is distracted sometimes, I confess. She bumped into someone there and spilled the apples. Silly girl."

I looked at the wedge in my hand, and saw the bruise, and heard again the apples falling around me on the cobbles.

"She has a temper, sometimes. And that Daniel Shady, oh he does rouse her anger! I don't blame her. He's—cruel. And treated thee cruelly at table. I'm so sorry! I don't understand the desire for cruelty."

"I don't either," I said, "and try to avoid such persons as Mr. Shady, when I can. Sometimes that is not possible, though." Then I ate that apple wedge, the bruised part first of all.

Mrs. Bringhouse got up, went to a little closet under the stairs, and brought out Mama's clothes, all washed and folded. She held them out. "Bring down what thou hast on, in the morning, and I shall patch the trousers."

"Yes, ma'am."

"And for goodness' sake, don't fall again," she said.

"No, ma'am. One torn pant leg is enough."

She nodded, then suddenly tilted her head and frowned at me, and I could see in her frown that she had done her own figurin', and now suspected it was likely me that her daughter had bumped into at the Goose Fountain.

I took another apple wedge and looked away.

"Be careful up the stairs," she said, as she lit a candle in its holder and handed it to me. "I wouldn't want you to fall again."

INTERLUDE

by Reverend Charles Campbell

As Isaac recounted his unlikely meeting with Rachel Bringhouse at the Goose Fountain, and his exchange with Mrs. Bringhouse about the incident later that evening, during which he handled a wedge of the very apple he had recovered from the fountain, I felt suddenly that some history had begun to emerge at that moment between him and Rachel Bringhouse. A certain brightness came into his expression, but which he then quickly extinguished. I would have liked to question him further, but he looked away from me and told how, passing into the attic quarters through the narrow door, he had been rudely accosted by the despicable Daniel Shady, who had no doubt been lying in wait for him. The troublemaker threw back his covers, and in a loud voice which awakened his fellow apprentices, demanded to know "How in God's name a nigger could be allowed to sleep in the same room with him and his fellows. I listened with growing impatience as Isaac then recounted Shady's expounding of the outrageous and quite bizarre notion that Isaac's breathing would "infect" their bodies "with pestilential airs," rendering their persons subtly damaged in mind and body by morning, perhaps for good. Shady concluded this menacing tirade, so Isaac said, by jumping from his bed and throwing open all the sash windows, one by one.

At this juncture in his narrative, I felt compelled to interrupt. "Did anyone come to your defense?" I asked, hopeful that one of the other apprentices had demonstrated a Christian courage of conscience. He replied that yes, Charles had, saying in a mocking tone that if Shady was so bothered he ought then to sleep downstairs in the kitchen. But of course, his rebuke was met only with scorn.

I put down my quill then and inquired how Isaac had responded to all of this. He replied, in a remarkably even voice, that if left to his own choice he would have rather gone downstairs to sleep in the kitchen, nearer the fire, and close to the door into the yard, where he could have easily gone outside to relieve himself, as he was used to doing, and contemplate the stars.

"But evidently you did not do this," I said.

He had shaken his head and said no, for that would only have given Shady satisfaction, and denied himself the pleasure of his frame bed and down pillow. He added that he had gone quietly to his bed, blown out the candle, and lain down on it, finding himself unwilling to undress, even in darkness, in the presence of "those white boys," even though Mrs. Bringhouse had laid out a night shirt for him. Shady had gone on railing that the "nigger might cut their throats while they slept," until at last Little Will had gotten from his bed and "pummeled him into silence."

Naturally, I was appalled by Shady's unwarranted behavior and hateful accusations. Yet even more than that, I was puzzled as to why Isaac was so taciturn in response. For I should have expected him to boil over in anger and demand justice. "You speak of the incident with no more emotion than would a newspaper reporter," I said, recollecting my own, brief employment in that profession. "Why was that?" Indeed, I continued, readers of Isaac's narrative, once published, would react similarly, I suspected. Their sympathies would more likely be aroused by a Negro protagonist who was stout in his own defense. His having slunk off to bed as he had done, without a word of open protest, might very well disappoint readers, and even cause them to close the book, heaven forbid.

Isaac looked at me for a long time with his inscrutable gaze, and then finally said, in a tone of mingled rebuke and pity, that perhaps I could have acted more forcibly under the circumstances than he had been able to do. That he had been no protagonist in a hero's tale but simply himself, a young man removed from familiar circumstances, trapped under a steep roof with three white boys, only just that day known to him, with but a narrow door for escape, and this across the room from his bed. That he had been schooled since childhood in the virtue of endurance.

And endure he had. For it was not only the insults at bedtime he bore, but those in the morning, when Shady spit in the washing bowl just as Isaac went to dip in his hands; and at the breakfast table, when Shady again objected to Isaac's very presence in the room as "tainting" their food, and refused to touch the sugar bowl or any tableware, if Isaac had touched them first, and then expressed dismay that Isaac should be allowed to use the same Necessary as everyone else, "when he could just as well sh-t in the dirt." These and a dozen other taunts and jibes Isaac recalled for me, before finally quoting his mother: "No matter what the white man say or do, just you keep on."

I confess that I felt chastened by these remarks, and perhaps for the first time there arose in me a sense of real sympathy for Isaac Granger, this old Negro who sat before me in his worn shop apron, unconsciously massaging his finger with the missing digit. "I am sorry," I said. "That must have been a miserable night for you."

To my surprise, he promptly retorted no, that had not been the case. "Once I knew the others were asleep—Shady snored somethin' awful," he said, "I got out of my clothes, slipped on that soft nightshirt Mrs. Bringhouse had set out for me, snugged myself under the covers of that frame bed, with the down pillow clutched in my arms, and imagined myself back home on Master Jefferson's plantation. That brought me peace. Comforting sights and sounds came to me, then: old Jacob braidin' rope and smokin' his slow pipe; Little George poundin' the hot iron on his anvil; John Hemings at work in his furniture shop, sweet-smellin' wood shavings curling onto the floor; Mama in her white apron among her pastry pots and pans—these and many other memories like fruit fresh fallen from the tree sweetened my loneliness there in that close attic room."

"Well said, Isaac," I exclaimed, remembering my own fond memories of home, before misfortune struck and I was forced to live with an unhappy uncle. "Well put. Memory is indeed a balm."

To my surprise, he chuckled and then remarked: "All was not melancholy, Mr. Campbell. There were some funny moments, now and then. As when I first went out to the Necessary and had to ward off the rooster Brigadier with a tree branch." He went on to say that he'd "come to an understanding with that rare bird after our confrontation," and from then on always brought out a bread crumb for him. And then there had been Jacob and Lydia, the Dempsey children who sometimes stayed with the Bringhouses so Rachel could care for them, and who normally sat on either side of her at table. "They were a handful," he said. On this one morning, he recalled, they wouldn't eat their oatmeal. Jacob had called it nasty and Lydia had agreed, so Rachel had tried to entice the children to eat it by warning them they would get no storybook afterwards if they did not. Still they only poked at their food. "So I piped up," Isaac said, "and told 'em that when I was a boy, and wouldn't eat my oatmeal—which for us was corn mush, never actual oatmeal with nuts and raisins as these children had—Mama would remind me about the Witchy-Woo, which had horns, and a sting in its tail, and lurked outside the door to capture children who didn't eat their breakfast." He shook his head and chuckled to himself. "I think I got a little carried away, for everybody at table got quiet, even Shady, who I'm sure must have thought, 'Oh, this is some old nigger superstition and ought not to be told under a Christian roof.'" Isaac tried to hold back, but then he just laughed. "Those children ate up their oatmeal at once," he said, and laughed again. "And Jacob he just couldn't get enough of that Witchy-Woo but must hear more about it day after day!"

I recognized then that Isaac possessed a particular affinity for animals and children, and they for him, perhaps because they all shared an awareness of vulnerability; in a world controlled by grown men—white men at that, I am sorry to admit, being one myself—animals, children, and the Negro were largely powerless, and so found, in their common predicament, a natural companionship. However, it occurred to me, this companionship, though comforting, might perhaps retard the development of the Negro character, in a world he saw as being beyond his power to affect. Had this been true of Isaac? Though weathered by experience and time-worn as he now clearly was, had he nonetheless remained at bottom a simple being, unwilling or perhaps unable to grow beyond this state? That he should have found solace, while clutching the down pillow in the darkness of Mr. Bringhouse's attic, in memories of Monticello, the very place of his enslavement, suggested that he had, and would, remain so. Yet despite his persecutions at the hands of Daniel Shady, his circumstances were otherwise fortuitous: he was off the plantation, apart from "Old Master," able to experience the vitality of Philadelphia, and personally resolved to learn the trade of tinsmithing. Would he overcome the obstacles set against him, and seize what opportunities might present themselves in his new life?

I was hopeful that he would, but only his story would prove my hope was not unfounded, and so I waggled my quill pen at old Isaac and tapped the open page of my notebook. Still, he remained silent for some minutes, no doubt thoughtfully sifting through his memory those momentous days of his youth before at last deciding how best to continue. So he nodded at me, half smiled, and began to speak.

PART III

CHAPTER  TWENTY-ONE

*At my bench at last, trouble with
Shady, the awl and shears*

On that morning when I stepped through the door of Mr. Bringhouse's tin shop to really begin at long last the first full day of my apprenticeship, as eager as I had ever been in my young life, I was of course confronted by Daniel Shady. "Don't stand there idle," he said, brushing sundry bits of tin and such off his bench, then scattering them across the floor with his boot. "Clean up the goddamn mess."

I had better prepared myself for his insults by this time and shook my head no. "That is not why I was brought here," I said.

He complained at once of my insolence and said he would have no *intransigent* n— in his shop. But when I looked at his bench, the mess it was in, I couldn't see how anybody, Negro or not, would ever decide to work in a shop of his. "Excuse me," I said, "but that pot you are working on, do the handles line up?" They most certainly didn't.

"Don't you go copying me," he burst out, pulling the pot into his lap and turning away from me on his stool. "Learn the trade on your own."

Mr. Bringhouse, with his sleeves rolled back and leather apron on, had ignored this exchange as he went pickin' through a wooden box of tin scrap on a stout table nearby. A dozen or more pieces of fair size he then brought over and laid out on my bench. Then he faced me squarely and made a fist. "There are three fundamental skills to tinsmithing," he said. He raised a forefinger. "First, marking and cutting." He raised the next finger. "Second, shaping and crimping." Then raised one more finger. "Third, seaming and soldering."

I might have counted them as six fundamental skills, or three sets of pairs of skills, but such counting would have required six fingers, or holding two fingers together for each pair, complicated by having to hold up his two fists together, so maybe that's why he shortened the list to just three. To be sure I understood, he went over the three in the same order, raising his fingers again, one by one, as if I were too dull to take in those skills the first time. "And each of these skills," he then continued, "requires a different method and the appropriate tool—the shears, the crimp hammer, and the solder iron." Bringhouse looked over the tools lined up on the shelf below the window. "This," he said, pickin' up a hammer with a square head, "is thy shaping and crimping hammer, which I briefly demonstrated for thee yesterday, if you remember."

"I do remember, Mr. Bringhouse," I said, but wondered why he did not first show me the marking and cutting tools, to match up with the first fundamental skill.

"There are different crimping hammers," he went on, "each one for a specialized task, but this one is the most common, for general purposes." Then he picked up the soldering iron, with its long metal rod and wooden handle, which he had also shown me the day before, and explained how best to stoke the little solder stove. Then he frowned. "Shears?" he asked aloud. "Where are the shears and awl?" He rustled among the tools under the window, cast his hand over the bench, bent down, and looked on the shelf under the bench. He was distressed by the general disorder. At last he turned to Shady and held out his hand. "Daniel," he said, "hand me thy shears for a moment. Also thy awl."

Shady objected, sayin' that he would on no account lend his shears or awl, or any other tool of his, lest my handprints upon 'em permanently degrade their usability. Mr. Bringhouse, in a level tone, pointed out that said tools were on loan only, while Shady was engaged as an apprentice. But Shady would not concede this, insisting that on the previous day Mr. Bringhouse himself had allowed him to claim both shears and awl and he therefore expected that as a good Quaker and surely a man of his word Mr. Bringhouse would abide by that agreement. He even pressed me into the argument, as a witness to their conversation, insisting I defend his right to the tools. But I stood silent, waitin' for Mr. Bringhouse to intervene. Yet he only put a hand to his head, closed his eyes a moment, and then looked at me with a tired face, as if I should be the one to extricate *him*.

Shady settled the matter by flingin' down the shears on my bench. "Fine," he shouted. "Keep your dirty shears." Then he grabbed up the awl, a slender spike with a round handle, and stabbed twice at the air with it, once for me, I supposed, and once for Mr. Bringhouse, before plungin' its point into my bench top and rushin' from the shop, as he had done the day before.

Mr. Bringhouse watched him go, took a deep breath, and then asked me, quite simply, "What again are the three fundamental skills a tinsmith must learn?"

I was shocked all over again by Shady's impertinence and Mr. Bringhouse's unwillingness to defend me in any way, but was more than happy to return to the business I had come so far to learn. "Number one, markin' and cuttin'," I said. "Number two, shapin' and crimpin'. Number three, solderin' and seamin'."

"Very good, my boy," he said, gratefully patting my shoulder, "very good. So let us begin with the first fundamental skill." He worked loose the awl stuck in my bench top and held it up. "*This* is for marking. A pencil will do, but an awl actually *scores* a line in the tin, which reads better." He took a straight edge from his apron pocket, held it firmly down upon one of the tin scrap pieces, and along it began to scribe a firm line with the awl. Almost at once, however, he stopped and examined the point, which was dull. "No decent line can be scribed with this," he said, shakin' his head.

"Let me," I said, takin' the awl gently from his hand, and goin' to work on it with a small file. I had it sharp as a pin point in no time. "Scratch a line with this," I said, and handed it back.

So he did, a fine scratch, straight and true, from one side of the tin scrap to the other. "There now," he said, "*that* is a line we can follow." He took up the shears Shady had thrown down, but they were dull, too, the jaw edges nicked and the action tight, and they soon jammed in the tin. Mr. Bringhouse had to pull 'em loose with both hands. "I despise the misuse of good tools," he said, in a trembling voice. "It is a *sin*."

So I offered to sharpen the shears, too, and he readily agreed, and so I went to work again, this time at the stake, and with the additional satisfaction of using a heavy file I found on Shady's bench, though the handle was broken off. Mr. Bringhouse meanwhile walked to the next bench, to inspect Charles' work, and then to Little Will's bench and his work. After using the big file, I continued with the small file that I had used on the awl, sightin' every now and then along the jaw edges until I had got out every nick and ding. Charles loaned me a whetstone to finish with, then I touched a drop of oil to the pivot point, where the rivet was, and worked the shears until the action was smooth. "Dandy now," I said.

Charles and Little Will came to see, and after them Mr. Bringhouse, who took up the tin scrap once again, and cut with the shears a fine, clean line, with not a burr or sliver. "Excellent, Isaac," said Mr. Bringhouse, holdin' up the cut tin for all of us to see. "Excellent!"

Then he had me try, both scribin' with the awl and cuttin' with the shears, three straight lines, while he watched me close the whole time. Then he took down a fairing strip hung on the wall and had me mark and cut curved lines. I found I liked cuttin' curved lines, and double curved lines better still, and even double curved lines that turned back upon themselves, so much so that I would have used up every decent scrap of tin in that box. What remained were saved from my hand by the ringin' of a bell.

"Goodness," said Mr. Bringhouse, snappin' open his timepiece, "It is past noon." He smiled at me. "I believe I have gotten so absorbed in watching you that I forgot all about our dinner."

Charles and Little Will put down their tools at once and went on to the house. But I was so eager for the work, I kept goin' until Mr. Bringhouse pressed my hand, and reluctantly I put down the awl and shears and followed him out of the shop, well satisfied with myself.

CHAPTER TWENTY-TWO

Shady offers a pipe, I suffer a wound at his hands, Rachel tends me

Back in the Quarter, on Master Jefferson's plantation, we took our dinner at night, after Papa got back from the fields and Mama came up from her pastry kitchen. There was no sit-down meal at midday, only what time and morsels there were between chores. Even for us Grangers, and the Hemings, and other domestics, daylight was for workin', not eatin'. We were better off in that respect than the field hands, right enough, but to sit down comfortable in the middle of the day when the sun was shinin', and eat hearty? Oh, that I had never known before I came to sit at Mrs. Bringhouse's table. I remember well that first midday dinner: beef in gravy, mashed potatoes, green beans, biscuits, and mincemeat pie to finish. Can you believe that, Mr. Campbell? I couldn't. But it would have been impolite for me to not partake, so I filled my plate not once but twice, as the other apprentices did, for I thought surely there would be no more sustenance provided until the followin' mornin'. But come to find out, we had a third meal, countin' breakfast, that very evening.

But now, to come back to that midday meal, the first day of my apprenticeship, after I had finished, and rinsed my tableware, I went right out to the shop, for I wanted only to work on scribin' and cuttin' tin scrap. But Shady stopped me. He'd left the table early, and now sat on the doorstep of the shop, smokin' his clay pipe. "You can't go in there," he said. "Not for another thirty minutes. You go in now and you make everybody look bad, and I won't have that, not from you, I won't."

I was surprised by his familiar tone, and suspicious. But I set off to one side on a log, for I had nowhere else to go and owned no timepiece to know when thirty minutes was up.

"Smoke?" he said and took from his shirt pocket another clay pipe.

That he would offer one of his own pipes to me, when he had railed so about my even touchin' his tools, surprised me still more. "No," I said, "I don't smoke. Never learnt the habit." I had tried the weed that way once, but my Papa caught me and swatted it from my hand and gave me such a talking to as I will never forget. Didn't I know tobacco was the money crop? he told me. Didn't I realize Old Master's whole big plantation depended upon the income from tobacco? That every ounce must get to market? That otherwise *everybody* stood to lose? And here I was smokin' it, like I was some prince. Smokin' money, I might as well have been, he said.

Shady, though, had never been talked to that way, I didn't suppose. He was among those who was meant to buy the tobacco Papa and so many others worked to harvest and bale and get on batteaus to float down river to market. So he sat smokin' peaceably for a few minutes, untroubled by all that, and wouldn't have cared if he had known. Then he spat on the ground. "I don't have anything against you people," he said. "You have your ways, peculiar though they may be. But I can live with those, for the most part. After all, we have our ways, too. You understand me?"

I nodded, slowly, and wondered what was comin' next.

"Then you also ought to understand," he said, takin' the pipe from his mouth," that I only want my rights, like any man would. It's only natural. If those rights get threatened, well, then, it's just my bounden duty to defend them." He shrugged. "Sometimes, righteous anger gets the best of me, I admit." Then he pointed at me with the stem of his pipe. "Now don't you play dumb on me. I know you understand, behind that black face of yours."

Up until then, I had no idea of "rights," the way he spoke of 'em. I think I had just assumed that life was a matter of takin'. Takin' and keepin', and that by force, when you got down to it. The white man took, and the black man was taken from. But Shady had argued for his rights by sayin' that it was only *natural* he should want to defend them, just as any man would. If that was so, I thought to myself, then I must have rights, too, and even Shady must know it, if he were put to it and would answer honestly. So I have him to thank, in a way, he with his pointin' pipe stem, that day as we sat at the shop door.

Our conversation, if you can call it that, ended when Charles and Little Will came out of the house and we all went back into the shop together. As Mr. Bringhouse was not present to give me further instruction, I took a larger scrap of tin, nearly two feet square, though damaged along the edges, that I found leaning up against the wall, and worked out on paper by pencil sketch a set of four spiral curves, which when tacked together at top and bottom, could hang from a tree and spin in the wind, and maybe scare off crows from the garden. Then I laid the fairing strip to the tin sheet, scribed with the awl those spiral curves, and took up the sharp shears to cut them out.

I got so absorbed in the work that I all but forgot about Shady plinking away beside me. But he had not forgotten about me. For just as I squeezed the shear handles together, and the jaws began to close along the first scribe line, Shady struck the elbow of my cuttin' hand, the tin sheet twisted in my holdin' hand, and a sharp edge like a knife blade opened a cut just between my thumb and forefinger. I dropped both shears and tin and squeezed my hand tight over the cut. It hurt somethin' awful. Blood welled between my fingers.

"Clumsy nigger hurt himself!" yelled Shady.

"Bastard," shouted Charles, who must have seen what happened, for he rushed by me and pitched straight into Shady. These two in their struggle knocked into me. My shirt got pulled, I fell and tried to scoot out of the way. One or the other of 'em caught hold of the scrap box, which struck the floor and broke apart, scatterin' tin everywhere. Then Little Will leaped over me and got hold of 'em both by the hair.

That's when Mr. Bringhouse showed, furiously swingin' a long-handled broom and swatting all four of us with stingin' blows. Shady held up an arm, Charles turned his shoulder, Little Will backed away. But Mr. Bringhouse swatted 'em all again, and even turned on me, indifferent in his rage. Then at last he stopped and looked in shock at the broom, now broken in his hands. "Get up!" he demanded, flingin' the handle away, "Get up, all of thee!"

I only managed to lean against my bench, blood from my clenched hand dripping on the floor.

"He's hurt," said Charles, pointing at me.

Shady cursed me again.

Mr. Bringhouse rushed to my side. "Did I do this, poor boy?" he whispered.

"I may pass out," I said, the words soundin' strangely in my ears.

Mr. Bringhouse had me sit on a stool and put my head down, and the next thing I knew I was lying on the floor, with my hand held up in the air. Rachel Bringhouse had knelt beside me.

"Relax your fingers," she said. "Can you do that for me, Isaac?"

I nodded, and relaxed my fingers as she instructed, and felt her bend open each one, ever so gently, and as she did so a deep feelin' of well-being spread through me. I felt her press a cloth into my hand and heard her say, "I'm going to have to stitch this wound." Then, in a louder voice, she called out instructions to get catgut from the kit, cut to about twelve inches, thread the curved needle, cut strips of clean cloth two inches wide, bring pinches of the aloe leaf.

I felt her one hand squeeze the cloth in my wet hand and lay her other hand upon my forehead. Never had I felt a touch so gentle, and I lay quiet, comfortable with her skills, though of course I had no experience with them. I was happy in her care, which surprised me, for I had been trained from a young age to fend for myself and depend on no one. Then I felt the cloth in my palm pulled away and a cool, thick jelly laid upon my skin, and Rachel's finger gently pressin' it into and around the wound. I heard her ask for a helper, but Little Will and then Charles declined, claiming dangers from contact with my blood. Finally, the boy Jacob was brought, and Rachel instructed him to pinch the skin just ahead of the cut, and I felt the squeeze of his little fingers.

"Now, Isaac," Rachel whispered, "this is going to hurt. Stay still."

I nodded.

"Clench thy teeth if thou must and try to think of something pleasant."

I could think of nothin' more pleasant than being just where I was that moment, with my head now upon a folded blanket. That is until a worry shot through me. "Will my hand be workable again?" I asked, openin' my eyes and looking up into her face. For if not, what good would a one-handed tinsmith be to Mr. Bringhouse, or more important, to Master Jefferson? For to be a useful workman was the whole sum and purpose of my life, and I daren't think what might be my fate, if my usefulness were impaired.

"Oh, worry thee not about that just now," said Rachel, and just as quick as she said those words I didn't. The worry just fled away from me like a storm cloud, and all at once, like the mornin' sun, I felt myself light up inside, and knew my *worth*. This is hard to describe, Mr. Campbell, and may sound foolish I know, but that's just how it was for me in that moment. My worth in the world had nothin' at all to do with how well I could work, or if I could work at all, or what I could produce and how quick. None of that. No trace even. Just *worth*. As I was, even lyin' on that floor.

"Curse if thou must," Rachel said, and then I felt the needle hard against my skin, and the point break through, and the hole open as the rest of the needle came through, then the rough catgut after that. I hissed through my teeth, then grunted. Twice more she pushed the needle through, and twice more I felt it break through one side and come out the other, and the catgut dragged through after it, what felt like a yard or more.

"There," she said, "I'm just going to pull the wound closed now."

"Jacob," I said, "you got a real future as a surgeon, long as you eat your oatmeal every mornin'." I winced again as she tied the knot twice and clipped off the extra. Then I sat up and looked at Rachel's handiwork. There was a raised fold of flesh, almost exactly between thumb and forefinger, with the cut line at the top, and and three loops of fine thread, with a knot at the top of each loop.

My worry returned. "No chance I'll lose my hand to infection, is there?"

"Not if we keep it clean," she said, folding a fresh square of cloth, dippin' it in a bowl of water, and cleanin' away the blood stains. "It must be washed every day and treated with aloe."

"When can I use my thumb and forefinger again?"

"In a few days."

"Well," said Mr. Bringhouse with a deep sigh, "that was a scare. But they'll be no more work for thee this day, Isaac. Take him to the house, Rachel, so he can rest."

I got to my feet and walked slowly to the door, she beside me.

"Poor shit," said Shady, "he ought not to be in this trade. Thank God he didn't hurt somebody else."

CHAPTER TWENTY-THREE

I meet Old Tapper, and listen in at the kitchen window

Once outside, Rachel guided me toward the house, but I didn't want to go inside like some invalid and lay down. Lookin' toward the animal stalls, I said, "Who's that old horse over there?"

"That's Tapper. He pulls the tin wagon."

"Why *Tapper*?"

She didn't answer but walked me over to his stall. When we got close, I climbed one-handed onto the first rail, clamping the top rail with a forearm, and reached out my good hand to the animal, but he shifted his head away.

"Rap on the rail," Rachel said.

So I rapped on the rail, and Tapper stamped with his right foreleg. Then I rapped twice, and he stamped twice.

"He was at one time a circus horse," she said. "Which also might be why he's ornery sometimes."

"I am familiar with ornery in a horse," I said, slowly reaching out my hand again, "and stubborn." I could see bridle marks behind his ears, and when at last he turned his head toward me, I scratched, and he leaned into my fingers. "You could use a good rubdown," I said, lookin' into his watery eyes. "Then maybe a ride out of this narrow yard. How would you like that? I sure would." Then I scratched down his neck,

feelin' the hardness of old welts, and tugged gentle on his
mane. I got down off the rail, for my stitched hand had begun
to throb and the worry rose in me again. "The hand feels
better already," I said. "Let me go back to work."

Just then Mr. Bringhouse came out the shop door. "Why
are the two of thee not up at the house, yet?" he called out.

"The fresh air does me good, Mr. Bringhouse," I answered.
"If I may walk around some yet, I will soon be ready for work
again."

Rachel agreed that, yes, fresh air was having a beneficent
effect, and added that she needed to impress upon me some
further instructions for my convalescence. He shook his head
and went on to the house, and she then turned to me with
a scolding look. "You are not ready for work," she said. "If
you tear those stitches, the wound cannot heal and may get
infected. You could lose your hand, maybe your whole arm."

"But I cannot be off work for a few days!" I objected. "Not
even one day. For I was sent here to work, and work I must,
lest Master Jefferson send me home as useless for the task."

"If you'd been more careful," she said, "this would never
have happened." There was a bite to her words.

I noticed that she had not been usin' "thee" or "thou,"
which I liked, but what she said made me mad, and I told
her that I had been careful, of course I had, I'd worked in a
blacksmith shop since I was a boy, which was considerably
more dangerous, that it was Shady who had been the cause of
my wounding, and on purpose, too.

That made *her* mad, and she stamped her foot. "Oh, I hate
him," she said. "I *must* tell Father."

I got around in front of her then, and told her to please

not do that, lest I appear a tattle-tale in his eyes, and more trouble yet. What she could do, I said, was ask him to move me to a different bench, away from Shady, maybe put Little Will where I was.

She watched me carefully, for I had gotten a little heated. I didn't know what she thought, me a Negro, tryin' to tell her father how to run his shop. Without thinkin' I took hold of her two hands in mine, the one good and the one wounded, but then at once let go. I had forgotten myself entirely in the urgency of the moment. "Look," I said, "I can be good at this work, I know I can, and prosper your father's business. I just need the chance to show what I can do, and I can only do that at my bench, not mopin' about in the house."

She nodded. "Then come inside," she said. "We can speak with him."

On no account did I want to be present at her side for any such thing. That would put me in real trouble, I was sure of it. "Let me wander about the yard awhile and you speak to him on your own," I said.

She stood still a moment, then touched my sleeve and said that when she went in she would open the kitchen window part ways, but keep the curtain closed, so that I could step close and remain hidden from view, and that if I were to pump a glass of water I could stand idly there and drink, while listenin'.

This I promised to do, and watched her turn and go into the house, then open the kitchen window part ways, and pull the curtain closed, just as she said. I took a slow turn about the yard, seein' Tapper pawin' in his stall, the shop door closed, the sow lying peaceful in her mud, Brigadier at his perch on the roof of the Necessary. After that, I walked to the well pump, filled a glass, drank it empty, pumped another, and stood close to the window, sippin'.

It was Mrs. Bringhouse I heard first. "Oh, now, James, he's a good boy, black or no."

"But the trouble he's caused, Catherine," answered Mr. Bringhouse. "And only his second day here."

Then I heard Rachel speak. "But Father, Daniel Shady is the cause of trouble in your shop."

"I never have trusted that boy, husband."

There was a moment of quiet in the room. Brigadier crowed behind me. Then Mr. Bringhouse spoke. "He's not much of an apprentice, I'll grant thee. But his father pays me handsomely to have him here and we need the money."

"James," said Mrs. Bringhouse, in a stern voice I had never heard her use. "What of thy principles as a Quaker?"

"*I* wouldn't keep Daniel Shady," spoke up Rachel, "if it was up to me. Not for one more day!"

I heard what sounded like a cup banged down on the table. "Daughter!" said Mrs. Bringhouse, "how dare thee speak to thy father so."

To my surprise, Mr. Bringhouse came to Rachel's defense. "No, Catherine, she's right," he said, in a tired-sounding voice. "I know I am lax on Daniel. But I have a business to run and bills to pay."

"I know that," said Mrs. Bringhouse in a rising voice. "But must Isaac, this poor Negro, who knows nothing of your business, and is not to blame, suffer the consequences?"

"We all must suffer, Catherine, each in our own way."

I felt suddenly very uncomfortable listening in on this family conversation, even if it did concern me. I thought it strange that Mrs. Bringhouse spoke her mind so strongly, and Mr. Bringhouse so readily gave in. Was this the usual for Quaker husbands and wives? It was the opposite in our family, father bein' the strong and unbendable one, with Mama more often bein' the peaceable one even if that meant takin' the blame.

Mrs. Bringhouse was not done with her husband. "'We all must suffer?' Gracious, James," she said. "What sort of answer is that? Our task is to relieve suffering, if we can."

"I know," he answered. "But I am persuaded by my circumstances, even against my conscience, that I had rather send Isaac back to Mr. Jefferson than discharge Daniel Shady and lose his father's payments."

I waited, my water glass half empty, and feelin' a gloom settle over me. So I was going to get sent home, I thought, with no decent chance to prove myself. Then Rachel spoke up, describin' my idea for movin' apprentices around, so as to separate me from Shady. But I got so anxious I could not bear to listen and set the water glass back on the well pump and walked over and visited with old Tapper, scratchin' behind his ears as before and countin' his many welts, then went back to the kitchen window. Mr. Bringhouse was in the middle of a long explanation for why changin' benches would not help, because he had done that before with a previous apprentice, not black, mind you, and Daniel had been just as abrasive, well perhaps not in the same way. In short, he concluded, I would have to remain where I was, "but only for twelve months," at which time Daniel would complete his apprenticeship, and Mr. Bringhouse, from the generous payments of Daniel's father, would have paid off the mortgage.

"Oh, James," said Mrs. Bringhouse, "twelve months is such a heavy burden to lay on that boy."

"He must simply learn to endure Daniel," said Mr. Bringhouse, "as I have, and prove himself at the bench. Otherwise, I fear, he must go."

"You saw his wound," said Rachel. "It must be given time to heal! He cannot properly work at his bench with stitches in his hand."

"We mustn't encourage laziness in him, daughter. It is after all the natural inclination of his race."

"Father!"

"In any case, the Negro heals more quickly than the white."

With that, I turned on my heel and strode back to the shop. I am sorry, Rachel, I said to myself, as if she, too, were listenin', but stitches or no stitches I would have to prove myself at the bench, just as her father said. As for Shady, I would not endure him; I would best him.

CHAPTER  TWENTY-FOUR

Shady taunts, I persist, and so prove myself

With a good night's sleep I felt better, and I came through the shop door the next mornin' firmly resolved.

"Well, look," said Shady, "the one-handed cripple is back."

But I paid his insult no mind and got down on my knees and looked over the tin scrap box still lying broken on the floor. It was sturdy, though, and not so badly damaged as I first thought, and workin' slow with my bandaged hand, I tacked a few loose nails back in place and set it upright again. Then I scooted with it along the floor, pitchin' back in all the tin scrap that had fallen out.

Shady laughed to see me. "I like the sight of you down there," he said, dropping in five pieces, one at a time, very slowly. "Maybe now you will understand your proper station in life."

As Charles helped me heft the scrap box back up onto the table, Mr. Bringhouse came over. "Set me to work again," I begged.

He was skeptical, but I raised my bandaged hand and wiggled the last three fingers. "These work fine," I said. Though it hurt, and Rachel no doubt would have told me not to, I then wiggled my forefinger and thumb. "These, too, almost."

"I won't accept shoddy work," he said, "even if thou art injured."

"Oh, you shall see no shoddy work from my hand, Mr. Bringhouse," I said. "For I am not inclined to laziness, as some might think, and only want the chance to work hard and show my worth."

He frowned at me a moment, then brought out his timepiece, and I felt his impatience as he told me I must move along in my learnin', regardless of my hand, which I assured him I would. He reminded me that I risked infection, but I promised to be careful and change the dressing daily, as Miss Bringhouse instructed. Still he hesitated, timepiece in hand, so I just took hold of the shears with my good hand, managed with care to brace the tinsheet steady with my bandaged left hand, the tin sheet still spotted with my blood, and began cuttin' honest and true along the curved and double curved lines, and even double curved lines turned back upon themselves that I had earlier marked out.

"You will *never* learn tinwork," said Shady. "No *nigger* can."

I put down the shears. "Then you needn't worry," I said. "I can be no threat to you."

Mr. Bringhouse snapped his timepiece shut and went over to observe Little Will at work at his bench, then came back my way to Charles, and finally again to me. "Gracious," he said, "will thee cut all my tin into curved lines?"

"Mr. Bringhouse," I said, "set me to make something of purpose."

He looked over the tin cuts I had made, picking up one piece of tin and then another, rubbing his thumb along the cut edge of a double curve. "Perhaps something simple."

"Not too simple, I hope."

He looked at me over the top of his spectacles, then went to his own bench in the far corner, plucked down something from a shelf, and brought this back. He put it in my hands. "Can thou make this?"

It was a tin strip about ten inches tall and four inches wide, with a hand hold at top, and a pattern of punched holes. "Why, this is a grater," I said, "just like what Mama uses in her pastry kitchen."

"What would be thy method to make it?" he asked.

I looked it over good. "Cut the strip first, then fold the edges over. After that, punch the holes with a nail and mallet, then shape the hand hold. That would be my method."

He looked at me in surprise and then nodded. "Good. Good. Then proceed. One piece of advice—tin work requires a light touch. Not the heavy hand of the blacksmith."

I soon found I liked the light touch of tin, which was better for my hand anyhow. It was quicker to work than iron rod, too, with no heating and shaping at the forge, the sheet so thin and even, half-made almost, even before I put my hand to it. So I cut out the shape, folded the edges, punched the holes, and shaped the handle. Even with my bandaged hand, the work went along fairly well, and I was happy with the result.

But Shady scoffed. "Any fool can do a grater."

I shrugged, markin' out another. "You would know, I suppose."

Mr. Bringhouse took a look at the first one, then showed me how to roll the edges, rather then fold them, on a very narrow stake he called a bisk iron. So I rolled the edges on that second grater just as he showed me, and went on to make a third, and was so caught up in the work that Mr. Bringhouse had again nearly to drag me away to the midday dinner. It was good to eat, and good to rest my bandaged hand, but I was eager to work again.

Shady stood smoking out in the yard, and when he saw me, moved in front of the shop door, as he had done the previous day, except this time he leaned against it. "I thought I made clear to you yesterday," he said, "that we all got thirty minutes of free time after dinner." He blew smoke at me. "That wound of yours don't give you privilege."

"Free time is for white folks," I said, then raised my bandaged hand. "Plus, I am slow."

He pointed the pipe stem at me and tipped his head back. "I'm watching you."

"Fine," I said, noticing a considerable scar under his chin, "go on and watch."

"You have some trickery up your sleeve. I know it."

I shrugged. "Trickery? The Negro is too simple for that, you ought to know." I took hold of the door latch.

He took the pipe from his mouth and knocked the bowl upside down against the door. A wad of ash, with a hot ember in the center, fell upon a nest of leaves just beside the wooden step, and flamed up. I stubbed this out with my shoe and went in, thinkin' as I did so that he would gladly burn the place down with me in it if he dared.

I finished the third grater and went on to a fourth, when Mr. Bringhouse came to my bench. This last one I put into his hand, and he turned it over and over. "*Quite* good."

Shady was back at his bench by then. "Bringhouse, you missed the *errors* he would have made," he said, "if I hadn't been close by to correct him."

Mr. Bringhouse acted as though he had not heard this

remark, walkin' briskly to the shelf again and then back, holding another tinwork, along with a leather pouch. From this pouch he took pattern pieces and laid these out. Then he held out the tinwork to me. "This is a pepper canister. As before, what would be thy method to make it?"

I took the pepper canister in hand. It was a tube, in two parts, not so big around as a rolling pin, or so long, and the top tube slid snug down over the bottom tube. I explained that after I had traced the patterns and cut out the parts, that my method would be to make the bottom tube first, and from that make the top tube to fit down smoothly over it. I wasn't sure how to close the tubes, which he called *cyclinders*, at top and bottom, so he showed me how to flare the tube ends and fix them in place with the crimpin' hammer and then the solder iron. I was glad for the instruction. He taught me how to heat the iron in the little solder stove to just the right temperature, how to apply the flux, and in what amount, and how to melt the solder so it flowed clean and bonded properly. Then I put my hand to the solder iron, and done as he showed me, all the steps, and soldered up every crimp and seam of those two pepper canisters. Mr. Bringhouse was well-pleased with my work. Shady complained bitterly that I had received more attention than I deserved, and he so little. But I kept on, workin' slow and steady all afternoon until nearly dusk, when Mrs. Bringhouse rang the supper bell. But I was almost finished with a third canister. "All I lack is to solder the crimp," I said to Mr. Bringhouse. "I don't mind workin' late." Charles and Little Will, and then Shady by himself, had gone to the house by then.

"Mrs. Bringhouse would never abide that," he said. Still, he tried the fit of my third canister, which was so good he slid the two cylinders into and out of each other three or four times. Then he set the canister down. "Isaac," he said, pausing to draw a deep breath, "you have a *gift* for this work. And I don't say that lightly. For I have been in this business twenty years and have lost track of the number of apprentices I have employed." Then he drew another deep breath. "If thy work had been reported in the newspaper, and I had not been personally witness to it, well, God forgive me, I expect I would be skeptical. And thy one hand still healing, too." His voice tailed off.

I could hardly imagine my work being reported in the newspaper. "Just keep me at the work, Mr. Bringhouse," I said, "that's all I ask."

The next mornin', after gettin' into my clothes, which was a slow business, I unwrapped my hand and found the thumb pad a little swollen and tender, and when I got downstairs, Rachel insisted I show her. She lifted up my hand and took it in hers, a hand so slim and white, to mine so square and so black.

She pressed all around the wound, very gentle, with the tip of her forefinger. "Does that hurt?"

I said no, then said, "not much," but I don't think she believed me. For she led me out to the well pump at once, and washed the wound good with lye soap, dried it, rubbed in more aloe, and bound up my hand again in a fresh bandage cloth.

"How did you learn about all of this?" I asked. "How to stitch and mend and bandage?"

She had learned, she said, from a house servant by the name of Marge. "Such a capable woman!" she added.

I was unable to hide my surprise "'Marge,' did you say?"

Rachel looked up from my bandaged hand. "Why, yes," she said. "She's the head house servant for the Dempsey family, which owns a lovely manor on the north side of the city." Then she described how one day, while she, Rachel, was acting as governess and tutor for the children Jacob and Lydia, Jacob had come in crying because he'd fallen and cut his foot. So Marge had sewed him up and made Rachel watch, and then taught her the rudiments.

I was sure by then that this Marge must be the very Marge who was beloved of Raymond the farrier, the one who had made me promise to deliver his message from *Hot Stuff*. At the time, it seemed unlikely I would ever have to make good on that promise, but not so, now!

The other apprentices were nearly finished with breakfast by the time we came back inside, and there was little time for me to savor the porridge with nuts and dried fruit, and an egg on toast besides. I would be late out to the shop, I feared, and could fairly hear Mr. Bringhouse snapping his timepiece open and shut.

When I came through the door, Shady groused that I was being given undeserved "allowances," referring bitterly to my time spent idle as Rachel tended and dressed my wound. He would have gotten no allowances then or now, he complained, but must always scrap for attention. Where is the justice in that? he wanted to know. "Soon you shall expect privilege as your *due*!" he burst out.

"I have no privilege," I said, "except the privilege of working here by you." Then I stoked up the solder stove and heated the iron to finish the third canister. By supper that day

I had gone from pepper canisters to tea cans. And the day after, Thursday, from tea cans to tinder boxes, which continued into Friday, when I switched from tinder boxes to cheese molds.

Before breakfast, each of the several days that followed, Rachel soaped and cleaned my wound at the well pump, daubed on aloe, and changed the bandage. By Saturday mornin', my hand was remarkably well healed, and just after breakfast she was able to clip each stitch just under its loop, and pull out the threads, one by one. There was a little blood as she done so, but only a very little, which she washed off, and then she inspected the wound marks very close, and gently rubbed on the aloe ointment. The feel of her finger kneadin' the thumb muscle brought life fully back into my hand. I was whole again! Thankfulness just rose up and flowed through my whole self, and I could barely hold myself from telling her so, but dared not, lest I be too warm at it, especially with Mr. and Mrs. Bringhouse both present, and Shady scowlin' from behind them. The best I could do was open and close my hand in demonstration. "There now!" I said, with a smile I could not hide, "that's mighty good."

The three fundamental skills of tinsmithin' had become for me, even in those few days and despite my hand, almost second nature, and so I took aim at more complicated tinsmithery, beyond the simple copying of pattern pieces, such as a two-window lantern of my own design, with prism mirrors. Mr. Bringhouse was reluctant at first to allow me such license, but little by little he relented, to see what I could do. Then it was that I really came to love workin' the tin. There were moments at my bench when I lost myself in what I did. Oh, there was a real liberty in that!

Shady, for all his taunts and jibes, kept a superstitious

watch on me, at first to expose my failures, if he could, but then from fascination, I guessed. For my skill so exceeded his, and me a nigger, too, that he became obsessed to discover my secret, neglecting his own work, such as it was, to fix upon mine. I knew, or felt, that he saw me in a way that Charles and Little Will did not, and envied what he saw and even hated himself for such envy, which he knew very well he ought not to have had, as he was supposed to have been superior to me by natural law, but wasn't, which galled. I don't know! Can't know, I guess. Maybe don't want to know. What I do know is that the more I loved the doing of my work, the more he envied, which only spurred me on, and kept me at my bench as many hours as Mr. Bringhouse would allow.

CHAPTER  TWENTY-FIVE

*From lantern to ledger book, then
lesson from Rachel*

The next day, a Saturday, called by the Quakers Sixth Day, I set to work again on my two-window lantern with prism mirrors. The other apprentices, though, did not pick up their tinwork, but got out pencils, and began writing in a narrow book, each one.

Shady, seein' I had no book nor pencil, asked why I had not the same, then struck his forehead with the flat of his hand. "How could I have forgotten! You're *illiterate*, that's why." He leaned toward me, as if to share a secret. "But that's all for the best, don't you agree? *Those* skills are the province of the *white* race, and quite beyond you."

Oh, that was a spur to me, that he should speak so! It made me all the more want to write in a narrow book, just as he was doin', he and Charles and Little Will. It had not been so with me back at home. Hardly any of us bondspeople on Master Jefferson's could read or write, and mostly we could carry on just fine without knowin' those skills, and no time for the learning of them anyway, even if we had been allowed. Though I had been strongly taken up with the idea of me readin' from a book that time Old Master found me in his library, I soon put that aside, and set my mind to the work of tinsmithin', as was intended for me. But now, stung by Shady's mockery,

I keenly desired to learn how to both read and write, and so prove his mockery empty. "I *do* know letters," I said.

He studied me a minute. "Name 'em for me then. Name even one." He held up a finger. "*One*."

I could've, too. With knowin' the letters from the Georgetown Road sign and toting Old Master's books into the house that day with James, why I knew a goodly number, a dozen or more. But would I let Shady force me to speak 'em? Oh, no, Mr. Campbell, I would not! So I just sat at my bench, silent as a stone.

"C'mon, now," he said again, "you said you know letters. Or were you just lying?"

I shrugged.

"Damn you, nigger!" he said. "You are so uncooperative! Then he struck his fist against his book, and went back to writin', with exaggerated strokes, as though he were penning words with a shaved-tip goose quill as Master Jefferson would do, and not with a short pencil.

When Mr. Bringhouse came into the shop, he walked down the line, hands together at the small of his back, observin' each apprentice at their book, startin' with Little Will. When he came to me, he said, "Go to my office, please," and pointed.

His office was in the corner, by his bench, and I got up slowly from my stool, feelin' punished, and walked over to it and went in. I sat down in a hard-back chair with a worn seat cushion and wondered if he was going to send me back to Master Jefferson for my want of readin' and writin'. But I wasn't *supposed* to know those skills. Old Master would have disapproved if I had known. So what could be my sin that I would require a private talking to? My tinwork was exceptional, Mr. Bringhouse himself had said so. Maybe, I worried, he just needed some reason to get rid of me and the trouble I'd brought on, and this would be it. So I was prepared for the worst when he came in and shut the door, and I was all alone in that closed office with him. He squeezed by a cabinet and sat down behind his desk, which had on it many neat stacks of paper and a small stone on top of each stack. He turned an inkwell in his fingers, picked up a quill pen and set it back down, then pushed a clay mug to one side. He looked at me. Then he leaned over, pulled open a drawer in his desk, and brought out a narrow, black book, same as what Shady and the other apprentices had. "This," he said, tapping it with a finger and then holding it up, "is a ledger book, used for keeping an account of all business transactions. For a tinsmith must be both tradesman and businessman. I require that every one of my apprentices learn to use one." He laid the book back down on his desk.

"Then it has to do with numbers," I said, with relief. "I know numbers. Master Jefferson insisted on it. For he doesn't like wastage, no he does not. So in the smithy, my brother and me, we keep a close track on every rod and bolt and bar of iron, and how many chain links struck in a day's time, and how many door hinges and pot hooks and every other kind of thing, for Mr. Jefferson he insist we keep a record. Which we did. Sometimes even on paper." It was the most I'd said in one go to Mr. Bringhouse since I'd got to his house, but I thought he would appreciate the detail, being a businessman himself.

He visibly brightened, and I felt better. "The practice of numbers is an edifying exercise, as well as practical," he said. "However, the book is mainly for keeping track of the names of customers, descriptions of work, dates of payment, and so forth. Some numbers, yes, but mostly not."

Then he handed the book across the desk to me. "Open it," he said.

I did, and found the pages inside empty of words, but drawn with lines, both red and blue, all in neat order.

"Look at the front cover again," he said. "Read the word there, if thou can."

Near the bottom was both a number and a word, written in gold. "I read the number 'one' and 'two,'" I said.

"And the word."

I looked at that word and tried with all my might to make the meaning of it come into my mind. I could at least see the letters, or I thought I could, but they were written in a script I could not decipher, no matter how hard I tried. I shook my head. "No, Mr. Bringhouse," I said, "this one I can't seem to read."

"Open the ledger."

I did.

"Now, on the inside of the cover there, read those words, if thou can."

"All of them?"

"Any of them."

There were big words and small words, and medium length words, too. The small ones were all crowded together. I searched for any word I might be able to read, but just could not make out one, from so many. I tried at least to pick out letters here, and found some—"L," "R," "B," and in two places, "T." But that was it. I was illiterate, just as Shady said, and Mr. Bringhouse had now proved. I deeply felt my ignorance, how entrance to the world of books and writin' was closed off to me. I was accomplished in tin work, yes, but what I dearly needed to be able to do just at that moment was *read*. And I could not. No matter how I concentrated my attention, I could not make out the meaning of those words. "No sir," I said at last, "I can't. Can't quite read any of 'em."

"That's going to be a problem," he said.

"Well, now, Mr. Bringhouse," I said, struggling to hold back the tears, "I am acquainted with books, more than most, Negroes or white. I truly am! For I have been in Master Jefferson's library, and I don't suppose any man in the whole country could have more books than he. Once, I reached down of those books to give into his hand. And carried in armloads of books to his Philadelphia house, and helped his manservant set 'em up on the shelves, all alphabetical."

Mr. Bringhouse studied me the whole time I talked and pulled at his chin just as I finished. He leaned forward and folded his hands on the desk. "I believe," he said, "in the right of the Negro to advance. And I am willing to assist. But I do have a business to run, thou must understand. I teach an apprentice my trade, and in return he gives me his time." He cleared his throat. "So I *hesitate* to sacrifice too much of thy valuable bench time to the instruction of reading and writing. Dost thou understand?"

"Oh, yes, sir, I do," I said, and sat straight in my chair. "And I am certain that I can learn readin' and writin' as quick as any Negro can. Quicker. And if it takes time, why, then I will work longer hours at the bench, to make up for it, gladly I will." I stopped, and a worry crept in. "If Master Jefferson will allow. He does have his rules."

Mr. Bringhouse pulled at his chin again. "I have already spoken with Mr. Jefferson."

A chill went through me.

"He said, 'for limited purposes, only.' He even offered to seek a teacher for thee."

I could have jumped from my chair with gratitude.

"Unfortunately," Mr. Bringhouse added, "he was unable to secure one of adequate competency, for a reasonable fee."

"Oh," I said, and felt myself sink down.

Mr. Bringhouse picked up the quill pen again and twirled it in his fingers for a moment. "However," he said, "my daughter, with her teacher's conscience for the less fortunate, has volunteered her services." He laid the pen down. "So vigorously, I may add, that I felt *obliged* to accede to her demand."

I almost asked him to repeat what he said, for it sounded too incredible to be true. Rachel Bringhouse had volunteered—no, demanded—to teach me to read and write, and he, Mr. Bringhouse, had agreed? Again, as when she had inspected my healed wound and kneaded my thumb muscle with her finger, and a feeling of deep thankfulness had risen up in me, so now, too, the same emotion filled me, along with a desire to tell her so. The best I could do was thank Mr. Bringhouse, over and over.

He nodded, and briefly smiled. "Make no mistake," he said. "Though young, she is competent, *especially* with regard to Negro education, as she is well-acquainted with the pamphlets of Anthony Benezet. But a teacher is no better than his pupil. Thou must do as she says."

"Oh, yes, sir, I will."

"And study as she directs."

"*Exactly* as she directs."

Mr. Bringhouse stood up and I stood, too. "Thou shalt begin thy lessons on Monday," he said, "just after midday dinner."

CHAPTER  TWENTY-SIX

The Society of Friends, Thaddeus Oleander Principal, and the confession of Mr. Bringhouse

The prospect of my lesson, even if it was two days away, so worked upon my mind that I tossed and turned that night, finally got up early, dressed in darkness, and went downstairs quiet in my socks, shoes in hand. If I could not sleep then I would begin work.

Mrs. Bringhouse was bent over at the hearth, stirring the embers into flame.

I tried to tiptoe by, but she heard me. "Good morning, Isaac," she said.

I bowed politely and answered in kind.

She stood up, poker in hand. "Where art thou going?" she asked.

Out to the shop, I told her, as I hoped to get an early start, for I was eager for the work, with all that Mr. Bringhouse had taught me so far, and wanted nothin' better than to please him. I thought she would heartily approve.

But she shook her head. "This is the day we worship the Lord," she said.

"Oh, I'm sorry," I said, "I forgot it was Sunday."

"No, *First* Day. We don't believe in *pagan* names, but simply call the days by number."

I didn't know what "pagan" was, but was afraid to ask, having already made two mistakes with her. "Can't I still work on this day? Master Jefferson would let us, if we wanted, though he did not require it. Except for necessary services."

"Oh, no, Isaac. We do no serious work on First Day, except to clean and tidy up, before going to our Friends meeting."

I said I was sorry for not knowin' about this, and promised in future I would be more thoughtful about my activities on First Day, then asked if I might at least go out to the shop, stir up the embers in the stove, and tidy my bench. This, with a smile, she allowed I could do, sayin' that "cleanliness was next to godliness." So I slipped on my shoes and went across the yard. The air was chill, and the sky by now just turning the faintest gray of dawn. Tapper stamped and Brigadier crowed. Once in the shop, I stirred the coals, broomed the floor, and began to tidy my bench. I was enjoyin' the peace and quiet when Shady came through the door and at once directed me to clean around his bench, too. I held out the broom and pan for him, and said maybe he would like to try, which set him off, naturally, for he would not "touch them dirty things," now that my hands had been on 'em. Then in that peculiar way of his, he settled down and tried to make me understand how sensible his objections were, nature having made us different on purpose, he said, his kind to rule, mine to serve. There should be no offense on my part, as God had decreed it all. It was something of a sermon, which he earnestly delivered for my benefit. Then Little Will walked in, listened a moment, then promptly took the broom from my hand and himself began sweepin', tellin' Shady that I was Mr. Bringhouse's problem and not to drag the whole shop into it for God's sake. He was too big to argue with, and Shady went mum, for which

I was glad, until Little Will told me to get on out of there, which I did, but wondered if the two of them would then be puttin' their heads together against me.

Rachel greeted me in the kitchen, with more attention than I was quite comfortable with, since Mrs. Bringhouse was present, and one last time inspected my wound, or the scar of it at least. After breakfast, Mrs. Bringhouse laid a set of folded clothes in my arms, washed and ironed, my "Meeting clothes," she said.

An hour later we all set off walkin' to the Friends meetin', the Bringhouses in front, apprentices behind.

"Why is Shady not with us?" I whispered to Charles.

"Oh, he is not allowed in Meeting any more," he whispered back, explainin' that whenever anybody spoke in favor of manumission, he would jump to his feet and denounce it as a sin against God.

I asked what *manumission* was.

"*You* of all people ought to know," he said. "*Manumission* is where a slave owner decides to free a slave of his."

It was an awkward moment for me. I should have known, and that I didn't seemed at once to open a gulf between us. He was free, I bound. He did not notice this gulf, I don't think, and I tried my best to pretend it was not there. "So you say Shady is not allowed in the Friends meetin' anymore," I asked, "on account of his having spoken against this manumission?"

"That's right."

What a pleasure it was to hear those words. At least in a Quaker church, a man such as Shady could be scolded and expelled, and this was the very church to which we were going! So different from all the other churches I had heard of, which seemed mainly organized to scold the Negro. But

Master Jefferson didn't believe in the usual religion, so we were not made to go to such churches, nor any churches. Though sometimes a black exhorter would come around through the Quarter to preach, not at all about obedience, but about Moses and his people gettin' free from old Pharaoh.

We all turned from Front onto Walnut, walked a block, then turned north on Second. A carriage went by, then a wagon, with a dog in back that barked at us.

"Of course," said Charles, "and meaning no disrespect to you, but the Negro should not *outright* be freed. He should *earn* it, with some *meritorious* service."

"What is meritorious service?" I asked.

"Service beyond the usual," said Charles. "*Well* beyond the usual. Service worthy of commendation, praiseworthy service."

Rachel, just in front of us, with the two children in tow, stopped so suddenly I almost bumped into her. She twisted around and looked at Charles. "And who is to say what is meritorious?" she said, and then without waiting she answered her question. "Not the slave, that is sure! Even though the bondsman—and bondswoman—who by their daily tasks from dawn to dark support the cushioned life of the slave master. Is not that tireless labor of itself meritorious?"

I thought of Papa, who bore on his back and in his worried mind the responsibility of Master Jefferson's tobacco harvest, and Mama, who must run her household, raise her children, tend the garden, and yet be responsible for the complicated daily pastries sent up to the Big House, and the heaps of laundry—all sent back fresh and ironed for the Jefferson family and even their guests if need be—and manage pressin' the barrels of apple cider in the fall, and I didn't know what else. Yes, by any measure Papa and Mama, and many others like them, performed meritorious service!

Rachel stamped her foot. "Meritorious service!" she said, with a look of disgust on her face. "It is but a ruse, an impediment, to prevent the slave from gaining freedom, not an aid to his seeking of rightful liberty!

The children tugged at her hands. "Let's go! Let's go!"

Charles shrugged and turned his hands palm up. "Don't get mad at me," he said. "I'm just quoting the law."

"A law written by slave masters!" she said, and let loose the children, who raced on up the street. "Who hope to entice the poor Negro to divulge information about conspiracies and insurrections."

"Well," said Charles, "conspiracies and insurrections *are* dangerous to the general stability, you know."

I saw a flush rise in Rachel's cheeks, and wished she'd stand long to deliver her rebuff, for there was beauty in her anger. But instead she lifted her skirts and went after the children.

Charles shook his head. "She's pretty. If only she didn't have opinions."

"She's entitled," I said.

He looked at me. "Maybe among *your* women," he said. "Not among ours, at least those of decent respect."

I wanted dearly to stand up for Rachel just then, but feared that trouble might come from that, especially if it got back to her father, and he should decide to forbid my lessons with her after all. I pointed ahead. "We better catch up," I said, and off we went in a foot race.

Once caught up, we walked in silence to the corner of Market Street, where we passed through a broad opening in a brick wall and walked across a yard laid with the same brick, and came to the Meetin' House itself also neatly made of that red brick, and with the double doors wide open.

"Good Morning, Friend Bringhouse," said a man standing just inside, greeting Mr. Bringhouse.

"Good morning, Friend Parker."

"And who is this friend?" said the man, turning to me to shake my hand.

"This is Isaac. Isaac Granger Jefferson. Our new apprentice."

The man let go my hand. "Well, friend, you may sit up there with that fellow." He pointed to way up in the back corner where sat a white-bearded black man all by himself.

"Go on, Isaac," said Mr. Bringhouse, takin' little Jacob by the hand from Rachel. "We shall meet thee after the service." Then, followed by Little Will and Charles, he and the boy went off to sit with the men in their pews. Rachel, with Lydia by the hand, and Mrs. Bringhouse behind, went to sit with the women in theirs, so that men and women faced each other, with an open space between. There was much rustling of skirts, whispered talk, and creaking of pews as people settled in their places. I went up the steps to the back corner, where the white-bearded black man sat on the last and highest pew, all by himself. His coat, though pressed, was frayed at the cuffs.

"I was sent up here to sit with you," I said.

He swung his eyes to me but hardly turned his head. "We all equal in here," he said, "just *some* is more equal than others."

I sat.

"I warn you," he said, "there's a penalty to you settin' there."

I looked at him in surprise. "What penalty?"

He briefly smiled. "You'll know." A moment later he handed me a kerchief. "You might want to cover your nose."

I was soon glad for the kerchief, and slid away from him on the pew, but he leaned after me. "My apologies," he whispered. "Constitutional *necessity*, which I *choose* to see as an advantage. Keeps white people away."

"White people?" I said through the kerchief. "What about *any* people?"

He didn't answer but pulled at his beard and leaned back to his place and sat straight.

Down below us, the Friends all now sat quiet, many with their heads bowed. Rachel turned to her mother, then looked straight ahead, then all at once, up toward me. She caught my eye, and I right away looked away and then up, as if studyin' the rafters—then remembered I had the kerchief still over my nose. I jerked it down, and in doing so saw in one corner three letters stitched—T.O.P. "Top!" I said, too loud.

"Shh," said the bearded man, puttin' a finger to his lips, "you in the House of God. Then he pointed to the letters. "Them's my initials. *Thaddeus Oleander Principal*. And worth every syllable."

"What kind of name is that?"

He looked at me as if I ought to know better. "My *slave* name was 'Tick.' Do I look like a tick to you?"

"No, sir."

"So there you are," he said, and then after a pause, "so what's *your* name?"

"Isaac Granger Jefferson."

Thaddeus raised an eyebrow. "As in *the* Jefferson?"

I nodded. "The very same."

"He's a fine man, from what I've heard."

"Yes, sir, he is."

"Though still a slave master, don't forget."

"Of course, I don't forget," I said, suddenly ashamed.

"You kin to him?"

"No."

"That's good," he said, and slid away from me.

Then a man in the front pew stood to his feet, folded his hands together and said, looking this way and that, "the Meeting of the Society of Friends is now convened, this First Day morn, fifteenth of the eleventh month, in the year of our Lord, seventeen hundred and ninety. May the Light within us shine forth. May gentleness and decorum mark our words." Then he sat down. All was quiet for a time. I looked down at the floor, where a nail head was not quite pounded all the way down, and then saw another. I would have started with a smaller rod, to make a trimmer nail. Where two boards met, the end of one had split.

Finally, a bent man with a bald head spoke up, five pews down from us. "Over and again my neighbor says to me, 'I am a veteran of the late war. I fought under General Green, and still have a bullet in my leg to prove it.' Then this neighbor *castigates* me for having refused to take up arms, saying, 'true patriots fought and died.' He is highly *resentful* that I should enjoy the life and prosperity which, he claims, *they* deserved."

There were murmurs and nods at this.

"What do I say?" said the man, opening his arms. "What do I say to my neighbor?"

I wondered if anybody would have an answer, until a skinny woman in black skirts and black bonnet got slowly to her feet, keeping one hand on the pew back. "Turn away from that neighbor, Friend Karl, turn away. Don't let his spite fester in thy heart."

She sat down, and a big man with wide shoulders across from her stood up. "I counsel thee to speak boldly and frankly. Remind thy neighbor that General Green was *disowned* by the Society of Friends. We are committed to peaceableness, yes, but that does not mean we are required to submit to abuse. We are good, honest, and productive citizens."

No sooner had that man set down, than a small woman in a gray shawl got up. "Gentleness, Friends," she said, raising her hand in the air. "Oh, gentleness. Even if we are provoked, let us be as the lamb, meek and mild. Remember Christ, who opened not his mouth before Pilate. Who loved the world though the world did not love Him."

A respectful silence followed.

Then a hump-back man with a little cross hung about his neck stood to his feet. He smiled to one and all and cleared his throat.

Thaddeus leaned over to me. "That there is Mr. Dunn. He is never *done* speaking."

He proved it that morning, I can tell you, for he began gravely to speak of history, and time, and the '*brief span of human life,*' of robin redbreast and the stars a-wheel in the heavens, until all at once a woman sittin' in the pew right across from him fairly jumped to her feet. "Heavens, Henry. Thou hast said enough. Prithee, sit down."

"That's *Mrs.* Dunn," whispered Thaddeus, "bless her soul."

Mr. Dunn promptly sat down, and a long silence followed. A now familiar odor arose about me, and I put the kerchief to my nose, and slid farther away from Thaddeus on the pew.

And then Mr. Bringhouse, neat-built Mr. Bringhouse in his pressed white shirt and dark coat, rose slowly to his feet. Somehow, I dreaded to see him stand there. "Good Mistress Wright spoke of gentleness," he began. "She admonished us to be as meek and mild as the lamb. To love, as our Lord doth love." He halted, looked down, and ran his hand through the curly hair over his ears. Then he looked straight ahead. "Those are hard words for me to hear this morning. For I have not been gentle these past days, nor as the lamb. But as a *beast*. I have not loved but *hated*. Hated so deeply that I struck my own apprentices with a broom, to hurt, to *wound*. And this," he said, his voice dropping low, "against a poor Negro, most of all, who was entrusted to my care." Then he turned, and all the men turned with him, as he lifted his hand and pointed up toward me.

"Uh oh," said Thaddeus, "here comes the dreaded remorse."

"Will you, Isaac," said Mr. Bringhouse, in a loud voice, "forgive me?"

I saw Rachel put her two hands over her face, and I wish I could have done the same, or somehow shrunk down underneath the pew and took hold of those two nail heads, as if they could hold me fixed to the floor. But there I sat, looked at by everybody in that whole congregation, until Thaddeus Oleander Principal, mustering an odor of uncommon strength, managed to turn away the faces of a considerable number of worshippers in our general vicinity. I was so relieved that I didn't even require the kerchief.

Mrs. Bringhouse came out of her pew and went to her husband. "James," she said, "my dear, dear James."

All at once, everybody stood. Hands reached out, side to side, until all the Friends were connected, like links in one long chain, windin' from pew to pew, and across the space to the pews on the other side, joining both men and women. Thaddeus and me looked at each other. He pulled at his beard and stood, and I stood with him. He reached out his hand, a dry hand, and I took it. "Don't we make a lovely pair," he said.

"Bless our good and stalwart Friend, James Bringhouse," spoke out the man who had opened the Meetin'. "May peace make its home in his troubled heart. May forgiveness release his conscientious mind. May the divine light, which shines in us all, shine the more brightly in him, this day."

CHAPTER   TWENTY-SEVEN

*Billey Gardner introduces himself,
James Hemings lords it over me,
I report to Master Jefferson*

Mr. Bringhouse held out both hands to me after Meeting, but I could hardly bear to look at him. Mrs. Bringhouse held onto his arm and nodded at me.

"I must get right on to Master Jefferson's," I said, "for he's expectin' me," and then did my best to get past the Quakers who crowded around to wish me well or add their own forgiveness. One even took me by the hand and said, "Friend Bringhouse, he is a good-hearted man, thou must believe it." Their attentions I'm afraid just made me all the more uncomfortable, as if I now bore some responsibility to them, as well, and be the good Negro they expected me to be.

Outside the Meetin' House, Miss Bringhouse caught up to me. "That must have been awful for you!" she said. "It was for me. I'm sorry."

I looked at her in the bright sun. The bonnet brim shaded her face. "Your father meant well," I said. "Now please, I must get on." And so I left her there, without any thanks for her honesty, but I just had to get away. I walked quick back to Second Street, then up Market, and turned left on Eighth. I put my mind to what I would say to Mr. Jefferson, but all I could think was "trouble." Trouble with Daniel Shady, then the trouble of my cut hand, which had nearly put an end to my tinsmithin', and now this trouble with Mr. Bringhouse, who must confess about me in public, and then of course the knockin' into Rachel—or Miss Bringhouse as I must certainly remember to call her in the Master's presence, should she be mentioned—at the Goose Fountain. None of this would be what Mr. Jefferson expected to hear from me, or I would like to tell. Yet he knew things, he always did, beyond what you might suppose, Mr. Campbell, and he might bring these subjects up on his own. Maybe as distraction I could get him to talk of his tinkerin' back home. For he had a little workbench there, behind his library, and from time to time he would show me the keys and locks and small chains he forged. He was as neat a hand as ever you saw at makin' such things. Was there nothing he could put his hand to, and not do it well?

When I came to his house at 274, with its many windows and white shutters, all in a regular order, bottom story and top, I stepped up to the door and raised the brass knocker.

"Don't," said a voice from behind me.

I turned around, and there on the walk stood a Negro of middle years, with a big basket held in both hands, stacked up with clothes almost to his chin.

"That's the front door, son," he said. "The help is supposed to go around to the back door." He motioned with his head. "You should know that."

"I'm not the help," I said.

"Oh, I see. You came to talk politics and books with the Big Man, I suppose."

"No," I said, "I came here to report. He is my Master."

The man set his basket down. He straightened his vest and tugged his shirt cuffs even. "Your *Master*, is he?" He put his hands on his hips. "Now, if he was my Master, I would never think to come in at the front door. Such *poor* taste. But I don't have no Master anymore, not like *you*."

I stepped down from the door and walked over to this man, who had intruded so bluntly into my affairs, and asked him just who did he think he was.

He straightened a blue scarf in his breast pocket. "I don't *have* to tell," he said. "Not to a *youngster* like you." Then he drew in a breath and puffed out his chest. "You need some luck in your life, that's your problem. And I am *it*." He grinned.

I didn't much care for his high-handed manner and told him he could keep his luck to himself, whatever it was.

He brushed at his one sleeve, then the other. "Don't be so hasty, young man," he said. "*Gardner* is my name. Mr. Billey Gardner, proprietor of Gardner Business Associates." He took a step forward. "I serve only the *best* clientele."

"That explains the basket of laundry, I guess," I said.

Gardner grabbed my sleeve.

I told him to let go, and he did, finally, but only after tellin' me that I should show some respect for my betters.

"Fine," I said, and shrugged. "Then let me by and I will go in the house by the back door, just to please you. Master Thomas Jefferson is *waiting* for me."

"You could at least say *good day*."

I stepped around him.

"Good day, Mr. Billey Gardner." Then I walked along the pathway into the back garden.

"Good day to *you*," he called after me. "We shall meet again. For it is *historic*, you and me!"

I knocked on the back door, waited, knocked again, and finally James Hemings opened, but blocked the way in. "I see who you been talking to just now," he said. "That man is *always* looking for his angle." He tapped me on the chest with his white gloved hand. "Just don't let that angle be *you*."

"Oh, you need not worry about that," I said. "I am no fool."

He let out a short laugh. "We'll see."

I waited for James to get out of the doorway, but he did not move and insisted that I describe my purpose in being there, which he must have known, but nevertheless required me to repeat: "I am here to report to Mr. Jefferson, on my week's work in Mr. Bringhouse's tin shop."

This did not gain me entry, however, for he then had to describe, as if I didn't know, that Mr. Jefferson was an important man with important business, that in fact he was Secretary of State to President George Washington himself, and that he, James, was charged with the particular duty of protecting Mr. Jefferson from *pestering*.

"I am not pestering," I protested. "He *told* me to come. Every Sunday, after the Friends meeting. So here I am, as instructed."

James looked me over, and had me retie one shoelace, and tuck in my shirt, which was tucked in but he made me tuck it in differently. "Now wait," he said, and went in the house, shutting the door.

I turned around and looked out over the garden, with its flower beds, and tree plantings, and rocks arranged. No doubt Mr. Jefferson had a book for it all, in which to mark what flowers bloomed and in what order, and tree buds by date.

Finally, I heard the door open and turned around. "Just don't talk on and on," said James, and let me in at last. I followed him down the hallway to another door, past the library, where he knocked, and opened it some and spoke softly to Master Jefferson, who spoke softly back. Finally, James stood straight and ushered me by, tuggin' up my trousers as I went past.

Master Jefferson sat tall behind his broad desk, with books about, some open, some stacked. His writin' machine was before him. With this machine, its wheels and little connectin' bars, he could write two letters at the same time, one a perfect copy of the other, and these copies he stowed in order, in a desk drawer. He took loose his hand from one of the quill pens, and smiled at me. "Well, Isaac," he said.

"I can stay," said James from behind me.

Mr. Jefferson took loose the pen he wrote with and pressed the nib against a paper to get all the ink out. "That won't be necessary," he said.

"Are you awfully sure, Master?"

Mr. Jefferson did not answer, but laid aside this first pen, then took out the second pen, that wrote the copy letter, and cleaned it, too.

"Well, I shall stay close by," said James, "should the boy become a bother." Then he bowed, backed out the door, and closed it without a sound.

Old Master opened his hand toward me. "Sit, Isaac," he said, in the pleasant voice customary with him. "Do sit."

After I had pulled up a chair across the desk from him and sat down, he leaned back in his own chair, reached up his long arms, folded 'em back in like wings, and cupped his hands together behind his head. "Of the writing of letters there is no end," he said, and smiled. Then he looked at me. No, searched me, for a long minute. He was good at that, searching a person with his eyes. "Those aren't your clothes," he said.

"No, sir," I said. "Mrs. Bringhouse lent them to me, washed and ironed."

He nodded.

I wasn't sure if there was somethin' wrong about that. "But my clothes will come back to me tomorrow," I said, "also washed and ironed, I'm sure. She believes in clean clothes and a clean house."

He nodded again. "And your hand," he said, "what happened to your left hand?"

My heart jumped. "Why, nothin' Master. Nothin' happened to my hand."

"Then why is it you are rubbing your palm with your other thumb?" he asked. "You have been doing so since you came in here."

I looked down at my hand. Sure enough, I had been doin' that very thing, without even knowing it! There was no help for it, now, I must tell. "Nothin', Master Jefferson," I said. "Or nothin' much happened to my hand. Just a little cut." I held up my hand, palm toward him. "See?"

He leaned forward over the desk. "Those look like suture marks," he said. "Stretch out your hand. Let me see."

"Oh, it was just a little wound, Master. The Miss Bringhouse she sewed it shut." I wished at once I had not mentioned her at all.

Mr. Jefferson took my left hand in his right, and then with his left forefinger felt the scar, and touched the six red spots, one at a time, where Rachel had pushed the needle through. His touch was nearly as gentle as hers. "Neatly done," he said. "She's quite an accomplished young woman." He let go of my hand and leaned back in his chair, and again searched my face.

"My hand is fine, now," I said. "No trouble doin' any work,

no matter how difficult." I spread open my fingers, then touched the tip of each one in turn to my thumb.

"Tell me," he said at last, smiling again, to my relief, "what have you learned this first week in the tin business?"

This question I was happy to answer. "The three basic skills, Master. First, marking and cutting. Second, shaping and crimping. Third, seaming and soldering. Already, I've made graters, pepper canisters, and cheese molds. Started on a two-window lantern with prism mirrors, even. Mr. Bringhouse he is well pleased with my work."

"That's quite a useful list," he said. "I may ask Mr. Bringhouse to have you make a pepper canister for me, then. The one in this house is poorly done."

"Oh, yes, sir. Be pleased to."

"How about the other apprentices?" he said, straightenin' the three books at one corner of his desk. "Do you get along with them?"

I hesitated. "Mostly. They have been with Mr. Bringhouse some time, though, and not all have taken kindly to me, bein' the newcomer, and—Negro. But I have worked to catch up, and believe I can best 'em all, in time."

Mr. Jefferson held up his hand. "You be careful there, Isaac. You don't want to *offend*."

"I only mean to do my best work," I said.

"Of course," he said, and put his hand down. "That is what I expect. I just don't want to see you be the *occasion* of trouble. That, too, reflects on me, you understand."

"Yes, sir, I *do* understand," I said, "and by no means do I want to be the cause of trouble to you. Oh, no. Believe you me, that would be the furthest thing from my mind."

He put up his hand again, and I was afraid I had said too much, which he might take as a sign that I was hidin' some trouble I had been in, which of course in a way I was. He shifted in his chair, rested his chin upon the fingertips of one hand, and again searched me. He had the deepest eyes of any man I ever met. He took in more, he understood more, he kept more in that ever-thoughtful ocean of a mind of his. I was afraid he might ask other questions about the wound, or maybe send James Hemings down to the shop to inquire about my troubles further. Instead he simply asked, "How about your table fare. Is it satisfactory?"

"Oh, yes, Master," I said, cheerful again. "More than satisfactory. For breakfast, porridge with nuts and fruit, and milk on it. Milk *and* sugar. Yesterday mornin', eggs, two each, with sausage and fried potatoes. For midday dinner, hot soup or stew and white bread. Even at supper there is meat, sometimes dessert. Mrs. Bringhouse, she makes the *best* apple pie."

"Don't let her spoil you, now," he said.

I knew then that maybe she had spoiled me, and that I shouldn't have made so plain what sumptuous fare I enjoyed at her table. I hadn't meant to speak so, it was just that I'd never had such food, and felt almost as though I'd always been hungry, and now at the Bringhouses for the first time could fill up and stay filled. But I thought it wise to correct myself. "But honestly, Master Jefferson," I said, "the cornbread and pork we get from your hand is all I really need. It's more to my taste anyhow. Mama she can do wonders with but little." Of course, she supplemented with kitchen scraps, and tradin' for nuts and berries from other slave families, and what she could get from our garden, but I wouldn't have wanted to mention all that, lest Mr. Jefferson cut our allotment.

Then he asked about my sleeping arrangements.

"I have a frame bed," I said, more careful now. "But I would sleep better on the floor, for the mattress is too soft, and them *sheets* and blanket is hot to sleep under, and the down pillow is *itchy*. Not at all like our comfortable pallet bed at home. But I will adjust, I guess."

Mr. Jefferson dipped his head and smiled just a little and looked at me. "The Quaker meeting this morning, how was that?"

"There is no preacher," I said. "All sit quiet, till one or another of 'em get to their feet and speak what is upon their heart."

He nodded, then drew a deep breath and let it out. "If I did choose to be outwardly religious," he said, "I believe I would choose to be Quaker."

"Yes, sir," I said, and then wondered if that included manumission.

Master Jefferson folded his hands on the desktop. "It's all a new experience for you, isn't it? This living and working in Philadelphia, apart from your family and the routines of Monticello."

"Oh, yes, Master, it is," I replied, surprised at his question. For in some fashion or other he seemed to have wondered what it was like to be me, wondered perhaps about the difficulties. I hadn't supposed until that moment that he would have been all that curious about my experiences, what they felt like to me, when he had so much else on his mind. It shouldn't have surprised me, maybe, for he was curious about so much. But I didn't want him to be overly curious.

Then he said, "Don't forget my purpose in bringing you here."

I thought I knew what my purpose was and didn't need to be reminded. Or maybe I did. He was plumbing for somethin'. What could that be? Yet he expected me to be simple, and simple I must remain to him. "Oh, I shan't," I burst out.

"And what *is* that purpose, again?"

"Why, to learn the tinsmith trade."

"That is not all."

I rubbed the scar in my palm again, then looked at my sleeve cuffs, still with the crease in 'em. Then I looked back up at Mr. Jefferson. "I can't think what," I said, scratching my head.

Old Master smiled. "*Generating income,*" he said. "That is your purpose. Tobacco is never a *dependable* business, and it is my intention therefore to *diversify* my enterprises. So I desire that you become a competent tinsmith, yes, and supply the needs of my plantation for pots and pans and so forth. But I am also eager that you produce admirable wares of remarkable craftsmanship which will fetch a good price and be coveted throughout Virginia and beyond. The *financial solvency* of Monticello, Isaac, may very well *depend* upon it."

The weight of his words sank heavily in upon me.

"Well," he said, drawing his writing machine to him, and loading first one quill pen and then the other with ink, "I must complete my correspondence, and you, young man and faithful servant, must return to your trade."

He laid in two sheets of paper, and I rose from the chair.

"I shall see you again next Sunday," he said, adjusting the wheels and bars. Satisfied, he took hold of the first pen. "And bring me a sample of your work, will you? I am eager to see your progress."

"The pepper canister you asked for? Or two-window lantern with prism mirrors?"

He smiled at me again, that mysterious smile of his which conveyed both compliment and demand. "Whatever you think will most please me."

I wished he had been more specific. He was pleased by all kinds of things, but was so particular at the same time. "Yes, Master," I said, then bowed, backed to the door, then stood and took hold of the doorknob, but turned to look at Mr. Jefferson one moment. He was bent over his letter, the quill feather moving above his fist as he wrote. I loved the look of him just then, he was so *concentrated* at the work, which I could understand, and know the pleasure of. But oh, I wished I could form words on paper as he did, not works from tinsheet as I did, but *ideas*, made from the *substance* of his mind.

Then I opened the door quiet as could be, stepped out, and closed it back as quiet again, leaving Mr. Jefferson all alone with his writin' and his thoughts.

CHAPTER TWENTY-EIGHT

First Lesson with Rachel, slaphand, and a scoldin' from Mrs. Bringhouse

On Monday, or Second Day mornin', I set about to finish the two-window lantern with prism mirrors, makin' the little door to swing neatly open and shut, yet tight enough that no stray gust of air could put the candle out, and the top funnel-shaped to shed the rain. I worked right through midday dinner, ignorin' Shady's objections, so I could turn my attention full and complete to my first ledger book lesson. Clearin' my bench of tools and tin, I laid open the narrow book and waited for Rachel to come through the door.

I had to put up with Shady first, who came in, put away his tobacco pipe, and demanded to know by whose permission I could sit with a ledger on that day and at that hour. Charles, following Shady in, told him to mind his own business for once. Little Will ignored all this and went to his station and began workin'.

At last Rachel showed, thank goodness, holdin' writing slates, with a chalk in each hand. Shady, suspicious, wanted to know why.

"Because," she said, "*I* am going to teach Isaac here to read and write."

He said nothing back for a moment, being surprised, I think, at the stoutness in her voice. I was, too, and suddenly saw her differently. Saw not just her round face and blue eyes, nor slender frame, but the fiber in her, if I may call it that, the heartwood, the forged iron.

Shady said it was "illegal to teach a nigger to read and write."

"*Never* use that word in my presence again," she said, stampin' her foot.

"Who are *you* to *regulate* my language?" he burst out. "I shall speak as I see fit."

"Do so elsewhere, then," she said, setting one slate and chalk in front of me. "For I am charged by my father to teach this *Negro* to read and write. And while it may be illegal to teach him these skills in thy backward state, it is not illegal for me to do so *here* in Philadelphia."

I was amazed to hear her talk so boldly in my defense.

"Well, it ought to be illegal," he grumbled. "No good can come of it, *if* he can learn at all." He watched as Rachel set down her own slate and chalk beside mine. "Probably I shouldn't worry, though. Being but a *girl* and weak-minded yourself, you can be no fit teacher."

Rachel gave him then such a look of fury that he went silent and turned to his work. Now, I thought, we can finally begin our lesson. But that was not to be the case, for just then came a sudden bangin' on the outside of the big rollin' door, and the words "tin shipment!" shouted out, and the squeaky door pushed open on its track by Charles and Will, and a driver backin' in a heavy wagon and his helper calling out commands of "slow," and "whoa," and "set the brake!"

The two men unlashed the tin sheet piled in the wagon bed, but the pile was not straight, and one sheet slid off and clanged to the floor and then another, and one horse rose up in its harness and the other snorted. Little Will got hold of one horse and called Charles to get the other, and Shady banged his hammer on his bench and pointed at Rachel. "See what you done?"

That was enough for her. She told me to take up my slate and chalk and then follow her into the house.

Mrs. Bringhouse stood over her work table, kneading dough.

"The shop was too noisy for a lesson," Rachel told her.

Mrs. Bringhouse stood up and turned to us, her hands white with flour. "Well," she said, "there's certainly no place in my *kitchen*."

"Then where?"

"How about the dining table?"

"Mother! That is all set out with plate and tableware. I need a place *designated* for the purpose. The front room would do."

"I keep that room for special, Rachel, thee know that."

"Mother, Isaac must have lessons, if he is to learn his ledger book. Father said so."

Mrs. Bringhouse stuck both her hands in her apron pockets and looked at us. I tried to lean away from Rachel a little bit, lest she get a wrong idea. "Well," she said at last, "I suppose thou mayest use the front room, at least this *first* time."

I was glad Rachel had found us a place finally, and so followed her again, this time around the hearth and over to the door of the front room, which she opened, and then waited for me to go through.

But I would not. "Oh, no, Miss Bringhouse," I said, "*You* go first. It is only proper."

"But I wish to welcome you, as my pupil, to your first lesson." Then at once her eyes got wide and she put a hand over her mouth.

"Is there something wrong?" I asked.

She took her hand down. "I used the *familiar* address with you."

"Is that so bad?" I asked.

"But it is not proper," she said, "and I am here to teach you proper speech, in the Quaker manner. I should have said, I welcome '*thee* as my pupil,' not '*you* as my pupil.' I should have said '*thy* first lesson,' not '*your* first lesson.'" She stood for a moment quiet. "I was not *taught* to be familiar," she said, almost to herself, "but *formal* in my address. Even to friends and family." Then she turned and looked at me, her smooth brow wrinklin' just a little. "You," she said. "*You.*"

There had been at least one other time when she had used what she called the familiar address with me, and I had let that slip by without mention, but here, in this room, just between the two of us, she had crossed over a kind of fence line, accidentally maybe so, and had boldly decided to address me, who by any measure she ought to have kept distant, as one more familiar to her than either father or mother. That was pleasing to me, but also dangerous, I feared.

Fortunately, the moment passed into the ordinary. "Well then, Isaac Granger," she said, "I welcome *you* to *your* first lesson."

I was still uncomfortable walking in front of her, to be first in the room. Yet she would not budge from where she stood until I had bowed again, gone by her quick, and then stood waiting for her to go by me.

"Please," she said, extending out her hand, "take your place at the table, there by the corner hearth."

This made me still more uncomfortable, but I at least went to the table, and stood behind the chair farthest from the hearth, so she could have the warmth. She told me to go ahead and sit down, but I would not. "Now, don't make me be difficult again, Miss Bringhouse," I said, "you come and sit down first. You must understand."

"But if I invite you to sit, please do me the courtesy of obliging," she said. "It is just between you and me. No one else need know."

So at last I pulled out the chair and sat down with great care. "Now you," I said, "do me the same."

She nodded, smiled, and closed the door.

I got to my feet. "No, please don't close the door."

"Why not?" she said, her hand upon the knob.

"Please, just leave it open."

Still she stood with her hand upon the door knob. "But I don't understand. With the door closed, we can have *quiet*, to better concentrate on the lesson."

"It's plenty quiet in here, even with the door open."

Just then there came sounds from the kitchen, a pot falling to the floor, then talking.

"You see?" she said.

I felt as if I were about to suffocate in this small, tidy room, all alone with her. "Please," I said again, half gettin' to my feet, "just humor my poor self, will you, and open the door."

She shook her head and then swung the door wide open. More noise and talk from the kitchen. "Will that do?"

I didn't want to make no more fuss about it, but still I

had to object, and she finally got the door to a point between open and closed that we could both agree on and I sat back down. Then she walked from the door to the little table, and stood at her chair, and I stood up at mine, we both very formal. Finally, she laid the slates and chalk upon the table, so they hardly made a sound, and then seated herself, looking straight ahead as though there were no one else at the table but her, and tucking her skirt and apron around her. As she began to sit, so did I, just as careful. But it was a small table, and I felt my knee touch hers, and pushed my chair back. She looked at me, and I dropped my eyes, which found her hands, folded together like a tent. They were so white and delicate. Those hands had touched mine, in treating my wound, and I had accepted that, but here, in this room, all alone with her, I could not get over the sight of her hands. I pushed my chair back a little more.

"You *can* look at me," she said.

I could have, and had before, sure I had. But here it was different. "I thought I was to look at my ledger book."

"You don't have your ledger book," she said.

"Oh," I said, embarrassed at myself, "how could I have forgot? Let me go run and get it." I rose from my seat then, for I suddenly wanted nothin' more than to be gone from that room. But she touched my hand, just the lightest touch, and that made me sit right back down.

"Never mind the ledger," she said, pullin' back her hand. "We don't need it for this lesson."

"If you say so," I said, and kept my eyes fixed straight down at the table top.

"But I do need you to look at me."

I didn't know why she had to need that. It made me not want to. "I have ears, you know."

"I know you have ears, Isaac, but how will I know you are really hearing me, if I can't see your eyes?" She tapped the table with her knuckles and I raised my eyes, but no farther up than the neck of her dress, which had two buttons, one above the other, just at her throat.

"Come now," she said, "am I now so *objectionable* to look at, after you have seen me at the breakfast table, and cleaning your wound by the well pump?"

Those circumstances seemed entirely different to me just then, but I did look at last, and saw just how blue her eyes really were.

"Your eyes are brown," she said.

I hadn't ever really looked to see what color my eyes were, and felt embarrassed, and wanted to check in a mirror right then. "Now can we begin our lesson?"

"Yes," she said, clapping her hands together. "We can begin by learning the alphabet. Do you know what I mean by the word *al-pha-bet*?" She bent her head to me and said the word very slowly, as if I were a child.

I did know what the word alphabet meant, but the way she talked bothered me, and so I pretended ignorance. "It has a lot to do with readin' and writin', I bet."

"Yes," she said, again very slowly, "that *is* true."

I got the idea from the way she looked at me that she knew I was not so ignorant as I pretended. "Well then, we can move on to letters, can't we?"

This caught her by surprise, which I am sorry to say pleased me a little. "You know letters?" she said, her eyes wide.

"Oh, dozens," I said, wavin' my hand as if I'd been acquainted with 'em for years.

She sat back in her chair. "Dozens? How?"

I was going to say how I'd gone about it in clever ways, as proof that I knew way more than she realized, when I suddenly thought that might not be such a good idea. For what if she were to tell her father what I had said, and he told Master Jefferson? Even if he had given permission that I should be taught to read and write for the ledger book, I wouldn't have wanted him to know I'd already been tryin' to acquire letters of the alphabet on my own. "I forget."

She leaned forward again, looking puzzled. "Well, it doesn't matter how *many* letters you know. Just name the ones you do know."

"I forgot."

She turned her head away, and then back. "You forgot *all* the letters, the *dozens* you told me you had learned?"

"I guess so. Every one. Negroes are weak-minded, you know."

"Oh, I don't think it's weak-mindedness, Isaac!"

I shrugged.

She put a hand to her forehead. "Why are you being so difficult?"

I felt badly then, for she did not deserve such treatment. Who but her had volunteered to teach me? What if she decided to quit? I would have doomed my chance to learn, all on account of mistrustfulness. That wouldn't do. So I suggested that maybe she could just start me off at the beginnin' letter, and maybe some of the others would come back to me, though I suspected she was still skeptical of my supposed forgetfulness.

Then she picked up a chalk, wrote on her side of the slate,

which she turned to show me, and pointed at her marks. "This," she said, "is the letter 'A.' The first letter of the alphabet. Also, the first vowel. Say it after me, please."

I watched her mouth open and her lips shape the sound "A," and then the words, "In Adam's Fall we sinned *all*."

I repeated the words after her: "In Adam's Fall we sin *all*."

"Not *sin* all. *Sinned* all. Past tense."

"That's what I said."

"No, you didn't. Let's try again." She laid the small tip of her first finger, pink under the nail, to the bottom of her lower lip and tapped. "*SINNED*. It's the 'ed' at the end you miss. SIN-N-N-DAH. Do you hear it?"

"I hear. *Sinned*."

"In Adam's Fall, we sinned all."

"In Adam's Fall, we sinned all."

"Good," she said. "So that's 'A.' Now, there are twenty-six letters in the alphabet, from the letter 'A' to the letter 'Z.' From these twenty-six letters are made all the words in the English language."

I considered this. "The alphabet is like tin sheet, then," I said, and explained that all the tin pans, pots, cups, salt cellars, pepper grinders, and whatnot could be made only from tin sheet. And no tin thing at all could be made without there first being the tinsheet. But she at once objected that it wasn't at all the same, for with the alphabet it was possible to build and rebuild words forever, whereas with tin sheet, once that sheet was all cut up and made into pans and pots and so forth, no more things from it could be made. I said well you could take those things apart if you wanted, and make them into new things, but she said a person could do that, yes, but what a bother it would be and do that enough times and there'd be nothing but a heap of scraps, each one no bigger than a thumbnail, or smaller. I still objected, on the principle of the thing.

"Shall we spend the rest of our lesson arguing?" she asked.

"I'm not arguin'. Only thinking." I thought that's what we are to do here, is think." I did not want her to suppose I knew nothin' on my own, except what I was told.

"We have twenty-five more letters to go," she said, put out, "and shall never be done at this rate."

"So what are these twenty-five other letters?" I said, feelin' put out myself, and as if I didn't know some already. "Name 'em. I have a good memory. Just name 'em one by one."

"I'd rather sing them."

"Sing them? I thought letters are for readin' and writin'. You don't need letters to sing."

"Somebody has to write songs down, eventually. If other people wish to sing them."

"Not the songs I know, they don't."

But she had had enough of my argument again, and so turned partly away from me in her chair, sat straight, lifted her head a little, and sang all the letters in order, from A to Z. She had a beautiful voice, much stronger than I would have guessed. I was so taken with the sound of it, and the cadence of her song, that when she was done, and asked me to name the letters in order one by one, as I said I would do, I could not.

"I didn't hear any letters," I said, "just the song of it."

So she said she would sing it again, only this time I must sing it with her.

"I ain't much for singin'."

"Oh, but you must try. If Jacob and Lydia can learn to sing it, forward *and* backward, then I'm sure you can, too."

I knew very well she meant to dare me not to, but I couldn't not try and still own my self-respect, so I nodded and she pitched right into it again, only slower, and I stumbled along beside her, my voice deep beside her high one. Then we sang it again, and yet again, and by then I had the tune and those letters comfortable together in my mind.

She clapped her hands once we had finished that third time. "Good, good. Now you sing the letters."

That I did not want to do, not all by myself, with her only as audience. But I decided that if she was going to make me, that I would sing as well as I was able. I drew a deep breath and really got my voice into it and the couple or three times I forgot a letter, she pitched it in, and so I got at last to Z, and hung on that letter pretty good.

"Goodness, Isaac. I thought you said you didn't like to sing."

"Depends on how I feel." So I went on and sang it again.

Rachel watched me close and smiled when I had done. "Then it's true what I've read. The Negro possesses a *natural* aptitude for music, though untutored and oft concealed."

I had to think about that for a minute. "So what else have you read about the *Negro*?"

She touched her cheek, then looked at her hands a moment. "That he has devised *unusual* ways of expressing the gladness and sorrow of his burdened soul."

"Is that so," I said. "Like what unusual ways?"

"Like, 'slaphand,' as it is called in a book of mine."

I could hardly believe that slaphand would be in a book, and so had to ask what exactly her book said about it.

"That it is an *artform*," she answered, "native to your race, which uses hands and body for percussion and cadence, *sometimes* accompanied by performance."

"You sound like a book yourself," I said, and then explained how the actual doin' of slaphand was altogether different than a book description of it.

She sat up straight. "You *know* this slaphand? You can *do* it?"

"Oh, well, Miss Bringhouse. Not like some I know, back home. Caesar, now, he could *really* go at it."

But it was enough for her that I claimed I could do slaphand at all, and so she begged me to demonstrate. Believe me, Mr. Campbell, I felt awkward about the business, but she was so eager I finally relented. I started out simple, showin' her how to slap one hand against one elbow and the other hand against her other elbow, then her two elbows together, then her two hands, then back to hand elbow, hand elbow. I thought that would put an end to it, but she got excited and asked if she could try, that is if it wasn't only for Negroes.

"Goodness!" I said, "it's for anybody. Go ahead and try."

Which she did, except she wanted to know how *high* to lift her elbow, and just exactly *where* on the elbow she should slap, and how *hard* to slap.

"Rachel," I said, and caught myself, feeling again as though in using her personal name we had crossed over another kind of fence row. "I mean 'Miss Bringhouse.

"Oh, never mind that!" she said, wavin' her hand. "I call you Isaac, don't I?"

"Alright, then, Rachel, you're takin' too much trouble with it all. You mainly just got to enjoy yourself and make it up as you go along. Why don't you try again?"

"I'm afraid I might make a spectacle of myself."

"Well, I made a spectacle of myself singin' the letters song, so you're going to have to make a spectacle of yourself doin' slaphand, I guess."

So she tried again and did get her hands and elbows goin' every which way, and struck her bonnet crooked. I'd have laughed except she was so serious to learn.

"I tell you what, let's do the letters song *with* slaphand. Then you will have somethin' you know to go by. How would that be?"

She liked that idea just fine, so I had us both stand up and move away from the table and onto the woven rug, so we had some room. "Now stand and face me. I mean, please, if you will."

So she did, and after takin' a deep breath she nodded for me to go ahead, and I slapped both hands together on 'A,' one hand to one elbow on 'B,' and other hand to other elbow on 'C.'

But she just stood and watched. "I will," she said, "I will. But let me see you do it first, all the way through."

But I found I didn't much like the idea of slap handin' in front of her, all by myself, as if I was no more than a circus act for her to watch.

"Naw," I said, and went back to my chair at the table. "I lost the interest in it. I came in here for my lesson, not for this foolery."

She came halfway toward me. "This *is* our lesson."

"Well, it isn't the lesson I expected."

"Fine," she said. "Fine. Be that way, then. But don't ask me to teach you another lesson, for I shan't. I shan't!" Then she stamped her foot, folded her arms tight and turned her back on me.

"Look, I'm sorry, Rachel," I said. I'm awful sorry. I lost my head. But I'm all revived now and will do the slaphand alphabet just as you asked. In fact, I *want* to do it."

She turned back around and dropped her hands to her side. "I'm sorry, too. I have a temper, I know I do. Sometimes, it gets the best of me."

"Just sit," I said, "and let me go at it." And so I began, slappin my hands together on 'A,' one hand to the opposite elbow on 'B', tother hand to tother elbow on 'C.' And then I went for speed, from elbow to hip to knee to ankle to shoe sole and back up, and then down again, singin' my way clean through the alphabet, and toppin' off with a turnaround twirl on 'Z.'

She jumped to her feet and clapped her hands. "Oh, I have never seen anything like that. Never. I am ready to try."

"Now, don't hold yourself too stiff," I said. "Loosen up, shake your hands. Good. Now shake your whole self."

And she did, she really did, and she laughed as she did, too.

"You look like you ready, now. Get your hands up, then."

She got her hands up.

"Then here we go," I said, and off I started on 'A', she slappin' right along with me and we singin' our way together through the alphabet, coming downhill after 'P,' then faster after that, and when we came to 'W and X and Y then Z,' I got fancy, sank to my knees, and coming back up, spun around twice. Rachel, she spun around twice, too.

That's when Mrs. Bringhouse came through the door. Rachel had spun around yet again, she liked that part so well, and by accident swept off the table with her hand one of the writin' slates, which crashed to the floor. Mrs. Bringhouse's mouth fell open and her eyes got wide. Rachel, a little dizzy, bumped the table, steadied herself, and blew out a big puff of air. Altogether she wasn't very ladylike, and I wanted to crawl under the rug, but could only wish I was somewhere else.

"What," said Mrs. Bringhouse, "is going on here?"

"Oh," said Rachel, with a big smile, "Isaac was teaching me *slaphand*. A most *refreshing* experience."

Of course, her mother demanded to know what slaphand was, and Rachel, drawing a kerchief from her apron pocket and pattin' her forehead, said with an exaggerated flourish that it was an *"exhilarating* Negro art form." I could have about died.

"I *thought*," said her mother, walking over to the table and picking up the slate from the floor, "that I could entrust thee in this room to give Mr. Granger here his reading lesson, as thy father intended. But I see that I was *mistaken*."

"No, mother," said Miss Bringhouse, "thou art not mistaken. I did give Isaac his reading lesson."

"If you please, Mrs. Bringhouse," I said, taking a step toward her, "she did. She is a very good teacher, too, your daughter is. She taught me the letters song, from start to finish. I never thought I could learn it, but she kept me at it, she sure did. I can sing it for you, would you like that?"

"No, Isaac," she said, "I don't need thee to sing the letters song. I know it very well." Then she looked at us both. "I just *do* not understand how thee two went from memorization of the alphabet to movement which looked perilously close to dancing." She faced Rachel. "Thee! Raised at my knee, a good Quaker, *dancing* in my house."

I had not supposed Mrs. Bringhouse could be so upset, and thought for sure our lessons were done, but Rachel she protested that she was a good Quaker, just as her mother intended, and proved it by teachin' me, who had been deprived of basic literacy, a great tragedy, especially as I had thirsted for knowledge even from a young age, and that bein' so she, Rachel, had employed every technique to my advantage, which included reinforcement of learnin' skills through the use of different methods simultaneously, as Mr. Benezet taught. "Thus, mother," she concluded, extendin' her hand toward me, "Isaac already knows his alphabet, backward and forward."

I hoped I would not be asked to demonstrate.

"Nevertheless, thy father would never approve. Certainly, thy anticipated trip to England is in jeopardy."

"Oh mother, please, no!"

She ignored Rachel and turned back to me. "As for *thee*, young man, this may be the last straw."

I hung my head.

"Mother!"

"I am truly sorry, Mrs. Bringhouse," I said, raising my head back up. "You have been so good to me, and Mr. Bringhouse, too, and now to be taught by Miss Bringhouse, well, it is more than I could ever have expected. I got caught up in the lesson, you see. But it shall never happen again, such antics. *Never*."

Mrs. Bringhouse folded her hands together at her waist and looked at me. "I would not have thee sent back into slavery, Isaac," she said. "Nor do I believe my husband would, in his heart of hearts. But decorum, modesty, decency—these are not paltry virtues. Your presence, in this room, alone, with my daughter—" She stood there, mouth open, unable to finish her sentence. So she turned to her daughter. "And as for thee, Rachel," she said, "I had hoped that you, at least, could be trusted." She shook her head. "It is doubtful these lessons can continue."

INTERLUDE

by Reverend Charles Campbell

In the course of narrating the past several chapters of his story, Isaac referred to me by name on several occasions, as you may have noted, kind Reader. These occasions endeared him to me, for I understood that he was no longer simply speaking to a future generation, or to some segment of the disembodied "reading public," but to me, Charles Campbell, an amateur historian, orphaned at a young age, troublemaker in his youth, failed haberdasher, etc., and then a pastor, now retired, of the Presbyterian church, and recently widowed, alas. Thus, I began to feel it was my obligation to represent him aright, not merely as an object of curiosity whose unusual life would make for little more than pleasant reading at a seaside resort. No, I began to see that it was my business as his amanuensis, so to speak, to present Isaac Granger as I now understood him to be: an observant, sensitive, remarkably thoughtful young man, wise for his years, set out in the broad world after the narrow bondage of his childhood and early youth. Indeed, I felt myself so sympathetic with him that I have been moved on occasion to improve his diction or expand his vocabulary in my transcription of his speech; it was the measure of my growing affection. Thus, while I decided to preserve some traces of his dialect—maintaining his contraction of the present participle, as in "readin'" for "reading," occasionally, I largely corrected other variances, such as his use of the verb "set"—as in "I set down"—for the grammatically correct "sit."

When Isaac related the incident in which Mrs. Bringhouse broke in upon him and Rachel doing slaphand together in the lesson room, he became so wrought up with remembered anxiety that I put aside my notebook and offered to suspend any further record of the episode. But he shook his head, saying, "oh, don't you do that, Mr. Campbell!" and went on to say, rather mysteriously, that the spirit of the Negro was subterranean, running hidden and out of sight like an underground river. "But isn't that true for all men?" I asked. He smiled at that and said if it were so then I should understand his fears. When I asked, quite honestly, what fears he was referring to, he looked at me as if I were a simpleton. "Why, fear of being lynched!" he said. I was simply astonished at this answer, as you can imagine, and begged him to explain. "I was alone in a room with a white girl," he said with a shrug. I protested that while this circumstance might indeed be dangerous for him elsewhere, surely not in *that* room, of *that* house, for as he himself had described, Mrs. Bringhouse was a kindly woman; her husband—even with his faults—was a man of principle and a Quaker; and Mr. Jefferson, though a slaveowner, was a gentleman, and a man of wisdom and charity. In short, it was preposterous that Isaac could ever have been *lynched*—God help me—in Philadelphia, of all cities! Isaac had toyed with a scrap of tin as I argued my objections, and then said, "if not lynched, then jailed."

Though imprisonment seemed nearly as unlikely, I had so expended myself upon objections to his fears of execution that I could do no more than shake my head. Thus, we sat silent for a long while after that, for I could think of no adequate words to cheer him. He coughed, and then expelled from his mouth a wad of phlegm into a small dish, and I feared that the state of his health was worse than he had admitted, and that I might soon be attending his final hour if he continued in such a frightful state for long.

I have never been a humorist but found it in me to say at last, "well, evidently you were not hanged. If you had, then we both must be in Hades." At this, he burst into laughter, saying that my remark was truer to the mark than I realized, which caused me to think that I had never fully appreciated his courage in living through those times in Philadelphia with the Bringhouses—nor, for that matter, his courage living through our present times, in Petersburg, when the cry of abolitionists has become so strident, and Southern states have become so intransigent. The peaceable Free Black is caught in the grindstone between the two; yet Isaac, it seemed to me, showed remarkable composure under these trying circumstances.

Rachel had persuaded first her mother, and then her father, that Isaac's "antics" in the lesson room were no crime and no danger to her but were instead the demonstration of a spontaneous exuberance, the inner light of God in him made manifest, and ought to be celebrated in a Quaker household, and not punished. She so succeeded in her argument that she was permitted to continue her lessons with Isaac every Monday. Isaac still could not thank her enough, even these many years later. "I cannot say my fears entirely vanished," he said, "but so long as she was on my side, I felt mainly safe." He shook his head then. "She cared about me. *Me!*"

The only hitch, he said, letting out a hoot, was that Mrs. Bringhouse was required to be present. She sat in one of the corner cushion chairs, with a basket of knitting in her lap, and though she said "don't mind me," frequently did mind the lesson, jumping from her chair and crying out "bread!" when she heard the letter 'B,' spoken, or "goose!" when she heard the 'G,' and running from the room, in the one case to check her rising dough, in the other the baking fowl, and then returning from one or the other of these kitchen chores—and others suggested by alphabet letters—to insist that the lesson be started over. Finally out of exasperation, Isaac sang out the alphabet letters "lickety-split from 'A' to 'Z'" the moment Mrs. Bringhouse collapsed into her chair again, and Rachel promptly launched into a regular sermon on syllables and vowels, long and short, and consonants with their complexities, and the proper use of "a" and "an" and the difference between "farther" and "further," and so on. This sermon and her exertions to the kitchen so exhausted poor Mrs. Bringhouse that she fell asleep in her chair, the ball of yarn rolled out of her lap, and her head fell forward on her big chest. All of this was for Isaac a comical scene, which he related with such skill that he set me to laughing. My plodding prose cannot do him justice; yet I wish you to understand, patient Reader, how rapidly Isaac could shift from a somber state of mind to a delighted one; from a tragic view of human life to a comic one. This ready shift I considered to be proof of his resilience, which I found most appealing in him, and, if I may so confess, so needful in myself.

With her mother asleep, Rachel was able to teach Isaac without interruption how properly to write, with chalk upon the slate, in round-hand script, the letters he had learned by song. This was, he said, "a most powerful experience." But it was attended with difficulties, for he found it awkward to hold and operate the writing chalk properly, as he was left-handed. Though Rachel urged him to switch, he had been adamant, saying, "the left is my lead hand and will be so till death." I admired his courage in resisting her well-meaning though unfortunate instruction, because I, too, was born left-handed, but unlike Isaac conceded to the insistence of my tutor and changed to my right. The better to instruct him, Rachel had come around to his side of the table and gently lain her small white hand upon his large black one, "like an angel come down to earth," as he put it, to adjust his fingers, and guide his strokes upon the slate: one down, then another down, beginning at the top of the first and equal in length, but angled away; the two strokes joined by a third, crosswise, to make the letter A.

I could all but see Rachel's shapely figure, bent over Isaac's broad back, her slender arm in its trim, soft sleeve hovering just over his muscular arm in its rough cotton. To touch is the most intimate of sensations, and to touch hands, even if for the studied purpose of forming letters, surely must have aroused in them profound feelings. Furthermore, they were young, he "near to sixteen" by then and she, "a healthy seventeen." While each of them were bound by the unique conditions of their particular lives, they were not yet invested in these conditions, as their elders would have been. And they were imbued with that optimism which is so delightful in youth and so confounding to adulthood.

Working through the alphabet, letter by letter and stroke by stroke, they at last came to the letter 'I,' and Isaac, recognizing this as the first letter of his name, asked that Rachel show him how to write out his name in full. So she did, and when he had completed this task, he sat back and looked at the word "almost in awe," there before him in chalk upon the slate. "It is a Biblical name," she had said. "For Isaac was the name of an Old Testament patriarch." He had asked what a "patriarch" was, and she had answered: "A father of the human race." He raised his eyebrows at this and asked, looking at her askance, "you're not going to tell me that Rachel means *mother* of the human race, are you?"

He had meant this light-heartedly, I am sure, yet she had answered, with some heat, that the "Rachel of old had never been given that honor! She only bore many children and died in childbirth." She turned away from him, then, looked first at her mother, mumbling softly in her sleep, and then out the window. "I wonder," she had said, "do you ever imagine how your life could be different than it is now?"

It was an unexpected question, Isaac told me, for he had assumed, mistakenly as it now appeared, that with all her advantages—living in a fine brick home as the daughter of a prosperous tinsmith, being well clothed and well fed, able to read and write, employed from time to time as a governess for a prominent family—being in short, privileged and white, and whiter than most, that there could be no life for her which was better than the one she presently lived.

Then suddenly, scribing an "S" upon his slate, she had asked him what it was like to be a *slave*, and did Isaac ever imagine himself not being one? He hadn't liked the question, he admitted to me, because he realized that he had never seriously pictured himself *not* a slave. It had been too far beyond his comprehension, that state of untrammeled liberty. Oh, yes, he had pictured himself with land and his own house somewhere in Freedom Land, while bumping along in his coffin box. But that was all idle dreaming to pass the time! In actual fact, he had learned to make do in his circumstances, which were not altogether so bad on his Master Jefferson's plantation. Now he felt ashamed of this "making do," for Rachel apparently had more dreams that he had, with less reason. "Every man has got a Master to serve, you know," he said. To this she had responded that her husband would be her master.

"Husband?" Isaac had said, with more shock than he would have liked to let on, I suspect. "You have no husband!"

"I will have," she had said, then wrote his name upon her slate: "Henry Chapman." A true teacher, she used this uncomfortable information for Isaac's instruction, as she sounded out the name, letter by letter. "I have been betrothed to him since I was thirteen," she had said.

Then Isaac got up from his stool, went to a corner cabinet with one door missing, and lifted down from the top shelf an object wrapped in cloth. This he brought to me, and unfolding it with care, as if it were a museum artifact, laid it in my two hands. It was a writing slate, about ten inches high and eight inches wide, with a narrow frame of wood, cracked in places. Chalk dust still adhered to the surface of the slate. "This is the very one," he said, "which Rachel taught me from." I took my forefinger and traced the letter S in that fine white dust, and then smelt of this chalky dust, and tasted it, too. Rachel Bringhouse had once handled this slate, I thought to myself, and felt as if her presence were suddenly in the room with us. Then, as he opened his hand to take back the slate again, I saw upon his palm, between thumb and forefinger, a pink scar, a good inch long, with three pink dots on one side, three on the other.

"Is that the scar from your wounding?" I asked, looking up at him.

He nodded. "It still hurts, now and again."

"May I touch it?" I said, in a trembling voice.

He did not answer, but left his hand open, and so I reached forward and ran my finger up and down along the scar and touched each of the stitching hole dots. The skin of his hand was rough and calloused, but warm, and the scar smooth. I had a sudden desire to travel with my finger along his thumb, and then up each finger, especially the smallest one, missing the digit. But he withdrew his hand, and I gave back the slate, which he carefully wrapped and put away again in its treasured place.

The experience of seeing the writing slate and touching Isaac's wound so moved me that I found it difficult to pick up my pen and go on with the transcription, and Isaac apparently found it equally difficult to go on with his story. Thus, we sat awkwardly in silence a moment or two, before going outside for a glass of water from the pump. It was a makeshift affair, the spigot partly broken off, the handle wobbly, and evidently repaired numberless times. I felt distinctly out of place, sipping water in my good suit, among all the Negroes going about their business, this way and that, talkative and gregarious, as is their nature. I considered how like Isaac's situation my own was at that moment, though in reverse, and how uncomfortable he must often have felt, and apt to be reticent in behavior and speech as a consequence. It seemed the least I could do, in consideration of this, to doff my hat to a pair of brightly clad women going by, and offer a "good day" to a man with a shoeshine box in hand, though I declined his services.

Having refreshed ourselves in this way and again taken our seats in his shop, I picked up my pen and just as I bent to the page of my notebook, I wondered what remarkable fate, or accident, or providence, if there be any, had brought Rachel Bringhouse, so principled, so educated, and so inquisitive, into the life of our young protagonist Isaac Granger Jefferson, who had now begun to awaken to himself. Mr. Jefferson was but the agent of their meeting, I thought; his need for revenue merely the cause; and the tinsmith shop of James Bringhouse only the setting. Through them all, some greater mystery was at work. Oh, dear me, I loved them both, contemplating thus! And feared for them, as much.

PART IV

CHAPTER TWENTY-NINE

*Primer to ledger to a poem
called "Slavery"*

At the next lesson I had, with Mrs. Bringhouse again in the room, this time darnin' socks, Rachel had me scribe out the alphabet on the slate once more. When we had done with that, she then drew out of her apron pocket a little book, *The New England Primer.* This book, she told me, had been used to teach children the rudiments of readin' and writin' for more than a century, not myself among them, I might have added, nor any children of bondspeople. Then she laid the book gentle on the table, opened the cover, slowly paged through lists of letters, then words, short and then longer, until finally she came to a page with the letter A beside it, and the rhyme she had already taught me from before: *In Adam's Fall We Sinned All.* She asked what I saw, so I studied the picture and then said, "I see a tree, with a snake wound 'round it and in the branches. Here on the left side of the tree is a woman standin' naked and on the right side, a man, also naked." Both were giants, according to the picture, for they were as tall as the tree. The woman held what might have been an apple in her hand.

"Heels and toes, heels and toes," burst out Mrs. Bringhouse from behind us. "If heels and toes were a penny a patch, I'd have a pie by now!"

"Mother, please," said Rachel. "I'm teaching."

"Daughter," she said, "that drawing is for *moral* instruction, as well as instruction in the alphabet. Please make that clear. We have no idea if he had any such instruction under Mr. Jefferson, and most likely none at all among his ancestors in Africa."

Rachel spoke up stoutly on my behalf, however, and maintained that I had been provided with such instruction, especially from said ancestors. I supposed this was true, though I really hadn't any idea for all I knew of Africa were two smooth stones Mama kept, which she said came from her people in the motherland and prevented what she called "haints." But I got my share of moral instruction, believe me, from both her and Papa.

"The woman," I said, "she must be going to feed that snake. I didn't think snakes ate fruits, but this one has a human face, so maybe so."

Rachel laughed outright at that. "Oh, no, you have it all wrong. The snake is Satan, and he is tempting her to eat that apple, which if she does, she will surely die, her and everybody else down through history to the present day."

"That's a heavy penalty," I said. "Why?"

In answer, she set about to explain in detail all about the Garden of Eden, and the Tree of the Knowledge of Good and Evil, and how Adam and Eve were not to eat of it—though they could eat of every other fruit or vine—for they would die if they did, they and all of their descendants. But they did eat of it anyway, Eve first, being no match for Satan, who said they would be as God and live forever if they ate, and she believed and took a bite and then gave both lie and apple to Adam who also ate. Upon eating the apple, they knew they were naked and were cast out of the Garden forever, and thus began as punishment mankind's travail ever since.

It was a lengthy explanation which I found puzzling in several respects, but at least by the end of it Mrs. Bringhouse had fallen asleep, as she had done in the first lesson.

"She hardly gets any rest," said Rachel, looking over at her.

"Same with Mama," I said, which caused me to think about her and Papa and my brothers and the routines of life day-to-day down there on Master Jefferson's plantation. But I didn't want to think of all that, for to do so made me feel how far distant I was and how alone, so I looked at the picture again. "Well," I said, "neither Adam or Eve are black. That's one good thing. We don't get the blame for the whole business of sin, white people do."

Rachel looked at the picture again herself and said she had never noticed that before. "*Eve* gets all the blame," she said, leanin' toward me. "But honestly, I think Satan didn't come to her because she was weak-minded, but because she was more thoughtful than Adam. She considered the apple first, before eating of it, the being as God and living forever if she did, and so, naturally considerate of her husband, she was moved to share the apple with him, so that he might enjoy such benefits, as well."

Then she leaned back in her chair and looked at the hearth fire. I thought how different the tale would have been if she had been in the tale not Eve, which caused me to picture her naked beside the tree, as in the Primer illustration, and so I stopped that picture. "Could we get on with the rest of the rhymes and pictures in this book?" I asked.

So we did, all the way through the letters to Z and its

rhyme and picture, "*Zaccheus* did climb a tree, his Lord to see." The Lord must have been a long way off, judgin' from Zaccheus' high perch in that tree.

Then at long last she told me to open my ledger book, and gave me a wood pencil to write with, instead of the chalk, so I could get down to the business for which these lessons were intended. But she had first to open the "model ledger" and show me how it was laid out, with each page divided by blue lines into columns, the columns identified from left to right as "Customer," "Work to be Performed," "Date," "Payment Rec'd," and "Etcetera."

Mrs. Bringhouse mumbled in her sleep, and Rachel turned and watched her with attention until her mumblin' ceased, and then turned back to me. "Now," she said, "you see under the heading Customer are six names." She counted these down. "And for each name," she said, pointin' with her own pencil, "in the appropriate column, a description of work to be performed, date of bill, payment received, and some note or other, if needed, under 'Etcetera.'" She lifted her finger from the page. "I would like you to copy this information into your ledger, in a clear hand—all the letters regular and between the lines—just as you see." Then she handed me the model ledger, which I set next to mine, took up the pencil and, going to the heading Customer, attempted to sound out the first name, but couldn't very well. Rachel came around to my side of the table and pointed with her finger at the name. What I noticed was her finger, not the name. It tapered so neatly from the knuckle of the hand to the nail. My fingers did not taper but came square to the ends. "Surname is given first," she said. "'Tanner,' separated by a comma, then Christian name, 'Benjamin'." Then we sounded out the name together—*Tanner, Benjamin*—her fine tapered finger movin' from syllable to syllable. She would have gone on helping but I resisted, eager to prove myself, so she went back to her chair, took a different book than the Primer from her second apron pocket, and began readin'.

So by myself I wrote out *Tanner, Benjamin*, with the greatest care, picturin' myself as I did so with spectacles on, goin' over my own account book in just this way, by candlelight, many years hence, after a long day of profitable business. What a fine picture that was!

Then I wrote, under Date—*2 Aug,* and under Work to be Performed, 1 *set cups & plate (12).* And under Payment Rec'd—*.50 cent, owe .50.* This Benjamin Tanner had not paid his bill complete for the set of cups and plate. What if he had been my customer, I wondered, and he decided not to pay a black tinsmith like me? What could I do to get the money? *Nothin',* I suspected, which caused me to put the pencil down. So much for the fine picture of myself. Well, then, let it be a business for Negro customers only. But how many of them would be poor and could not pay? Or would ask a favor, that I accept what money they could spare, even if it was only half? And suppose this were to go on, week after week, and bills pilin' up?

"Isaac," said Rachel, looking up from her book, "are you having trouble? Do you need help?"

I shook my head and went on writin' with the pencil again, this time for the customer, *Haddon, Eliz. Mrs.* She *had* paid the seventy-five cents for work done—salt and pepper boxes. I got down through two more customers and had to stop, for my hand had begun to cramp. I rubbed the thumb pad, and up each finger from the big knuckle. Then went on through

Aldham, Harold; *Hicks, Edward*; and *Savery, William*. Only
two more customers to go, I said to myself, and went right to
work on those two—*Ashbridge, Anna, Miss*, and *Clackerhorn,
Matthew*. When I had done, I sat back and stretched. How, I
wondered, did Master Jefferson sit for those hours every day
at his writin' desk? I stood up and bent side to side. Rachel
was so absorbed in her book she did not notice. I walked in
place. Still she did not notice. Then I flapped my arms like a
bird.

That did it. She fairly jumped from her seat. "Oh!"

Her exclamation woke Mrs. Bringhouse, too. She suddenly
sat up on her cushion chair, looked around as if she were just
back from a long journey, and said, "Well, now, everything
seems to be in order, here. I shall return to my chores, then."
And so saying, she straightened her bonnet, gathered up her
basket of socks, and strode from the room.

Rachel watched her go, frowned, then looked at me. I said
I was sorry, that I hadn't meant to disturb her mother like
that. Rachel collected herself and raised up the book so I could
see. "This," she said, tappin' the cover, "is by the renowned
poet and abolitionist Ms. Hannah More, of Bristol, England,
the title being, *Slavery*." Then she got smartly to her feet,
smoothed her dress, and holding the book out, began to read
aloud:

> *"If Heaven has into being deigned to call*
> *Thy light, O Liberty! To shine on all;*
> *Bright intellectual Sun! why does thy ray*
> *To earth distribute only partial day?"*

I had never heard such language, with its rhythm of
syllables and music of rhymes. Why, Rachel herself was the

poem, I tell you! The way she stood, her body all awake, and she rising up almost on tiptoe, her voice larger than I had ever heard it. I was very taken with her performance, could not take my eyes off her! Then she stopped, let the book down, and turned to me, her eyes wet with tears—which was not at all what I had expected. "Whatever is wrong?" I asked.

"I am so sorry, Isaac," she said, wipin' at her tears with a cloth drawn from her apron pocket. "So *very* sorry."

"Oh, now, Miss Rachel!" I said with honest concern, "now *I* am sorry to see *you* so sorry, what is it in this poem that could make you feel so bad? You must explain to me!"

I felt so shamefully ignorant in speaking so, but she only smiled, sat down, and then spoke of how the poet used the Sun as *symbol* of another kind of light, namely *Liberty*, and then had questioned why this Sun does not shine its light of liberty over all the earth equally, but leaves some parts and the peoples who live there in darkness, or "partial day."

I asked what parts of earth, and what peoples this Sun the symbol of liberty had left in darkness, and she answered from the poem, saying, "sad Afric quenched in total night." But that only made me annoyed, and I got to my feet. "By which you mean *Africa*, I suppose. Why, it is as light there as it is here! Else how could the people hunt game, collect firewood, build houses, hoe in their gardens, do all else that is needful for life?" Then Rachel got upset, and said I had already forgotten what she had just taught me, that this night was not the *actual* time between dawn and dusk, but a metaphorical night of *injustice*, and to prove the point she stood up as I sat down, paged forward in the book, and read aloud again, only this time in slower and even mournful tones:

Wheve'er to Afric's shores I turn my eyes,
Horrors of deepest, deadliest guilt arise;
I see, by more than Fancy's mirror shown,
The burning village, and the blazing town:
See the dire victim torn from social life,
See the sacred infant, hear the shrieking wife!
She, wretch forlorn! Is dragged by hostile hands,
To distant tyrants sold, in distant lands . . .

She closed the book, sat back down again and looked at me, and I could see the tears about to come into her eyes once more, and so looked away. I did not understand all that the poet said, but got the gist, and said that was a sad time, truly it was, and unjust in every way, but it had not always been dark there. For there were old ones in the Quarter down home on Master Plantation that sometimes spoke of their time in Africa as children, and it seemed to me that they must have enjoyed as much Liberty as anyone! I was sorry for them having been snatched by slavers and brought over to this land, with all their suffering on the way. But why, I asked, "why must you read of this to me? I carry no spear and pound no drum! I know no more of burnin' villages that you do!" My place is here, I said, here in this country, and then rapped my knuckles sharp on the table and said again: "Here!" At once I felt the strangeness of my words, for this was not my place, either—not at all, this room in a Quaker house in the city of Philadelphia! How could I ever think so? "Oh, that poem of yours is difficult," I burst out. "Right enough I feel partial!" For I was a bound slave, yet sat here talkin' poetry with this white girl, who was no longer "this white girl" but Miss Rachel; no, Rachel. My lessons with her made me feel nearly free or only half bound. Neither quite the one nor quite the other; a more complicated predicament than Uncle Bob's comparative and absolute. "Here I catch the sun one way, or catch it another, but never entire, no. Instead it is always that *partial sun* I find myself in." I shrugged my shoulders and turned up my hands. "What am I to do?"

Rachel sat back in her chair, lookin' pleased with herself. "Poetry is meant to move us," she said, "and I see it has moved *thee*!"

What she said only made me feel restless, and irritable with myself, for I had not been trained up to be moved in such a way as this, but rather was taught to take instructions well, to cause no trouble for anybody, and make the best of my circumstances. And so I done, or tried to. But that was only partial, and partial wouldn't do!

Then Mrs. Bringhouse came in, and so I closed up my ledger book and went back out to the shop. Such was my introduction to the poem *Slavery* by the Miss Hannah More.

CHAPTER THIRTY

*A challenge from Mr. Bringhouse,
contest with Daniel Shady, forty-eight
cups with graceful handle*

Daniel Shady hated that I should be excused, by permission of Mr. Bringhouse no less, every Monday afternoon to be taught by his daughter skills which he insisted ought to have been forbidden to me. It proved to him his complaint that I was given preferential treatment never afforded him, when I ought not to have been educated in anything other than menial work. His gall was so bitter and his intention to "restore right order" so determined that he lost no opportunity to pester, to meddle, to rebuke, and otherwise undermine my efforts to excel at the tinwork and mock my ledger lessons. He would resort to so small a thing as puttin' a tack, point up, on my stool seat and mock me when, going to sit down, I instead jumped up from the prick of it. Then I would not sit before seein' if the tack was there, which sometimes it was and sometimes wasn't, until I forgot, and sat, and again jumped up from the prick, and he took fresh pleasure in his game. I had little doubt he would have burnt me to ash, if there was some way he could do it and not be found out. Yet he continued at the same time intensely interested—obsessively so—in even the least of my tinwork at the bench, as though he believed I possessed some fearful secret which he could not for the life of him divine. I knew that the quality of my work, which I continually undertook to improve upon, exposed to view his own poor craft, and sharpened the knife of his anger. So I kept a careful eye on him, even when absorbed in the task at hand, lest he once again seek to wound me, or otherwise impair my progress in the trade I had undertaken to learn. Yet I knew the day would come when his pent-up hatred would split open the seam of his soul and burst out to scald me.

That day came on a Saturday, or Sixth Day, mornin', when Mr. Bringhouse rushed into the shop and cried out, "Cups!" He cried it out again, and shook aloft in his hand a drinkin' cup, shiny as silver. I watched him in surprise, as did the other apprentices, for this was not at all the usual Mr. Bringhouse— sober, punctual, and anxious. Telling us to "gather around," he then turned the cup over and over in his thick fingers, so we all could see. "A pint in capacity," he said, "plain and functional, neatly done, *and* with a graceful handle." He ran his finger smoothly along this handle, which looped up from the rim generously outward and then curved nicely back inward where it was soldered just above the base. "Not the usual ring handle," he noted, then handed the cup to Little Will, asking him to take a good look and pass it on, but Shady reached in and took it from Charles, and then gave it straight back to Mr. Bringhouse, for he would not take it from my hand, nor pass it to me, either.

Mr. Bringhouse held the cup aloft again, walkin' back and forth in front of us as if he were his own parade. "Now," he said, "we have before us a *rare* opportunity. A New York buyer, boarding in our city, found me out, yesterday after Meeting, and expressed his earnest desire for many more cups, exactly like this one, with its graceful handle." He stopped and turned to us, his face alight and his shirt untucked. "*But* this buyer must have these cups by five o'clock this evening, when he will arrive to collect them. *So*," he said, rappin' the cup with his knuckle, "I have decided, that the man among thee who makes the greatest number of acceptable cups by that signal hour—shall be granted a full day off and a dollar in his pocket."

This dangled reward was enthusiastically received by the other apprentices, Shady especially. As for myself, I had no idea what I would do with either a day to myself, or the dollar. The challenge itself was enough incentive, a rare opportunity to further demonstrate my worth to Mr. Bringhouse, and secure, if that was possible, the abiding approval of Old Master.

"A man could *cheat*," said Shady, "and make a fast cup, *poor* in quality." He bobbed his head toward me. "*That* one *will* cheat."

"No cheating," said Mr. Bringhouse. "I shall be around to inspect, be sure of that." He handed out sets of templates to each of us—cylinder, bottom, and handle—then drew out his timepiece and looked at it. "It is just now seven o' clock," he said, "which means each of thee has ten hours. So clear thy benches and begin."

Now, it was a principle with Mr. Bringhouse that a good and proper tinsmith should make one tin work at a time, from start to finish, and only then go on to the next. This, he said, would ensure the "integrity of craftsmanship" and best satisfy both customer and tinsmith. I knew the method, though not his phrase for it, having been trained in it by my brother, Little George, in his smithy. All the craftspeople along Mulberry Row worked in this fashion, so far as I knew.

But I had begun to think there was another way, faster and more efficient, which was to proceed first by the makin' of parts, in total, and only then to begin assembly of these parts. I saw no reason that I could not also preserve integrity of craftsmanship.

Shady first, then Little Will, and after him Charles, jostled and argued to get new tin sheet from the rack, but I stayed at my bench, took what sections of sheet I already had, and scribed out, with the templates, enough parts for four cups—four cylinders, four bottoms, and four handles—and laid these, each in a separate stack, to one side.

By then, the three other apprentices were back at their benches, and I was able to take a new tin sheet from the rack with no interference and little time lost, record this on a nearby paper as required, and begin work. I scribed out parts on this new sheet, fittin' the templates so as to get the most parts, with least waste. Master Jefferson would have been pleased, I thought, as I counted the shapes scribed out and found I had enough for twelve cups.

Shady, cranin' his neck, said I was doing it all wrong.

"Too late, now," I said, and shrugged.

But he persisted, shouting out the same complaint to Charles, and then Will by name. Neither answered, though, for they were already hard at work. Then I took up the shears—with half an eye on Shady—and cut out all the parts, careful as could be, and laid each part, when cut, upon its proper pile.

"Cup one!" called out Charles, holdin' it up.

I went back to the rack, got a second sheet, and repeated the whole process, only faster this time, with even less waste, then took up the shears and once again began cuttin' out the parts—cylinders, bottoms, handles.

"One cup, and two!" said Little Will, holding these up, one in each hand.

Shady complained that he would have had three by then, only I was such a bother and distraction that he could not concentrate. He banged his hammer on his bench, I think to distract my concentration, but I went right on cuttin' and stackin' neat piles of parts.

There was no more talk for a good while, just the sound of shears and hammer, and the smell of solder.

"Three cups done!" called out Charles followed by Little Will's call: "Four here!"

Charles disputed the count, so William held 'em up. I saw they were nicely done, too, and then counted up my stacked cup parts and found I had enough for the makin' of twenty-eight cups. I considered for a moment whether I could assemble that many parts into finished cups by five o'clock, and decided so, if all went smoothly, and more, maybe. So I took a chance on myself and went back to the rack, got one more sheet, and began again—scribin', cuttin', and stackin'. Add on the additional twelve and I would have forty cups. *Forty*. If I could just get them all made in time.

"Five!" cried out Charles, followed at once by Little Will's answer: "Six—and seven!"

Shady cursed over his one cup, only partly finished and that inferior, I could see. He stared over at me, claimed I was cheatin', and altogether quit on his cup to watch me begin assembly at last. I took up the top-stacked cylinder part, rolled over the top edge, flanged out the bottom one, bent the side seam, and fitted into this the matchin' side edge, and hammered this snug on the bick iron. This I had done ten times, and stood up the ten finished cylinders, when Mr.

Bringhouse came in through the shop door and came walking down the line.

"Six, Mr. Bringhouse," said Charles. "You see, six!"

"Eight!" said Little Will, "and the ninth nearly done."

Mr. Bringhouse rubbed his hands together with delight, I saw, and inspected each of their cups in detail. Then he came to my bench. He didn't rub his hands together this time but held them behind his back. "What are we doing here, Isaac?" he said. "Cups with no bottoms?

"Nor handles!" cried Shady.

"Now, Daniel," said Mr. Bringhouse, "let the boy answer."

I explained my method.

"Have I not preached integrity of craftsmanship?" he said. "This is mere replication of parts."

"Beggin' your pardon, Mr. Bringhouse," I said, "but I think not. And if you will let me continue with my method, I believe I can demonstrate both integrity of craftsmanship and more cups at the same time."

He ran his fingers through the hair above his ears, checked his timepiece, and then said, "go ahead then, demonstrate."

Shady bitterly objected and wanted to know how it was the "nigger" could be allowed such freedom and he not, and then reversed himself, and said go on Bringhouse give him such freedom and so hang himself by his infernal "method" and show what downfall awaited, which he, Shady, had warned of all along.

Even for the patient Mr. Bringhouse, Shady's harangue was a chore to listen through, and he announced, pointing to his time piece as proof, that it was "now nine o'clock—two hours gone," then went to his own bench by the office, took out templates and tools, and himself began to make cups.

Meanwhile, I continued with the makin' of the cylinders, ten more to make twenty, and ten more after that to make thirty. I had got so good by now that I fairly flew through their assembly and saw with satisfaction how fine the side seam of even the thirtieth was, equal to the side seam on the first cylinder.

Charles called out ten, almost eleven, and Will twelve. Shady, I saw with mingled satisfaction and dismay, was attemptin' to copy my method, scribin' out on his tin sheet, with templates, cylinder shapes, bottoms, and handles, all neatly arranged. He who had always struck me as careless and inattentive, and only able to taunt, now took up the shears and cut out cylinder shapes one after another with proper care.

Then Mrs. Bringhouse's dinner bell rang, and Little Will and Charles set down their tools and went out the shop door. I stayed put though, and crimped the edge seam on the thirty-eighth cylinder. Shady had not stirred either but kept at his cuttin'. Mr. Bringhouse insisted we must go in to mid-day meal, "to be fair," which I could agree upon, except that now that I had my method workin', I just wanted to continue on.

"You cheat," said Shady, puttin' down his tools. "But I'm going to take your method and beat you anyway. *Think* about that when you sit down to eat."

So I did, though he did not, saying he felt ill, and would rather take fresh air in the yard, but when I had rinsed my plate and fork, before anybody else, and came out the kitchen door, I saw he was not in the yard, but at his bench, hard at work. He grinned at me when I came through the door. "I like this method," he said, "and have about caught up."

He had about caught up by takin' twenty of my cylinder

shapes and settin' them side-by-side on his bench and was well along at puttin' the bottoms on these. "You can't expect to keep all these to yourself," he said. "Because you're not a *real* apprentice, and never will be. No *slave* can be an apprentice." He took another of my cylinder shapes in hand and looked it over. "This one," he said, "is shoddy and will never do." Then he dropped it on the floor and stamped it flat with his boot heel. He leaned over, picked it up, and held it out to me. "Here," he said, "fix it back."

I took the cup without a word and set it down very carefully up on on my bench, for a dangerous anger had sprung up in me. "Keep 'em," I said, in an even voice, "keep those cylinders I made. They were only for *practice* anyway." That took him back, I could see, so I went on to the tin rack, got yet another sheet and began scribin', cuttin' and stackin', all over again. By mid-afternoon, I had again completed the twenty cylinders Shady had taken, and was crimpin' on bottoms, as tight and fast as I could go. But Shady, too, was goin' fast, and by using my cups had got ahead of me.

Mr. Bringhouse, who had been at his bench since right after mid-day dinner, was as concentrated on his work as any of us. He now turned, drew out his timepiece, and clapped his hands. "Four o' clock, fellows," he said. "Four o' clock. One hour to go. Bear down on it, now." Then he went back to work.

"Seventeen, eighteen," said Little Will.

"Sixteen and Seventeen!" said Charles, holdin' 'em up, and then at once takin' up his shears again.

I counted my finished cups, in pairs—two, four, six, eight, on up to thirty-eight. Only two more and I would have forty. That left the handles to bend, and fit, and solder. I might just be able to do it. But where were the two last cylinders?

I searched again among the cups with bottoms, but the two cylinders were not to be found.

Shady stood up and watched me. Then he held up two finished cups, handles and all, one in each hand.

He had stolen from me again.

"I *told* you I would beat you," he said, then sat down on his stool, yawned, then picked at his teeth with a fingernail. "Oh, I shall enjoy that day off, with a dollar in my pocket."

I turned away in disgust, meditated briefly upon my desire to kill him and the recklessness of such an endeavor, and then stood up tall and went to the tin rack for one last sheet, and set to work on it at my bench.

Shady demanded to know what I thought I was doin', there was not time to make more cups, let alone finish the ones I had not yet put handles on, further labor was useless, he, Shady had as good as won that day off and that dollar.

"I don't need no *day* off, and don't *want* no *damn* dollar either," I said, with temper enough that even I was surprised.

Shady got to his feet then, and *he* went to the rack, and *also* pulled *himself* out a short sheet, laid it up on his bench, and began scribin'. And so we went at it, that last hour, and though Charles and Little Will called out their cups, the two of us, side by side, paid no mind, but only cut, crimped, and soldered, Shady at his bench, I at mine. And when Mr. Bringhouse pulled out his timepiece and called the hour, we neither of us stopped, or even paused, but went on with the cylinders, bottoms, and handles, as though it were Judgment Day and lightning would strike if we quit. Charles and Little Will came up to watch, and Mr. Bringhouse with them, then Mrs. Bringhouse came out of the house to call us in to supper but stood instead quiet beside her husband. Then Rachel came near and held aloft my two-window lantern with prism mirrors. Soon afterwards, Daniel Shady, heaving a sigh, set down heavily upon his stool, with two more cups from the short sheet held up to show.

But I, I went on: three, four, five, six, seven, and eight. Eight cups to add to the forty, not counting the ten Shady had stolen. Forty-eight cups, all quality cups to boast of, each with its graceful handle, generous in its curve, outflowing, good in the hand, and neatly curving back into the solder joint. Then at last I put my hammer down, and arranged those cups in rows, and Miss Bringhouse moved the light over them, and they shone silver, and so I went into the house and up to bed. And none dare speak to me, not even Daniel Shady.

CHAPTER THIRTY-ONE

Sunny Mr. Bringhouse, Rachel intercedes, Shady begs

I felt myself shook awake the next mornin' and opened my eyes to Charles pullin' on my arm. It took me a moment to register his words: this was Meetin' day, had I forgotten?

I sat bolt upright with a question. "Did the New York buyers show?"

"No," he said. "Mr. Bringhouse read out their note at table. They were delayed and shan't be here until tomorrow as they have their own church to attend this day."

I felt my spirits sag at this news, the more as I was so late out of bed. "Why did everybody leave me to sleep?" I asked, peevish, and got up to dress.

Charles faced away, to give me privacy. "Mr. Bringhouse said leave you be. 'Our young lion needs his rest,' he said. 'Let him have two days off,' he said. Why, at table you were all he could talk about."

I laced up my shoes and made the bed.

"Shady hated that, of course," said Charles, waving his arms. "I am happy to see him humiliated, though. He *deserves* the humble pie, the way he treats you. It's horrible, just horrible."

I suppose Charles meant well in reportin' Mr. Bringhouse's warm words but I was afraid more trouble could be in store for me, and I went hesitant down to breakfast. Neither Little Will nor Shady were at table, which was a relief. Mr. Bringhouse was all smiles. "Don't thee bother about the usual chores before Meeting," he said, usherin' me to my seat. "Charles can take care of those." Charles left the room, noddin' at me as he went. Mr. Bringhouse called upon Rachel to "bring on" the porridge. She smiled briefly at me and I watched her slender hand upon the ladle stem and saw the slight bone at her wrist. Then she sat down across from me, Jacob and Lydia on either side of her as usual, both eatin' their porridge without a murmur of complaint but walkin' their fingers like animals along the table between mouthfuls.

Mr. Bringhouse himself passed me the milk. "Marvelous work, yesterday," he said, pushing the sugar bowl to me. "Marvelous. Thy method was something to behold. Yes, I am a committed disciple already." He beamed at me. "A day off and a dollar in thy pocket is too small a reward I fear."

"I'm sorry, but I don't want those things," I said. "They would be trouble for me, I'm afraid."

Mr. Bringhouse looked at me in astonishment, for he was a frugal man. "Is there anything I can give thee?" "Anything at all?"

"Yes, sir," I said, "there is. Since the New York buyers will not be here until tomorrow, may I borrow one of the cups I made to show Master Jefferson this afternoon?" I said. "He asked to see a sample of my work."

"Oh, goodness, yes," he said, relieved, I think. "By all means." He declared again what a powerful impression my work had made on him, and how eagerly he anticipated the morrow, when those buyers should likewise behold my work. Then he hesitated, toying with his teacup. He was only worried, he said, that they would find it hard to believe a Negro could do such quality work and be so quick. He ran his fingers along the table edge. "I hope they are not *put off* when they find out."

Rachel spoke up then, sayin' that should make no difference, that my handiwork was clearly superior, and that her father ought to claim me proudly as his apprentice!

Her mother had to ask her not to speak so to him and Mr. Bringhouse answered her that he only wished it was that simple. "They may decide it will be difficult to sell the cups if it were known they were Negro-made," he said. "Begging your pardon, Isaac."

His remark stung, especially after his high compliments, so I excused myself, sayin' that perhaps if I put an extra shine on those cups he had so praised, perhaps those New York buyers might overlook that I was a Negro.

But goin' out the kitchen door I grumbled. "Beggin' your pardon!" I muttered to myself. What would Thaddeus Oleander Principal have to say about *that*, I wondered. Both Little Will and Charles were over by the animal stalls, straightening up equipment. Shady, I guessed, was probably somewhere out of sight, smokin'. I pulled open the shop door, happy at the prospect that I could be by myself for a few minutes at least. But I was not by myself. Shady stood at my bench, with one of my cups in his hands.

I came right over to his bench and stopped. "Seems to me I remember you said my touch was contaminated," I said. "And here you have your hands all over a cup I made."

Slowly, he put my cup back down and rubbed his hands on his trousers. "Maybe I was wrong," he said. "Maybe we have more in common than I thought. I am the only one that kept up to you," he said, in a strangely subdued voice. "I could have been every bit as good as you are. I just wasn't favored, like you have been."

"That's what you always say!" I answered. "But there's no truth to it, and you know it."

He flung open his arms. "It *is* true!" he said, staring at me and waiting, as if he expected me shortly to agree. "You get all the attention from old Bringhouse. The rest of us? We might just as well be bit characters in some poor novel, for all *we* count. And *me*? Why, I only get attention because I am *objectionable*. You are to be the hero here, I know that. You arouse sympathy, but I *never* will. You have kindness, but I have not; it isn't in me." He rubbed his forehead a moment, uttered a sigh, and looked at me again. "So show your kindness, will you? Set a few of your cups on my bench, why don't you, so when the New York buyers come tomorrow morning, I will have something decent to present. Will you do that for me?" He took up from his own bench one of his cups, and pointed out where the solder seams were rough, and how the handle curve was pinched. "I can't show this," he said angrily. "Not when you got all those fine cups of yours so close by."

"I am sorry you feel that way," I said. "I only aimed to see just how good I could do."

"Don't shame me, for God's sake!" he cried out. "You got forty-eight cups there. You can spare one. Just one." He held up a forefinger. "*One.*"

I shook my head. "I can't do that. Mr. Bringhouse would know."

He struck the bench with his fist. "Bringhouse be damned!" His jaw worked. "Then sell me one. Sell me a dozen. I got money."

"They're not mine to sell."

"Oh, now, you are not going to hide behind that excuse, are you?"

"I am not hiding," I said, holdin' up the flats of both hands. "But I came a long distance to be here, and resolved to prove my worth." I waved my hand over all of my cups at once. "I cannot give the proof away."

"Goddamn it, nigger," he burst out. "I'm only asking for *one*. What do I got to do, beg?"

"Don't for God's sake beg, Shady."

But he shuffled from foot to foot and finally got down upon his knees anyway. "Condemn me if you will," he said, puttin' his hands together in a prayer and lookin' up at me beseechingly, "but I beg you now. *Please*, sell me a cup, or *make* one."

"No," I said, and turned away. "I got to go to Meetin', now."

"Then after, for Chrissake."

I turned back. "I got to see Mr. Jefferson then."

Shady stayed knelt, hands still pressed together. Tears welled in his eyes. "Look at me. *Look at me*. Look how pitiable I have become. Abasing myself before you like this. My God, nigger don't leave me in this condition!"

But I did leave him in that condition. Plucked up a cup of mine nearest to hand, turned on my heel, and walked out while he shouted curses at me as I went.

CHAPTER THIRTY-TWO

*Billey Gardner at me again and
Mr. Jefferson calculates*

When I told Thaddeus Oleander Principal at the Friends Meeting that mornin' about my confrontation with Shady, he stroked his chin whiskers and said, "Some white people is like gnarly wood. They's just plain cussed."

But it's not just white people that can be just plain cussed. For who should I meet right afterwards, as I stepped up to Mr. Jefferson's door with my shiny cup in hand, than the troublemaker Billey Gardner.

"Ho there, Tin Cup," he said, with a broad smile. "You beggin'?"

"No, I'm not beggin'!," I answered back, incensed.

He looked me up and down. "Then what you doin' with that beggin' cup you got there?" he said, shakin' his finger at me.

I did not appreciate his question nor his general attitude, and told him in no uncertain terms that this was no beggin' cup but my own handiwork, newly made, and which I had brought on purpose to show Master Jefferson.

Billey set his basket down then and took an altogether different attitude. "May I see it?" he asked politely, holdin' out his hand.

"You may not," I said. "I have shined it up special for Old Master, and don't want your finger smudges on it."

"Oh, now, young man," he fawned, "humor an old man, for goodness' sake. I shall not smudge your precious cup." He held out his hand and pointed at every finger. "See? "Every one clean. C'mon now, don't you be so selfish! I only mean to admire."

I stood there, unconvinced.

"Ah, now, Isaac, show some mercy! Will you turn me away disappointed?"

He went on like this for several minutes, acting out his sentiments like a stage performer, until I could bear it no longer and thought I might just break a smile. "Stop it!" I said and held the cup out. "Touch it by the handle only."

He took it from my hand gingerly, turned it every which way, looked inside and then pretended to take a drink from it. He could not get over that I, who was so young, could have made this fine cup all by myself and he kept asking, "You made this? You really did? You sure?" Then he got quiet, tilted his head, and said to me very directly, "You ever thought about goin' into business?"

I had pictured myself, now and again, in spectacles and with a quill pen, settlin' up a day's accounts some evenin' far into the future, but that was all idle daydream. But actually going into business, in the serious manner he seemed to have in mind? Why, I'd never given it a moment's serious thought. I was bound to Old Master and took for granted I always would be. So of course I'd never thought about going into business.

"You could sell this cup," he said, rappin' it with a sharp knuckle.

That seemed like a kind of treason to me. "Don't rap," I said, and grabbed for the cup.

But he was quick and jerked it away. "Correction," he said.

"*I* could sell this cup and sell it *right* now, too. This and every other cup you could make, just as fast as you could get 'em into my hands. You make, I sell." He snapped his fingers. "Just like that we're in business and makin' money. *Good* money."

The way he said this, with such pure confidence, made the whole ridiculous idea seem momentarily achievable. He spread his feet, and stretched out his hands, holdin' up my cup and pointin' into the sky. "I have read," he said, "how in Paris, France, a new invention, a hot-air balloon, sailed with majestic dignity high over the city, to the wonder of all its citizens."

I looked up into the sky where he pointed, half expectin' to see such a thing.

"Now, the day will come," Billey went on, "when just such a balloon will float high over this city of Philadelphia." He grabbed me by my shirt front. "And when that day comes," he said, his eyes bright, "I see our name in big letters emblazoned on the side of that balloon: *Gardner and Granger, Tin-works*."

The thought of seein' my name—well, *his* name first followed by mine—floating high up in the air like that was so extravagant, if not downright unlawful, that I felt obliged to remind him of a certain down-to-earth fact. "You already got a laundry business."

Billey looked at me in disbelief. "Laundry!" he exclaimed. "You call that a business, takin' care of white people's dirties? Why, it's but a step up from slave work." He kicked the basket. "No, that ain't no decent business. *Nor* handling transactions now and then for crippled old Mr. Madison back in Virginia, who *still* treats me like his nigger boy, expectin' I will not ask an honest fee, out of loyalty, you know. Naw! I need a business with *prospects*, and room for *extension* and *advancement*." He spread his arms wide.

I had been a disappointment to him, I could see that, and felt badly for it. But he still had my cup, which he wouldn't give back, and my sympathy soon evaporated, for he began to question me. What if I did show this cup to my master, and he got all pleased, then what? Take it back to Mr. Bringhouse, I said, so's he could sell it and the others to the New York buyer. That, and anything else I make. And then what? Well, I don't know, I said, go back to Old Master's plantation in Virginia and do the same for him.

Billey just laughed. "I don't hear a lick about *you* in all of that," he said. "Thank God you met me. I *told* you our meeting was historic." He held my cup behind his back and got right up in my face. "Now, it is high time you start thinking of yourself as a *man*," he said. "A man of *independence*. A man of *worth*. A man," he said, again spreadin' wide his arms, as if to encompass the whole city, "who believes he *deserves* opportunity to make good, and *understands* how to *seize* that opportunity. *Are* you such a man, Tin Cup?"

"Stop with the Tin Cup, will you?" I said. "And for the last time, give me my cup back!"

He shoved the cup at me. "Fine," he said. "Be that way! Take your *precious* cup. Shine it up good for your ol' Master. Make him happy." Then he picked up his laundry basket and walked off through the flower bed, all mulched for the winter. Halfway through he stopped and turned around. "You know what?" he said, juttin' out his head at me like a turtle. "You suffer from a lack of imagination. A *lack of imagination*. Think about it."

James Hemings rushed out the door just then. "Gardner!" he shouted, wavin' his arm. "Get out of there! *Git!*"

Billey Gardner stopped again, set down his basket, poked about in the greenery, pinched off a long sprig, stuck it in the button hole of his coat lapel, picked up his basket again, and sauntered off.

"Miscreant," said James, as he let me in the door. "Stay away from him, you hear? Now get in there and report to Mr. Jefferson. You're late."

I went down the corridor and knocked lightly on Master Jefferson's door, but hearin' no answer quietly opened it, stepped inside, and stood silent. He sat behind his wide desk, with papers and books upon it, bent over his prized writin' machine with the two quill pens goin', each one scribin' away on its separate sheet of paper. A small stove, burnin' coal, stood just to his left. Two windows to his right, the curtains drawn back on one, looked out onto another little garden.

After a moment he said, without lookin' up, "You can sit down, Isaac."

So I set on the wicker chair right across the desk from him and waited, uneasy.

Still he went on writin' for some time, and I thought he had forgotten about me, absorbed as he was in the high business of expressing his thoughts on paper. At last he sat back, lifted out the one quill pen, cleaned the nib of ink, did the same with the second quill, and set the two aside. He leaned back in his chair, which creaked, and began to rub his wrist. "Change of weather goes right to the bone break," he said. He rolled back the sleeve and rubbed up to the elbow. He stretched out his long arms to both sides and then straight over his head. He drew in a big lungful of air, blew it out, and brought his arms down again. "I should rather be out on my horse," he said, turnin' enough to look out the window, "touring my farms, instead of sitting at this desk, hour upon hour." He rubbed his hands together and looked at me. "So. Is that a sample of your work you have there?"

"Yes, Master," I said, shinin' up the cup one last time on my sleeve and handing it across the desk to him.

He reached out and took hold of it in both hands and turned it slowly in his long fingers. He hefted it by the neatly curved handle, set it on the desk top, hunched down and turned it slowly around. Then he put on his spectacles and held it up close, lookin' over every seam, then set it down again. He took a glass of water which stood at one corner of his desk, and poured from it into my cup, almost up to the very top. Then he sat, arms folded, and watched. "No leaks," he said, at last.

"No, Master, no leaks."

"The handle has a pleasing beauty," he said, "I appreciate that."

"I hoped you would."

Then very carefully he lifted my cup to his lips and took a sip. Then another. "Tastes better from tin than glass, I believe." He took an honest drink this time, and then set my cup back down. "Tell me, how long did you take to make this cup?"

It was a question I had expected, he bein' a man for time and cost. "Well, Master, I didn't make this cup, nor the others, in the usual manner, one at a time, start to finish." Then I described the method I had employed. He listened carefully, and I could see in his expression how he began to realize that

I was capable in ways quite beyond what he had supposed. It was a precious moment.

He sat quiet a minute. "And just how many cups did you produce by this method of yours?" he asked at last.

I was quiet a spell. Then I let the number drop. "Forty-eight."

He audibly drew in his breath. "Forty-eight? And each of them as good as this one?"

"Yes, sir. Every one. And no other apprentice did as many. Not near."

Mr. Jefferson nodded. "And how long was the day?"

"Mr. Bringhouse started us at seven in the a.m., and we was to quit at five in the p.m., but I kept on, he let me. Worked by candlelight at the end." I counted hours on my knuckles. "I would guess I worked twelve hours, more or less."

"Let's figure a straight twelve hours," he said, takin' a stub pencil and scribblin' on a paper scrap. "Fifteen minutes," he said after a bit. "Took you just about fifteen minutes per cup, Isaac."

I pointed out that I had hardly taken any time for mid-day dinner, nor for supper, so he made allowances: thirty minutes per day for meals, which still came out to a "presentable" forty-six cups in a day, rather than the forty-eight. Then he took his stub pencil and began adding up the cups per day, proudly announcing the totals: 246 cups per week—with Sunday off, 946 cups per month, and a grand total of 12,546 cups per annum, with Christmas week excepted as usual.

He put the pencil down and tapped on my cup, which sat with its pretty handle gleamin' on his desk. "Such industry," he said. "You ought to be proud. *I* am, Isaac, and furthermore, I feel considerably more comfortable now about the financial future of Monticello. I nearly wish I could set you to work tomorrow in your own shop—which by the way I am designing—on Mulberry Row. Yes, I have a fine future planned out for you."

I nodded, picturing myself, a one-man tinnery, workin' hour upon hour, day unto day, month after month, year in and year out, until I could no longer lift a hammer nor see to crimp a seam, no good to anybody by then, and worth only pennies to sell, a pitiful old man whose only escape was the grave. In the contemplation of this miserable destiny, I felt the full weight of my servitude settle down upon my spirit like a shroud.

"You would not always be doing cups, of course," he added brightly. "Once you become established and your reputation expands, I expect customers from all points of the compass will come seeking your services." He smiled.

"I expect so," I said, without any enthusiasm and wishin' I had not described my method, which after all had only served to add to my labor, from now to the moment of my demise.

Just then James knocked on the door and entered. I was almost glad to see him. But he looked at Master Jefferson and said, "Do I need to show this boy out now?"

I wanted to burst out in answer, "Oh, yes, please do, James! Show me out of here, I need fresh air." Of course I said nothing at all.

"I shall be done with him shortly," said Master Jefferson.

"You sure? He does go on."

"Now, James."

James gave me a glarin' look and backed out the door, closing it as he went.

Old Master half turned in his chair and looked out into the garden again. He began to hum. His hum went on for a minute or two, a tune I recognized as one he played on his violin sometimes. When he had finished the tune, he turned back to me. "*Quality* and *quantity*, Isaac. That is how we shall make money."

"Yes, Master," I said. "We wants to make money, sure enough." But I knew that no amount of money would be enough.

He rapped twice on his desk and James opened the door not one second later. "Now, you may show Isaac out," Master said. "And be kind to him, James, will you? For I consider him an *investment*, who shall earn me handsome dividends, in time."

James was not kind to me, as he led me out of the house, for he resented Mr. Jefferson's compliment of me, and made me know it, as I knew he would. But I paid him little mind. Instead, walkin' back to Mr. Bringhouse's place, I thought of Billey Gardner, standin' in the garden, pointing back at me. His words rang in my ears: "You know what you suffer from? A *lack of imagination.*"

CHAPTER  THIRTY-THREE

Broomin', New York buyers,
Shady thrown out

T hat next mornin', a Monday, or the Quaker Second Day, Mr. Bringhouse hurried us apprentices through breakfast. "Get thee out to the shop," he ordered. "Put thy tools in order and set out thy cups, for the New York buyers will be here at eight." He snapped out his timepiece. "That's thirty minutes from now." But he held me back, with a tight pinch of the sleeve, until the others had gone out the kitchen door. "Now, Isaac," he said, "stay thee in the house, this once."

I looked at him, how he pressed his lips together and furrowed his brow, as if pained by what he said. "My cups are the best of the lot," I said. "My place is at my bench."

"Ordinarily, yes," he said. Then he hemmed and hawed, and said he meant no disrespect, and ought to have forewarned the New York buyers about me, yes he should have, but he was only asking of me a small inconvenience, this one time, and of course there was Daniel, whose behavior could be so disruptive, and no one would want his resentful outburst in front of such men, with so much at risk, and such opportunity, surely I could understand that. "I myself," he said, lookin' at his hands, "am proud to have thee work for me, as thee know. Thy tinwork is truly exceptional, Isaac. I mean that in all sincerity."

You need not have said all that, I could have told him, *I understand perfectly well you want me out of sight, no need to pretend.* "Thank you, Mr. Bringhouse," I said. "But I would at least like to see for myself if these New York buyers consider my work as exceptional as you do. So how about this: I am present, but only to broom and tidy up, so that they may see just what a clean and orderly business you run."

He brightened. "And thou would keep respectfully out of the way?"

I nodded.

He warmly shook my hand and snapped open his timepiece. "Mercy! Get out to the shop and take up thy broom, Isaac. The buyers shall be here any minute."

So I did as he said, and sweeping over to my bench, saw at once that a cluster of four of my finished cups were yet again gone from their place, and sat now in the middle of Shady's bench. I set the broom aside, reached out with both hands and took hold of my four cups all at once.

Shady caught hold of the handle of one, careful not to let any part of his hand touch mine. "Don't you dare shame me like this," he whispered. At once enough anger boiled up in me to consume both him and me, and Mr. Bringhouse, too. "Don't you dare threaten me," I said back, in a level voice. He had never heard such a direct rebuke from me, nor, I guessed, from any Negro, and I could see the surprise and maybe even fear in his eyes. He slowly withdrew his hand and I took away my cups from his bench and put them back where they belonged. Then I took up broomin' again, as if it were all I ever did.

It was only a moment or two later that in through the door came Mr. Bringhouse, followed by a tall man and a broad one, both in overcoats.

"So this," said Mr. Bringhouse, opening his arm, "is my shop, and these are my apprentices, William Wharton from Lancaster, nearest to us, Charles Shippen of our own city, next to him, and Daniel Shady, of Maryland, at the far end."

"Of *the* Shady family?" asked the tall man.

Mr. Bringhouse nodded. "The very same, Mr. Gibson."

Then the broad man asked if they might see the wares, and Mr. Bringhouse said, "Certainly, Mr. Huntington," and ushered the two of them over to William's bench, where they picked up this cup and that, passed a cup or two between 'em, and spoke one with the other in low voices. Then Mr. Bringhouse brought 'em to Charles's bench, where they did the same. As they moved on to my bench, I broomed over that way to better watch and listen.

"*My!*" said Mr. Gibson, picking up one of my cups and turning it over and over in his hands. "*Outstanding.*"

"*Extraordinary,*" said Mr. Huntington, pickin' up another.

They kept pickin' up my cups, one after another, exclaimin' as they did so, my pleasure in accomplishment building with every additional compliment. "Never seen the like," they concluded.

Then Mr. Huntington turned to Mr. Bringhouse, "Which of your apprentices is responsible for this fine work?"

I tried to summon the courage to speak up for myself, broom or no broom, but Shady stepped right in front of me. "Mine," he said, and bowed. He passed his hand over my bench. "Yes, all mine."

Mr. Huntington warmly shook Shady's hand. "Well done,

young man," he said, "*very* well done." Then he went on merrily to say that he believed he may have had some business dealings with Shady's father at one time or another, and what a pleasure it would be to renew that acquaintance.

Where was my anger, now? For it seemed to have vanished. While I was able to rebuke Shady in private, among all these white people gathered together I felt disappointingly timid. Which of the New York buyers in their big overcoats could possibly believe an outburst of ownership from a poor black man with a broom? It was an idle tale to suppose so. I looked at Mr. Bringhouse, but he turned away.

Then suddenly Charles spoke up. "Not true!" he said, interruptin' Mr. Huntington's chatty conversation. He pointed at Shady. "Those are not your cups and you know it."

There was some confusion between the New York buyers, with furrowed brows and looks back and forth.

Shady pointed back at Charles. "He's just jealous," he said. "It's the price I have to pay for being exceptional."

Mr. Gibson turned to Mr. Bringhouse. "What is the explanation here, good sir?"

Mr. Bringhouse looked at the toe of his shoe a moment, then looked at Mr. Gibson. "The explanation is—that the cups in question were made by—the Negro there," he said, nodding toward me, "incredible as that may seem."

The two buyers looked at each other, then back to Mr. Bringhouse. "You swear to it?" asked Mr. Huntington.

"Yes, I swear to it," he said, and hung his head. "I am deeply sorry."

"No, no, don't be sorry!" said the two of them together. "This is splendid," said Mr. Gibson. "Marvelous," said Mr. Huntington.

Mr. Bringhouse raised his head and looked at them in surprise.

"What is your Negro's name?" said Mr. Gibson.

"Isaac. Isaac Granger Jefferson."

"Jefferson?" asked Mr. Huntington. "Do you refer to the Mr. Thomas Jefferson who authored the Declaration of Independence?"

"And is now our esteemed Secretary of State?" said Mr. Gibson, in excitement.

"Why, yes," said Mr. Bringhouse, a puzzled look comin' into his face.

Mr. Huntington pointed at me while lookin' at Mr. Bringhouse. "So that must mean that Isaac here is a *slave* of Thomas Jefferson, am I correct about that?"

Judging by the look on his face, Mr. Bringhouse did not at all understand what the man was getting at, nor did I. His insistence on knowin' for certain that I was a slave made me fearfully uneasy, though.

Mr. Bringhouse admitted that yes, regrettably, I was a slave of Mr. Jefferson. This information immediately caused Mr. Huntington and Mr. Gibson to dance a little jig with each other, lockin' arms to circle one way, then lockin' their other arms to circle back the other way. I stood there watchin', perfectly bewildered, same as everybody else, even Shady. The men finally stopped, unbuttoned their overcoats, and stood there panting, gleeful as chickens in a bag of seed corn.

"Gentlemen, gentlemen, please!" said Mr. Bringhouse, no doubt uncomfortable with their dancin', "what is the explanation for thy unaccountable good humor?"

Rather than answer directly, Mr. Gibson motioned me to come over to him. "You can put the broom down," he said.

Which as soon as I did he threw his arm over my shoulder and pulled me toward him. Got me in a bearhug, he did, made still tighter when Mr. Huntington came over to my other side, and threw his arm over my shoulder, too. I was squeezed so tight I could barely breathe, but maybe that was worth the sight of Shady standin' transfixed, his mouth open, eyes wide.

"The fact is," said Mr. Gibson, releasing me from his grip, "there is now, throughout the North, a wave of sympathy for the downtrodden Negro." He then launched into a history lesson, with frequent additions and asides from Mr. Huntington, how that many Negroes had fought bravely under President Washington in the War of Independence, and all enlightened citizens agreed it was a national shame, given such service, that the Negro, in the decade and more since, still had not achieved his full and deserved rights and worse yet, remained enslaved under awful conditions in the South, even though it was their labor that supported the economy of those objectionable states, which exerted their power in Congress or out, legally or even illegally if need be.

"We are therefore *confident*," said Mr. Huntington to wind up the lecture, "that we can successfully market the exceptional wares of this fine Negro craftsman to the *tens of thousands* of discerning citizens who believe as we do that this young man—here he clapped me on the shoulder—and many others just like him, deserve liberty and justice."

His speechifying overwhelmed me like a sudden rain shower. I was soaked to the bone with it, so to speak, but was not sure whether I should be happy about it or not.

"In short," said Mr. Huntington, "we can make a fortune with young Isaac here."

"Indeed," said Mr. Gibson, "we are *so* confident of this,

that we would like to make another order, this very hour, for as many cups, and more, as he can produce."

Here the two New York buyers separated from me, as if I was being presented.

"This is wonderful news," said Mr. Bringhouse, foldin' and unfoldin' his hands.

"We would *prefer* to deal exclusively in the work of your Negro, you understand," said Mr. Huntington.

Mr. Bringhouse, looking dismayed, protested that it had been his understanding that they would take the full complement of cups made by all four of his apprentices, pointing out that together they had used up several sheets of tin in the making of said cups and expended thirty hours or more of labor, and that he, James Bringhouse, was responsible for paying these expenses, and surely they could understand, being businessmen themselves.

The New York buyers listened patiently through it all, spoke in whispers for a moment afterwards, and agreed that yes, they would take the wares of William Wharton and Charles Shippen, out of consideration for Mr. Bringhouse's plight.

Mr. Gibson turned to Shady. "Chin up, young man," he said. "There's always a chance, if you work at it."

"Don't you judge *me*," said Shady, slappin' his chest, "you hypocrite in a great coat!" Then he turned and pointed at Mr. Bringhouse. "And don't *you* judge me by my performance at the tedious exercise of cutting, crimping, and soldering. I am better than all that!" He looked slowly around the shop, taking us all in, and then shook his head, as if he could not believe what he saw. "By God," he said, "I have wasted my time here long enough. O*ne* day I shall manage my *own* shop,

much more prosperous than this *shoddy* affair." At the word
"shoddy" he plucked up his shears and flung them in fury at
Mr. Bringhouse, who ducked just in time. Mr. Huntington and
Mr. Gibson, gathering up as many of my cups as they could
manage, trundled hurriedly out the shop door. Shady took up
his solder iron and holding it up like a dagger, advanced on me.
I got hold of the broom again and raised it up like a cudgel.
The New York buyers, I saw, had come back in the door, and,
with heads down, had rushed to my bench, and gathered up
more of my cups. Shady, hearing them, turned and flung the
soldering iron. It struck Mr. Gibson full in the back and he
leaped in the air, but still clung to my cups and rushed out the
door after Mr. Huntington.

Shady grabbed up his hammer and once again advanced
on me. "Go ahead, nigger," he said, "strike first! I dare you."

I almost did, for I had more reach on him, but once again in
the door came Mr. Huntington and Mr. Gibson to fetch the last
of my cups. What a compliment they had paid me, I thought,
just as Charles tackled Shady from behind, and down they
both went in a scramble. Shady struck him in the nose with
a hard elbow, and Charles fell back, gushin' blood, and Shady
backed himself into the corner by his bench. Blood-spattered,
he stood with that hammer of his held high, his eyes wild,
teeth bared like an animal.

"Daniel!" cried out Mr. Bringhouse, "put your weapon
down. Peace."

Shady's answer was to spit, and then grab hold of one of the
cups on his bench, and fling it at the poor man, striking him
in the forehead with such force he fell back upon the ground.
Then he flung another and another. Little Will jumped in
then, and I after him, but Shady tore and scratched and bit

with such fury it took help from bloody Charles to keep him pinned down and pry the hammer from his hand.

Mr. Bringhouse stood over us, his whole body tremblin'. Blood dripped onto his shirt collar. "Out!" he cried. "Out! Get this man out of my shop!" And he took hold of Shady, too.

Yet it was not easy, even with the four of us, to wrestle him out the door and across the yard. A cold rain had begun to fall. Mr. Bringhouse opened the wagon gate. "Pitch him!" he commanded. "Go on now, *pitch* him into the street."

And we did. He landed hard on the cobbles, and lay there in a sprawl, soiled and mussed, then stared up at us just wild with hate, and blood upon his brow. We scrambled in behind the wagon gate doors, closed 'em tight, and dropped the brace into place. Shady flung himself against the gate doors again and again with such force I thought they would burst open. He screamed out vengeance upon me. "One day, nigger! One day!"

Mr. Bringhouse stood there in the yard, drippin' wet, his head down, cryin'. I had to lead him into the house, where both Rachel and Mrs. Bringhouse came to comfort him, while Shady went on screamin' in the street. Even inside the kitchen I could hear him, until at last his cries became a moan that finally sank away and ceased altogether.

Mrs. Bringhouse then called us into the dinin' room for mid-day meal, but I was too worked up to eat so went out to the shop again, where I banked the stove coals and sat a spell. Getting to my feet finally, I picked my way through Shady's cups all scattered and thrown about, and the blood spots upon the floor. My bench was clear of all my forty-eight cups, sure enough. Only a card lay there, with on it the words, "P. Huntington & S. Gibson, Broker of Fine Wares, NY."

CHAPTER THIRTY-FOUR

*Quill pen, Master Jefferson's
Declaration, Rachel's
surprisin' lesson*

Only when Little Will came in, and then Charles, did I leave the shop and go back into the house. For it was my lesson time with Rachel. She was already at the table, readin', but looked up at me when I came in. "I'm so sorry about what happened," she said.

I nodded and sat down in my place across from her.

"It was past time for Shady to be gone," she said, and frowned. "He was *awful* to you."

I opened my ledger book and paged forward.

"*I* hated his fixed ideas, his *prejudice* against the Negro," she said. "I don't know how you put up with him for even a single minute!" She toyed with her sleeve. "He wasn't like that when he first came here, he really wasn't. He *seemed* so decent."

Just like dry old Mr. Cary could be decent with Old Master one minute, I thought to myself, and the next minute whip me at the gate. But Shady was the last subject I was interested in discussin' at my lesson. "Am I going to learn how to write with the quill pen today?" I asked.

Rachel closed her book and put it back in her apron pocket.

"Don't you have anything to say?"

"Miss Bringhouse—" I began.

But she cut me right off. "Don't you call me '*Miss Bringhouse*. How long have you lived under our roof, now? How many lessons have we gone through? Charles doesn't call me 'Miss Bringhouse.' Nor does William. So why must *you*?" She loosened the bonnet bow under her chin. "I thought we had settled that my name is Rachel, so I would be most grateful if you would please use it." She had gotten flush in the cheeks. "Especially now."

I lifted my hands, then set 'em back down again. I looked at my ledger book, then at her. "It's like this, Miss Bringhouse," I began.

She slapped the table and stood up.

"I'm sorry," I said, and stood up, too. "It's habit, that's all it is. A habit of respect."

She slowly sat down, and then I sat down, but she would not look at me.

"I have told you before, *Rachel* is a beautiful name. It's just that I don't want anybody to get a wrong idea. You understand, it's dangerous for me. And you, too."

Rachel looked at me finally, then looked away again. "You don't have to speak to me as if I were a child."

"I don't mean to. I just need to be sure you understand."

"Then you must understand me. I don't like you to treat me like I was a delicate porcelain doll, and that's what I feel like when you call me 'Miss Bringhouse'." She had to explain the word "porcelain."

I nodded. "I suppose so. Well, I'm sorry."

"This is not the South," she said, slapping her hand lightly against the table and leaning forward. "This is not

Virginia. This is Philadelphia. A Quaker city. We have a *whole* community of Free Blacks, here."

"I know. It's called 'Black Town.' My Papa told me about it."

"Well, then, there you are. So you need not always keep me at arm's length, with your polite address. I appreciate your manners in doing so, but I would greatly prefer you call me by the name I know myself by, which is simply *Rachel*. I call you Isaac, after all."

I could have said, "That's different," that Masters always spoke in the familiar to their bound slaves, denyin' them even the small dignity of a "polite address." Even here that seemed to be so. I would have appreciated a "Mr." in front of my name, now and then. "Your parents might take offense if I call you by your name, 'Rachel'."

"Why should they?"

I shrugged. "I just hate to take the chance, even here in Philadelphia, which believe me I had rather be in than Richmond, say, or Williamsburg."

She looked at me a long moment. "Then can you at least call me Rachel, here, in this room, during our lessons? Can you do that much for me?"

"So long as your mother is not present. Where is your mother, by the way?"

"Oh, she's decided we know how to behave, finally."

"Well, that's an accomplishment we can be proud of, I guess."

"I did have to argue the case," she said. "But she at last relented, and even said she rather enjoyed our company."

"But she mostly slept."

"You might be surprised."

I tried to think in our last lesson what I might have said because I thought Mrs. Bringhouse was sleepin'.

"Well, then. Let's go on with our lesson today, shall we, *Isaac*?"

"Yes," I began, and almost said, "Miss Bringhouse" yet again. But I just could not bring myself to call her simply, Rachel. "Yes," I said, "let's go on with our lesson, *Miss Rachel*."

She looked at me, then let it pass. "Now," she said, "the quill pen."

"The quill pen," I said, and smiled.

The quill pen was harder to learn than the pencil by far, as I had to load the nib with ink just so, and turn the split tip exactly right, and press down with only so much pressure, to keep the line even, with no spottin'. Rachel was patient with me, and said I was progressin' nicely, and I liked the look of my clean black lines on the white practice paper. So I went to load the nib again, just as she showed me, and said, "How about I write out some more entries in my ledger book?"

"Let's try something else." She looked at the framed paper on the wall. "How about this?"

"That's a lot of words," I said. "I'll be at the work for days."

"Oh, I only mean for you to copy *one* sentence from it, one of the most *renowned* sentences ever written."

I asked what 'renowned' meant, and she explained, and I wondered just what sentence this could possibly be.

She took down the paper framed in glass and laid it on the table, then brought her chair around to my side.

"Now," she said, tapping the glass, "do you know what this is?"

"Somethin' important, I'm sure."

"Very important. It's the *Declaration of Independence*."

"The Declaration of Independence," I said, soundin' out each syllable, as if that would somehow bring the importance of it into my mind. "I see."

"This document declared our independence, as the United States, from Great Britain. We weren't any longer colonies in rebellion, but a nation at war with the King of England and his armies."

"Oh, I know that war," I told her. "I was in Richmond when the British drew up cannons and fired three rounds and knocked off the top of a butcher's house. One of the British officers called me 'Sambo,' and put a great monstrous red coat on me. Yes, I know that war."

"Do you know about 'taxation without representation,' or the Boston Tea Party, or the Continental Congress?"

I wished I could have said, for my own self-respect, that I knew somethin' about these things, but could only shake my head.

So she told me about those things, and about Patrick Henry with his "Give me liberty or give me death," speech, and about General Washington and his ragged army at Valley Forge, and the dashin' Marquis de Lafayette, the French nobleman who offered his services at great personal risk, and how General Cornwallis surrendered at Yorktown, and much else besides. I could not believe how much history had gone on, and how little I knew of it. All I did know, I was too ashamed to say, was what I had seen, or other people, mostly bound slaves like myself had seen, and told me of. All that sort of thing was but bits and pieces, not at all the broad picture, which Rachel was able to see, and then tell out to me in order.

"The whole war went on for seven long years," she said,

"and though it actually began at Lexington, this paper was at the bottom of it all."

"This very paper?" I said.

"Not *this* paper," she said. "This is a newspaper, the *Philadelphia Evening Post*, from July 8, 1776. It was the very first newspaper printing of the Declaration, so father had it framed. The original Declaration was written out—with a quill pen—by none other than your Master, Thomas Jefferson." She stopped, and lightly slapped her cheek. 'Listen to me! *Master* Jefferson. I mean *Mister* Jefferson. For I don't believe in his mastery over you."

I was very glad, and even flattered, to hear her correct herself for my benefit, as she had done. Still, I couldn't help but feel proud that it was my Master, and not any other, that had written out this important Declaration, so renowned in the world.

"And at the very heart of his Declaration," she said, "is the one sentence we will copy." She ran her finger down the glass a little way. "Here we are. Let me read it for you: *"We hold these truths to be self-evident, that all men are created equal, that they are endowed by their Creator with certain unalienable Rights, that among these are Life, Liberty, and the Pursuit of Happiness."*

She had to explain "self-evident," and "pursuit," and most of all, "unalienable." But when I had got those, I said, "Let me look," and leaned forward. "Now read it again, if you would, only slower, and let me follow along."

Afterwards, I sat back and considered the words. "I don't see it," I said.

"Don't see what?"

"Don't see that all men are created equal. Why, it is the

plainest thing in the world that all men are not created equal. One man is short, another tall. One fast, another slow. One crooked, another straight. One sharp, one dull." I hesitated, then said, "One black, one white. There is no end to the unequals."

"But you don't understand, Isaac. Those are all outward traits you are comparing. What *is* equal is our worth. What is equal is our *value*."

I shook my head. "I still don't see it. One man may harvest a heavy bundle of tobacco in a day, another but a small. What each has done is of different value, and that is how a man is measured. One man may cut two cords of wood in a day, another not even half that. And you would call those two men equal in value?"

She shook her head and then looked at me, puzzled. "Don't you understand?" she asked. "These are *still* but outward measures of value you describe. I mean the *inward*. Not what a person can *do*, or produce, or accumulate, but what they *are*, intrinsically, in themselves."

Once she explained "intrinsically," I understood this was a whole different way of lookin' at things, but I held stubborn to my point. "Well, then," I said, "since you seem to be so blind to the matter, what about the *slave*? The slave is not equal by *any* measure. He is property and can be sold for money. Whatever he may mean *intrinsically,* to himself or anybody else, means nothin' at all in the market, or by the law."

I had spoken too much again, and wished I could take it all back in, and that just made me madder. I jumped to my feet and slapped my pantleg. *"Nothin'."*

Which made her jump to *her* feet. "What about *women*?" she said.

That stopped me.

"*Women* are not in this Declaration of Independence, either," she said, rappin' the glass. It only says all *men* are created equal." She shrugged her shoulders and opened her arms, as if to put herself on exhibit. "What about *us*?"

I had to admit it was a question I had entirely overlooked. For she was a head shorter than I was, and slender of build, almost slight, and with her voice, even in anger, being light, well, I guess because of all this, and maybe because of how I was taught, and just how it had been for ages and ages, I just never actually thought of a woman as *important*, I am ashamed to say, that is in the way that a *man* was. Mr. Jefferson, who was tall and well-studied and owned a vast plantation, he was important, of course. Papa, with his strong voice and decided views and rank among the field hands, he was important. Mr. Bringhouse, who owned his own shop and business and was built stout, he was important. Even Shady, or Shady most of all, with his scowl and bushy hair, he was important. Numberless others—all men, as myself. Strange it was to think of all these, so different in build, temper, and position, character, yet all of one group nonetheless. They had all the importance in the world, nearly, or outward importance anyway. Not the woman. Not Rachel, nor Mrs. Bringhouse, nor even Mama, when you got down to it. They all were *essential*, I understood that, but it was to the *man* I looked for direction, for he held the law, or the whip, and kept the books.

"Did you know," she said, slowly, and looking squarely at me as if I were also implicated, "that if I were to have children and then were divorced—and only the husband can declare a divorce—that I could not have custody of the children? Did you know that?"

That she would already at her age be thinkin' of marraige, and then of children, and even divorce, shocked me. Those subjects had never even entered my mind up until then. Yet she had *meditated* on those subjects, and no doubt others that were connected, though she was hardly more than a year older than me. "No," I said in amazement at her, "I did not know any of that."

"Did you know," she went on, "that if he should die, his estate would not pass to me, and that I could have no say in the matter whatsoever?"

I wanted to say how could I, that I would have no say in any "estate" any more than she would. But that would have been a selfish objection. "No," I said, "I didn't know that either."

"That I cannot keep my own money, if I were to earn any?"

"No."

"That I cannot own property?"

"No."

"Cannot go to a college or even a trade school?"

I stood up from my chair then, for I had had about enough questions put to me, as though I were to blame for any of her unfortunate conditions. I went across the room and turned about at the bookshelf. "Look," I said, "I didn't know any of this, and if I sound sour to you, I am sorry. I just never considered what difficult circumstances you might be in. I never thought of it! I got my *own* difficulties, in case you hadn't noticed." I threw my hand up in the air. "I thought if you were white you just *must* be free. In most every way, even if you are a girl. Or a woman, I don't know."

"A woman."

"Yes, a woman, Miss Rachel."

"For goodness' sake," she said, also getting to her feet, and then stampin' the rug, "please don't call me *Miss* Rachel. I don't call you 'Mr. Isaac,' do I?"

"No," I said, "you don't. And I wouldn't want you to."

"So just call me Rachel, will you? In that way at least we can be equal, or try to be, you and I."

I nodded. "Rachel it is, then."

She smiled. "Thank you, Isaac."

I did my best to smile back. "You're welcome, Rachel."

"There, isn't that better?"

"I suppose."

"Even if I am a woman—a young woman," she said, patting her chest where her heart was, "I *feel* life. I *desire* liberty. I wish to *pursue* happiness."

The look of her in that moment, and the sound of those words in her voice, stirred me deep down. If she could so dare to feel and desire and pursue, why then couldn't I? "Can you teach me to copy out that sentence with the quill pen now?" I said, with a genuine smile this time.

But just then Mrs. Bringhouse burst in the room. "Gracious on me, daughter," she said, "what art thou teaching Isaac that is taking so long, all the Law and all the Prophets? Mr. Bringhouse is waiting for him in the shop, with a new order to fill."

CHAPTER THIRTY-FIVE

First errand to tin pots, Master Jefferson inspects, Charles and me have our differences

Having got rid of Daniel Shady at last, Mr. Bringhouse hired on a Mr. Drexel to fill his place. This fellow had his own tools, brought his own lunch of fish and bread which he ate alone at his bench, and smoked his pipe upside down, I don't know how. He hardly said a word as he worked along, except now and again, "Oh, fiddlesticks." So the shop was blessedly peaceful and Mr. Bringhouse kindly to me. He lingered at my bench sometimes, just to chat. "I spoke last evening with Mr. Jefferson," he said one day, as I worked on a set of fancy tinder boxes, "at the Philosophical Society. He expressed the hope that in time your tinware would be sold as far west as the Mississippi." Mr. Bringhouse marveled at that prospect, sayin' that the country was getting larger by the day. "Imagine, Isaac! Thee, a *Negro*, working here in my shop and known to the very edge of civilization."

I did try to imagine, and thought of Billey Gardner, standin' in the garden shouting out about my lack of imagination. But I wasn't so sure I wanted to be known to the very edge of civilization, as I had more than enough cups, plates, pans, pots, butter molds, lanterns, snuff boxes, and so on to make as it was, not to mention what Mr. Huntington and Mr.

Gibson ordered. But the very idea of my growin' reputation inspired Mr. Bringhouse's confidence in me, and so another day he told me Master Jefferson had said to him that I should learn the full range of tin work, and he, Mr. Bringhouse, had recommended I learn the skill of tin coatin' copper pots, a service always in demand. Master Jefferson liked that idea so well, Mr. Bringhouse said, that he had promptly requested I tin his copperware. So it was that one happy mornin' I found myself sitting alongside Charles as he drove the tin wagon, pulled by old Tapper in harness, out the wagon gate.

"Now Charles," said Mr. Bringhouse, strikin' the sideboard, "teach Isaac well. Step by step."

With all the tin coatin' gear aboard, we clanged and rattled west on Walnut to Eighth, then turned north toward Market, Tapper's hooves noisy on the cobbles. Hawkers called out their wares, two gentlemen in a phaeton with a matched pair went by at a fast trot. A crippled boy begged at a corner grog shop, an old man pushed a cart filled with grain sacks. Charles had to pull Tapper to a sharp halt when three women, all with baskets, stepped out suddenly between two vegetable carts, both heaped with onions, of a type which Mama back home had never even heard of, I don't think, but which Mrs. Bringhouse used in her cookin' nearly every day.

Just as we came to Seventh, out of an alley came a heavy wagon loaded with split wood. I saw two painted words on the side and suddenly realized that I had not sounded out their letters first, but just all at once *knew* by sight what words the letters made: *Fire Wood*. I was surprised and pleased at myself, let me tell you.

Loaded as it was, the wagon came but slowly into the

street, though pulled by a strappin' big horse. Two fellows set up on the seat.

Charles waved his arm and shouted. "You, Benji. Get that shambles of yours out of my way!"

The driver looked over at us and brought the wagon to a stop, blockin' our way. "Shambles?" he shouted back, "Why, *you* got the shambles." Then the other fellow shouted. "Who you got there with you? Your *boss*?" Both fellows laughed at that.

"Hold the wagon where it is," said Charles, handin' me the reins and hoppin' down to the ground. He ran over to the Fire Wood wagon and then he and those two fellows began to talk and laugh and push at each other. One began to smoke, and then they all three did. Tapper swished his tail, then bent down his head and nibbled up some loose straw scattered by the curb stone.

I waited, watching the three go on smokin' and talkin' until finally I got impatient and called for Charles to come on back and let's go. But he waved me off, and the other two fellows laughed and slapped at their knees, so I told Tapper, "Go on," and slapped his rump with the reins. Up came his head, still with straw ends in his lips, and forward we went at a goodly pace. Charles he didn't like that and shouted for me to stop, but I didn't, and he broke away from his friends then, cursin' me and runnin' for all he was worth and finally caught Tapper by the bridle. "Stop this wagon, I tell you!" he said.

I stopped it. "We have a job to do, and I mean to go do it."

"Why, you know nothing of tinning pots," he said, after he had caught his breath.

"I know what time it is," I said, pointing up at the sun. "And the time is gettin' on."

"Those are my friends," he said, cockin' his thumb back toward 'em. "We got time."

"You ever been in Mr. Jefferson's kitchen?"

He railed at me for askin' such a question.

"Well," I said, "I expect nearly every kind of pot and pan known to man is in it. We need to get there and get started, if we mean to finish before the stars come out." I held out the reins to him.

Charles stood a moment, looked once across to his friends, then climbed up and sat down. But he wouldn't take back the reins. "You drive," he said, "since you know so much."

He was mum after that until we made the turn at Eighth. "You embarrassed me back there."

I asked him how I could have done that.

"You *ought* to know," he said, put out, as if it should not be his responsibility to explain.

I could guess, but I did want to hear him explain. "Tell me."

He turned on his seat to face me. "I gave you an order," he said, "plain and simple. I said 'Stop this wagon.' But you didn't. You chose to ignore me." He waved his hand around, as if trying to catch the words he needed. "I don't stand on color, you understand. But it's only common decency—you being Negro and all." He turned away from me then.

I kept my eyes on the street ahead. "It may be common, Charles, but it ain't so very decent. Not to me it's not."

"But it would have been so easy for you. Now I shall have to endure no end of ribbing from my friends. What harm could there have been in obeying me, especially in a request so simple?"

I pulled the wagon to a stop and turned to Charles. "Are you my Master?"

He shifted on his seat. "Now, why would you ask me a fool question like that?"

"Because you talk to me as if you was," I said, in a level tone.

"Well, you don't have to be so *prickly* about it," he said, glumly.

We went on in silence for half a block until I swung the wagon left onto Market and pointed out Master Jefferson's house. Charles remarked that he hoped to live in such a fine house one day, and I drove the wagon up the alleyway to the back gate, where I brought Tapper to a stop, wrapped the reins, set the brake, and hopped down to find James. But he was already waitin' for me at the door, with his coat pressed and shoes shined. Hands folded behind his back, he rocked back and forward on his heels. "You lost, Granger?" he said, and smiled.

"No, James, I am not lost. We are here to tin Old Master's kitchen pots, as Mr. Bringhouse instructed us to do."

"Don't you get smart with me," he said, and went back in the house.

"What's *his* problem?" said Charles, still on the wagon seat.

"He wants to make sure I know he's important," I said. "The trouble is, we got to do as he say or he can make things hard on us."

Charles stood up and stepped over the seat into the wagon box. "You bring out the pots and pans, and I shall get the tools ready."

"But Mr. Bringhouse said for you to teach me step by step," I reminded him. "To start with, I must learn the tools."

Charles looked at me. "Some would say you are uppity," he said.

I stood straight and looked at him. "But not you. You don't say that, do you?"

He hemmed and hawed. "Oh, well, then!" he said after a moment, "come here and help me lift down the forge."

This forge was not at all like the forge in my brother's smithy, with its big bellows and stone fire pot. This one was compact, and set on three legs, and had a pedal to turn a fan inside a tube and blow air up through the charcoal. Charles handed it down and I set it away from the wagon some, as he told me, and then took from him a short work table, which I set by the forge. Then I laid out on the table, in order, the tools he gave me, naming each one as he did: "tongs, flux, brush, tin bars, and these are wiping mitts." I filled a water pail, and then got leather aprons and gloves from under the seat, while Charles struck a kindlin' fire in the forge, and brought up a flame with the pedal fan.

"Let's go get those kitchen pots," he said, and headed for the house door.

I jumped ahead, though. "Now, Charles, you remember what I said about James. He has got to give the say-so, before we enter the house. He's very touchy about his domain."

I knocked. We waited. I knocked again. Finally, James opened, and in the stiff way I knew he expected, I described our present purpose and the necessity at this point of fetchin' the pots and pans from the kitchen, if he would so allow.

"Are your shoes clean? And the white boy's? I want no mud in this house."

"They're clean."

"Show me."

So he inspected first my shoes, right and left.

"You can do better," he said. "Rub them on the mat, there."

So I rubbed 'em on the mat. "Do the same, Charles," I said. "Will you please?"

I'm not sure how he felt about bein' so beholden to a black man, but James had such a scowl on his face that he looked at me a minute, shrugged, and then rubbed his shoes.

"Now then," said James, mostly to me, "follow close. At a *decent* walk."

In the house we went at last and on to the kitchen. James opened cabinets, above and below, and we got our arms full with those pots, and the ones hangin' at the hearth. "Don't forget these above the Rumford stove," he said, pattin' a broad iron plate set on a brick box. So we had to make a second trip.

James tailed us the whole time. "Don't knock those pots together like that. You sound like an army on the march."

"He's awfully sour," said Charles, once we got outside.

"Well, he has a good side," I said, surprised at myself for findin' any compliment in myself for a man so derogatory to me. But he belonged to Mr. Jefferson, as I did, and besides, we were both black, and were inclined, in the presence of Charles, to exhibit, if not exactly kinship, then some measure of fraternity, even if often irritable. "But I admit, his good side don't often show."

After I had taken Tapper to the stable for hay and water, I added more charcoal to the forge for a good, white flame, and Charles put on the heavy gloves, then set a big skillet on the coals to heat. "We only tin the inside," he said, "not the out." He kept turnin' the skillet. "I want the whole bottom evenly warm, and only then do I brush on the flux. You got to put it on quick, but even." He pointed. "See how it goes red and then sizzles?"

I dropped another charcoal in the fire pot and kept pumpin' the pedal.

"Now the tin," said Charles. "Hand me a bar."

The tin bars were no bigger around than a hazel switch, and about a foot long. I handed one to Charles. He touched the tip to the skillet, and almost at once it melted. "See it shine like silver?" He pushed the tip all over the inside, until he had only a nub left. This I took from him with a cloth and laid it to one side in the wagon box. "The whole business goes quick," he said. "Don't linger." Then I gave him a wipin' cloth, and he showed how to wipe the inside, going all over a couple of times, careful not to miss a spot. After that he took tongs and dipped the hot skillet in the water pail. "Don't dunk it all at once," he said. "Just the bottom to start." The metal hissed when it touched the water, and a thick steam rose. "Touch again, then dunk." He handed me the tongs, and I put on gloves, and touched, then dunked the skillet as Charles had demonstrated, and brought it up again, bright with water and shine.

"There," said Charles. "All done. Just towel it dry. Hand me the next one. That stew pot there."

But I dearly wanted to practice the methods I had seen him demonstrate, and was afraid I'd not get the chance. So I spoke up. "How about you melt the tin on," I said, "and I do the wipin'? Might go faster."

He thought about that a minute and allowed that I could be right, so I pumped the forge and he tinned and I wiped, and we together worked our way through a fair number of pots and pans without a break till midday. Then we sat under a tree to eat the bread and cheese Mrs. Bringhouse had packed. An upstairs window was open, and from it came the sound of a violin.

"Very nice," said Charles. "The instrument has a *spacious* tone."

I had to have him explain "spacious" to me, and then asked how he knew about the spacious tone of a violin.

"My uncle had one, and I got to know it well. I played it every chance I could."

I looked sideways at Charles, just then takin' another bite of bread. Here I had thought he was only a tin apprentice and white, with hardly any more detail about him than that. "But you play no more?" I asked.

He shrugged. "My father wouldn't let me. Told me it was time wasted, and I couldn't afford that, and neither could he. He expects me to pay one hundred dollars when I get done here, for the time he lost having me to work for Mr. Bringhouse."

"One hundred dollars!" I exclaimed, for it was an awful sum.

"Oh, yes," he said, nodding. "So I am in a hurry to finish."

Then we went back to work, only traded chores. I did the heatin' and tinnin', and he the wipin' and washin'.

So intent were we upon the work that I didn't notice the music had quit, nor that Master Jefferson had come out to watch, until he spoke. "What temperature is your flame?" he asked.

Charles and me both stopped and looked up at him. He was dressed in a worn old coat, and his hair was not tied back. James would have looked the better man beside him, in his gloves and bright waistcoat, if he were not black, which he almost was not.

"I don't know what temperature, sir," said Charles. "I only know if the tin melts, the flame is hot enough."

"I expect it would be approximately 500 degrees Fahrenheit," said Mr. Jefferson, "as the melting temperature of tin is 450, or nearly that."

Charles looked at me, then back at Mr. Jefferson. "Yes, sir," he said, "that does sound about right."

Mr. Jefferson nodded. "What are you using for flux?"

"Rosin, I think."

"Sal Ammoniac might be better," said Mr. Jefferson, takin' out his small book and pencil, and writin'. "It's a dependable formula. The rosin likely has impurities."

"Yes, sir. I shall tell Mr. Bringhouse."

Then Mr. Jefferson said not to mind him, he had just come out for air and to stretch his legs, and we could go on with our work, which we did, only it was hard not to mind him, and so we were both glad when he went back in the house.

"So is that actually Mr. Thomas Jefferson?" asked Charles, putting down his wipin' cloth and lookin' at me.

"The very same," I said, with considerable pride.

"Is he a tinsmith by trade?"

"Oh, gracious no!" I said, amused. "But he could be. He knows enough to be most anythin'."

"Well, then, what does he do?"

That was a tall question. "He works for President Washington."

"President Washington!" said Charles in surprise. "Doing what?"

It was astonishing to me that here was this white boy innocently inquiring what me, a bondsman, knew about such things. I certainly didn't want to disappoint his curiosity though, so I made the most of what I did know, which was little. "Oh, important work," I said. "State House work."

Charles got a look on his face as though he was reflectin' on this information. "And he's your Master," he said at last.

"Yes," I said, and felt no shame in saying so. "He's my Master."

"He doesn't look like a Master, nor act like one, either."

Now it was my turn to be curious. "How would you know?" I asked, "what a Master looks or acts like."

Charles shrugged. "From books I have read."

I was astonished again. "You read books?"

"Some," he said. "Slave narratives, if I see one. The Masters in those are always cruel and deceitful. I would not stand for it. I would run off, no matter what the risk."

Suddenly I felt badly about myself, wonderin' if I had the courage to run off. I ought to have, I thought, if Charles could claim the courage to. "Well," I said, "it's not so easy as all that."

We worked right through the dinner hour till dusk, and the last pot done. Then we carried 'em all back into the kitchen. James for once helped out. I got Tapper back into his harness, and Charles loaded up the mitts, tin bars, cloths, the whole affair, and shut down the forge, which we put back up in the wagon and tied down. When we put in the tailgate, Charles said to go on and drive, since I had got us there, and could now get us home. I unlashed the reins, unlocked the brake, and we set off, down Market Street this time.

"We have done a day's work," said Charles, leaning back. "Bringhouse ought to be happy. But mainly I hope his daughter shall notice. Isn't she a beauty?"

I turned to look at him, and saw he was starin' up into the clouds. "I wouldn't know," I said.

"I guess you wouldn't. Oh, but I am just aflame for love of her." He lifted his hands up into the air, as if he was about to catch hold of an angel. Then he brought his hands down and looked at me. "Of course, you wouldn't know anything of that rare emotion, it is beyond the Negro."

I looked at him. "*Beyond* the Negro, you say."

"I'm serious, Isaac! It's nothing personal, you understand. It's just that the Negro is not made for *depth* of feeling nor *height* of comprehension."

He said this without a trace of personal contempt for me that I could tell. "And just how do you come to know all this about the inner workings of the Negro soul?" I asked.

"Oh, all the books say so," he said.

"I thought you said you mainly read slave narratives with cruel masters," I pointed out, slowing Tapper around a stopped wagon with a broken wheel.

Charles waved his hand. "Well, it's common knowledge."

"I don't know much about common knowledge," I said, gettin' Tapper back up to speed, which wasn't much. "I'm not privy to that. So you got to *prove* what you say about the relative 'depth of feelin'' and 'height of comprehension' between the white and the black."

"Well, then," said Charles at once, "experience proves it!" He got all excited. "Listen, Isaac, have you ever had a sweetheart?"

I wasn't so sure I knew what a sweetheart was, so asked.

"A girl you are sweet on, of course. Now, have you?"

That was a question that had never been asked of me before, and I had to think. But really, there wasn't one. Not Doll's daughter, Emmy. We were just little then, and she got the chills and died. Not that girl I caught crawdads with, the summer before I was put to work with Little George, and she and her Mama were hired out, then sold. Now, Millie, maybe, for a little while, till she got mad at me when I ran off with her one shoe—it was a mean thing to do, I admit, even if it was one shoe, and useless—and after that she would never speak to me again. If I was honest about it, the only girl I had ever gotten to know well at all was Rachel Bringhouse! But *sweet* on her? Sweet on a white girl? Oh, my goodness gracious no. Absolutely not. I could maybe count her as a friend. If you could count a white girl as a friend, which was a stretch. And a dangerous one at that.

"Oh, Charles," I said, "there have just been so many with me, I don't know where to begin."

"That's exactly what I mean," he said, not catching my facetiousness at all. "Your emotional attachments are by nature shallow and changeable. But my heart," he said, puttin' his hand upon his breast, "burns deep and strong." He raised up his voice then. "Ah, Sarah Tilghman! She swore undying love, until *Randolph Chews* came along and then she couldn't bear to see me anymore. Oh, the bitterness of memory. But it shall be different with Rachel. I only await the opportunity to speak with Mr. Bringhouse."

The right front wheel went over a bump just then, which is about how I felt, for a moment. It was not jealousy—pray not that—but I doubted as Rachel had ever spoken so openly to Charles as she had to me, and me back to her, and the truth was I didn't much like the idea of Charles intruding on that, or tryin' to, even if he didn't know of it, which he hardly could. I drove on in silence for a block or so. "She could be spoken for, you know," I said at last. "Her father being prosperous."

"But I am in thrall, don't you understand? That is the *depth* I speak of. And where the heart leads, I must needs follow."

In the light of lanterns ahead I saw a gang of men in the street, and halted Tapper. "Is the Negro curfew enforced here?" I asked, my heart beginnin' to pound.

"Oh, we have no such curfew," said Charles disdainfully.

I was not so sure. "You better take the reins, and I will hide myself under the seat."

So I hid, and he even pulled a tarp over me, and I lay still, as the wagon rattled over some rough cobbles.

Then a voice shouted out. "Whoa, there."

The wagon stopped.

"Where you going at this late hour?"

"Home, Mister," said Charles, in a weak voice I had never heard him use. "Been a long day."

"Get out your money."

"Ain't got no money, Mister. I only do the work."

"What you got in that wagon?"

"Junk."

"We'll see about that. Boys, see what he's got in there."

I heard the tailgate being jiggled at.

"Take what you want, Mister," said Charles. "Only it's poisoned."

The jiggling of the tailgate stopped.

"Poisoned?"

"Yes, Mister. My brother died of it. We work with *chemicals*. Now I got to do the work alone."

There was a sudden quiet.

"Aw, get your poison cart on out of here, then!" shouted out the voice. "The gall to pull up among us. *Scram* with your poison."

I heard a slap against the wagon sideboard, and felt Tapper buck in the reins, and then the wagon lurch forward. There were more angry shouts, and then the sound of rocks against the tailgate, and in the wagon box, and one dinged against the forge.

When the ruckus died off, I got out from under the tarp and set up by Charles. "That was good," I said. "That story about your brother poisoned."

"Don't you make fun. He was poisoned. Poisoned in the manufacture of gunpowder for the war. He was my twin and still I miss him."

"I'm sorry," I said, and meant it, for I realized he had a depth that I had missed after all, assumin' he hadn't any, or not much. He assumed the same of me. It was the common mistake of most people, I guessed. What is more, it seemed to me that from knowing Rachel I had found more depth in myself than I had thought I had, or even should have. Was it the same for her, from knowin' me?

On that question, I pulled the wagon up to Mr. Bringhouse's yard gate, Charles jumped down and opened it, and in we went.

CHAPTER THIRTY-SIX

A letter, an errand, a detour to the Dempsey estate

Two days later at the breakfast table, Mr. Bringhouse, after putting on his spectacles, read out a letter from Old Master:

> "*Dear Sir,*
>
> *I bring to your happy attention the excellent work of the two apprentices sent to my residence Friday last, one being my own Isaac Granger. Both performed their task of tin coating my kitchenware with admirable diligence and attention. My compliments to yourself who have taught them so well. I shall certainly commend your business to my friends and acquaintances.*"

Havin' read out this letter, Mr. Bringhouse carefully folded it back up, put away his spectacles and looked at me with a smile that just beamed. "Well done, my good man," he said, "well done! My wife and I, and our daughter Rachel, too, we all of us commend thee." Then, rubbin' his hands together with satisfaction, he announced that he was sending out Charles and I that very mornin' to just such an acquaintance, one Henry Knox. But Charles stood up from his place wobbly, said he was doin' poorly and must seek his bed, and without another word climbed the stairs to quarters. After some hesitation, Mr. Bringhouse asked if I could perform the service alone and I said, "Yes, sir, in a pinch, but I had rather Charles were with me, so if you don't mind let me go up and look in on him." Mr. Bringhouse nodded his approval, and so I bounded upstairs to quarters, and found Charles already in the bed and with his nightcap on. He was not eager to see me, who he said had been so generously complimented by Mr. Bringhouse, with his hurtful mention of "dear Rachel" and not a word included for "poor me, Charles." Then he complained mournfully that his fever was now desperate as a result, it having already been severe from his having lately learned that Rachel—his "fair Rachel," this time— was betrothed to another. Then he moaned that I had not the capacity to understand his suffering. I sat with him a moment longer, but he turned his head to the pillow and began to sniffle.

When I told all this to Mr. Bringhouse, minus the laments for Rachel, he said he had no choice but to send me out on the tin wagon alone, for he did not want to let this excellent opportunity pass by. Little Will and Mr. Drexel could not go, he added, for they were needed in the shop, and neither knew the least thing about tin coating.

So I harnessed up Tapper, loaded the tin wagon, and off we went. I had no trouble findin' the Henry Knox residence, which was a large and comfortable place on Filbert Street, and only two blocks or so from Old Master's place. Mr. Knox himself came out the front door to greet me. He was a stout man, and his belly stuck out, which made him have to lean back for balance. There was a soup stain on his waistcoat.

"I am here to tin pots," I said.

He leaned toward me and cupped a hand behind his ear.

"Here to what?"

"Tin pots!"

"Thin pocks?" he shouted.

"No, sir," I said, and cupped both hands around my mouth like a bugle. "*Tin pots.* James Bringhouse sent me."

He frowned and pointed to his ear. "Cannons!" he fairly bellowed, standin' so close I could smell the horseradish on his breath. "From the war! Ten pounders!" He fumbled in his waistcoat pocket, pulled out a small book and pencil, like what Mr. Jefferson kept. On a blank page I wrote out the words—TIN POTS—and handed back the book. He read, smiled broad, and gripped my hand as though he would wring it off. I don't think I had ever been so proud of myself. For I had proven I could write, and not just in the lesson room, with Rachel to call upon, but here, all on my own, with practical purpose, and good enough to be understood.

"I had several Blackies in my command!" Mr. Knox shouted, so loud my ears hurt. "Fine soldiers! Fought like the very devil!" His stomach bumped against me as he shouted, and it was so hard I wondered if maybe a cannon ball had gone down his gullet by accident.

"Yes, sir!" I shouted back. "Now where should I park my tin wagon and set up the forge?"

That was too many words at once to get across by either shoutin' or writin', yet I managed by parts of both and certain hand motions to make him understand, and so at last I set up right there at the front curb, with even an oat pail and water bucket for Tapper. I went in to the house, got the pans, and set to work, and when all was done wrote out the work in my ledger book, as well as I was able—1 larg pan, 2 smal pan, 1 larg stew pot, 1 smal skelit.

"Come again!" bellowed Mr. Knox, thumpin' me so hard on the back he nearly knocked me over.

As the weeks went on, Mr. Bringhouse sent me out alone on tinnin' errands quite often, even as the demand for my tinwork in the shop grew. Good luck for me, it was a warm winter that year. Though chilly in the mornings, it was often so hot by mid-day that I had to shed my coat. Why, I even saw white boys swimmin' in the Delaware, and wanted so bad to do the same, if I had dared, and found myself a place out of view.

At first, I only went out to whatever customer I was sent to, and then came straight back to the shop, and showed the ledger book to Mr. Bringhouse, who made up the bill and sent it off by post. Sometimes I myself would deliver the bill if it was on my way to another customer, and neighbors of these customers would see me at work and ask could I do their kitchen pots, too? I would say I must ask permission of Mr. Bringhouse, and so would return another day to do the work, but after awhile he let me go on and do the jobs just as they came up, and write out the bill there, and even take the money.

So in this way I came to know Philadelphia as well as the village of Charlottesville almost, or so I liked to tell myself, from the Northern Liberties above Pegg's Run, down even into Southwerk, and all the way west to the Waterworks on the Schuylkill. Even met a workman there, Thomas Gordon by name, who showed me a Fifty-Five Dollar Continental he had found stuck in the filters. Though ragged, he hoped it would someday be valuable again and he could retire on the profit.

I often thought as I set off to tin pots here or there, that I had in truth been all about this great city, or much of it, just as I had so broadly boasted to Mama I would. And not walkin', either, but drivin' a horse and wagon! Oh, she would have been so proud, had she known.

Meanwhile, my lessons with Rachel went on, week to week, though sometimes not, when she served as a governess, most often for the Dempsey children, Jacob and Lydia. At times, she stayed with them at the Dempsey estate, it being such a distance away. Even with these interruptions, our lessons they had gone far past the ledger book. We read out the poem *Slavery* from start to finish, in turns, though I struggled some, and we argued over it, as we had done that first time. I granted, though, that it was a mighty work and wondered why there was not one similar written for our country, which had need of it as much, if not more. Besides *Slavery*, Rachel brought in poetry by Robert Burns, the Scotsman; rare adventures of a man called Robinson Crusoe, shipwrecked alone on an island; and a big storybook called *The Mysteries of Adolpho*, about Emily St. Aubert, who had about the most outlandish life any woman ever could have. Also, she brought to our lesson one day *The Interesting Narrative of the Life of Olaudah Equiano*. This Olaudah was a Negro, enslaved to begin with, who by his wits and learnin' travelled the world, went into business, and got his freedom. I had never supposed that any Negro could have such a life as he!

These books we could not read entire, there was not time for that in our lessons, but Rachel would mark out considerable sections, which we went through together. By this means I learned of many subjects and unusual lives, but also and most important, I learned of her, and she of me, sometimes through disagreement. Oh yes, we had some rousin' arguments!

However, all changed in the spring of 17 and 91, just as the shade trees began to leaf out, and flowers in the Buryin' Grounds showed buds. For one Monday mornin', Mr. Bringhouse came to my bench with a request for tinnin' services from a Dr. Cornelius Sharp.

"He is Negro," said Mr. Bringhouse, "a barber, who operates quite an establishment by all accounts, and is singularly prominent in the Negro district, which is thriving. I wouldn't dare send anyone else but thee."

As if I would want to go. For there still lingered in my mind Papa's warnin' about *Black Town,* because of which I made sure to skirt the Negro district on my tinnin' errands, especially Spruce south to Cedar, and Second west to Seventh, even when it would have been more sensible to go through, rather than around. Now, a part of me *did* want to cross through, but another part was afraid I would seem too much the outsider, or even traitor, even black as I was, sittin' up on the white man's tin wagon.

Not only would Mr. Bringhouse not dare send anyone else, but this Dr. Sharp expressly requested that I alone should be sent to him. When I asked why this was, Mr. Bringhouse only shook his head and said he didn't know. "What I do know," he added, "is that he has but a single item he desires thee to tin coat." This was stranger still, though again Mr. Bringhouse could provide no explanation. He only added to the mystery by sayin' that Dr. Sharp had promised to pay handsomely for my services. Pay handsomely, when he had but a single item to tin coat? What could this item be, I wondered? Not somethin' explosive, I hoped. Or maybe it was just something simple, only enormous in size. But what could that be?

Regardless of my misgivings I would have to go, so Mr.

Bringhouse gave me his address: 423 Pine. Which would put it right in the Negro district! Well, I thought, if he only has but one thing to tin coat, and it were not dangerous or otherwise difficult, I could be in there and gone out in no time. Yet I had hardly driven the tin wagon out of the gate and headed Tapper up the street when here came Billey Gardner runnin'.

"Whoa, there, Tin Cup!" he called out.

I snapped the reins, to put a little trot in Tapper's walk.

"Tin Cup!"

I did my best to ignore him, but he dodged through traffic, wagon and foot, came up almost flush with Tapper's nose, and dropped his laundry basket. Tapper about ran the two of 'em over, man and basket, before I got the wagon halted.

"What do you think you're doin'?" I said, standing up, reins still in hand.

Billey paid me no mind, but walked all around the tin wagon, inspectin'. Tapper tried to nip him. But he ducked away, and said, "My, my. How we have come up in life, since last I seen you."

"I'm on business, Billey, and must go." I sat back down.

"Business, is it? And just what business is that?"

"Tinnin' pots. Busy with it, too."

"Oh, I see," he said, his shoulders slumping. "You too good for the likes of me, now? Can't be seen talkin' to poor, pitiful Billey Gardner toting around his baskets of white people's dirties?" He clucked his tongue. "And you just a youngster, too."

I stood up again and spread my hands, to show myself in full. Mrs. Bringhouse's ample table had done me good. "Do I look like a youngster to you?"

I could see from his face how he saw I was growin'. "Now," I said, sittin' down once more and takin' up the reins. "I can't leave this wagon parked in the middle of the street, I got to go. Got a customer waiting."

But Billey got himself in front of Tapper again, just far enough ahead that he could not be nipped. "And just who is this *fine* customer, Mr. High & Mighty?" he asked. From the way he laid on that word *fine,* it was clear he didn't suppose the customer was fine at all, but more likely ragged and miserly.

"Dr. Cornelius Sharp," I said, expecting him to be some impressed.

But he was more than impressed, he was *transformed*. His whole face changed. His eyes got wide and his mouth dropped open. "*The* Dr. Cornelius Sharp?" he said, astonished. "You going to tin pots for *that* Dr. Sharp?"

"There likely is no other."

He slapped his hands together and began to walk back and forth, exclaimin'. "That *is* something, now. That *really* is. Think of it. Little ol' Isaac Granger Jefferson going to tin pots for none other than the *esteemed* Dr. Cornelius Sharp. I got to hand it to you, Tin Cup, you done good. I mean *real* good. You don't *know* how good." Then he came around to my side of the wagon. "Which is why," he said, "you need *me* up there on that wagon seat with you." He then proceeded to explain that given Dr. Sharp's stature in the community I would need an *envoy,* and that he, Billey, was eminently suitable to perform that function. But when he told me just what an envoy was, I knew that he was most certainly not suitable, and in fact that I needed no envoy at all, for Mr. Bringhouse had sent me, and Dr. Sharp already knew my errand. Still, Billey he held out to be an envoy until I got exasperated, and anxious, too, for by this time there were a dozen carts, hard trucks, and loaded wagons tryin' to get around us on one side or the other and cursin' as they did so.

"Well you might give me a lift at least," he said, relenting, "as I am going that way anyhow."

I objected that it was not my wagon and not for me to take riders, but he begged and pleaded, and finally took a coin out of his pocket and laid it up on the wagon seat. I knew better, but took the penny anyway, pushed it into my pocket, and told him to climb up, as the frustration from other drivers in their assorted vehicles was dangerously mountin'.

Billey grinned. "You got pluck in you after all, Tin Cup," he said, and told me to take the basket of laundry.

I set it in behind the seat, and Billey clambered up beside me. Then I snapped the reins, called out to Tapper, and on we went, though the curses continued for half a block. Billey was all smiles and talk. I was in for a real treat, he said. There wasn't no man in all the city like Dr. Cornelius Sharp. He had a way about him. You could feel it. "Even *white* people feel it," he said. "They speak respectful to him— 'Would you be so good as to clip my hair, Dr. Sharp?' 'Would you be so gracious as to shave my beard?'"

"Where did he come by *Doctor*?" I asked.

"Oh, he come by it natural," said Billey, flinging up his hands as though the "natural" had drifted down upon Dr. Sharp from the skies. "He don't need no certificate. For he has been beat down and got back up. He has been tried and tested. He *sees* the cause and effect. He *divines* the principalities and powers." Billey rubbed his hands together. "And besides all that, he knows how to make money. I mean, *money*. You want to know how?"

"I guess you are going to tell me."

"You bet I am going to tell you," said Billey, slapping his knee. "For I have made a study of it. He treats his customers as if they were the finest specimen of mankind as ever walked through his door, that's how. He shapes their hair. He trims their beard. He oils their face. Why, he straightens their tie and presses their coat, and has a man to shine their shoes. And *then* he sends 'em out the door as God's gift to the known world." Billey winked at me. "The other thing is, he never, I mean *never* takes on a customer that ain't dandy rich."

I had to wonder yet again, after hearin' all this, just what in the world must be this one thing, and one thing only, that Dr. Sharp wanted me to tin coat. But I could not wonder for long, for up ahead, wagons were halted. "Look here," I said, "more traffic."

"Oh, now, Tin Cup, don't you worry. I shall get us through. Stop this wagon and let me down."

"What you going to do?"

"You'll see. Just set up there and look solemn." Then he took Tapper by the bridle, and pullin' him forward, cried out in a mournful tone, "Funeral wagon! Funeral wagon comin' through! It's a sad day when Death comes on such a bright morning. Funeral wagon!"

It was like Moses parting the Red Sea, the way that crowd moved aside, carriages and wagons and tradesmen and hawkers with their carts. I felt the fool, setting high upon my wagon seat, solemn as could be, with Billey in front still callin' out, "Funeral wagon, funeral wagon!"

After goin' some distance in this fashion, we got through the traffic sure enough and Billey climbed back up in the wagon, very pleased with himself, and said I ought to give his penny back and one more with it, for the favor he done. Then of a sudden as I turned Tapper's head south on Second Street, he caught hold of my arm and said for me to turn north, which is the direction he needed to go, that it was only a short detour but would save him much walkin' with the laundry basket. He carried on so that I did turn north after all, but after a block or two, I stopped the wagon and demanded to know just what his destination was exactly, and how far? He said the Dempsey estate, to deliver the laundry stowed under the seat, for goodness' sake.

"The Dempsey estate," I said, and right away thought of Rachel, and then thought that I might like to see the place where she was governess. And since I only had but the one piece to do for Dr. Sharp, I thought there would be time, wouldn't there? "How far is the Dempsey estate?" I asked.

"Not far," said Billey, "if this old nag had some speed beside 'walk'."

I snapped the switch above Tapper's rump once or twice and he got up to a decent trot, and held it, more or less. All the tin equipment in back began to clatter and bang. Just as we got to Market Street, I saw a tall, big-shouldered man, right in the middle of the street. Black he was, too, but he stood there like he was white and owned the place. A group of black men stood about him, but he was the one that stood out, with his dress coat, red vest, and gold neck scarf.

"Herc!" Billey called out, standin' up and wavin' his arm. "Herc!"

The man didn't turn our way, so Billey did not even wait for me to stop the wagon, but scrambled down and hopped off, then ran over to the man. "Tin Cup," said Billey, turnin' and wavin' for me to come on, "get on over here and meet my man Hercules."

I wrapped the reins and got down off the wagon, regretting that I had turned the wagon north as Billey said. The sun was high in the sky by now.

"Hurry up!" said Billey, "Hercules don't have all day to wait on a slow poke like you." When I got close, he threw his arm around my shoulder. "Herc," he said, pullin' me with him right through the circle of other men, "I have *about* made up my mind to go into *business* with this young fella. He's trouble now and again, as the young will be, but I shall get him shaped up."

I looked at this Hercules in wonder. His hair shone and he had a gold tooth. He opened his big hand to me, a ring on every finger. "Let the young man speak for himself," he said, and smiled broad, and I saw a second gold tooth. "What business?"

"None yet, sir," I said, as he took my hand, nearly crushing it in his own. "I'm apprentice to the tinsmith, Mr. James Bringhouse. I'm out tinnin' pots today."

"What's your name?"

"Granger. Isaac Granger Jefferson."

Hercules shook my hand in his up and down, and his smile got bigger. "*Granger*, you say. Sure! I know your daddy, Great George. How's he doin'? Still slavin' on Old Man Jefferson's farm, I suppose?"

His tone, which began so jovial, ended serious, and left me confused.

"Yes, sir," I said, "that's my papa. But he's goin' to be overseer one day."

He let go my hand and shook his head. "Ain't no fun in

that, son. I'd rather slave in the *culinary* arts, myself." The men around him clapped when he said that.

"Herc here is personal chef to the Big Man," says Billey, "President George Washington."

"The kitchen is my kingdom, that's right," said Hercules, takin' hold of his coat lapels in both hands. "And Mr. Washington, Master or not, he *know* it." The men clapped again at this, and some whistled. "Say, how is James Hemings? He still in the kitchen?"

"No," I said, "He's Mr. Jefferson's manservant now."

He shook his head again and let go of his coat lapels. "Oh, that James. He want *so* bad to be high and mighty. But Bob Hemings now, I like Bob. You ever see him?"

"He brought me here to Philadelphia. Part ways, anyhow."

"Well, when you see him," says Hercules, and touched my shirtfront with a big forefinger, "you tell him, I got the money ready." He laughed big. *Three* gold teeth. "Stop by my kingdom sometime. I got a pair of stew pots and a brazing pan you can tin." Then he turned and swung on down the street in fine style, the circle of men after him.

Once back up in the wagon and on our way again, Billey leaned back in the seat, hands behind his head. "See?" he said. "I *know* people. The *right* people. Got you a customer already—my man Herc."

I snapped my fingers with impatience and Tapper jerked ahead a step. "I *never* said I was going into business with you."

Billey sat up in his seat and looked at me. "Tin Cup," he said, "a man must *seize* opportunity. Why, with your skills and my connections, we could turn a dollar now, we could." He slapped his knee.

I didn't want to hear any more about his business ideas.

"This is Vine Street, Billey." "We're going to be clean out of the city soon. I'm turning this wagon around."

"No, no. Don't do *that*. See that rise ahead? The Dempsey estate is just up there."

We still had to go a long block, then cross a little bridge over Pegg's Run, and *then* finally up the rise. Tapper put his head down and trudged to the top.

"There it is, the Dempsey estate. It's a sight, ain' it?"

It was. A great brick house, with porches and balconies and colored windows, set back among the Chestnut trees, all in bloom. Three Negroes, well-dressed, worked about the lawns, one on his knees in a flower bed.

"Well," said Billey, "are you going to set here and gawk, or are we going to get on?"

Tapper was winded, but I clucked him into a slow walk, and on we went, under the trees and up the long drive to the house. All was quiet about the place. If it had been Mr. Jefferson's, there'd a been a dozen workmen, changin' this and buildin' that.

"Like I said," said Billey as he patted me on the knee, "I *know* people, the *right* people. Now, hand me down my laundry basket."

Which I did, and then bid him good-day, and made to turn the wagon, but he strenuously objected, askin' how was he to get back, and I said that he'd asked for a ride and I'd given him one, but now I must continue my errand. But he objected that was no way for one business partner to treat another, and I repeated as before that I was not his business partner, and he said, "Aw, Tin Cup, don't be that way," and I said, "Quit with the Tin Cup," and he said I was heartless, he would only be a minute, until finally I became so exhausted with this back and forth that I waved my hand and said, "Go on. Just hurry back."

Of course, Billey was not right back. So I sat on the wagon, while Tapper stretched his neck to nibble grass, and I looked up at the house, and wondered where Rachel was inside, if she was at all. I saw there was a tower on the back side, with windows at the top. Was she up there, lookin' down at me just now? What must I look like to her? I leaned back a little, and held the reins easy, and looked out across the lawn, like a comfortable man of the world. Then I thought she would wonder what I was doing here, with her father's wagon. That brought me back to myself. Where *was* that Billey? I was just about ready to get down out the wagon and go after him, when here he came back around the side of the house. He held up two pots, one in each hand.

"What took you so long?" I said.

"Couldn't leave my basket of clean folded laundry just settin' on the porch, now could I? Besides, I must be paid. But not before Boss Marge must check *every* shirt and petticoat, I tell you! They don't call her the *Boss* for nothin'."

Boss Marge! Yes, there could be no doubt in my mind, now. This was *the* Boss Marge that farrier in Fredericksburg told me of. I thought of Beulah once again, and trottin' on her back proudly down to the Rappahannock, and remembered the disaster which followed, and had to put my head down, lest tears show.

"Well," said Billey, "don't make me stand here, Isaac Granger, take these pots." He held them up. "You *do* tin pots, don't you?"

"Not those pots I don't," I said, as if they were the most infernal things ever crafted.

"You got to," he said, in a plaintive voice. "I promised."

"Promised," I repeated, droppin' Tapper's reins. "Promised what?"

"Promised as these pots would be tinned up and brought back shinin' like new. I swore on it. Swore on your reputation."

"My *reputation*," I said, strikin' my forehead. I was about to add, "I have no reputation," but then realized that in fact I did, all the way to New York, and what was more to the moment, with Dr. Cornelius Sharp. I never expected to have a reputation, believe you me, Mr. Campbell. It just wasn't supposed to be anything a slave would ever expect to have, or seek, not in the way Billey spoke of it.

"I let it be known," he went on, "that you were the finest tinner of pots in the whole of the city of Philadelphia. Probably in the whole state of Pennsylvania. Could be you are the best tinsmith all the way to the western wilderness. You got a lot to live up to it now, young man." He shook the pots. "I can't stand here all day like this. Take 'em."

So I took the pots, and Billey climbed up and sat down beside me again. "Look at that," he said, pattin' the pots in my lap. "Here I got you a *second* customer." He set the pots down behind the seat. "Now, get this wagon on back to Dr. Sharp's establishment. We late."

CHAPTER THIRTY-SEVEN

Jumpin' boy again, Sword of Judgment, a question of my worth

We rattled back down Third Street at a good trot, for Tapper was only too happy to be headin' back in the general direction of home. Billey, so talkative up until then, became unaccountably quiet, which I was happy for. But as we passed Spruce, he all of a sudden piped up that the man had tribal marks on his cheeks, and when I asked what man, he said, why Dr. Sharp, who else. "He was marked out to be chieftain as a boy, you see," he went on. "But he got snatched up and brought over on a slave ship. He still acts the chieftain, though."

This strange information only added to my growin' unease at the impending business with this most unusual man Dr. Sharp. What if he was also an impatient man? For here I was at mid-afternoon, rather than early morning, and not yet arrived at his house.

I slowed Tapper at Pine, and we swung left. At once I saw the street was poorer, with cobbles missin' here and there, and houses needing repair, and then after half a block realized everyone I saw—doin' business in the street, walkin' on the curb, or up talkin' on the porch steps—was Negro! I saw many shades, too, some quadroon, others near as white as James, and yet a few as black as me. You must understand, Mr. Campbell, it was a shock, even though, yes, I knew we were headed to Black Town, but I had forgotten all about it, what with Billey's interruptions and detour to the Dempsey estate. Now, though, it struck me where I was, and I slowed Tapper to a walk, and just gawked. For in all the business that I saw goin' on—the hagglin', the walkin' and talkin', the goin' into doors and comin' back out, the sittin' and smokin', the sweepin' of steps, the vendors with their wagons and carts in the street—there was not a white face to be seen. This was not like the Quarter, either, back on Master Jefferson's plantation, oh, no! That could be lively at times, yes, it could, but here, oh my lands there was a buzz about it all, a zest, a zing, a bubblin' up *vitality*, with laughter mixed in from here and there, and angry voices, too, and the music of banjo and drum from somewhere. Two old men set over a card game played on a barrel head, children ran by, a man and woman together were doin' slaphand, for goodness' sake. *Real* slaphand. And there were two gents in tails, and their women in furs, as fine as any visitors that called on Old Master. I supposed these must be the troublesome Free Blacks. But they did not look troublesome to me, nor did the other Negroes of every sort, high and low, goin' on about their business. And me, among 'em! Once I got over the strangeness, I felt *comfortable*, comfortable through and through, like surely, I was come home at last, even though I had never laid eyes on the place until just then.

Billey gripped my arm and pointed. "There it is, *The Paladin*."

The signboard was pegged out in brass letters, with a

bright picture of a barber with razor and brush. I sounded out the words below the picture—*Fine Grooming for Men.* A bright-painted spring phaeton was parked out front, and three trim horses were tied up nearby.

"See that tavern next door?" said Billey, in a reverent whisper. "Dr. Sharp owns that, too. And the bakery, there. Along with some other businesses, so I have heard. How many I don't know."

I pulled the wagon to a stop, and Tapper gratefully dropped his head down to snuffle along the cobblestones. I pointed. "What's with those men there, sittin' side by side on the curb like sparrow birds?"

"Errand boys," said Billey. "If Dr. Sharp have some little thing to do, he calls for the first man in line to do it, then the next one wait his turn and so on." Then suddenly, without a word of explanation, Billey clambered down out of the wagon.

"Hey!" I asked in surprise, "where you goin'? I thought you were goin' to be my envoy."

"Oh, you don't need no envoy," he said, backin' away. "At least not me." He looked this way and that, as though he was about to be nabbed. "Look, Isaac, I had a run-in with him one time. Thought maybe now I could face him. But I don't think so." Then he turned on his heel, dashed down an alley, and was gone.

For all the bother he had been, I regretted Billey's absence now. I could have used an envoy after all, I admitted to myself, but now must face this mysterious and powerful Dr. Sharp all on my own.

Tapper, though, with his usual unconcern, only bobbed his head and swished his tail. I took hold of his bridle and walked him to a rail, and there lashed the reins. I scratched down along his mane and rubbed his soft nose. "Wish me luck," I said, then standin' tall with shoulders back, as Papa always told me to do, I walked across the street to *The Paladin*. I came up to the windows and saw inside mirrors all along one wall, and four big padded chairs, a gentleman in each, with four Negroes, all fine dressed, clippin' and shavin'.

I reached for the door handle.

"No, you don't," came a deep voice from behind me.

I turned and there stood over me a big man in a blue suit.

"I was sent to do tinwork," I said nervously. "For Dr. Sharp. Mr. Bringhouse sent me."

The man shook his head and pointed his thumb over his shoulder. "Not here. Around back."

I stepped off the curb and started back across the street to Tapper and the wagon, when I felt a tug on my sleeve. I saw a boy had hold of me, the very same boy I met when first I rode into the city on Odin, for goodness' sake! I was happy to see 'im.

He smiled big, showin' a front tooth gone.

"Well," I said, "look at you."

"I works for Dr. Sharp, now," he said. "Follow me." He let go my sleeve and ran off a ways. "Come on, Mister!" He waved for me to come on and ran a ways farther.

I unlashed the reins, and Tapper pushed his nose against my hand, lookin' for a feed. "Later," I said, and climbed up onto the wagon seat. I looked for the boy, and saw him a block on, nearly. He jumped up and waved, I clucked Tapper into motion and headed down the street toward him. He pushed open an alley gate and ran all the way back to me.

Then he jumped up and down. "Can I ride, can I ride?"

"If you sit still."

He scrambled up into the wagon, squirmed across me, and set. Then stood up and turned around. "What you got in back?"

"Tin works. Now set yourself down, like I said."

He set, more or less.

I turned Tapper down the alley, which opened out into a yard, with a great tree in one corner, and a stone bench under the broad branches.

The minute I stopped the wagon, the boy climbed over the seat into the back. "What's this? What's that?" He had to touch everything.

So I got back there, too, and showed him this, and showed him that, and how to hold it, and what it done.

"Is somebody goin' to meet us out here, or what?" I asked.

The boy blinked up at me a time or two, jumped clean out the wagon like a frog, then ran across the yard and in the house. I waited a moment, and then went to the business of liftin' off the tailgate, gettin' out the work table, and arrangin' in order the mitts, and flux, and tin bars, and wipin' cloths. I got down the forge, and set the fire goin' with the foot pedal, watching the house door every now and again as I did so.

At last a very old man came out, some stooped, and thin as a rail. He had both hands held out and stretched across them an object of some kind about three foot long, wrapped in white cloth. It could be no pot, that was sure. This man came very slow and dignified across the yard, settin' each foot just so as he came, but his left leg dragged just a little.

I took my foot off the forge pedal and he came up to me

and stopped, and stood there, very solemn.

"Well," he said, "you going to make me stand here till Kingdom come or what?"

"No," I said, surprised to hear him speak, and so brusquely, too. "Set it on the wagon here, where I took the tailgate off."

He nodded, and did so with exaggerated care, and then began with his bony hands to lay back the cloth, until the thing inside was all in view. But I could make no sense of it. At one end were two half balls, then higher up two quarter moon shapes, then what looked like a prunin' hook. All I could think was, *wicked*, a *wicked* lookin' thing. And old, for it was scarred, and dented here and there, and showed rust.

The old man pulled loose the cloth from underneath, neatly folded it up, laid it over the wagon side, and looked at me. He had no tribal scars on his cheeks. "Can you tin this?"

"I don't know," I said honestly. "What is it?"

The man looked at me gravely for a long minute. "*Ngulu*," he said, as if speakin' a magic word.

I had to ask again.

"*Ngulu*," he said, with the same tone of reverence. "The Sword of Judgment."

I looked at the pruning hook end for a long minute. "Judge what?"

"Whatever Dr. Sharp determines."

I saw now that the other end, opposite the pruning hook, was a hand grip, above the two half balls. I could feel the power of the thing. "Is it safe to touch?"

"So long as Dr. Sharp give permission, it is."

"I never tinned anything like this before," I said. "I'm used to kitchen wares and so forth."

The man raised his chin a mite and studied me again. "So can you," he said, in a voice almost threatening, "or can you not?"

I hesitated but was determined to measure up. "Well, yes," I said, "I suppose I can. I have my tools laid out, as you can see."

"Careful now," said the old man, "rust or no, this sword will cut." And so sayin', he turned and walked stiff and slow back across the yard and into the house.

I found out just how right he was when I nicked a finger on the blade edge and drew blood. After that I was more careful and kept right at the work for I don't know how long. I wished I'd had Little George's big files with me, but made do with the two files I did have, then sand, and finally a good whetstone. By then my hands and shirt sleeves were red with irony dust. Once I had wiped the whole sword clean with a cloth dipped in my water bucket, I stoked up the fire again, set the tin bars near, put on the heavy mitts, and went to heatin' *Ngulu* so as to apply the flux.

But just then I felt a tingle up my back and knew somebody was watchin' me. I raised up my eyes enough to see, sittin' there on the bench under that one great tree, none other than Dr. Cornelius Sharp himself. Oh, it had to be him all right, no doubt. He sat there like a boulder rock, big like that, heavy like that, and dressed all in white, which made his black face blacker still, and his two hands, set one atop the other on the head of a walkin' stick. Kingly he was upon his bench under that great tree, as if turnin' over in his mind all the country he ruled, like a king would do.

I could hardly pull my eyes away from him, but pull away

I did, and went to work tin coating *Ngulu*, which was a trick. For I had to turn the thing over and back, over and back, and make sure I kept my fingers away from the cuttin' edge, and keep the forge fire at the right color, and melt on the tin bar with no drip and even all over. I had to work extra quick with the wipin' cloths, turnin' the sword by the hand grip, over and back as before, and double-checkin' to be sure all was coated. When done and satisfied, I cooled it in water, I spread the cloth open again at the tailgate, and set down *Ngulu* carefully upon it.

That was when Dr. Sharp got to his feet and came to me, not slow so much as *deliberate*, and with *purpose*, swingin' up the tip of his walkin' stick at every step, and settin' it down again ever so exact. When he had come right up to me, he leaned that stick against a wheel rim, set his feet apart shoulder width, and stood as if from there he would never be moved again. The tribal marks were upon his cheeks, sure enough, four scratches at a slant on one cheek, four on the other. He smiled, slow and even, then looked at the sword.

I watched his head move as he looked and held my breath.

"Fine work," he said, in a voice so deep it seemed to rumble. "Fine. Now show me you can use it."

I begged his pardon and said I was sorry but didn't know what it was nor how to use it.

He smiled a slow smile. "You do know, young man," he said, in that rumblin' voice of his. "You have the shoulder for it. Step back and take a cut."

I looked down at *Ngulu*, shinin' there upon its cloth. It was a beautiful thing, but fearsome, too. It was one thing to scrape and sand and tin it, but another altogether to handle its power.

"Go on now, don't be bashful. Pick it up and take a cut."

So at last I gingerly picked it up with both hands, one above the other, tight on the handgrip. Then I stepped well back from the wagon and took a light swing.

"I mean a *man's* cut," said Dr. Sharp. "That's a sword of *authority* you got there. A chieftain's sword. *My* sword. It deserves better from you. Put your body into it, son."

I took two more steps back, set my feet wide, adjusted my grip, raised *Ngulu* back up over my shoulder, and swung it with all the strength I could summon up, and grunted as I swung, just like Little George taught me to do when I swung the heavy sledge. My God, it felt good. I raised the sword back up over my head yet higher and swung again—and yet again. And I grunted louder every time.

"There now," said Dr. Sharp. "There now, that's it."

He reached out his hand to take the sword from me, but I held on.

"Let go now, boy," he said, and there was a note of threat in his voice. "Let go."

Slowly I stepped back to the wagon and laid down *Ngulu*, the Sword of Judgment, there upon its soft cloth once again.

"No," said Dr. Sharp, "I mean for you to hand it to me."

So I picked it back up, gentle in both hands, and held it out for Dr. Sharp, and he took it easily by the grip in his one big hand, and raised it straight up above his head, where he turned it, side to side, to flash bright in the late afternoon sun. Then he let it down slow across his shoulder, like a tree cutter would his axe. "You can tell Mr. Bringhouse," he said, "that I shall post payment in the morning. With a *healthy* bonus."

"I will tell him. And *thank you*, sir."

He nodded. "Now I have a question for you." His face was

so black, it was blue. "What is your worth?"

"My worth?" I asked, not understanding.

"In dollars and cents," said Dr. Sharp, looking at me now as if I were one of his subjects, whose answer was required and upon which my life hinged. "What are you worth to your Master in dollars and cents?"

"I have no idea. Never thought about it," I said, suddenly ashamed, as if I ought to have known to ask it years before, even if I was a little boy.

"Think about this," he said. "If your Master was to set you up on the auction block, what price would he put upon your head?"

"Master Jefferson would not do that!" I protested.

"You are his *slave*, are you not?"

"But he is a kindly Master."

Dr. Sharp was not moved. "You are his property," he said, "and property can be sold. Any Master will do so, in a pinch."

I wished just then that Dr. Sharp would set back down under that tree, or go in the house, and leave me be to pack up. But I mustered up courage enough to inquire why he asked all these questions of me.

"Because," he answered, takin' his cane in hand again, "if you can tell me your worth, I shall purchase you away from your Master and set you free, Isaac Granger Jefferson."

"Purchase my freedom!" I burst out. "My *freedom*? What do you care if I am slave or free?"

He bent his head a moment, as if he were listenin' for some sound from underneath the ground, and then looked at me again with his penetratin' eyes. "I *resent* ownership of the Negro as property by the white man," he said. "If there is a chance to spring loose the trap, I will do it."

"But why me, Dr. Sharp?" I continued. "Why spring *my* trap?"

Dr. Sharp took hold of my shirt front with his big fist. "I *particularly* resent ownership of the Negro by the good Mr. Jefferson and crave opportunity to make him own up to the lie he has become. And *you* are the means to do it." Then he let go of my shirt front and lifted down the Sword of Judgment from his shoulder with his other hand. "Wrap it up, if you please."

I did as he said, fold by fold.

Then Dr. Sharp snapped his fingers and out from the house and slow across the yard came the old man.

"Virgil," said Dr. Sharp, when his man got close, "take back *Ngulu* from Isaac Granger, here."

I carefully took up *Ngulu* in its wrappings and solemnly gave it back to Virgil, who bowed, turned about, and walked as slowly back to the house as he had come from it, with an air of ceremony all the way.

"Now then," said Dr. Sharp, "talk to your Master. Get from him your worth in dollars and cents and then come see me. In the meantime, here's a down payment on your freedom." He plucked from his vest pocket a big coin. "Open your hand."

I opened my hand, and he put down upon it that coin, with a crown and shield on the face.

"That's a gold Spanish dollar. Now go on, Isaac. Be a man and go learn your worth."

CHAPTER THIRTY-EIGHT

*That Spanish dollar, Master
Jefferson's grand plans, hot-air balloon*

It was a terrible thing, that gold Spanish dollar. Never in all my life had I ever held such a coin, been given such money. No one I knew ever had. Not even *laid eyes* on such a coin. Why, I even doubted if any of the Hemings's had. Yet here I was, alone among all of Master Jefferson's bound slaves, with a gold Spanish dollar in my pocket. I was rich with it. And scared to death I would lose it, or be found out, and forced to explain. More than that, it demanded action of me. It pressed upon my conscience, it challenged my courage to question Old Master, to extract from him my worth in dollars and cents. So I kept that coin secret on my person at all times and fingered it in my pocket again and again all the day long. I clutched it in my hand at night and would not rise before I had again rolled it through my fingers. I studied it, front face and back. There were words all around the rim, which I could not read, and on the front, the head of a king, with crown on, and on the back a picture, the sun with its rays shootin' out like spears, rising up from behind a branchin' tree. The more I studied that coin, the more mysterious and valuable it became to me, and the more it demanded of me that I speak up to Master Jefferson.

But I could tell nobody about that coin, not even Rachel—
lest I would have to say where I got it, and why Dr. Sharp had
given it, and what he expected me to find out because of it,
which would only bring up how fearful I felt. That I didn't
want her to know about. How fearful, and weak, and cowardly.
How much the pitiful slave, who even in his deepest self found
it hard to disobey, and only wanted to be left alone to go about
his humble business. Yet another part of myself rose up angry
against this and wanted to break and strike down and cast
aside. But such destruction would gain me nothing, I knew. I
simply had to gather up my determination, cool my fears, and
open my mouth to ask the mighty question.

Yet Sunday afternoon after Sunday afternoon, when I sat
down in the chair across from Old Master, this great, tall white
man at his broad desk, with the writin' machine before him,
and books all about, who had been to the far off country of
France on the nation's business, and now worked as Secretary
of State for President Washington, and was besides all that a
kindly Master, who had been so good to Papa and Mama, and
had chosen me out specially to be a tinsmith apprentice here
in Philadelphia—well, when all that came up in my mind, I
could not bring my mouth to ask the question, no matter how
mighty. Instead, I sat there quiet and ashamed, and answered
his questions as required, and then bowed my way out, and
could hardly keep the pitiful tears back as I did so. Oh, I
wanted to fling that heavy Spanish dollar into the Delaware
and be done with it. And very nearly did, on more than one
Sunday, but could not. Could not! For it had become the very
symbol of my freedom and of my bondage.

It was James who at last provoked me. "It has unfortunately come to my attention," he said, one Sunday afternoon

after yet another miserable failure of my resolve to speak up for myself, "that you have had some *dealings* with that *so-called* "Doctor" Sharp. I had *hoped* you would have had the good sense to know better." He spat into a flower bush, and I watched the spittle hang from a bud. "*Apparently*, I was wrong."

"James," I said, feeling the salt rise in me, "I only done what Mr. Bringhouse told me to. He sent me on a tinnin' errand to that Dr. Sharp, and so I went. For Dr. Sharp would have none but me to do it."

James eyed me suspiciously for a moment. "Mr. Jefferson told me to keep a watch on you. With good reason." He poked my chest with a forefinger. "For you is young, and foolish, and *troublesome*. And Mr. Jefferson don't like troublesomeness from his *property*. He likes *peace*. Peace and harmony."

I pushed his finger away. "Don't lecture me, James."

He got up in my face. "Look, here. I won't say this but one more time. Stay away from that Dr. Sharp character, you hear me? He's dangerous, and he's sly, and you, boy, are gullible."

That done it. That kicked up my determination a solid notch or two. "Get out of my way," I said, and opened the door.

"What do you think you're doing?" he said, moving to block my way.

"There's one thing I forgot to ask Mr. Jefferson," I said, and pushed by him. "Thank goodness you reminded me."

Old Master was already hard at his writin' again.

"Isaac!" he said, lookin' up. "Can't you see I'm at work, here?"

"Yes, sir, I can," I said. "And I am sorry to disturb you, but—well, it's urgent that I speak with you."

He motioned with his hand and I took my seat.

I thought my heart might pound out of my chest. "I have a question, Mr. Jefferson." I had never called him just "Mr." before.

He noticed this, took off his spectacles, folded them, and set them to one side. He did not speak, but simply waited for me to go on, watching me all the while with his deep eyes.

I felt my determination want to ebb but held it in place. "In the tin business," I said, "I have learnt of worth."

"Worth," he repeated, in his quiet, searchin' way.

"Yes, Mr. Jefferson," I said. "The worth of property. In dollars and cents."

He pushed his writin' machine to one side and folded his hands together on the desk. "What property exactly do you mean?"

I felt along my pant leg for the coin in my pocket to help me hold my determination in place and find the proper words to answer back with. I described the ledger book, and how I kept track of customers and work performed and so forth, but especially the price charged, and payment received, of a cup or pot or pan. "That property," I said, "to begin with."

Master Jefferson smiled, and I began to feel more comfortable. "To calculate the worth in dollars and cents, of a particular cup, or pot, or pan is no mean exercise," he said, warmin' to the subject. "There is the labor to account for, minute to minute, and the materials utilized—tin sheet, solder, flux, charcoal, incidentals, and of course, wastage." He raised a finger in the air. "There is also what I call *dilapidation expense*, which includes equipment repair, replacement of tools, building upkeep, and a host of other items, general and specific." He drew a deep breath, apparently satisfied with his inventory, and, I thought, relieved that my question had to do with no more than such things as these. "The accounting of expenses is long, but the accounting of profits? Short, I am afraid."

I expressed my appreciation for his understandin' of property, and promised to pass along his wisdom to Mr. Bringhouse, who was sure to agree. Then, again feelin' of the gold Spanish dollar in my pocket, I said, as innocently as I was able, that I was thinkin' of the worth of other property, too, beyond just tin works.

Old Master made a fist of one hand and with the fingers of his other hand, traced the veins from the wrist up to the knuckles. "I did not prepare your assignment with Mr. Bringhouse," he said, again looking at me, "with the expectation that you would also contemplate the complications of property." He paused. "I believe I made it plain you were to learn the tinsmith trade."

I nodded agreeably. "I know, Master, believe me I know," I said. "Done my level best at the learnin' of the trade, too. I hope you have been satisfied, so far."

Now it was his turn to nod. "Very satisfied, Isaac."

I drew a deep breath. "Mr. Bringhouse told me your very own words, that I should learn the 'full range of tin work,'" I said. "And I have taken those words to heart, Mr. Jefferson, and would include the business angle, the way I see it. Which brings me again to the matter of property."

He traced his veins again. "What property exactly do you have in mind, Isaac?" he asked.

I thought from his look that he might now comprehend what property I meant, but I had to go on and say it, nonetheless. "If you please—human property."

He turned over his hand, and this time traced the palm

lines, taking his time at it. "Are we speaking here of human property in general?" he asked, finally. "Or of a *particular* human property?"

He was only waitin' on me to get to that particular. But he would make me go there step by step, and watch me as I did so. I felt the sweat under my arms.

"A particular," I said. "A particular human property, Mr. Jefferson."

After a long minute, he said, "And just who might that be, I wonder? You can speak freely to me, Isaac. We are family."

It was simple what I had to say. Only one word: *me.* And of course, he knew by now. And yet I could not seem to bring that simple, one-syllable and two-letter word up to my lips.

"Well," he said at last, "so we are finished here? I have work to do."

"No!" I burst out. "No, Master, we aren't quite finished. "Me. It is *me. I* am the particular property. *Myself*, Isaac." I looked down in my lap, embarrassed by my awkward speech.

But Mr. Jefferson said nothin', nothin' at all, and so at last, I looked up. And there he sat, unmovin', like a cat, with his eyes fixed upon me. To my surprise, I saw no anger in 'em, though, but disappointment, I think. He bent his head a little and rubbed back and forth across his forehead with his fingers. Likely our exchange had brought on a touch of migraine. "How is it," he asked, looking away, "that my kindness leads so often to the severing of connection?" Then he put his hand down and did look at me. "To calculate the worth of human property in dollars and cents, in both the general and the particular, is such a disagreeable business. Especially when it touches upon those who labor so for my happiness. How could I ever put a price on you, Isaac Granger?"

Then he turned away from me again and looked out the window. "Have I ever told you," he said, "the story of how I acquired your mother?"

I knew it, for Mama had reminded me of it now and again, but never had I heard it from him. "No, Mr. Jefferson, you have not told me that story."

He turned back from the window and looked at me. "Soon after I was married to Mrs. Jefferson, she sent me up to Goochland County. 'I will have none but Ursula in my kitchen,' she said to me. 'Don't come back here, Thomas, unless you come back with her.'" Mr. Jefferson smiled at the recollection of those words, for he deeply loved his wife, all agreed to that. "I had to pay a pretty price for her, mind you. Then on my own account, I hunted out your father, and bought him, too. That was a happy day, Isaac, when I settled your parents together at Monticello. And there they have raised you—you, and Little George, and Bagwell." He smiled again. "You ran all about the place as a boy, even surprised me in my study one morning, remember?"

I did remember, and remembered another time, too, when I got caught in the dumb waiter he had in his dinin' room. He never found out, but Mama paddled me anyhow.

"You were so inquisitive," he went on, then shook his head. "Just into everything. What a boy. I saw your promise, even then. And as I watched you grow, I cast about for an opportunity worthy of your promise. It was only after considerable trouble, you understand, that I was able to arrange your apprenticeship with James Bringhouse."

"I am grateful to you, Mr. Jefferson," I said, and meant it, too. Likewise, thought what a tether my gratitude was, however deserved, and knew that he knew this, and held me with it, which made me resentful. It had always been this way with his favored slaves, who must soothe his feelings, which were sensitive on this point, lest he feel slighted, or his generosity go unrecognized. But I only recognized this, in myself and him, only just then.

"I hope you are grateful," he said. "I trust you are. However, in the event you are not content here, I *can* send you back to Virginia." He extended his hands toward me, as if in invitation. "With no ill will on my part. None whatever. Perhaps that would be for the best."

"Oh, no, Master!" I said, fearful he might do just that. "I am *very* content here. Content and hard at work."

Mr. Jefferson watched me as I said all this, felt him tryin' to plumb the cause of my discontented mind, and question about property.

"Pull your chair around to my side here," he said, suddenly amiable. "I have something to show you."

So I pulled my chair around as he reached back to a cabinet, took hold of a rolled paper that lay on top, and then spread it out flat on the desk. "Hold the one side," he said. Then he put a weight on the other side and moved his hand slowly over a drawin' he had done, nearly as large as the paper, with many markin's and numbers, all done fine and neat. "This," he said with enthusiasm, "is the tinsmith shop I plan to build for you." He ran his finger along the wall lines: front, side, back, and t'other side. "It will be a considerable structure," he went on, "as good as any on Mulberry Row. Sixteen feet broad, ten and one-half deep." He traced along one wall line with his finger. "There will be a line of windows here, for good light on the workbench. Solder stove over here. Rack for tin sheet to this side."

He pointed out everything, for he had it planned down to the last inch.

"I have taken the liberty of asking Mr. Bringhouse if he would come down to Virginia for six months," he said, "when the time comes, and supervise the building of cabinets and work benches, and equip your shop with all the necessary tools, gear, material, and accessories. In short, I mean to provide you with the most up-to-date tinsmithery in the whole of western Virginia."

Havin' finished his presentation, Mr. Jefferson leaned back in his chair and folded his hands behind his head. "There now, Isaac!" he said, "what do you think?"

What I thought was, how far I had come from that moment in my brother's smithy— which seemed now a century ago— when full of myself at the prospect of adventure in a far city and the learnin' of a trade—I had cocked my elbows and crowed like a young rooster. Now here was I in truth living in that far city, working as an actual tinsmith apprentice, and a good one, too, and sitting across the desk from Old Master himself, who was not telling me what to do, but asking me what I thought! Oh, and I had a lot I could answer his question with, too! For now, thanks to Rachel Bringhouse I was no longer ignorant, praise be, but could read and write. I could keep a business ledger book. I could recognize *symbol* and *metaphor* in poetry, and discuss all manner of books, both literary and philosophical. I even knew Old Master's Declaration of Independence—had studied it, knew by heart its most important sentence: "We hold these Truths to be self-evident . . ." And I was now also *experienced*, having weathered Daniel Shady's bitter contempt for me, his taunts and jibes and his wounding of my hand; I had been cajoled and pestered, and yes even tempted by Billey

Gardner's bold and even outlandish business proposals. I had myself handled *Ngulu*, the Sword of Judgment—had swung it over my head and heard it whistle in the air! And right here and now, Old Master had shown me detailed plans that he himself had drawn for a tin shop to be all my own! A shop to be larger than any other on Mulberry Row, equipped with all the modern gear by Mr. Bringhouse himself.

So what was my worth in dollars and cents? I didn't know, and wouldn't have an answer for Dr. Sharp, for Master Jefferson had not told me. But was I disappointed, or upset with myself? No! Far from it. For I figured the question was too small by half. For who could judge the worth of all I had learnt, and experienced, and contemplated in thought? Who! But even as I struck upon that word in my mind, I knew who: Mr. Thomas Jefferson. *He* knew my worth, and he knew that I had begun to know, too. And here I had expected to surprise him with my question of dollars and cents! Oh, but I was sure now he had suspected; seen that I had grown in both body and mind—could not have missed it! So he had drawn up those fine shop plans, prepared them for me like a trap to secure my loyalty, and someday gain from the sale of my tinworks an income for his plantation. Oh yes, I knew all this was so, for I felt the pull of loyalty to him, as he sat across the desk lookin' at me, more powerful than I had ever felt it in all my life. And yet, I resisted! Loyalty and then resistance, back and forth in me, I felt 'em strong!

"Isaac?" I heard Mr. Jefferson say. "I asked you a question. What do you think of my plans for your shop?"

"Oh, Master," I said, "It all so—grand."

"Yes, *grand*," agreed Mr. Jefferson, relishing the word. "For only grand will do, in this as in all things."

When I stepped out on Market Street, I could have shouted! Could have spun in a circle and just shouted, I was so proud of myself, felt so strong and good clean through. And just then—hardly believin' my eyes—I saw an *actual* hot-air balloon hovering high above the Wharf Market, as if Billey Gardner had somehow conjured up the one that sailed over Paris, France and summoned it here. I ran the next five blocks at a sprint to get a closer view, where I was prevented from going any farther on account of the people clogging the street, looking up in wonder at this marvel of modern times. A basket hung under the balloon, with two people in it, dressed in bright coats and wavin' down at the onlookers from a height of eighty feet or more, I guessed. This balloon, with its basket and passengers, was moored to the ground by great ropes, and at the firing of a signal gun, the ropes were let go, and the balloon, to everyone's astonishment, drifted slowly out over the Delaware and began to lose altitude. The persons in the basket dropped out bags, and flared a gas jet, and the balloon rose up again, to applause and cheers, and coasted south above the river. The crowd began to thin out then, but I resumed my run, past the Goose Fountain and all the way to the pier, where I watched that balloon with its bold passengers drift ever farther south, on its way to the great ocean, I supposed. The whole scene was like a *symbol* to me. My hopes rose, my confidence lifted. "You, world!" I shouted out over the river, "just watch what I shall make of my life!"

Then I turned south on Front and fairly danced back to Mr. Bringhouse's establishment, for I was full of new ideas for shapin' the tin. And could not wait to confide in Rachel all I had been through on that precious day.

POSTSCRIPT

by Reverend Charles Campbell

After concluding his uplifting description of the hot-air balloon, his old face aglow with remembered excitement, his finger pointing into the air as if the airborne contrivance were again passing overhead, Isaac sat quiet for several minutes. Then with a certain agitation he got to his feet, picked up a half-finished tin pot and said, with a deep sigh, "That must be the finish for now, Mr. Campbell. I have a business to attend to, and a wife to care for. Come back another time."

Though I was intensely curious to know what followed this extraordinary episode with Mr. Jefferson, I saw plainly that he was at an end for the present and could hardly begrudge him; we had been at it, with few interruptions, for several weeks, he juggling both his work and recitations to me. Therefore, lest I offend him, and he refuse altogether to continue, I closed my notebook, packed away my pen and ink, and took my leave, only pausing to give him my card and beg him to contact me promptly by post when he was ready.

Before engaging a coach for the journey home, I diligently scoured editions of the *Philadelphia Evening Post*, other newspapers of the period, and miscellaneous records, hoping to corroborate Isaac's account of the hot-air balloon near the Wharf Market in the late spring of 1791. Alas, I could find no such account or record. Perhaps it had been simply an unrecorded instance, so local and spontaneous that no one thought to report it officially. Or perhaps his active imagination had conflated his own experiences and attendant elation with another such event, for it was no more than two years later, in 1793—in Philadelphia and observed by President Washington himself—that the first manned flight of a hydrogen-filled balloon took place in America, albeit from a prison yard.

At the risk of tarnishing my own cherished reputation as a historian, though as yet unrecognized, I decided, after considerable deliberation, to include his description of the sighting verbatim, whether precisely accurate or not, for it stands out neatly as an unusual but fitting symbol—just as Isaac said—of his emerging hopes and dreams. Yet even as I write out this careworn phrase, "hopes and dreams," I realize what a gulf must separate my own understanding of these, and his experience of them. For while my earliest dreams, now laughable to me, were to be first a sea captain and then a trapper in the western wilderness, and that of my youth to set up as a haberdasher—at which I proved to be a miserable failure—they were dreams, nonetheless. None of these would have been open to him. Indeed, despite all his exhilaration as he proclaimed himself to the Delaware River, no dreams at all were open to him, I supposed, beyond the satisfaction of pleasing "Old Master" at whatever work he was assigned to.

Hot-air balloons, though they may be inspiring to view as they float grandly aloft, are susceptible to disaster by fire, or explosion, or becoming entangled in trees, or struck by lightning, with attendant horrific loss of life. Thus, Isaac's excited recounting of that magnificent balloon he had witnessed, though auspicious, filled me with unease. For surely, portentous events lay ahead of him. Dr. Cornelius

Sharp, equipped with his peculiar *Ngulu*, Sword of Judgment, and bent upon using Isaac to confront Mr. Jefferson, would certainly not rest until he had achieved his object. What cataclysm might result when these two powerful figures, from their separate worlds, collided in argument? What would be the consequences for Isaac? And what of his deepening relationship with Rachel Bringhouse? That he, a young Negro as dark as ebony, and she, a maiden of the fairest hue, should have any relationship at all was fraught with danger for both of them, and Isaac at least was conscious of this danger. Yet the heart oft must have its way, regardless. Surely in those long Monday afternoon lessons, when they set aside the ledger book and communed over poetry, argued over philosophical papers, and questioned each other regarding their separate and very different lives, a bond of imperishable character must have developed between them. Because Rachel had shown herself to be curious and bold enough to ask pointed questions, and Isaac, prompted by her example, had begun reciprocating with his own questions, there was every reason to suppose that they were coming to know each other better than anyone had ever known them, even, I dare say, their own parents. And better known to themselves, too, I would wager.

Was romance involved? I leave that for you to consider. For myself, romance is a broad field which can encompass a tender look, a softened voice, a sensitized touch—and no more. For the common slave master, all such intimations of affection, however innocent, could only signal miscegenation, the vilest of sins. Though Thomas Jefferson was broadly liberal in his views, generous by nature, and the author of the Declaration of Independence, a document which shall ring down through all the ages as the finest and most succinct expression of human liberty, he was nevertheless a man of his times and susceptible to human frailty—as we all are. Even ministers of the Word of God, I confess, have their moments of weakness—their bouts with the lusts of the flesh. But I wish to be no apologist for Mr. Jefferson. History must be his judge. Yet I surmise that, as for other men of his class, the mixing of the races was an abomination. What would be the consequences, for both Isaac and Rachel, should he begin to suspect the worst?

Begging your forgiveness therefore, I am obliged to leave you with the foregoing narrative as it stands, and these questions to ponder, with the promise that just so soon as Isaac Granger Jefferson agrees to further cooperation, we shall again resume, and with God's grace and good health— both his and mine—complete this signal narrative, hurry it into published form, and thence into your waiting hands, Dear and Patient Reader.

With regards, I am, most sincerely,
Reverend Charles Campbell

END OF BOOK ONE

ABOUT THE AUTHOR

Sculptor and author Lawrence Bechtel began his journey toward the writing of *The Partial Sun*, his debut novel, and Book One of the *The Tinsmith's Apprentice* series, with two bronze portrait sculptures: the first of Thomas Jefferson and the second of Isaac Granger, who had grown up as a slave at Monticello. During the  course of this work, and the extensive research it involved, Lawrence read about Isaac's brief account of his time in Philadelphia as a tinsmith's apprentice and felt compelled, finally, to write a historical novel built from that account. This began with a long process of finding Isaac's voice, encouraged as he did so by the words of E.M. Forster from Howards End: "only connect."

A former English teacher at Virginia Tech, book reviewer for *The Roanoke Times*, and creator of three CDs' worth of short stories, Lawrence is presently working on the sequel novel for this series.

OTHER BOOKS BY
LAWRENCE REID BECHTEL

That Dazzling Sun, Book 2 in The Tinsmith's Apprentice trilogy, continues the vivid coming-of-age story of Isaac Granger, slave to Thomas Jefferson, begun in Bechtel's marvelously adept debut novel, A *Partial Sun* in which Isaac begins his complicated apprenticeship at age fifteen as a tinsmith in Philadelphia in the fall of 1790.

In this second book, Rachel Bringhouse, the tinsmith's daughter and Isaac's tutor, sails off to England to work alongside the famous social activist and poet, Hannah Moore, writing enthusiastic letters to Isaac and which Isaac answers back with assistance from the irrepressibly poetic cook's helper, Ovid. Meanwhile, Billey Gardner, the feisty and opportunistic former slave of James Madison, pesters Isaac with notions of a business partnership; the charismatic Dr. Cornelius Sharp uses Isaac to confront Jefferson as a debt-ridden slave owner; and the Reverend Richard Allen provides Isaac with a most surprising document.

When an exuberant Rachel returns from England with a key insight and Isaac's hated nemesis Daniel Shady reappears, bent on revenge, the book rises to its crescendo, in which Isaac must rise to his own power and bargain at last with Thomas Jefferson on his own terms.